William Bernard Ullathorne

The Autobiography of Archbishop Ullathorne

With Selections from HisLetters

William Bernard Ullathorne

The Autobiography of Archbishop Ullathorne
With Selections from HisLetters

ISBN/EAN: 9783337120931

Printed in Europe, USA, Canada, Australia, Japan

Cover: Foto ©Raphael Reischuk / pixelio.de

More available books at **www.hansebooks.com**

The Autobiography

OF

Archbishop Ullathorne

WITH

SELECTIONS FROM HIS LETTERS

London : BURNS & OATES, Limited.
New York : Catholic Publication Society Company.

I am now in the middle of the 4th Lecture, having written a new one by way of preface, and think I am getting on somewhat better with the book.

I may God bless you and all under your care, and remain

My dear Mother Prioress

Your Devoted Father in Christ

+ W. B. Ullathorne.

P R E F A C E.

The Autobiography of Archbishop Ullathorne was written in the year 1868, at the request of an intimate friend, and with no view of publication. It was revised by the writer towards the end of his life, when he both inserted some passages bearing reference to a later date, and omitted others which he appears to have considered less suitable for general readers. It is from this revised copy that the greater portion of the following pages has been prepared.

The Autobiography is not carried on later than the year 1850. Comparatively few letters have been preserved that would illustrate this earlier period of the Archbishop's life ; but subsequent to that date a large number exist, from which a selection has been made so as in some manner to carry on the history to the end. In a letter addressed to the friend for whose perusal the original Auto-biography was drawn up, the writer remarks : "Two objections to giving such a narrative have made me somewhat reluctant to comply with your request. One is the necessary egotism of such a narrative, and the other, the fact that the external and visible outlines which are all that I can touch on give no fair representation of that veritable life which is wholly of the soul." In selecting the letters to be given to the public, which form the Second Part of this publication, and which will fill a separate Volume, it has been the desire of the Editors in some degree to supply the want here alluded to, by choosing those which present the reader with some of the stores of spiritual wisdom which enriched the mind of the writer, rather than such as would merely illustrate his public Episcopal career.

Unfortunately, the Archbishop did not live to complete the revision of his autobiography, the latter portion of which, as here published, has had to be drawn from the unrevised copy. Besides the Autobiography, he left a collection of anecdotes, written at rather a later period, which it was his intention to have woven into the narrative in their proper place, an intention he never had leisure to carry out. These, therefore, have now been either included in the body of the narrative or added as illustrative notes. A few passages in the Life have, for obvious reasons, been either omitted or briefly summarised, according to what would seem to have been the purpose of the writer ; but all such abridgments are included within brackets.

ST. DOMINIC'S CONVENT, STONE,
September 10th, 1891.

AUTOBIOGRAPHY

OF

ARCHBISHOP ULLATHORNE.

CHAPTER I.

BIRTH AND EARLY RECOLLECTIONS.

I WAS born at Pocklington, in Yorkshire, on the 7th of
May in the year 1806, and was the eldest of ten children.
My father was a grocer, draper, and spirit merchant, and
did half the business of the town, supplying it with coal,
before it had a canal, and, in the absence of a bank, dis-
counting bills. His father had descended from gentle
birth, but owing to a singular incident he became a shoemaker, and afterwards a farmer. For his father was a
gentleman of landed estate in the West Riding of Yorkshire, which estate he acquired through his marriage with
Miss Binks, to whom it came as heiress of Mr Binks, who
had married Miss More, a lineal descendant of Sir Thomas
More, the Chancellor and Martyr, and the sister of Mrs.
Waterton, who is commemorated by her grandson, the
celebrated traveller and naturalist of Waterton Hall, in his
autobiography.

The estate was forfeited through the insurrection of
1745 in favour of the claims of the Stuarts, after which my
grandfather and his brother Francis were taken in charge

2

by Dr. Lawrence, of York. The two boys, however, were so terrified at the discovery of a skeleton in a cupboard in their bedroom that they both ran away. My grandfather apprenticed himself to a shoemaker, his brother fled to London, and there engaged himself to a chemist, and thus the turn in the fortunes of the family was completed.

My dear mother was a native of Spilsby, in Lincolnshire, of which county her father was Chief Constable. Sir John Franklin, the Arctic navigator, was her cousin, and next-door neighbour in their youthful days. She well remembered Sir Joseph Banks, of Captain Cook's exploring expedition, under whose influence young Franklin went to sea.

My father met my mother in London, where they were both engaged in Townshend's great drapery business in Holborn ; he converted her to the faith and then married her, after which they commenced business in Pocklington on their own account. As my father was a popular character, and my mother was greatly esteemed and respected for her gentle kindness and her good sense, their children were much noticed and every house was open to them.

I was sent to learn my first letters from a Miss Plummer, the daughter of a Protestant clergyman, who lived to a very advanced age. At home, I learnt to say my prayers at my mother's knee ; and although she was engaged all day in business, yet, with the aid of a confidential servant, devoted up to old age to the family, she contrived to keep us in good order and discipline. Indeed, a grave look from her was always a sufficient correction. My imagination as a child was extremely vivid, and communicated a sense of life to much that I looked upon in nature. I can recollect being led, by the hand as a little child, past a garden covered with snow, through which a group of snowdrops and crocuses peered out, and they seemed to me to be living creatures coming up in their innocence from the earth. The corn in the fields was to me a great mystery, especially when it turned from green to brown ; and when cut and gathered into sheaves, I thought they had killed the corn to make bread of it. Another childish experience that set my mind a wondering, was the exercising of the militia on the public green, in those warlike times. To see all those red-coated, black-gaitered men with feathers in their hats, moving, like one will in all their bodies, at the voice of a man with a different shaped hat, was the cause to me of many surmises. The nurse used to subdue us into good behaviour by the threat that Buonaparte was coming ; and I used to picture him as a little man with a big cocked hat and a great sword in his hand, going in his solitary strength and sternness from house to house, killing all the people. Now and then a sailor would pass through the place, deprived of a leg or an arm, holding in his one hand or dragging on wheels a little ship, and singing with brazen lungs about " We boarded the Frenchman," which led to talk among our elders about the wars, and set the children's minds on their first wonderings about the great world abroad.

How shall I recall the joys of my first remembered Christmas—joys, not of the eye or the palate, but of the imagination ? The being awàkened in the night to hear the playing and singing of the waits. Rude enough they might seem to other ears, but to the child, awakened out of sleep, it was little less than celestial harmony. The young imagination, in its glow, peopled all the heavens with beautiful angels, flying happily among the falling flakes of snow, and singing the invitation : "Christians awake, salute the happy morn, whereon the Saviour of mankind was born." On the next day came the expected visitor, old Nanny Cabbage, in her red cloak and black bonnet, and, though a Protestant, producing from under her cloak her little houselein, with its holly, its two red

apples stuck on pegs, and between them the Child Jesus in
His cradle, when, courtesying to the family, she sang the
" Seven Joys of Mary," to the delight of the children.   Relic
this of the old Catholic times, which I fear has passed
away with many other traditions.   Things like these were
educating me, if we attend to the sense of the word, much
more than Miss Plummer's lessons in reading and spelling.

After being rigged in a suit of boys' clothes, the great
transition of childhood, my father took me with him to
York, where the walk by his side through the Cathedral *
gave me such an impression of awe and grandeur, such a
sense of religion, that for many a long day my imagination
fed itself upon that wonderful recollection.   I was told, of
course, that the marvellous structure had been the work of
Catholics long ago.   It did not so much astonish me as
elevate me by its sublimity.   The city walls and Clifford's
Tower perplexed my young mind as to their use and object ;
but after two or three explanations had failed I was told
that, "if Buonaparte came, they would get in there and
fight him out," and this satisfied me.   I can recall, as though
it were yesterday, the tender tones in which all my questions
were answered.   The father seemed to feel what was passing
in the mind of the child on that first great day of its development.   York Minster was visible, as a great and con-

* He had, however, been already used to gaze at the Minster from a
distance.   " Easter Sunday afternoon," he writes, " was a great festival
at Pocklington from an old tradition.   A large number of all classes
of the population, men, women, and children, went up to Spring Hill,
Chapel Hill, or Primrose Hill, for it was called by all these names, and
gave a distant view of York Minster.   There, by the ruins of the old chapel
and at the clear spring sat half Pocklington, the children with sweets
in their bottles, and the grown people with wine and spirits in theirs,
tempering them with water from the spring, picking violets and prim-
roses, and enjoying themselves with great freedom.   I have no doubt
this chapel was a place of pilgrimage in the olden days."   In another
letter he says : " It was Mr. Holmes, the solicitor, a great friend of my
father, who first introduced me to the " Arabian Nights."   I visited his
son some years ago, and took my last leave of old Pocklington, with a
look at York Minster from Primrose Hill."

spicuous object, from a hill near our residence, though some ten miles distant ; so I now could animate that mysterious mass of pointed stone, and recall its lofty arches, its gorgeous windows, and the figures of kings and bishops in their mysterious sleep, that stood in their niches or lay on their tombs.

Who can say how much of our future tastes and mental tendencies are unconsciously derived from the early impressions made upon us by the more elevated forms of art ? I can remember what an impression was made upon my mind by the first sight of a Greek statue. It was a Flora standing in the open air among rich foliage, and literally dropping honey, for the bees had made their combs within the wreath on the head and the folds of the garment. The colourless creature seemed to sleep with open eyes, as she stood in her beauty. And I suppose it was one of my earliest lessons in abstraction, for she seemed to be a spirit of a different world from that in which I lived ; with whom there could be no communication by speech, though she seemed to think even in her sleep. She simply made me very silent.*

There was a little chapel at Pocklington with only two windows in it, a small presbytery, and a long slip of garden. The priest was the Abbé Fidele, a venerable French emigrant, long remembered there and at York for his piety, simplicity, and charity. He used to kneel before the little

* This statue was one that stood in the grounds of Kilnwick Hall, near Pocklington. Writing, in 1887, to Mr. Hudson, a native of Pocklington, but then residing at Baddesly Clinton, near Birmingham, the Bishop says : " Kilnwick Hall was the first gentleman's mansion I had ever seen as a child, and with my quick imagination I was struck with the ideal beauty of certain statues of Greek form among the trees in the woods. The gardener pointed out a statue of Flora, in the folds of whose garments the bees had formed a hive, and the honey flowed down to the feet from the combs. I have never forgotten the impression of this, my first introduction to the sculptor's art, though I daresay the figures were nothing particular. But it was an opening of the young mind to the ideal."

altar in a Welsh or worsted wig, saying his prayers, until Miss Constable, the patroness of the mission, arrived in the vestry, which was also his dining-room and parlour ; he then rose up and entered the vestry, where in sight of the little flock he pulled off his wig, powdered his head, and came in vested with his two servers for the Mass. I was told at a later period that he had four written sermons, and that when he had read the first words of one of them the congregation knew the rest by heart. Other French emigrant priests occasionally visited our house, and I remember one was Dr. Gilbert, a man of great dignity of bearing, who told us dreadful narratives of his escapes from the guillotine. He was afterwards raised to an important prelacy in France.

It is very odd that our old nurse, who was so fond of us, and often heard our prayers when our mother was engaged, was a strong Methodist, and used sometimes to express in our hearing her contempt for priests and "their trumpery."

As soon as I was able to read, I got hold of a pictorial book of Bible stories, lent me by a lady, which gave me an early interest in the sacred Scriptures ; and, as I grew a little older, I used to read with wondering pleasure the Book of Genesis, and with still more delight the Book of Revelations, in the Protestant version (for I do not suppose that at that time my parents knew that we had an English Catholic version). My father had an intimate friend, a Mr. Holmes, a solicitor, a man of a bright face and cheerful ringing laugh, who was fond of reading good literature aloud. He was quite a character and passionately fond of the drama. He lent me the "Arabian Nights," "Gulliver's Travels," and other books, which fostered my imaginative tendency. Yet there were graver tendencies as well. The following anecdote is simple enough, but it records a great opening of my mind. A book of arithmetic was lying on the table where my father was busy with accounts. It was still a sealed book to my childish under-standing. I took it up and fell at the numeration table. To me it looked so complicated, with its many figures, that I declared I should never understand it. " No ?" he said, " let us see." He took me kindly between his knees and ex-plained it. It seemed so simple that from that moment I was never afraid of what looked complicated, but felt assured that it only required a key to make it clear and intelligible.

I was a heavy, clumsy urchin, with what a Protestant clergyman's daughter described as "large blobbing eyes," silent when not asked to give an account of my reading, but always ready to give that account. I cared little for play * and my parents did not know what they could ever make of me. My second brother was active and agile, and this made me look all the more lumpy in the eyes of my neighbours, and awakened many a joke at my expense. The climax of my literary enjoyment was when " Robinson Crusoe " came into my hands. I never tired of reading it, and of talking of it to anyone who chose to draw me out. I believe it did much to give me a taste for the sea, at a

---

* Among the Bishop's recollections of his childhood, however, were some which prove that he shared in some of the sports wherein boys delight, especially in the catching of what are known as " horsehair eels," which abounded in the " beck " or stream which ran through Pock-lington. The memory of these eels having been referred to by his correspondent, Mr. Hudson, he replies : " We also caught the hair eels as you did, believing them to be vitalised horse-hairs. We had another tradition about these horse-hairs, that if you put one on your palm when the schoolmaster called you up to be *feruled*, it would split the ferule. We also caught stickle-backs, which we called bull-heads." He also refers to a certain baker's shop, " which we youngsters also knew as a place where sweets could be got." " The keenness and piquancy of the Bishop's recollections of localities and people," writes Mr. Hudson, " remembering that he left Pocklington at ten years old, was quite exceptional. He overflowed in anecdote and artless memories about them. It is satisfactory to state that he had not forgotten his native tongue, but could speak with readiness of " t' house " and " t' man," and so on. Such reminiscences, mingled with those of Vatican Councils at which he had assisted, and Popes and Cardinals with whom he had associated, contrasted curiously.

later period ; and when in the course of my missionary life I sailed in fine weather past Juan Fernandez, all the dreams of my early life were reawakened.

We could not have been more than seven and eight years old respectively, when I and my next brother were sent to school at the village of Burnby, some two miles from home. The master of the school was a character and had a reputation, and my father had learnt English grammar under him. We went on the Monday morning and returned home on the Saturday afternoon, lodging at the village blacksmith's, whose wife had been my nurse ; not the Methodist nurse of the whole family, but another, whose conversion from Church of Englandism to Methodism with her whole family I witnessed with all the fanatical accompaniments of those times.

We slept in a dark attic under the thatch of their cottage, illuminated only by one pane of glass. As we sat, in the winter evenings, by the fire in the brick floored room which served " for kitchen, parlour, and hall," we heard a good deal of pious sentiment uttered in an unctuous drawl ; but there was much more vigorous talk on agricultural matters, intertwined with the gossip and small scandal of the village, of which the blacksmith's shop was the focus. Sometimes we got the privilege of taking a turn at the great bellows, or of hitting the cold chisel with the big hammer that cut the glowing horseshoe nail from the rod of iron, of which my brother was fonder than I was. And some-times we got a half-holiday to help to plant the family potatoes.

The schoolmaster, I have said, was a character. He was a grave, self-contained man, who, when he unbent at the firesides of the farmers, could talk of many things which to them and to us left the impression of learning beyond our aspirations. He was not only the oracle, but the man of business of the village : he adjusted his neighbour's accounts and surveyed their land, when we were sometimes called on to drag the chains and to plant the flags and pegs. All the village had been at school to "the master," and he lived week and week about at all their houses. At the house to which he came it was a sort of festive time : neighbours looked in in the evening ; he had his special armchair and his glass, and, when invited, would sing one of his three songs in a grave, sweet voice, or, between the puffs of his pipe, tell us stories of the war or of other men's travels. We had our annual barring out and our annual school feast, to which all the fathers and mothers, with their young men and maidens, were invited. It was the great event of the year. The school-house had mud walls, thatched roof, and a clay floor, but it turned out good accountants and land surveyors. The 5th of November was a high day for the school. After dinner the pupils got the keys of the church, rang the bells, sported among the pews, and fired off little cannon in the church until twilight came, when they were succeeded by the farm lads and lasses, who carried on the saturnalia until late in the night. Another custom savoured more of the old Catholic times. A funeral was rare, but when it occurred the whole population assembled, sang the psalms in procession to the old chants, and afterwards received a distribution of bread and beer at the house of the de-parted.

By express arrangement we were not to learn the Pro-testant catechism ; but as we sat over our books whilst it was said, we had it all from memory by simply hearing it repeated.

Still dreamy and clumsy, and getting a fair amount of gibes for it, I lived in my imagination. I remember going all the way back to school to search for my task-book. The master said : " What are you looking for ? " " For my book." " What is that under your arm ? " And there it had been all the time safe enough. The master had more than once hard work to conquer my pride, in which he unfortunately failed. For the more he thrashed me, the more I quietly, but desperately, stiffened my spirit to endure, and afterwards boasted that he had not conquered.

After a certain time we passed from the blacksmith's to lodge at the wheelwright's, whose wife was the daughter of the old village clergyman, and who had a brother-in-law the clergyman of a neighbouring village. Here we had better accommodation and pleasant company. I still bear the marks on my fingers of the chops they got from bungling with the great axe in the wheelwright's shop. Here we saw a certain amount of the Protestant clerical society of the high and dry school, which gave us no idea of there being much religion in it, and which strangely contrasted with the spirit of the devout Abbé Fidele. I remember that when the annual Sacrament Sunday came round, I think on Easter Day, it was preceded by a good deal of talk as of an event like the annual Christmas party given in the house. One of the daughters asked: "Mother, is Jim to go to the Sacrament?" She replied: "No, Jim must not go, he would drink it all up. You know it is only a little taste." Poor Jim was the big apprentice to the trade. Burnby was a lonely little place; we seldom saw a stranger, and if one rode through it on horseback at rare intervals, he seemed to me to come out of some unknown world, and to pass into another.

But a crisis came upon the village, hitherto so peaceful and united as one family. A group of Methodists appeared one evening upon the village green, praying and singing hymns. Week after week this group appeared on the green, sundry convictions of sin and conversion took place ; and among the rest there was one that made a great sensation. It was the case of a particularly steady young man, son of the chief farmer. He got his conviction and some visionary view whilst sitting on a stile, and became a Methodist of the Methodists. As Christmas approached there was much discussion as to whether he would come to the Christmas parties, or sing his good songs, or play at cards. He came to the parties, but neither sang nor played at cards. At last the blacksmith received the preachers into his house, and it became their chapel; but we had already left it for the wheelwright's. From this time the village was divided, and got uncomfortable in its social relations, and its old simplicity was sadly marred.

As to the old schoolmaster, I never knew until after years that he was devoid of any kind of religious principle. I saw him in his decay, about the year 1850, just before he died, in company with Bishops Briggs, Gillis, and Brown, on our way through Pocklington to the mansion of Lord Herries, to open a church at Howden. The poor old man had lost all his savings through the failure of a bank, and was helped in his distress by his old pupils. I asked him privately if he had done his best to make his peace with God, and he assured me he had.

The things I have described were not without their practical influence in opening my intelligence to the then existing state of Protestant and sectarian life. They awakened my curiosity though they presented no attraction to my youthful mind. We had our Sundays at home, but I am afraid that our prayers during the week were limited to the sign of the Cross, the Our Father, Hail Mary, and the Creed.

CHAPTER II.

LIFE IN SCARBOROUGH, 1815.

I SUPPOSE I must have been between nine and ten years old when my father transferred his residence and business to Scarborough. He there became popular by breaking down a system of union among tradesmen to keep up prices at a point agreed upon, and by cheapening the grocery, drapery, and wine trades one after another. Here I first saw the sea, the object of my aspirations from the time I had read " Robinson Crusoe," and I recollect all the circumstances of my first view of it from the top of the northern cliffs, and the expansion which that wonder of creation gave to my mind. My second brother and I were placed as day scholars at Mr. Hornsey's school, which had some reputation both as a boarding and day school. Hornsey was a genuine pedant as well as pedagogue, and the fact of his having published an English grammar and some other elementary books did not diminish the importance of the man. We stood in awe of him, and of his moral lessons, given with pompous intonation when occasion served. But we took more kindly to his son and to a second usher, who was preparing for the Anglican ministry. He taught his own grammar ; but though I was quick and fond of knowledge, he never explained or taught us to apply the principles of grammar. He was a well-meaning man of the high and dry Protestant type, and conspicuous from afar, with his portly figure, white hat, clouded cane, and decided strut. I think, however, that I got my mind more enlarged through one of the boys, who had a collection of voyages and travels, which he lent to his companions at a penny a volume.

Two of my brothers attended the school of a Protestant clergyman, who was assisted by his two clerical sons. It will surprise the later generations of Scarborough to know that this school was held in the transept of the old Church of St. Mary's, which was walled off for the purpose. It had formerly belonged to an Augustinian monastery. I remember how angry my father was, when he found that one of his sons, following the custom of the school, had put out the eyes of Queen Mary with a pin, in Goldsmith's "History of England."

Whilst our education was going on in these Protestant schools, we laboured under a great disadvantage in only having a priest at Scarborough one Sunday in six weeks. This was a great disappointment to my parents, who knew there was a good chapel and presbytery in the place, but did not find out that there was no resident priest until they had fixed their own residence. Mr. Haydock, the editor of Haydock's Bible, came once in three months; and Mr. Woodcock, of Egton Bridge, also came once in three months. They were both Douay priests, and as they generally dined at our house, I used to be much entertained with their college stories. On the five Sundays intervening between their sacerdotal visits, it was arranged that the flock should attend chapel morning and afternoon as usual, and my father and Mr. Pexton (who had been a Church student at Ushaw, but had given up the idea of the ministry) were appointed to act as readers on alternate Sundays. First the usual English prayers were said aloud, then all in silence read the prayers for Mass in the "Garden of the Soul," making a sort of spiritual Communion, and then the lector for the week read one of Archer's sermons, which my father did from his usual seat,

but Mr. Pexton stood before the Communion-rails facing
the people. In the afternoon the usual psalms and prayers
were said aloud and the children said their catechism to the
lectors. None of us youths had made our first Communion;
and as to' Confirmation, we had none of us ever seen a
bishop, either at Pocklington or at Scarborough. There
were only four in all England and Wales.

At twelve years old my father took me from school and
put me to his business, with the idea that if I returned to
school again, after two years of trade, I should better ap-
preciate the value of a school, and should be able to apply
my mind with more practical intelligence to such mercantile
education as I required. I trudged on for twelve months,
getting an insight into my father's three businesses, and
into the method of managing account books and money
transactions, but with no great taste for this kind of occupation. In the evenings I was indulged by being allowed
to follow my passion for reading, which I did by running
through all the books that tempted me by their titles in
the two circulating libraries then in the town. Voyages
and travels were still my leading attraction, though I did
also run through many rubbishy novels and romances. I
followed my reading after everyone had gone to bed, and
put my book under my pillow for a fresh start in the
morning before business began.

This miscellaneous and undirected reading filled me
with a strong desire to see the world, and as the only way
of accomplishing this, I set my mind on going to sea. To
this proposal my mother and father long and justly ob-
jected, but seeing that I was bent in that direction, they
yielded at last, still hoping that I should sicken of it after
trial. A Scarborough ship was to be my destiny, and I
was nearly put under the roughest and most cruel tyrant
that ever sailed from that port, a man who had hung up
his own son by the thumbs, and whose atrocities to his

apprentices had become a proverb among seamen. But providentially my father found out his character in time to save me from him.

Happily for me, a fine brig was going to be launched, whose owners were my father's friends, and which was to be commanded by a captain superior to the ordinary run of mercantile captains, a man of gentlemanly manners and feelings, and whose wife, a superior woman, always sailed with him. I can never forget the kindness of Mrs. Wrougham to me. Our officers and crew were also picked men, connected with decent persons in Scarborough. One of my father's assistants, a man of mature years, having taken a fancy to the sea, sailed in the same ship.

When, however, the Rev. Mr. Haydock came next Sunday to Scarborough, he looked very gravely on the notion of my going to sea. He saw its perils for a youth of my proud character, spoke seriously against it, and was evidently distressed. But finding it was all settled, he told me to go to him to prepare to receive the Sacraments before I left. But alas! in my boy's conceit, fostered by all this reading, by my fondness for isolating myself, and musing alone on the cliffs and sea beach, I fancied that the good priest was obtruding too much on what concerned me. I did not go to him at the time appointed, and even spoke of it to the shopmen and servants, who let me see that this did not edify them. Pained at my breaking his appointment, the good priest sent for me again, and when I reached the sacristy he made me stand at the door and gave me a grave rebuke, which did not advance matters. Had he been sympathetic perhaps he would have won me; but that is no excuse. I went to sea without the Sacraments.

CHAPTER III.

WE were proud of our brig, the *Leghorn ;* she was hand-some, quick, and easily handled. We literally walked past most craft of our kind and trim. I was cabin boy, and my dear mother had stipulated with Captain Wrougham that I should not go aloft for the first three months. We took out a cargo of merchandise from Newcastle to Leghorn ; went thence to Barcelona, and then to Tarragona, where we shipped a cargo of nuts for Hull. The nuts were brought by long strings of mules over the mountains ; were then sorted on long tables, by women in the stores, and shot out of sacks into the hold like corn. The captain treated me almost like his son, kept me a good deal aloof from the sailors, except in the night watches, and never let me go ashore except with himself.

I soon attracted the attention of the sailors by beguiling the night watches with stories from my readings under the lee of the long boat, repeating large portions, among other things, of Sir Walter Scott's earliest novels. This, with the knowledge they had of my friends, made me respected among them, although they did not fail to give me the rough side of their tongue now and then, especially for my want of smartness in action, the favourite quality of a sailor.

A specimen of this kind of regard for me was curiously exhibited at Gibraltar. As we entered the Bay and looked upon the tremendous Rock, with its projecting cannon, I was in a romantic rapture, not at all diminished by a shot sent between our masts from the batteries for neglecting to hoist our colours. Having care of them, I made but one step off the companion ladder, and pitched on deck the horsehair bag that contained them, and the ensign was aloft in a moment. My familiarity with Drinkwater's "Siege of Gibraltar" made the whole scene classic to my mind. But the captain, in his good nature, allowed the men to purchase private stores of rum ; and, of course, they all got dead drunk, so that the ship at anchor was left to the care of the mate, myself, and another boy, the only sober creatures on board, for the captain was ashore. The men lay sprawling half on deck, half in the forecastle ; one of them was so mad that he went to hit another man for some fancied offence, but finding that he had struck the boy Bill (myself to wit) he was so vexed that he flung himself overboard, and, had not the mate jumped into a boat alongside and caught hold of him, he would certainly have been drowned.

At Tarragona the men bought buckets full of the cheap, black Catalonian wine, and sitting round the bucket, bailed out the wine and drank it from the cans in which they cooked their tea and sugar on the cook-house fire until it was black and bitter. At one of these carouses, from which I always withdrew in disgust, they called on me, lying in my hammock, to have some, but getting nothing but silence in reply, they poured a can of it over me. It was simply fun.

Lumpy as I then was, and was called, I got drowsy in the night watches, and acquired the habit of walking the deck fast asleep. This was a serious habit, especially when having the look out for ships approaching, and it was necessary to cure me of it I walked the gangway steadily with folded arms, and turned without touching any fixtures as when awake ; but if anyone stood in my way there was a collision. Sometimes a noose was put to catch my leg, and down I came on my nose. Tar was

3

put in my mouth, and the burning substance so roused me that I seized a capstan bar to knock the offender down. Finally, they pitched whole buckets of water on me from the rigging, and shouted, " A man overboard "; and this kept me wakeful for some time to come.

The Spaniards who came on board used to take to me as being a Catholic, which I was rather fond of letting them know. Whenever a group of monks or friars, in their big hats and long costumes, appeared on the shore, the sailors had a laugh and rough joke at my expense. At Barcelona, the two Custom House officers placed on board to prevent smuggling compassionated me in their hearts as a Catholic boy among heretics. They were overheard planning a scheme to get me ashore out of their hands. The captain gave me sundry hints and threats which I could not understand. But many years afterwards when I met him, after I was a priest, he told me of this plot, and how anxious it had made him, feeling his responsibility to my parents.

The walls and bastions of Tarragona were still in a ruinous condition from the two assaults they had undergone in the Peninsular War, the French first taking the city and the English retaking it. Our captain, who had commanded a transport in that service, explained to me the English attack, of which he had been an eye-witness. The English approach was by a long viaduct spanning a broad valley. The Cathedral, with its cloisters and seminary, first revealed to my sight a great Catholic church with all its appointments, and enabled me to realise what York Minster once had been. Travelling, much later in life, with a venerable Spanish bishop, on comparing notes I found that he had been a student in that seminary at the very time that I was cabin boy in the harbour. How often do these encounters in after life quicken the memories of the past !

Reaching the Bay of Leghorn from Gibraltar, in this first voyage, the quarantine doctor came alongside, and decreed that as it was reported that the yellow fever was at Gibraltar, we must have forty days' quarantine, of which twenty at least must be passed at anchor in the open bay. This was a matter of unexpected consternation, for there was no fever at Gibraltar, and, besides the loss of time and consequent expenses, the bay was insecure and open to heavy gales. So the yellow flag was hoisted, our letters sliced, vinegared, and fumigated, and all communication with the shore, except by long poles with the boats bringing provisions, cut off. We rode out our twenty days at anchor in idleness, except setting up the rigging and doing odd jobs, and then came the doctor again. We had all to stand in a row and be inspected from his boat, and then to jump up and down to show our healthy condition. He then came on board and felt everyone under the arm-pits, after which he declared that we could enter the harbour, but must remain in quarantine for twenty days more. It was an awful day of rain and tempest when we hove anchor, a cold piercing *tramontana*, that searched into every bone ; and all the long day we toiled, beating against the wind, to gain the harbour. I shall never forget how desolate we were, wet to the skin and chilled to the spine. When we got into our berth at last, we were hemmed in by an Algerine on one side and a Greek on the other. Our men, unaccustomed to the Mediterranean, had strong superstitions about the Algerines, taking them for pirates ; and the long robes of the captain, his white turban and long cherry stick pipe reaching to the deck, gave him a solemn appearance, whilst his men looked a truculent crew. On the other hand, they were puzzled with the enormous baggy costume of the Greeks, who surprised them not less by their agility. The Algerines rushed over the side; it was simply to suspend a defensive beam to prevent the ships crushing, but so alarmed were our men that they determined to keep watch with handspikes over their shoulders. However, they soon got friendly with their neighbours.

For me, it was just that touch of romance which I enjoyed. The calm of the port, the change of those icy cold garments for dry ones, gave me a sense of Elysian enjoyment such as I never experienced before or since. I walked the deck with the new sights and sounds about me and a sense of revivification within me that approached to rapture. Our prime amusement during this tedious quarantine was the music-boats that played and sang around us. Among other compositions, we constantly heard Rossini's *Fra tanti palpiti*, which at that time excited a *furore* in Italy.

My ears had been attuned to music from childhood, for not only did my father play the flute and flageolet, but my brothers and sisters cultivated various instruments as well as singing, and formed the choir in the chapel. My father also amused himself with engraving plates and etching, so that our artistic tastes got a certain encouragement. Yet in Leghorn I found nothing to gratify mine except the well-known statue of the Grand Duke Ferdinand, with the four bronze figures of Algerines chained at his feet, about which the sailors had many legends.

Our passage home was beset with storms and contrary winds that delayed us six weeks between Gibraltar and Portsmouth. In the Bay of Biscay our fresh water had turned putrid, and its stench was horrible ; our bread was filled with cobwebs and maggots ; our beef (consisting of condemned stores from Gibraltar, which was all that was left), was, on the outside, like mahogany, though the inside was green : and the men cut it into snuff-boxes, like any other timber, as curiosities. It had probably been ten or twelve years packed in salt brine, and buried in vaults of the commissariat, should it be needed for another siege

Our first news from the English pilots was that George III. was dead, the Duke of Berri was assassinated, and the English coast lined with wrecks from the terrible gales we had encountered. This last news made us grateful that we had not reached the English coast earlier, notwithstanding our short allowance of rations and their detestable quality. How eager we were to get some fresh water after we had rounded the Isle of Wight to the quarantine grounds, and with what glee the men hoisted the first quarter of fresh beef on board ! Our long delay and the extraordinary number of wrecks had made our friends anxious about our safety. My father happened to be in the commercial room of a hotel in Hull, when a person came in and announced that the *Leghorn* was lost with all hands. He called for his horse, rode forty miles to Scarborough scarcely knowing what he did ; but had the discretion when he got home to say nothing of what he had heard. In a day or two after the news reached him of our safe arrival off Portsmouth.

After discharging our cargo at Hull we took horses on board for St. Petersburg. In our first voyage to the Baltic, when anchored between Copenhagen and Drago, such a heavy gale came on that we had to cut cable, leave a buoy over the anchor, and run for the open sea. There was a sort of ceremony on this occasion. When all was ready the captain himself took the axe and cut the cable. But when we got off the Isle of Bornholm the wind increased to still greater vehemence and a storm of sleet drove keenly in our faces. I and another lad were ordered aloft to furl the main-top gallant, prior to reefing the topsail. But when we got on the yard the folds of the sail were so full of sleet, it so cut our faces, blinding our eyes, our hands were so benumbed, whilst one of my shoes blew off, that we could do nothing except hold on. It was a critical moment, for we were on a lee shore without refuge. The curses sent up from deck did not stimulate us, so a man of light weight was sent up, and as we got down and jumped on deck crack came a rope's end across our backs.

In the same voyage we had to run into one of the Swedish Sounds, where, landlocked and in smooth water, we had to wait for the subsidence of the gale. Here it was my delight to ramble in the valleys gathering bilberries and strawberries, and lying on a green bank to listen to the sounds that hummed in the air of insects, birds, silvery threads of waterfalls, and the woodman's axe. Then the mate would take me with him in the jolly-boat with jib and leg of mutton sail, and we traversed the transparent water from shore to shore. So clear was the water that we saw everything distinctly at a great depth on the ground below. We saw oyster beds packed like tiles, and countless sea plants in great varieties of colour and form ; crabs also, taking their lateral walks ; polypi and anemones of brilliant hues, and fish pursuing their prey among the plants. The summer skies of the Baltic enchanted me more than those of the Mediterranean, for I had still much of the poetical element in my composition. Elsinore, with its memories of Hamlet; Copenhagen, with its islands and floating batteries recalling Nelson ; the beautiful landlocked bays of Sweden, into which we ran when the storms began to rage ; the short and almost nominal nights ; the magnificent sunrises ; the passing through the Russian fleet ; the tranquil sail up the Gulf of Finland ; Cronstadt, with its even then prodigious batteries; then the Neva, up to the magnificent quays of St. Petersburg, glowing with its metal domes and spires ; all these scenes worked on my youthful imagination like enchantment. The Russian people might not be very cleanly, the officials might require a good deal of bribing before the ships could get on smoothly ; but the summer climate, with its changing hues, was fascinating. When, at a later period of life, I opened Comte De Maistre's " Soirées de St. Pétersbourg," his description of his own fascination with the summer evenings on the banks of the Neva awoke a chord of memory unspeakably pleasant. Yet I was then but a cabin boy with my thoughts buried under a tarry cap.

Perhaps the most beautiful scene that I ever saw in creation was a sunrise in the Baltic. The summer nights in that climate were to me enchanting. The sun went down with a large glowing disc, and in a couple of hours was up again, so that one could read a good print at midnight. But on that wonderful morning the sun, as he rose, had fairly centred himself in a glowing sphere of amber, ex-panding beyond into a rich orange, which passed into crimson, and then into purple, covering half the hemisphere with these brilliant hues, whilst the opposite half-hemisphere was a pale reflection of the same, and the deck was chequered with those colours like a stained window. I once, and only once, saw a counterpart to this gorgeous spectacle, in a sunset in the tropics. It was on my first voyage to Australia. The whole western sky was banked up from the horizon with crimson clouds, presenting with their shades and salient lights the picture of a lofty moun-tain range, with a city piled in pyramidal form, like Algiers with its towers and battlemented walls, but all of glowing flame intense as a furnace. After a long gaze which seemed to subdue and entrance the passengers, the vision slowly passed away.

One of the sights in the Baltic was an extraordinary shoal of mackerel. The sea was as smooth as a mirror, and there was not a breath of wind. As far as we could see, and as deep as we could look down, all was mackerel, and there was not a square inch where their bright blue and silver backs were not flashing and crossing one beneath another. In vain we tried a variety of schemes, such as running lines from the jib-boom to the topsail ; we could not catch even one. The mackerel pursues its prey, and when running with a rippling breeze of from four to five knots an hour, may be caught as fast as the lines with a bit of white and red rag can be let down.

The cooking-house of Cronstadt was an institution worth describing. In the ports of the Baltic no fire was allowed to be lit in the harbours. For cooking, a great house was provided on shore close to the port. In that dingy receptacle fireplaces with bars were ranged all round with wood fires, amid an atmosphere rich in reek and all kinds of culinary odours, blending the tastes of all navigating nations. At a certain hour each ship sent its boat, generally rowed by a couple of lads, to convey the cook with his provisions to the cook-house. It was often my lot to pull an oar, and once or twice I did the cooking. What a jabber of languages there was, and yet a kind-hearted good fellow-ship, however incomplete the modes of expression among different nations. Now and then a little surliness, if one man trenched on another's bars ; now and then an exchange of sly grogs; but in the main it was a merry, though weird, scene. Then, as twelve approached, all the boats reassembled to carry off the cooks with the steaming products of their labours. I saw, at the landing, a French sailor conversing with a Russian, when they found out that they had been opposed to each other at the Battle of Borodino ; and then how affectionately they hugged each other, whilst tears came into the eyes of the soft-hearted Russian.

Then we moved near the famous statue of Peter the Great, by the Winter Palace; and many a legend did I hear of his doings, and of the eccentricities of the Emperor Paul, whilst I witnessed the worshipful attitude of the people towards the Emperor Alexander.

The churches seemed to me Catholic yet not Catholic, I could scarcely tell how : but I was greatly struck with the religious customs of the people. They made the sign of the Cross on all occasions, commonly repeating it thrice. They seldom passed a church without entering, or at least uncovering and kneeling before they passed it. Nor was this custom limited to the poorer classes. The priests, in their beards and Oriental costume, were often striking and reverend figures. Even our sailors were impressed by the signs of religion which they saw, and spoke of them with respect. I remember being in the serfs' Sunday afternoon market with some companions, when suddenly a bell rang out from one of the churches, and the whole market, trades-men included, knelt down in prayer. Whether it was something like our *Angelus* bell I cannot say. Our object in the market was to buy pieces of Russian duck or canvas with which to make sea clothing with our sail cloth needles. We took in a cargo of hemp at Cronstadt, the stowing of which by means of jackscrews was the work of the Russian serfs, whose brawny limbs were fed on nothing better than black bread of a very sour flavour and garlic. But they were kept in heart by glasses of fiery " bottery," which it was my office to give them at stated hours ; and they lightened their heavy labour by improvised chants sung in untiring chorus, under a leader, who gave the improvi-sations.

On returning to London, I made acquaintance with my relatives, who were very kind to me, and on alternate Sun-days, when I had leave on shore, I went to Mass with them at the Chapel of Somers Town.* They took me also, as a special treat, to St. Mary's, Moorfields, recently com-pleted, and looked upon at that time as a wonderful

---

* At the time when William Ullathorne was in the habit of attending Mass at the Chapel of Somers Town Margaret Hallahan was an inmate the Somers Town Orphanage.

advancement in Catholic architecture. It is a fact to be avowed that when abroad I had never tried to go to Mass, and probably I should not have been permitted to go alone. Yet I always stuck to the confession of my Catholicity and was proud of it.

The shipping trade was now slack, and a charter could not be got on 'Change for a new voyage. So the captain, who was part owner, resolved to put our beautiful brig for a time in the Newcastle and London coal trade. He would not, however, have anything personally to do with this dirty work, but stopped in London with his kind-hearted wife, and put in his place a coarse, rough Newcastle skipper, and under this ignorant man my fortunes were changed. We made a couple of voyages in this black trade, and everyone cried out against the degradation of so fine a craft ; but there was no remedy. What I vividly remember is, that when in harbour two of us boys had to land this captain (no better than a common sailor) each evening, that he might have his carouse with other coal skippers of the same class, whilst we poor boys had to guard the boat—no trifling thing on the Thames where the wherry-men, jealous of ship's boats, would not let us lie near the stairs, but compelled us to keep afloat in the tide, or to fasten on to some moored lighter for long hours. At last the skipper appeared with his fellow-skippers. Our boat had to carry them all to the smart ship, where they came for another glass ; and then we had to row the visitors, half drunk, to their own ships, getting nothing but abuse from them, and got back to bed between twelve and one in the morning.

I had two narrow escapes of drowning in the Thames. Another lad, knowing I had a constitutional fear of dogs, set one upon me by way of a joke. I sprang from the bulwark of our own vessel to the loftier side of the next in the tier, calculating on catching on a moulding with my fingers, and so scrambling on board ; but forgot at the moment that her sides had been newly tarred and varnished, so down I slipped between the two ships and sank beneath them. I could not swim, but being perfectly calm and self-possessed I paddled myself up with hands and feet. Alarm was given, the men sprang out of the hold where they were at work, and one of them seized me by the head from the fore chains just as I emerged. It was considered a great escape, as few who sank in the tideway were ever saved. The other case was in running down the Thames with wind and tide, having to get on board from a boat that hung by its painter. I seized the chain plates and the boat went from under me. I could not swing myself up, and was too proud to call out; but a voice from another ship cried out: "Captain Wrougham, that boy will be drowned there, under the main chains." This brought a pair of hands down on my collar and a fair share of abuse on my person.

Being in the Thames after our second trip to Newcastle the skipper one day got very angry with me, owing to a trifling mistake, and gave me a kick with his foot that wounded my pride to such a degree that I determined to abandon the ship. That night, accordingly, I packed up my bundle of linen, put on my best clothes, and sat all night in the cook-house on deck. I confided my secret to another youth, a respectable boy, who had been my schoolfellow, who faithfully kept it. About eleven some of our men came from the shore half tipsy, and one of them came into the cook-house for something he wanted; but as I sat low down on a bucket in the corner I escaped detection. About two o'clock in the morning I scrambled across the tier of ships in which we lay, got down into a lighter, and hailed a wherry at the landing. The man came and suspected me to be a runaway. We had a parley, and half-a-crown induced him to land me. I wandered about the streets of London, gradually working my way towards the

West End; answered the policemen and patrols, who were
suspicious of my bundle, in broad Yorkshire, as a simple
country lad going to see my relations ; received cautions in
a kindly tone about not letting anyone carry my bundle,
and in due time knocked at the door of one of my uncles,
who heard my tale, gave me breakfast, and then took me
to other relatives, three of whom agreed to drive me down
again to the ship, and there have an interview with the
captain.   My appearance thus accompanied produced a
great sensation.   It was thought on board that I must have
been drowned.   The skipper was nonplussed and had
very little to say, but referred my friends to the real captain,
who lived at some distance.   We went to Captain Wrougham,
who, as usual, was very kind.   He admitted the coarseness
of the man in command, and proposed that I should go to
my friends for the winter, and should rejoin the ship in the
spring, when he hoped to resume command and enter once
more on foreign trade.   I enjoyed the spectacles of London
for a time and then returned home.   But our ship was at
Scarborough before me.   The other owners were dissatisfied
with what the ship was doing and sent a special agent to
bring her home.   They agreed with my father to give up
my indentures and I was free.   Though always admired,
the *Leghorn* was never prosperous ; she was sold, and
finally sank in the Bay of Genoa.

In vain did my parents try to persuade me to give up
the sea.   I had not much taste for ship work, nor did I like
the rude society into which I was thrown ; but I was fond
of roaming to see the world, and was too proud to swallow
the handspike.   I had seen schoolfellows jeered at for
deserting a pursuit supposed to have perils in it, and
demanding a hardy disposition, and I believe that this
opinion keeps many a youth at sea after he has had a
sickening of it.

I spent the winter in studying the science of navigation

under an old sea captain, who had Norrie's "Epitome" off by memory, the table of logarithms included. He was clever, and had some half-dozen pupils, much older than myself. It was a strange sort of school; the old man kept no servant, cooked his own food, sometimes got tipsy, and then there was a fencing match between him and one of the students with two-foot scales. I learnt to work a ship's way, to keep a log book, and to take observations of the sun, which we did with our sextants in fine weather on Castle Hill.

In the spring I set sail once more. There was an excellent old couple of an old Catholic family residing at Scarborough, who had a brig called the *Anne's Resolution*. To this vessel, which was very inferior to the *Leghorn*, I was apprenticed for a short term, not altogether to my liking. I wanted to go in one of the Arctic discovery ships, or where I might see more adventures, but my father wished to sicken me of the sea. The captain was a good-natured man of ordinary abilities; the mate, who had been for a time at Stonyhurst and was full of Catholic faith, was a nephew of the owners, and bore their name. I had stipulated not to go again as cabin boy, but this threw me into the forecastle, among a set of men and boys whose conversation was the vilest imaginable. This did not at all suit my taste, for I always kept a certain self-respect. But after a time the captain became indisposed, and required more attention than, with the present boy, he could get. He therefore asked me as a favour to act as cabin boy. This touched my feelings and I consented. It had the further advantage of taking me out of the forecastle.

There was another youth on board, older than myself, who was not only steady, but very anxious to improve himself. This led to a certain intimacy between us. But we got into one or two scrapes together. With my vivid imagination I was passionately fond of the theatre, but always kept away from low exhibitions. When in the London Docks, and we had leave on shore in the evening, I induced him more than once to accompany me to Covent Garden; and when the play was over we wandered through the streets until six in the morning, when the dock gates were opened, and then we slipped on board before all hands were called. One morning, however, the mate appeared on deck before we returned, which put an end to our theatrical enjoyments. In these nightly wanderings we made it a rule to keep to the main streets, to enter no place of refreshment, and speak to no one.

Whilst in the docks I got a severe scald through upsetting some burning fat on my right instep, and being neglected gangrene appeared. The doctor who was called in declared that it was a hospital case and serious ; I was therefore conveyed up to my Uncle Longstaff's, who then resided in the Polygon, Somers Town. Through the affectionate care of my aunt and the skill of the family doctor my foot was saved, and in due time I returned to the ship. I was one day engaged in tarring a cable, when I suddenly heard my father's voice from the quay saying : "I see his eyes, but nothing else of him." I looked up and there I saw my father and uncle gazing at me. My father looked anything but contented, and coming on board said : "Do you mean to say that you like this?" However, I held on until we got to Memel, and there I found my deliverance.

When Sunday morning came in the harbour, Mr. Craythorne, the mate, said to me : "William, let us go to Mass." I fished up the "Garden of the Soul" from the bottom of my sea chest, and we set off through the flat town of Memel, with its numerous windmills for sawing timber, and its churches in the hands of the Lutherans, until beyond the town we reached a considerable wooden structure exteriorly not unlike a barn. There was a square yard of

grass in front of it, surrounded by a low wall, and on one
side the walk to the door was a mound surmounted by a
large wooden figure on a cross, round the front of which sat
a number of aged and decrepit people singing and soliciting
alms. The Mass had begun when we entered the chapel,
the sanctuary was profusely decorated with flowers, and
two banners were planted on the sanctuary rails, one of
which, I recollect, represented St. Michael the Archangel.
I vividly remember the broad figure of the venerable priest
and his large tonsure, which made me think him a Franciscan. The men knelt on the right side, the women on
the left, all dressed very plainly and much alike. With
their hands united and their eyes recollected, they were
singing the Litany of Loretto to two or three simple
notes, accompanied by an instrument like the sound
of small bells. The moment I entered I was struck by
the simple fervour of the scene; it threw me into a cold
shiver, my heart was turned inward upon myself, I saw the
claims of God upon me, and felt a deep reproach within
my soul. When we came out I was again struck by the
affectionate way in which the people saluted each other, as
if they were all one family. Whatever money was in my
pocket went into the poor box, and when we got on board
I asked Craythorne what religious books he had with him.
He produced an English translation of Marsollier's " Life of
St. Jane Chantal," and Gobinet's " Instruction of Youth,
which I read as leisure served.

The venerable figure of St. Francis de Sales and that of
St. Jane Chantal introduced me to a new world, of which I
had hitherto known nothing. A life filled with the sense
of God and devoted to God was what I had never realised.
Gobinet's "Instructions" again took me into my conscience.
Still there was much fancy in me, and I lived in a sort of
rapture of the imagination until we reached London. I
then wrote home and informed my parents that I wished

to leave the sea and return home. This was speedily
arranged, and I was again employed in my father's business.
My dear mother, however, unacquainted with the change
that had taken place in me, wrote to me before I left the
ship, expressing a hope that I should give no more trouble
to them than the rest of the family. I cannot remember
how it was, but though there was then a young priest
resident at Scarborough, to whom I went, and under whom,
at his request, I resumed the catechism, I did not at that
time make my first Communion. I took evening lessons
in French with Mr. Pexton, already named, and in walks
with him he interested me in college life and studies ; and
I renewed my old habit of general reading. But in the
midst of this course of life we happened to receive a visit
from a linen manufacturer of Knaresborough, who had a
son studying for the Church, at the Benedictine Priory of
Downside. He took a fancy to my brother James, who
had a fine boy's voice, and was a principal singer at the
chapel. He pressed him to go to Downside as a Church
student, and spoke warmly about it to my parents. But
my brother did not feel the attraction. Whereupon I
acknowledged how much I should like it, and made known
the altered state of my mind. My father wrote at once to
Dr. Barber, the Prior, and the matter was settled to my
great delight. As Downside is near Bath, I preferred going
by London on board a packet sloop. But whilst anchored
at the mouth of the Thames we were caught in a severe
January gale, and had to cut and run with about fifty sail
more—of whom one, a Dutchman, went down—and got
safe into Harwich, where, in consequence of floating ice in
the Thames, I did not delay, but went on by coach, and
arrived at Downside in the beginning of February, 1823,
being nearly seventeen years old.

The College, as well as Priory, were then packed in the
old mansion, with considerable contrivance ; but the new

College and chapel were in course of preparation. I made the twentieth boy in the school. The first thing that struck me was the good feeling and piety which prevailed among the boys, and the kindly relations which existed between them and their masters. The whole tone of things was in great contrast to all I had ever known, and threw a light into my mind as to the practical bearing of the Catholic religion. The next thing that struck me was the absence of worldly knowledge and experience in the Superiors, as well as in the monks, who nevertheless, by their great dignity, piety, and kindness at once attracted my reverence and veneration. It revealed to me a world in utter contrast to the world I had known before.

CHAPTER IV.

COLLEGIATE AND MONASTIC LIFE.

ARRIVED at St. Gregory's Priory, Downside, my life underwent a total and very earnest change. In these days it will scarcely be believed that until I went to St. Gregory's I had never been present at Benediction of the Blessed Sacrament, or heard the Litany sung, except at Memel, but it now came with great sweetness to my soul Such devotions in those days were chiefly limited to the few existing colleges and convents. Father Polding, afterwards the first Archbishop of Sydney, was our prefect and our director, and in him I found all that my soul needed.* To him I made my general confession, and he kept me long in training, for it was not until Christmas night, 1823,† ten

* In the dedication to a volume of sermons, published in 1842, Dr. Ullathorne thus expresses his obligations to his holy director : "You were my first, my constant, and my best instructor in the spirit of the religious life. It was you who early inspired me with that missionary spirit which counts self as nothing in pursuit of the salvation of immortal souls. And as I was brought up at your feet, so have I since been privileged to walk by your side in the Apostolic career, and to be guided by your light."

† A letter is preserved, dated Downside, January 7th, 1824, in which the writer, addressing his parents, informs them of this event. " I had the inexpressible happiness," he says, " of approaching Holy Communion for the first time on Christmas Day, and promised now to begin in earnest and serve God with all my heart, which, indeed, is a very poor return for all the mercies and blessings which He has vouchsafed to grant to such an unworthy being as myself. And now, my dear parents, I feel as if I were entering on a new being, so much happier am I than during my former course of life. . . . Much yet remains to be done ; and now I humbly and sincerely, and from my

months after my arrival, that I made my first Communion. I had now two things to look after, my studies and my soul, and in both had everything to make up ; for I had never understood before either in what real study consisted, or how the soul could be advanced towards divine things. I began the first with the Latin grammar and elementary books, and the structure of language dawned upon me as a beautiful thing and one of deep interest. For in my earlier days syntax was a locked up mystery for want of a proper teacher to draw its principles into application. I soon began other languages, for which I had a natural facility, and my private time was mainly given to history.

I was pushed up much too rapidly through the school, and consequently did not get my fair share of scholarship, even as it was then understood in our colleges. I got no Greek, but picked up the rudiments later on in teaching a class of beginners. I was passed on from class to class at each bi-monthly examination, so that in the course of twelve months I had gone through all the classes and stood by the side of those who had been studying for six or seven years. It is true I had a method of my own, which gave me more of the book than they who had completed their year in it ; but that was unknown to the masters. I first got up the lessons of the day as completely as I could, dodging the dictionary through all the roots and compounds of the words, and then went on in the book for the remainder of the time, so that I was soon ahead of the class by some hundreds of pages, yet had scarcely ever a mark against me. Then I made it a point of honour never to revise for examinations, having a

heart, ask your pardon for all the uneasiness, troubles, and disquietudes which I have caused you, which I hope you will grant through the love you bear our Blessed Lord, and through the goodness of your own hearts. I must also ask pardon of my brothers, for all the scandal which I have given them, when I ought to have set them a good example."

detestation of secondary motives as something mean, but
went on pursuing further studies. Yet the result was my
transfer to a higher class. But I have always regretted
this rapidity, which was beyond my own control ; for
though I have read most things privately, I have knowledge without due scholarship.

On the following Feast of the Epiphany I became a
· postulant together with four fellow-students. But the
postulancy was managed in a peculiar way. We still remained in the school and its dormitory as usual, but were
called up at five instead of six to attend Matins and
Lauds, and Meditation with the monks in choir. This
was the only thing that distinguished us from the other
lay students. We received the religious habit on March
12th, 1824, little more than a year after I had entered
the school. Although the taking the habit was made a
great ceremony, and Dr. Barber, the Prior, read us one of
his beautiful discourses, yet, owing to the times, it was
performed in a very primitive way. A small scapular was
placed over our ordinary lay dress, to be worn underneath,
and a large choir habit, kept for such occasions, was laid
upon the shoulders of each one, but kept to cover only the
last of the candidates.

During the novitiate we wore out our old coloured
clothes under an ordinary college gown, open in front,
and a trencher cap. Our master was a man of a warm
and tender heart, with true religious instincts, who
formed our souls to detachment and the spirit of the
Benedictine Rule with unction and genuine solicitude. We
were devotedly attached to him and affectionately united
with each other. After the duties of choir our morn-
ings were given to the study of the Rule, committing the
ascetic chapters to memory. As breakfast was not a con-
ventual meal, we daily asked for it on our knees, and before
it was granted the chapter of faults was held, followed by

such admonitions and instructions as might forward us in discipline. We then continued our classical studies for a considerable part of the day. Our master thought it well to exercise our memories, and therefore we had to commit to memory the Sixth Book of Virgil, the " Ars Poetica " of Horace, Pope's " Essay on Man," and various other compositions.

Whilst still in the school as a lay student, I had taken the " Spiritual Combat " as a text-book, and had made it a special study, applying its principles as well as its exposition of the soul's faculties and their use to my own case, and finding more systematic help in it than in any other book. And I have never ceased to recommend it as the most valuable of books for postulants when used as a text-book. Not only because it is so clear on the difference between the Spirit of God in man and the spirit of the world, but also for the help it affords to self-knowledge and self-conquest. It is exactly the book to lay the foundation on which to place the Religious Rule. To this book of principles were added the Lives of the Saints, and especially of the Fathers of the Desert, in whom the spiritual combat was most completely illustrated.

To return to the novitiate. Our work was not all study, manual labour was sometimes added in the old Benedictine spirit ; and there can be no doubt that the man who can handle a spade, or do some mechanical work, will have more practical sense than he who can only handle books, not to speak of this veritable association with our poorer brethren. Penances, those true searchers into nature, were sometimes rather eccentric in their character, as more effectually probing and bringing to the surface those things hidden to oneself, but needing to be known and corrected. Thus, after the time of meditation, a novice would now and then be called upon to write down what he had thought of, with all its wanderings and distractions, which gave the Novice-master the opportunity of teaching the just and right use of the faculties in that spiritual exercise. Our chief text-book for the religious spirit was the " Practice of Religious Perfection," by Rodriguez ; to which the master added instructions drawn from the Rule of St. Benedict. Here let me remark that however great is the value of Rodriguez, it ought to be adapted in a special edition for the use of Religious women. For there are certain points in it that only regard the Society for which it was written, and which are apt to mislead those numerous institutes of Religious women to whom they are not applicable.*

What took most hold of me, as an idea at least, was the whole doctrine of Christian and Religious humility ; and the example of the Fathers of the Desert had a still greater charm, at least for my imagination. This, however, introduced a disturbing influence, which set me a day dreaming and so unsettled me. Abbot de Rancé's book on " Monastic Life," his life and the four volumes recording the lives and deaths of the first members of his reformed monastery, took hold of me and linked themselves in my mind with St Bernard, whom I had taken as my patron Saint, and with his reform of the Benedictine Order. All this combined with the impression made on me by the Lives of the Fathers in the Desert, as drawn up by Bishop Challoner, had become to me what fiction had been to my earlier years— a grand, romantic, spiritual ideal, to be somehow realised and acted upon. I earnestly entreated my Superiors to allow me to go to La Trappe, there to live a penitential life, buried from and forgotten by the world. A visit from Mr. Walmesley, an English gentleman, skilled in medicine, who was a lay brother of that monastery, only increased my

* As, *e.g.*, the chapter on " Manifestation of Conscience," which the Archbishop never allowed to be used in the novitiates of convents of women subject to him.

desire. My Superiors tried to divert me from it, yet in the kindest and most considerate way. Yet the notion acted upon me in a way that for a time overpowered my fondness for intellectual pursuits, for which I more than once got a smart rebuke. When it came to the question of profession, I opened my mind anew to the Novice-master on the subject. He asked my leave to consult with the Prior. The result of their conference was to express to me their sincere apprehension of there being something of imagination in what I contemplated, and their fear that if I went to La Trappe I should most likely fail, in which case I should probably lose my vocation and return to the world. I was therefore advised to make my profession as an Anglo-Benedictine, upon the understanding that, if after a period of two years I was still of the same mind, putting aside the thought in the interval, they would offer no further objections to my going to La Trappe. On this advice I acted ; nor did I doubt, in later years, as I have known in similar instances, that all was a delusion. It left me, however, a valuable experience for the future guidance of souls.

Our novitiate was a happy one ; our numbers had been doubled during its course, and, isolated as we were from the professed Community, on whom we looked with great respect, as well as from the school, we were closely united with each other. We observed the rule of silence strictly, and even if one of us glanced through the windows by way of curiosity it was made the subject of self-accusation at next morning's chapter. The evening recreation became a valuable influence, and from time to time our master pointed out some incident, religious event, or pious history in an easy way, and turned it to useful instruction. Seldom did a priest visit the house from the mission but we heard something edifying about him or his work, and the occasion was taken for inculcating the true missionary spirit. That life, however, he used to tell us, was only for us, if called on by the President-General to enter upon it ; our real business there was to make ourselves good monks, and to leave our future disposal in the hands of God, Who would manifest His will through the voice of Superiors. This solid principle also was carefully enlarged upon, that the care of souls was an office so far beyond human powers that nothing could make it safe or effective but the grace attached to obedience ; that it was essentially what the Divine Revelation declared it to be, a mission ; and that mission consisted, not in selecting for ourselves, but in being *sent* by authority.

Four of us who had entered the novitiate together made our profession on Easter Tuesday, April 9th, 1825. It was a time of unusual fervour, as well in special preparation as in that greatest oblation to God of which man is capable. As I am in part recording the customs of those days in which the Catholic Church in England was first beginning to emerge into freedom, after its long state of obscurity, I may mention that our change of costume consisted in nothing more than a change from the old brown or blue clothes to what was then considered clerical costume, to wit, a black-tailed coat, shorts with gaiters, and a white limp cravat; and in the monastery a soutane, a college gown, and cap. For it was still a long time before it was considered prudent to adopt the religious habit. Father Polding still continued in the office of Novice-master, and we, as junior professed, remained under his paternal care. He still directed our studies, and under him we studied Rhetoric, Logic, and Mental Philosophy. During the year of Rhetoric our text-books were Cicero and a manuscript by Eustace, the author of the "Classical Tour in Italy," who was first a student and then professor of the Priory when at Douay, though never a monk ; Quinctilian and parts of Longinus ; whilst for private reading we had Blair, Rollin on "Sacred Eloquence," and Campbell's

" Philosophy of Rhetoric." But for my part I read everything the library could produce. A little debating society
was also got up later on, which some of the older monks
joined ; and thus one began to gain the habit of thinking
on one's legs before an audience. Privately, I felt the need
also of a certain physical training ; for though no longer
heavy and clumsy as in my sea-going days, because study
had reduced my system, yet I was stronger on the left than
on the right side, and had a lisp in my voice. I therefore
took to Austin's " Cheiromonia," and with the aid of dumb-
bells trained myself to freedom and ease of action until it
became natural to me. I stood for hours together, at my
studies, on the right leg to gain power over it; and, to cure
the lisp and get clear open utterance I repeated compositions walking up hill and with pebbles in my mouth,
when I had opportunities of doing so unobserved. We
also paid particular attention to pronunciation, making it a
rule to correct each other, and keeping " Walker's Dictionary" on the table for an authoritative appeal. And
here let me express my surprise that so little has ever
been done in the training of our clergy, to cultivate clear
and effective reading for Church use.

About this time I took up St. Augustine's "Confessions "
as a spiritual manual, which, next to the sacred Scriptures,
is the book of greatest profundity, whether as regards the
knowledge of God or of the divine operations in the human
soul; no book ever opened my intelligence so much by
setting before me the principles upon which human life
should move. It is a book for the heart quite as much as
for the mind, and reveals to us the divine operations of
grace in its conflicts with nature with wonderful clearness.
There is much truth in the remark that St. Augustine
formed the religious intellect of Europe.

From Rhetoric, after an elementary course of Physics, we
passed to Logic. Our text-books were Watts and the

" Port Royal Logic," after which we took up the Scholastic Logic in another manuscript treatise by Eustace. Here I found a study completely to my taste, for few things have fascinated me more than the analysis of mental operations and the study of the mental and moral faculties. I therefore found myself in a field of predilection when we passed to the study of mental and moral philosophy. Father Polding himself was an extensive reader and large thinker on these topics, and made the subject attractive. He first opened our minds with Reid and other Scotch philosophers, and after thus interesting us in philosophic thought, especially in the beautiful style of Reid and Beattie, passed us on to the Catholic philosophy. All the chief systems were analysed excepting those of Germany, which, at that time, were scarcely known in England. We were then set to analyse Hume, Berkeley, Locke, and Hartley, and to write essays upon them. Then we were introduced to Natural Religion, which brought me into contact with the " Pensées de Paschal," Paley, and the large works of Bergier and Bishop Butler. In private time I analysed and annotated most of these books on paper, and, which I afterwards regretted, burned a great pile of these papers before going to Australia.

Nor was the study of the Scriptures neglected. These occupied the Sundays, festivals, and an hour each evening. Besides the "Prolegomena," we studied the Psalms, with the help of Menochius, Bossuet, and South, and after studying one day wrote notes the next. We committed the Gospels of the Sundays to memory, and afterwards all the Epistles of St. Paul, except the one to the Hebrews, and studied a commentary on them. I never regretted the learning St. Paul's Epistles by heart in the Douay version. This exercise became invaluable to me as a preacher, though it gave me an involved style, which it took me years to shake off. I found South of great assistance in comprehending the style of the Old Testament, and a few lessons in Hebrew, which I privately obtained at Scarborough from a Jewish Rabbi, gave me an insight into the structure of that language.

Our Professor of Theology had no taste for Philosophy beyond the Scholastic Logic. He caught me one day in the library reading Smith's "Theory of Moral Sentiments," with "Coghlan on the Passions" lying by my side. "What are you reading?" he asked. I told him. "There is no theory of morals," he said. "No," I replied, "but there *have been* many ; and in its nature it is a system." Comprehending the significance of my "*have been*," he let me read on.* It became a habit with me to trace everything I could to its origin and principles. I endeavoured to think by principles, and the habit made me laconic in speech, for my style was a reflex of what was going on in my mind, and made me sometimes a puzzle to those to whom I spoke. One good *confrère* hit me with Horace's "*brevis esse laboro, obscuro fio*"—"In trying to be brief you grow obscure." And I sometimes heard my old nickname amplified into "Old Plato." I believe I was more or less a puzzle to Superiors as well as to brethren, and was left to do much after my own way. Thus I got into a habit of constant reading with very little relaxation ; and excessive reading overlays solid mental, as well as moral, discipline. I read far into the night, beyond the time for

* The obscurity of the above passage is thus explained by a learned friend to whom it was submitted. "In this passage reference appears to be made to the distinction drawn by St. Augustine ('De Civit. Dei,' l. 19, n. 1) between the moral systems of philosophers—'empty dreams' he calls them—'and the hope which God gives to us, and the substantial fulfilment of it which He will give us as our blessedness.' The word 'theory' is used in that loose sense so common in English writers, which takes it as equivalent to *hypothesis*, and hypothesis for *conjecture*. In this sense we have no 'theory of morals'; yet 'in its nature it is a system,' for it essentially implies subordination according to a distinct method—whatever method be adopted or principle of subordination assumed."

extinguishing lights, and consequently was often found wanting in choir when Matins had begun. Nor was this noticed, as it ought to have been, until at last I went to the Prior, acknowledged my fault, and offered to submit to whatever correction he thought best. After which I received a public rebuke.*

There is a certain class of persons in colleges and monasteries who, having a degree of intelligence and love of study, are more occupied within themselves than outwardly demonstrative, and who look more singular than they really, in their hearts, wish to be. Not being altogether comprehended, they are apt to be left too much to themselves, so far as is consistent with ordinary observance. Such persons require to be drawn out of themselves, not so much by admonition as by the kind and considerate converse of Superiors. But even sensible Superiors too often refrain from doing this from the mistaken motive that they may do more harm than good, although there may be stages where it would be so. But, in the main, those self-included characters, like ghosts, will speak when calmly spoken to. Their hearts want the relief of communing, and are only in a labyrinth for want of a hand to guide them out of it.

The Sundays and festivals, which were days of Holy Communion, were exclusively devoted to spiritual studies and the Holy Scriptures. We were accustomed to daily self-examination, and always took a chapter of Scripture, and another of the "Following of Christ," before proceeding to other spiritual reading; and towards Holy Scripture I had always a special attraction.

In the beginning of the year 1828 we began our course

---

† To this frank acknowledgment of his fault, it is right to add, on the authority of one admitted to his closest confidence, that whenever in later years the Bishop visited Downside he always assisted at the office in choir as an act of reparation for former negligence.

of Theology. Here, at last, I found a teacher who really taught systematically, and not only with method, but with considerable preparation and from an extensive accumulation of knowledge. I have always said that Dr. Brown, late Bishop of Newport and Menevia, was the only person from whose living voice I ever learnt much. All else was acquired chiefly through books. But here I found a teacher who spoke from the digested stores of his mind.

The study of the tract on "Religion and its Evidences" led me into a wide course of reading, and into the whole controversy with the Philosophers of France and England. The study of the Divine attributes and of the Holy Trinity elevated the mind and laid the deep foundation of all Theology. I found it to be the most spiritual of all spiritual reading. I may mention, as an instance of my method of work, that at a certain stage the professor placed in my hands the well-known treatise by Dr. Clarke on the Divine attributes. But with all its clearness, I found a link wanting in the argument where the transition occurs between material and spiritual existence. I referred it to the professor, who was equally perplexed. I then beat about until at last I found a hint, in the " Dictionnaire Theologique" of Bergier, that Clarke had drawn his whole argument from Tertullian. Referring to that deep thinker I found the link that was wanting in his books *Contra Hermogenem.* The science of the Incarnation gave a unity and depth to the sacred Scriptures such as I could not have understood before ; whilst the heresies through which that science obtained its wonderful development and accuracy completely explained the good which God brings out of the conflict between light and darkness. The previous learning of St. Paul's Epistles was a good preparation for the treatise on Grace, for which we had an excellent text book abridged from Tournely. But I also read some of St. Augustine's treatises against the Pelagians, which were chiefly enucleations of St. Paul, whose Epistles after that became a new book to me.

With respect to the treatise on the Church, I must admit that our professor was inclined, by his studies, to Gallicanism, and hence we had a good deal of Tournely and De la Hogue. This, however, did not altogether satisfy my mind, nor was it the view taken by Dr. Barber, our Prior, who had been trained by Dr. Eloy, a distinguished Doctor of the Sorbonne, who was first of his licence in that University, and whose views were altogether ultramontane. I consequently took up De Maistre's book, and Gallicanism was gradually cleared out of my mind. This reminds me to state, before I forget, that at the Council of the Vatican the public press completely misrepresented the line which I took on the discussion of the question of the Papal Infallibility. I was represented as taking a middle course. It was nothing of the kind. As a matter of fact, I never opened my lips on that question. It is true that I prepared a discourse upon it, and my name was put down to speak, but when my turn came I was so ill that I was unable to rise from bed. I got another Bishop to ask leave to read my address ; but it was ruled by the Presidents that it could not be read unless the author was present, and as there were more than forty speakers still on the list, the opportunity was lost. The sole object contemplated in that address was to propose the addition of a term in the definition which might tend to greater clearness. As I knew that impressions had been privately made on the mind of the Sovereign Pontiff with respect to my views, I solicited a special audience, in which I informed His Holiness that from the time of my theological studies I had always been an Infalliblist, and that all I desired was to see that the definition should be as clear as it could be made. But in fact the lines of explanation added to the decree before its promulgation accomplished all that I desired. With this explanation His Holiness expressed himself well satisfied.

Although our Dogmatic course was wisely conducted in Latin for the sake of accurate terminology, yet our professor decided to conduct the moral course in English, on account of the many and minute practical questions which belong to modern times and English customs. It was a happy circumstance for us, that just before we began this last study a Jesuit Father, on a visit from Bristol, introduced the great work of St. Alphonsus to the knowledge of our professor, together with the decrees in its favour. It consequently became our chief guide and saved us from the rigorism of Collet. At that time St. Thomas was little known in practice on this side of the Alps, except in quotations. Bishop Collingridge had also bequeathed a sum, at his death, for a reprint of the *Praxis* of Blessed Leonard of Port Maurice, which our professor superintended at about the same period. We thus had safe guides to Roman doctrines. Although our professor gave us the summary of many authors, when great questions were concerned he always left us free where the Church left us free; but we chiefly followed the conclusions of St. Alphonsus.

I long endeavoured to form to my mind a map of theological science in its order and logical sequence, getting the first start from the preface of Petavius, and so proceeding with time and study. For out of this intrinsic view of the whole system of Theology, there appears to me to arise one of the sublimest demonstrations of religion, a demonstration that well deserves a book to itself. During these studies, the late Father Dullard, who, with permission of the Holy See, had passed from the Franciscan to the Benedictine Order, left in my cell for safe custody copies of the best editions of St. Augustine, Tertullian, St. Bernard, and Bossuet. To these I devoted much private time,

and got initiated into the value of the Fathers of the
Church; which contributed much to breadth and freedom
of mind.   As to Bossuet, I never tired of him.   His com-
prehensive views tend so greatly to the enlargement and
elevation of thought.   Comparing notes, at a later period,
with such men as Abbot Guéranger, Cardinal Pitra, and
other men of that stamp, I found them ascribing much of
their mental enlargement to an early familiarity with the
pages of Bossuet, notwithstanding his Gallicanism.

Another book the study of which formed a real epoch in
the history of my mind was a collection of the works
attributed to St. Denys the Areopagite, which I read
when a deacon at Ampleforth.   Here I found Theology
in its purest form divested of controversy, and written
as if by a spirit with a pen of light; explaining also,
with wonderful lucidity, both the celestial and the ecclesiastical hierarchies.   These works I followed up with
the "Apostolical Constitutions," which exhibit the early
discipline of the Church in full detail.

I have thus recorded the great landmarks of my
reading, as a student, whilst regretting that the want of
earlier and higher scholarship has been an obstacle to the
better use of reading all my life.

CHAPTER V.

IN the month of October, 1828, I received the Sacrament of Confirmation from Bishop (afterwards Cardinal) Weld. I had never before seen a bishop, except Bishop Baines, when he officiated at the opening of the old Chapel of St. Gregory, the year after I arrived at Downside. On the same day I received the Minor Orders, and on October 12th of the same year the Sub-diaconate, together with my companions, Messrs. Kendal, Davis, and Dowding. On Ember Saturday, September, 1830, together with others of the brethren, I received the Order of Deacon. On March 3rd, 1829, the aged bishop, Dr. Collingridge, of the Western District, departed this life, and Bishop Baines, who had been his coadjutor, succeeded him as Vicar-Apostolic.

Soon after this event began the great conflict within the Anglo-Benedictine Congregation, arising out of the establishment by the Bishop of a great College at Prior Park, near Bath. Through his persuasions, the Superiors of the College of Ampleforth and several of the monks were induced to abandon their monastery and pass over to the Secular College at Bath. The Fathers of Downside not only stood firm to their Order, but even refused to give up a quota of their income to the support of Prior Park, rightly regarding the claim as uncanonical. The troubles arising out of this conflict are now a matter of past history which need not here be recapitulated.

5

Soon after this time my Superiors wished to advance me to the Priesthood, before I had completed the course of Theology. But apprehending there might be difficulties raised by the Bishop about dispensation from time and interstices, a petition was sent to Rome, through Cardinal Weld, the Protector of the English Benedictines. His Eminence replied that it belonged not to the dignity of a Cardinal to act as agent as well as protector ; and so, to my individual satisfaction, I escaped from what I thought a premature ordination. However, I was not destined to continue my studies ; but with the Rev. Mr. Sinnot, a deacon as well as myself, I was sent to assist the new Prior in restoring the Monastery and College of Ampleforth after the great desolation caused by the events above referred to. Soon after arriving there I was appointed Professor of Theology to a small class ; but by the time I had prepared the first lesson the Prior had changed his mind, put an Irish Franciscan to that office, and appointed me Prefect of Discipline over the school. Although those who remained constant to the Order after the great desertion stood firm, yet there was still a flavour remaining of the spirit in which they had been trained. The new Prior was from the old house of Lambspring, and an old missioner, and was not accepted with perfect cordiality, still less the two members from Downside. This spirit communicated itself to the school, which had too intimate relations with one or two Religious. So no sooner had the new Prefect appeared, than there was chalked up on the walls, " No Hunt, No reform." I let the students have their little triumph for the day. But the next morning, after prayers, I let them know how surprised I was to find a college of boys with the manners of a pothouse. I observed that if one or two of them had chalked the walls in a style insulting to an entire stranger, the rest must have concurred, or they would have removed the disgrace fastened on the whole

school. " I will not be severe with you," I said, " without
necessity : I will give you till the next recreation hour to
get the walls cleaned of their disgrace. If it is not done by
then, I will stop all the school work until I find out the
offenders. If I fail I shall conclude that the whole school
is involved in the guilt, and shall punish by decimation."
At the next recreation the walls were quite clean. Soon
after, I expelled one of the older students and flogged a
younger one, after which we became good friends and
understood each other.

Meanwhile I had received the Order of Priesthood,
together with Mr. Sinnot, from Bishop Painswick at
Ushaw. This, to me, great event took place on the
Ember Saturday of September, 1831 ; nor need I dwell
upon the great change which the Priesthood wrought in
my spiritual habits. Only those who, after long preparation, have entered under obedience into that sublime state
and office, can in any degree realise what the Sacrament
of the Priesthood does for the soul of the receiver. For
weeks after my ordination I seemed to feel the sacred
unction on my hands. The thought and feeling with which
the Priesthood inspired me was one of *sacrifice*, making it
appear to be the natural life of a priest whose soul had undergone a transformation into a new order of existence.
The ideas of *monk* and *priest* appeared to my mind's eye
in singular correlation with each other : the monk, as the
man spontaneously offered to God through the call of His
election of grace ; whilst the Priesthood, imparting the dis-
tinctive character of Christ to the soul, absorbed the hidden
life of Our Lord, and brought Him forth an open sacrifice
for the souls of men. The tremendous mystery of the altar
took visible form in my eyes, and was coloured to my inward sense as that Divine oblation of the Immaculate Lamb
which on Heaven's golden altar was ever offered before the
majesty of the Father, the earthly repetition of which made

by mortal man seemed to make the material altar stream with grace. As Prefect I felt reluctant to employ my consecrated hands in punishing boys sent up to me for the purpose. I believe this sense of sacrifice impressed on my soul at my ordination had a secret force and some conscious influence in rendering me prompt to respond to the call to the Australian Mission. Alas! that those deeper movements of the soul should slacken and suffer loss amid the strife and turmoil of subsequent life!

Soon after my ordination I was sent to the small missions of Craik and Easingwold on alternate Sundays. There I preached my first sermons, and did the Sunday duty. It was at Craik that Dr. Baines first began, and I found there a copy of " Archer's Sermons " covered with his marks for accentuation. It was there he first elaborated that style of enunciation which made him afterwards such a master of oratorical delivery. Some time before I received the Priesthood I had lost my dear father. He received the last Sacraments surrounded by his family ; and one of his assistants, who was likewise present, was so touched by this Catholic death-bed, the sacred rites which accompanied it, and the moving words of the priest, the Rev. Mr. Leyne, that he asked for instruction and to be received into the Church. It then came out that he had hitherto been the secretary of an Orange Lodge, which he at once relinquished ; and, as he subsequently told me, the object of that Lodge was to do all the harm they could to the Catholic religion.

Returning to Downside in 1831, I had scarcely settled down in my old monastery and begun to teach in the school, when Dr. Polding received briefs of appointment as Visitor-Apostolic to the Mauritius, where his uncle, Dr. Slater, was the Bishop. But he feared lest the intense heat of that island should relax his energies, and so respectfully declined the appointment.

CHAPTER VI.

MISSION TO AUSTRALIA.

THROUGH the recommendation of Bishop Brampton, Vicar-Apostolic of the London District, Dr. Morris, a member of the Downside Community, who had for several years been the only member of any regular Order employed on the London Mission, was then appointed as Apostolic Visitor to the Mauritius, which appointment he accepted. He naturally wished to obtain co-operators from the house of his profession, and accordingly made application to the Superiors of Downside. In reply to his application he was told that if I were asked I should probably not be unwilling to go. This impression was, I believe, derived from an incident which took place several years before that time. I had been suffering for some two years from an acute inflammation of the liver, combined with sharp and continuous attacks of ague. I was going with other young Religious, in company with Dr. Polding, in a post chaise, to Bath, to consult a physician, when Dr. Polding began to talk of the great want of missioners in Australia ; he spoke of the sufferings of the convicts, and observed that there was not such a field in the wide world for missionary labour. He gave his own ideas as to the way in which such a mission should be managed, expressed his attraction for it, and asked us which of us would be ready to join him. I at once declared myself ready to do so. This conversation had evidently been laid up in Dr. Polding's mind, and had led to the mentioning of my name to Dr. Morris. When, therefore, Dr. Morris wrote to me, I replied that I had about a hundred reasons against going to the Mauritius, and almost as many for going to Australia.

It must here be observed that the Bishop of the Mauritius had at that time a most extensive jurisdiction ; it reached, on the one side, to South Africa ; and on the other, over Australia and the South Sea Islands, including New Zealand. Dr. Morris replied that he equally required help for Australia, and asked me to go to New South Wales. I therefore submitted the question to my Superiors. The Prior at that time was Father Turner, an old Douay monk, a truly meek and holy man, whilst Drs. Polding and Brown filled the next offices. Dr. Polding advised me to wait, thinking that the time for the Australian Mission was not yet mature. But the Prior and Dr. Brown advised me to write to the President-General, who gave me up to the jurisdiction of Bishop Morris for the Australian Mission.

I therefore proceeded to London, where I received the kindest hospitality from my relatives ; nor can I ever forget the affectionate co-operation or the prolonged hospitality of my *confrère*, the Rev. Dr. Heptonstall, who was the Procurator of the English Benedictines in London, and had a small mission at Acton. At that time I had no prospect of aid from the Colonial Government, but was going out at my own expense. That is to say, I had a little legacy from my father, which I was allowed to use, and which was doubled by my mother and two brothers. My first work was to form a library, for I knew that the books I should require could not be found in Australia. I therefore spent months in the old book shops and among their catalogues, and gathered together about a thousand volumes of Theology, Fathers, Canon law, and sacred literature, in every language of which I knew something. I then made a visit to Scarborough, where I bade farewell to my dear mother, brothers, and sisters, never expecting to see them again.

Meanwhile a despatch had come from the Governor of New South Wales to the Secretary for the Colonies, which changed my position altogether. His Excellency represented to the Secretary of State that there was no authorised head of the Catholic clergy in that colony, that difficulties had consequently arisen between the Government and the senior priest respecting grants of land, and that it was desirable to obtain the appointment of a Catholic ecclesiastic invested with due authority. Bishop Morris was in consequence invited to an interview at the Colonial Office, and he informed the Secretary of State that he had an ecclesiastic in view, whom he could appoint as his Vicar-General for Australia, with residence in Sydney, who would have all the authority required. This was agreed to, and a stipend was assigned by the Government of £200 a year, an allowance of £1 a day when travelling on duty, and for voyage and outfit £150. The title assigned to me by Government, in documents, beyond that of Vicar-General, was that of His Majesty's Catholic Chaplain in New South Wales. I also received a letter from the Colonial Secretary, recommending me to the Governors of the Australian Colonies.

Dean Kenny, in his " Progress of the Catholic Religion in Australia," gives an anecdote about the spirit of my departure, as derived from Dr. Heptonstall, which I may as well put in its authentic form. Just before sailing I happened to meet, in the streets of London, my old professor, Dr. Brown, and our old Professor of Greek, Dr. Heptonstall. On bidding them farewell they expressed their surprise that, going out alone, to the furthest extremity of the world, and leaving country and friends behind me, I should be so calm and, apparently, so indifferent. I simply intimated that, having God with me, the authority of the Church and a great vocation before me, I felt I was in my right place and had nothing else to care for.

CHAPTER VII.

DEPARTURE TO AUSTRALIA.

I SAILED in the *Sir Thomas Munro*, on September 16th, 1832. A large ship is a very different thing from the brigs in which I had sailed as a boy ; and I was no longer a cabin boy, but a priest with a title expressive of responsible office. I had a good sized cabin which enabled me to enjoy retirement at any time. Although solitary as a Catholic, and unable to say Mass as a priest, and although I had but little in common with those around me, I never felt those long voyages tedious. I enjoyed the quiet and the absence of solicitude, and the retirement of my cabin, that floating hermit's cell. From my boyhood I had a good deal of the hermit in my composition, preferring to be alone, and having no attraction for society beyond the sense of duty. My attraction was to books and my own solitary musings. And though for many years I had the credit of putting out a good deal of practical energy, that was when duty called, and no longer. Archbishop Polding used to say, and with truth, that I required some exciting cause, or some difficulty to surmount, to draw out the sleeping energies within me. I never felt the disposition to take in hand the future before the present, and was thus saved from many useless solicitudes which torment the imagination. Experience has taught me that things do not occur as the imagination is apt to paint them by anticipation, and that by tormenting yourself with anticipations of events in which you are to be engaged you only jaundice your eyes and warp your judgment. Napoleon's remark that the eye of the general should be as colourless as his glass is applicable to all who have to deal with difficult human affairs. I did not therefore tease myself with the unknown future, but in some degree, on St. Augustine's principle, I "joined myself to eternity and found rest." And of that eternity I had all around me the image in the boundless sea joined to the boundless heavens, always the same, yet always living in a change that spoke of God's never ceasing action in the created universe. On how many tranquil evenings and starry nights did I drink in a deeper sense of God's grandeur as Creator and controller of the boundless air and ocean, and of the worlds that twinkled above me as from a point! There is nothing that inspires the sense of dependence on that sovereign will like the silent teaching of the trackless ocean through the process of the intelligence.

Early habits had made me indifferent to all but the necessities of life, and I discarded many of those useless encumbrances which people call comforts. In the cabin there was much more luxury than I needed, and I never troubled the twelve o'clock "tiffin," or the eight o'clock assembly over the spirit bottles. For many years neither tea, coffee, ale, wine, or spirits suited my constitution; I had steam enough within me to keep up the movement of life. Most of my companions made themselves miserable with the heat in the tropics; and certainly the pitch would sometimes bubble up from between the seams of the deck, and your sticks of sealing wax would melt together: but these good people unnecessarily put fire into themselves, and heated themselves through the imagination by thinking about it. By keeping below when the ship was cool in the earlier part of the day, and coming on deck in the evening when the ship was hot, I was always cool when my companions were in misery. By a little manage-

ment I saved myself this torment, and tried to impart
some of my philosophy to others, but without success :
they seemed to think that our natures were not the
same.

I had a sailor's heart for the poor fellows who manned
the ship, and though I never spoke to them but a word or
so on occasion, they seemed to know it by instinct, and
always showed me particular respect. I fancy they liked
to see the sturdy way in which I walked the deck in all
weathers, and that independence of circumstances which
came of the monk grafted on the sailor. Except the
privation, therefore, of the Mass and the Church services,
I was always inclined to regret when the voyages came to
an end, and the quiet and retirement that they afforded
me. They were a sort of prolonged retreat, uniting a
course of spiritual with a course of ecclesiastical study, by
which I in some degree made up for my abridged course
before ordination.

The rule of life which I adopted on board ship, and
which I followed on all future occasions, never failed to
give me influence on emergency. I followed a plan of
studies in my cabin, but after meals I mixed in the
general conversation. A long voyage at sea generally
contributes to good fellowship ; yet, as the passengers are
of a mixed description, and there is much weariness
arising from indolence, and as wine and malt liquor are
put twice a day on the table, and spirits in the evening as
well, people are apt to talk too freely, and to let out those
infirmities which are, ordinarily, family secrets. Hence
misunderstandings are apt to arise, and sometimes
antipathies. For instance, there was a very quiet Methodist
minister with his wife and family on board this ship.
They used the quarter deck, but had a large cabin, and
second class food by themselves. They were very un-
obtrusive and respectable in their way, but they were teased

and put upon by a number of young men, for no better reason than their own thoughtless amusement. But my reserved habits enabled me to act as their protector on various occasions, and as they suffered a good deal of discomfort I privately sent them presents of wine and other things, which had been sent as presents to me, but for which I had no occasion.

Feeling my deficiency in Ecclesiastical law, I made it a point of special study, and directed special attention to what concerned the authority and jurisdiction of a Vicar-General. For, by my deed of appointment, this extended over the whole of Australia, Van Dieman's Land alone excepted, which was left to the only priest then in that colony. I knew that I should be some four thousand miles away from my Bishop, with whom the means of communication would be rare and casual. Even the consecrated oils for the Sacraments were received from London, much after date, and there was the whole breadth of the world between these colonies and the Holy See. I felt, then, that I should have to act almost as if the complete authority of the Church were concentrated in my office, and to rely on my own resources.

We put in at the Cape of Good Hope, where, on landing, I found but one priest for the whole of South Africa. He was an English Benedictine from Ampleforth, and an accomplished man. His congregation, at that time, was a mixture from all the nations of Europe and the East, and they gave him much trouble, so much so that he often got into fits of abstraction and ground his teeth together. He was subsequently brought to England with the loss of his mind. This was the first opportunity I had of observing the impolicy of leaving one priest alone in a remote colony. Later on I was destined to see more of this evil.

We beat up against the wind under a heavy gale, and

bore such a stress of sail that we were mistaken by the people for a man-of-war. The bold and lofty mountain rising over the town, with the flat table at the top, was covered with its cloth of clouds, at the end of which hung a rainbow, whilst the descending sun threw an exquisite colouring over the vast and stormy scene. The Dutch have built Cape Town after the fashion of their streets at home, in broad straight lines and at right angles, void of all protection from the fierce winds, sun, and dust, so that even the gentlemen had to wear blue veils for the protection of their eyes.

Enjoying the hospitality of the Rev. Father, I was much interested in the novel vegetation to be seen on all sides, and the diversity of races, and especially with the social customs of the Hottentots and the Malays. I visited a particular friend of the priest's, and one of his chief supporters, who was quite a character. A West Indian Creole by birth, he had begun life as a player on the violin, and had risen to wealth by supplying the exotic gardens of Europe with seed, and its menageries with wild animals. He had lions, tigers, ostriches, and other wild animals ready in iron cages for shipment. His hospitable table was surrounded by a large family, and in the centre of his hall stood an immense basket of oranges for the free use, at all times, of his children. His establishment was a curiosity.

Setting sail again, we ran with a fair wind and stiff breeze all the way to the Australian coast, where, passing through Basso Straits, we entered the harbour of Circular Head, so called from a huge rock, or rather mountain of rock, in the shape of a drum, rising up from the sea, and covered with forest, that sheltered the bay within. Here were the head-quarters of the Van Dieman's Land Company, which had received from Government half a million of acres on which to establish an improved system of agriculture. The manager, Mr. Curr, was an English Catholic, and brother of a priest from whom I brought letters. The homestead was certainly in a flourishing condition, both as to vegetable and animal production ; but, with the exception of the manager, his family, and a few superintendents, the whole settlement consisted of convict labourers assigned to the Company. Here I had no juris- diction, and the only priest in the island, which was about the size of Ireland, resided at Hobart Town on the opposite coast. To the great surprise of all on board, I received no more attention than any other passenger. We were invited in parties, once, to dine whilst part of the cargo was un- loading ; but I was left on board like any other stranger, except that I was asked to baptise three of the manager's children, who were old enough to play with the stole and to make remarks whilst the Sacrament was being adminis- tered. The letters in which I described my first impression of the country, its singular trees shedding the bark instead of the leaves, the odoriferous shrubs and scentless flowers, the rich plumage of the birds, and the diversity of the shells and sponges on the shore—these and similar ones of later date were long preserved by my brother Owen, but were unfortunately destroyed by his widow.

From Circular Head we sailed for Hobart Town. No one will ever forget his first entrance into Storm Bay : its vast expanse and depth ; its basalt columns rising out of the cliffs like gigantic organs ; its numerous islands of basalt of varied and fantastic shapes, as we approached the mouth of the Derwent; and Mount Wellington towering 3,000 feet in the distance and marking the position of the capital. To enliven the scene, a shoal of black whales was crossing the bay and shore-boats were after them. We saw one that had been struck with the harpoon, flying rapidly through the water, towing the boat whose harpoon had struck the huge fish, the boat with its fore-timbers out of the

foaming flood, and the men sitting as still as death.
Another whale had been struck repeatedly, its spoutings
were red with mingled blood, and the harpooner, leaning on
the instrument, was forcing it into the exhausted body as
it lay upon the waters. We wound through the islands—
the pilot pointing out Brumdi amongst them, as producing
the best potatoes in the world—and entered the Derwent,
sailing up between its beautiful sloping shores until we
turned into Sullivan's Cove, when we beheld the city, with
Mount Wellington towering over it.

The one priest was absent on his annual visit to Laun-
ceston, on the opposite side of the island.   I was hospitably
lodged and entertained by Mr. Hackett, a native of Cork,
and a distiller; a man of information, popular among the few
Catholics, and influential in the town.   Meeting the leading
Catholics, all of Irish origin, I soon began to hear a sad
account of the state of Catholic affairs, which my own subsequent knowledge but too much confirmed.

I must refer to my two pamphlets, "The Catholic
Mission in Australasia," published in England in 1837,
and " The Reply to Judge Burton," published in Sydney in
1839, for the history of Catholic affairs before my arrival.
The first priest who arrived with authority in New South
Wales was the Very Rev. Jeremiah O'Flynn, who was invested by the Holy See with the title of Archpriest, with
power to administer the Sacrament of Confirmation.   He
arrived in Sydney, by the ship *Duke of Wellington*, on
August 3rd, 1817.   All those Catholics who remembered
him spoke with great reverence of his mild, religious
character, his great charity, and his fluency in speaking the
Irish language.   He was of a Religious Order, and, if I
remember rightly, a Capuchin.   There was no charitable
institution at that time for receiving the helpless poor, and
he took into his residence several aged and decrepit people,
whom he lived with and maintained.   But as he had come

without any authority from the Home Government, the Colonial Government, influenced by a strong anti-Catholic party, illegally seized upon him, put him in prison, and sent him back to England by the first ship. This tyrannical act produced a great sensation at home : Mr. Hutchison, of the Donoughmore family, member for Cork, brought the whole case before Parliament; and under the influence of Lord Bathurst two priests were sent out, Father Connolly and Father Therry, each with a stipend of £100 a year. They arrived in Sydney in 1820, but soon afterwards they disagreed, and Father Connolly went to Hobart Town, where he landed in March, 1821, and remained there without seeing a brother priest until 1833.

A state of things grew up under his *régime* which gave rise to many complaints. I found the chapel in a most disgraceful state, though the house was decent. Built of boards with the Government broad arrow on them, the floor had never been laid down, but consisted of loose planks, with their edges curled by the heat, and sharp as well as loose under the knees of the people. There was a coating of rough plaster on the wall behind the altar, covered with a black glazed cotton all over filth, that had hung there ever since the death of George IV. The altar, a framework of wood, had a similar black glazed cotton for the frontal, and the dirty altar-cloths were covered with stains. The space between the two ends of the altar and the side walls were refuge holes for all kinds of rubbish, such as old hats, buckets, mops, and brooms. There were no steps to the altar, but the same loose planks that formed the entire floor, and no seats for the people. The chalice and ciborium were tarnished as black as ink. I cleaned the sacred vessels, cleared out the rubbish from the sides of the altar, and laid smooth planks down across the front of it to make the footing steady. On two Sundays I preached to the people, who, unaccustomed to be spoken to sympathetically, were moved to tears.

Sir George Arthur, the Governor, received me with great courtesy, and invited me to meet at dinner the Protestant Archdeacon Broughton, who was on a visit with his large family from Sydney, and was afterwards the first Anglican Bishop of Australia. At a later interview the Governor opened up the subject of religion, and we had a long private conversation on the subject. He was himself a very earnest Anglican of the Evangelical school. He put certain questions to me, not mentioning that his friend, the Archdeacon, was at that very time writing a pamphlet on the subject, which I had afterwards to answer in Sydney. Yet I recall with pleasure the courtesies I received from Governor Arthur.

Father Connolly returned before I left Hobart Town; he expressed no discontent at what I had done in the chapel, as the people thought he would, but rather approval, gave me his own ideas of the state of things in Sydney, and we parted friends.

CHAPTER VIII.

ARRIVAL AT SYDNEY.

I MADE it a point of policy not to send any previous notice of my coming to Sydney, where I arrived in the month of February, 1833. I walked up straight to the priest's residence, and there I found a grave and experienced priest in Father McEncroe, who had formerly been Vicar-General to Bishop England in South Carolina. He had come from Ireland to Sydney the year previous with Mr. Attorney-General Plunkett, his wife, and sister. From him I learnt a good deal of how things stood. Father Therry had gone to Parramatta, but quickly hearing of the arrival of another priest, returned that evening. The housekeeper was the widow of the celebrated John Maguire, who kept the British troops at bay in the Wicklow Mountains after the insurrection of 1798 had been put down in the west of Ireland. At last he surrendered, on condition that he and his family should be conveyed out free to New South Wales. Father Therry had promised the gallant old man on his death-bed that he would protect his wife and family.

I looked so youthful that the first language of Father Therry, and even of his housekeeper, was naturally patronising; but after dinner I produced the document appointing me Vicar-General, with jurisdiction over the whole of New South Wales, as well as the rest of New Holland, after reading which Father Therry immediately went on his knees. This act of obedience and submission

6

gave me great relief. I felt that he was a truly religious man, and that half the difficulty was over. At his invitation I went with him that evening to the house of a gentleman, where I found myself in company with precisely the three persons with whom it was represented to me in England that I should find my difficulty. But, in fact, they were all very good men, and we became great friends. Still I was internally amused, for they evidently took me for a raw college youth ; and I humoured the notion, and was told at a later time that after I had left they had talked of sending me to Bathurst, then the remotest part of the Colony.

The next morning as I came from Mass in the little chapel, Father Therry met me and said : " Sir, there are two parties among us, and I wish to put you in possession of my ideas on the subject." I replied : " No, Father Therry, if you will pardon me, there are not two parties." He warmed up, as his quick sensitive nature prompted, and replied, with his face in a glow : " What can you know about it ? You have only just arrived, and have had no experience." " Father Therry," I said, with gravity, " listen to me. There *were* two parties yesterday ; there are *none* to-day. They arose from the unfortunate want of some person endowed with ecclesiastical authority, which is now at an end. For the present, in New South Wales, I represent the Church, and those who gather not with me scatter. So now there is an end of parties."

That day I went by coach to Parramatta, to see the Governor at his country residence. Sir Richard Bourke had recently lost his wife, to whom he was much attached, and was ill in bed. But he was anxious to have the Catholic affairs settled, and gave me an audience in his bedroom. The fine old soldier was one of the most polished men I ever met. In his younger days he had been a good deal under the influence of the celebrated

Edmund Burke, and was a man of extensive information as well as experience. The statue erected to his memory in Sydney bears recorded on its base the great measures by which he gave freedom and social progress to the Colony. Though not a Catholic, he had a great respect for the Catholic religion, and had many Catholic relatives and friends. He received me with great kindness, and we soon understood each other. I listened to his remarks, and then asked leave to see him again after I had inquired into the points of which he spoke. I returned to Sydney, and on the Sunday I announced my powers to the people from the altar, and stated that I suspended all affairs connected with the business of the Church for a fortnight, when, after making due inquiries, I would call a public meeting of the Catholics.

Father Therry was quite an exceptional character. He was truly religious, never omitting to say Mass daily even in difficult circumstances ; and up the country, when he could find no appropriate roof for the purpose, he would have a tent erected in some field or on some mountain side. He also said the Rosary in public almost every evening, gathering as many people as he could. He was of a highly sensitive temperament, and readily took offence, but was ready soon after to make reparation. He was full of zeal, but wanting in tact, so that he repeatedly got into trouble with the Government, and sometimes with the successive ecclesiastical authorities. Hence the long difficulties which arose after he was superseded as Vicar-General in Tasmania by its first bishop. Having passed from trade to his studies, he had sufficient knowledge of his duties, but was too actively employed to be a reader. Having been the sole priest in the Colony for some eleven years, he was very popular, not only with the poor Catholics, for whose sake he did not spare himself, but with all classes of the population. Being the one representative of the Church in those times, landed property was bequeathed to him in various places by Catholics who had no relatives in the Colony. This he always treated as his private property, though he never took much trouble about it. But in his will he bequeathed it all to religious purposes.

Government policy was still strongly in favour of an exclusive Established Church under the Crown. A Royal Commissioner, Mr. Briggs, was sent out to report on the condition of the Colony ; Mr. Thomas Hobbs Scott, formerly a wine merchant, accompanied him as secretary. On their return Mr. Scott was made the first Protestant Archdeacon of the Colony ; and on his arrival announced his intention to organise the Protestant Church, to establish parishes and schools, and to hand over to a corporation one-seventh of the land of the Colony for that purpose. This was accomplished by a deed under the sign manual of George IV. Moreover, in the orphanage established by Government at Parramatta, the children left without parents were all to be taught the Protestant religion. This new state of affairs was very alarming to the Catholic population, and Father Therry addressed a letter to the *Sydney Herald* (which was at that time also the Government Gazette) on June 6th, 1825, in which he signified his intention of forming a Catholic School Society, and also of doing his best to establish Catholic cemeteries, which would prevent many inconveniencies, besides avoiding collision with the Anglican clergy. But at the close of the letter he spoke of the Protestant clergy as entertaining for them, as it appeared in print, "*qualified* respect." Father Therry explained that this was a misprint, and that he had written the word "unqualified." Nevertheless the letter was made an excuse for withdrawing his small salary, and of excluding him from officiating in any Government establishment ; thus prohibiting him from

visiting the prisons, hospitals, and similar institutions.*
This occurred under the Government of Sir Thomas
Brisbane, and soon after the arrival of Archdeacon Scott
with the purely Protestant scheme of an exclusive
Establishment. It is said that Father Therry was offered
a small sum of money, £300, to leave the Colony, but of
that I never heard, and have no proof.

In the year 1829 Sir Roger Therry arrived as Solicitor-
General and Commissioner of the Court of Requests. He
was the first Catholic appointed by the Home Government after the Emancipation Act. On taking office, the
Protestant oath was tendered to him. He asked for the
Catholic one. The official replied : " Now that the point
of honour is settled, it can make no difference." " It
makes all the difference in life," replied Sir Roger. So
the Catholic oath was produced. In 1832 Father
McEncroe arrived, in company with Mr. Plunkett, his wife,
and sister. Mr. Plunkett came with the appointment of
Attorney-General. These two Catholic gentlemen, both of
high character, were the first men of position who were
earnest in the practice and support of their religion, and
their influence was of great value. Two other Catholic
gentlemen had come out with office at an earlier time, but
they concealed their religion until it was lost to themselves
and their families. It was a saying in Sydney when I
arrived that Lady Therry's was the first bonnet that had

* " Whilst still under this ban Father Therry went to visit a dying
man at one of the hospitals, but was stopped by the guard when
about to enter. Father Therry said : 'The salvation of this man
depends on my ministration ; which is your first duty ?' The guard
lowered his arms and permitted him to pass. On another occasion,
going to the infirmary to visit a sick person, the doorkeeper bade him
wait till he should have ascertained from the attendant surgeon
whether he could be admitted. Whilst he was away, Father Therry,
who knew all the passages of the place, gave the sick person the
consolations of religion, and on returning met the official, who told
him he could not be admitted."—Dean Kenny, " History of Catholicity in Australia," p. 51.

appeared in the Catholic congregation. But when I reached Sydney things had very much changed in that respect. In 1829 the Rev. J. V. Dowling also arrived, and made his residence at Windsor. These were the only two clergymen besides Father Therry whom I found in the Colony in 1833, and both of them had stipends from the Government.

The chief difficulty on my arrival regarded the church in Sydney, which Father Therry had begun soon after his arrival, but which was not yet completed. It was on a very large scale, with transepts raised to a great height, with walls of massive solidity, and with large crypts beneath. The Government had granted the site for the church, and an ample space for whatever buildings might be required in addition ; but it had never been conveyed to trustees, which the Government now required to be done. Moreover, Father Therry claimed an extent of land considerably larger than the Government admitted to have been granted, and there was no documentary evidence producible. The land in question formed part of Sydney Park, and the addition which he claimed would have made considerable inroad into the open space. The Government appointed its own surveyor to measure and mark out the grant, but Father Therry resisted, and the result was that the Catholic Attorney-General was put into a painful position, having received directions to bring an action against the Father, which was only stayed by my arrival.

On my second visit to the Governor I asked his Excellency to allow me to arrange that instead of six lay trustees, as demanded, I might be allowed to have three clerical trustees of my own appointment, and three lay trustees to be selected by the congregation. This, I said, would secure three very respectable laymen, in whom everyone would confide, but if six laymen were required it would lead to serious conflicts. Sir Richard at once understood it, and consented. " Anything reasonable," he said, " for the sake of peace." I then solicited his Excellency to join with me in completing the church for service ; for we had not a single church completed. In Sydney we had only the use of a Government building, used for the Court of Requests, where we had the Sunday services and a school on week-days. If the Government would complete the woodwork, including the flooring, I would put in the sixty large windows. His Excellency agreed to this also.

On the Sunday appointed for the meeting, I first said the Mass and then preached an earnest sermon on unity. I then took the chair, on my own motion, and knowing that several people had come prepared to rake up stories of the past, and to load my ears with grievances, I put a stop to all this by saying that we were not met to talk, but to vote ; that hitherto painful divisions had prevailed owing to the want of an authority, but as there was now a duly appointed authority all good Catholics would adhere to it ; and as to past troubles, the sooner they were forgotten the better. Let us put a ponderous tombstone of oblivion over them, and then leave them in God's hands. Let all the congregation, except the servants of the Crown (the convicts), put the three names they wish for trustees into the voting box. This was done. The three names turned up were those of Mr. Attorney-General Plunkett, Mr. Commissioner Therry, and Mr. Murphy ; the latter being a most respectable Emancipist, who had been unjustly transported, was now a wealthy man, and universally respected. I then appointed Father Therry and Father McEncroe, with myself, as the three clerical trustees. Thus ended our troubles, for the six trustees would now have to deal with the Government as to the extent of land to be granted. As I saw that all

were relieved and in good humour, I said I should be
happy now to hear any remarks that anyone was disposed
to offer. This brought out expressions of thankfulness
and unity from the leaders, and the meeting closed. I have
been thus particular in detailing the steps taken to
establish peace and order, because, after this stroke of
policy, it was never afterwards interrupted.

Passing from the meeting to my residence, I was met
at the door by a poor ragged Irishman, the only man in
tatters I had yet seen. He asked me if I would please
listen to what he had to say. "Well," I said, "what is
it?" In reply he poured out a stream of hexameter
verses, in perfect metre and harmony, describing the
meeting and all its incidents, winding up with a touching
thanksgiving for the peace restored to the Catholic body.
I asked my Irish troubadour, with some astonishment,
what reduced a man of his ability and elevation of mind to
such a condition. He replied : " I am a child of nature,
your Reverence ; and I cannot refuse the drink which my
countrymen give me in their generosity." Some years
later, when in the interior country, I called upon a wealthy
Catholic magistrate, who pressed me to stay for dinner,
promising me something interesting afterwards if I would
do so. I consented, and after dinner in rolled my
troubadour from the farm, in a fat and fine condition,
smiling all over his face. Standing by the door, he
resumed the history of my transactions from the time of
the meeting, rolling out a stream of sweet and harmonious
verses without halt or fault for an hour. He was a self-
taught man, a mere child of impulse, and spoke in tones
the tender sweetness of which I completely recall at this
hour. I never saw him again.

Writing home on the day of my arrival, with the window
open before me, suddenly there came a darkness. I
looked up, and there was the head of the chief of the

Sydney tribe thrust through the window to see what was going on. His black face painted red under the eyes, wild mass of hair, beetling brow, big jaws, crushed nose, white teeth, and naked shoulders ; the grin on his face ; the energetic nodding of his head, formed a picture so grotesque and unexpected that it required a little effort to return his greetings with politeness. Behind him was his *gin*, the poor princess of his tribe, peering out of the blanket with which she was enveloped. I gave them some coppers, and sketched them into the letter I was writing. We were the intruders into their dominions, not they upon ours, and their tribe had already dwindled down to half a dozen fighting men. Father Therry was habitually kind to these poor creatures, who camped and held their dances and their funerals in a valley by the seashore, about half a mile below our residence. He often fed them when in want. But there was no making any religious impression upon them. Any allusion to a God reduced them to silence. They had a fear of evil spirits, which they some-times showed at night, and imagined that the spirits of men after death came back in other forms.

Father McEncroe and I had once a most interesting account from two young men, of the Botany Bay tribe, telling us their traditions of the arrival of Captain Cook in that bay. When they saw the two ships they thought them to be great birds. They took the men upon them in their clothes, and the officers and marines in their cocked hats, for strange animals. When the wings (that is, the sails) were closed up, and the men went aloft, and they saw their tails hanging down (sailors wore pigtails in those days) they took them for long-tailed opossums. When the boat came to land, the women were much frightened ; they cried and tried to keep the men back. The men had plenty of spears, and would go on. Cook took a branch rom a tree and held it up. They came on, and they trembled. Then Cook took out a bottle and drank, and gave them it to drink. They spat it out—salt water! It was their first taste of rum. Cook took some biscuit and ate it, and gave them some. They spat it out—something dry! It was the old ship-biscuit. Then Cook took a tomahawk and chopped a tree. They liked the tomahawk and took it. Thus the first gift they saw the value of was the axe that was destined to clear their woods and to make way for the white man. Allowing for the broken English, that is an accurate narrative of the tradition of the Botany Bay tribe.

Dr. Bland, an old inhabitant, told me that in early days he had witnessed a fight between the Sydney and the Botany Bay tribes on the very ground before the house. After hurling their fourteen feet spears, they closed, and each struck his antagonist with his *waddy*, a club of hard wood, and then chivalrously presented his head to receive the return blow, striking alternately until one of them was laid prostrate. I was walking on one occasion with Father McEncroe on the same ground, when a young native fled across our path naked and unarmed ; a second, with his waddy, followed in chase ; whilst a third appeared in the distance. The first plunged into the Government domain, an aboriginal forest with walks cut through it. We followed by the shortest cut in the same direction, but only arrived in time to find the first man killed with the *waddy* of the second, who had fled. The third came up in terrible excitement, his naked skin fretted and his eyes bursting. He was the brother of the man who was slain. Finding life extinct, he sent up one cry and then rushed after the slayer. The police brought the body into our stable, and an inquiry was made. But it was found to be a case of native feud between two tribes following their own laws. The body was given up to the tribe to whom it belonged, and I heard the funeral rites performed that night in the valley below. Nothing could be done for the souls of these poor creatures, corrupted as they were among the Europeans. Some youths, however, from tribes more remote, were brought up in Catholic families and became regular communicants; but as soon as they reached manhood, the savage revived, they flung off their clothes, and rejoined their tribe.

Soon after my arrival at Sydney a venerable old man, who lived by splitting timber in the woods, came for his annual visit to go to his religious duties; for, like thousands of others, he lived in the bush a long way from any priest. He remembered the early days when Sydney was nothing but a penal settlement. He was a tall man, with white hair and a bowed head, with much refinement of speech and manner; an old insurrectionist of 1798. He spoke much of Father Flynn, and said with touching pathos: " If Father Flynn had been let remain, what would not have been done?" He had the sweetest and swiftest tongue of Irish I ever heard.

Another tall old man, with the same breadth of chest and shoulders, and the bearing of a chief, used to be led from the convict barracks every Saturday by a boy (for he was stone blind) to make his confession. And always, after concluding, he made a brief, but solemn, act of thanksgiving aloud for the gift of blindness, as it shut out half the wickedness in the midst of which he was compelled to live.

Bushranging, with its venturesome hazards, had an attraction to the Irish convicts, and some of the most desperate bushrangers were Irishmen. But it was a rule among bushrangers of all descriptions, English and Irish, never to touch a priest. They had a fixed idea that if they did they would never have luck again. So we always knew we were safe. Once, going on a sick call from Sydney to Liverpool, a man sprang out of the bush with a blunderbuss on his shoulders, and seized the horse's head. I was sitting in my gig, wrapped in a cloak, and at once disengaged my hands, whilst my servant prepared for a spring on him, when the bushman, seeing my face in the moonlight, ran off among the trees. The men in the condemned cells have told both the Bishop and the priests of particular times and circumstances when they passed them by, lying in wait in their hiding-places.

There were several soldiers in the 17th Regiment who went to their weekly Communion, and at least twenty-two who went once a fortnight. One young man I particularly remember, who was quite a contemplative. He had received the Carmelite scapular before he entered the army, and had persevered in a habit of prayer and fasting. He spent all his sentry watches in prayer. He had to stand sentry by the jail, close to the gibbet, one night after two men had been hung upon it; and such was his terror at the working of his imagination in that ghastly spot, with the shades of night around him, that, as he afterwards told me with a sense of gratitude, nothing but the earnestness with which he said his prayers, and so conquered his imagination, saved him from throwing down his musket and running away. The incidents of the barrack-room and the rigours of military discipline served him as subjects of self-mortification, and he certainly had a tender conscience and an habitual sense of the presence of God. He kept several of his comrades steady to their religious duties. I have often wondered what became of this young soldier, who had then gone on well and holily for several years.

There was a convict about thirty years old, far up the country on the Bathurst range, beyond the Blue Mountains, who was quite a contemplative. A shepherd, always following his sheep over extensive pastures, and except at lambing and shearing times, always alone, or nearly so, he spent his time in prayer and enjoyed his solitude. There was then no priest resident in all that country ; and his master was so pleased with his steady, reliable conduct, and the care he took of his sheep, that he let him come down once a year to Sydney to receive the Sacraments, and gave him five shillings to buy food on the way. He walked upwards of a hundred miles for this purpose, praying by the way. He would stop a few days in Sydney, and I used to give him half-a-crown to help him back, and then he returned to his wilderness. He had the gentleness of manner which the habits of prayer and solitude give.

I was often struck with the injustice that men constantly commit in generalising the habits of criminals, and leaving them not one virtue or humane quality. I have often sat at the table of lawyers and attendants at the criminal courts and have heard them discuss the criminals they had been engaged in trying, or hearing tried ; and have observed how natural is the disposition, even of shrewd men, to apply the principle, "he who offends in one point is guilty of all," in a sense certainly never contemplated in the sacred Scriptures. There the sense intended undoubtedly is that the offender against one point of law is guilty against the principle on which all law is based, and against the God Whose command is disobeyed, and against that love of God which is the object and end of all law. But men of the world have a habit, fostered specially in law courts and among those who deal with criminals, of concluding that "once a criminal, always a criminal ; " and that to have offended once implies a natural malignity ready on occasion to perpetrate every crime. Such monsters, however, are rare in human nature. I have often had the opportunity of comparing men, as from my scant knowledge I knew them inwardly, with the judgment passed upon them by those who knew the same criminals only by the outward evidence that is brought into the courts of justice. And I have seen the vast amount of practical truth embodied in the inspired sentence, "Man sees in the face, but God beholds the heart." This singular experience has forced on me the necessity of a divine judgment to rectify the judgment of men, more than all the high theories drawn up on the subject, from the treatise of the pagan Plutarch down to the reasonings of the Catholic De Maistre.

By Christmas night the great church was completed, and we began to have the services and devotions in a more becoming manner. The congregation became large and communicants were much increased. With the aid of the Government I also began a school chapel on the Rocks, among the rudest part of the population. Father Therry often made visits into the more populous parts of the interior. I visited various districts occasionally, and especially Maitland, on the river Hunter; St. Patrick's Plains, higher up the country ; Newcastle, at the mouth of the Hunter ; the beautiful district of Illawara ; Bathurst, beyond the Blue Mountains ; and sometimes Parramatta. Our usual way of travelling was on horseback, with a servant on another horse carrying the vestments and altar-stone. We always carried the Blessed Sacrament in a pyx in the breast pocket, not knowing where or when we might come upon the sick and dying. The Holy See has since pro-hibited this practice ; and recollecting that we often had to stay the night in taverns, and in more miserable places, I think there was wisdom in the prohibition. My oil stocks, through wearing a hole in the pocket, were lost in the desolate Blue Mountains. But, strange to say, a Frenchwoman passed that way, found them, and concluded that they must belong to a priest, and so they were finally recovered. A silver snuff-box lost in the same region was never recovered, although my name was upon it and I offered a reward for it. I valued it as a gift from my mother.

We generally used the police courts for chapels, but at

Bathurst I used the ballroom of the Royal Hotel, built over the stables, and at Appin I said Mass in a room of the tavern, where I preached against drunkenness. The innkeeper, a worthy Catholic, was rallied about this sermon; but he said: "We will take anything from his Reverence." I was breakfasting after my work in this inn, when I was told that a man wanted to see me. "Bring him in," said I. "Good morning, your Reverence," he said at the door. "Good morning to you; when were you at your duties last?" "Ah, it's not them, your Reverence." "Well, what is it?" "To tell your Reverence the truth, the other day I got drunk, and I promised my wife on my knees that I would not take a drop of drink for twelve months, unless through the hands of a priest. And if your Reverence could just let me take a bottle of rum through your hands to keep Christmas with——" "Well, I will make a bargain with you. Father Therry will be here about Christmas, and if you promise me to go to your duties with him, and only to drink it moderately, two glasses at a time with your family, you shall have a bottle of rum." It was brought in and paid for, when the man held it up to the light, and said: "It looks very nice, wouldn't your Reverence have a little drop?" "Come," I said, "you want the bottle opened. It won't do; go and keep your promise, and mind this, I shall inquire if you do keep it." "But," he said, "your Reverence must touch the bottle; that was in my oath."

Wherever we went the Catholic innkeepers entertained us and our horses, and would never accept payment. When we reached a township, the first day was spent in riding round the country, visiting all the settlers, Protestant as well as Catholic, to ask leave for the convict servants to come to Mass and the Sacraments next day. The whole of the next day was occupied with people coming and going, and perhaps a second day was required for Communions. The heat was often intense, and after riding round both man and horse were exhausted. To approach a farm required a little management. The moment you appear, a whole chorus of barking dogs rush out to meet you; and there you must stand surrounded with them until someone comes to take you under protection, after which your claims to hospitality are admitted and you are greeted with a wagging of tails. But woe to you if, after a hard day's ride, one of your first salutations is : "What a pity, we are just going to kill ; " for this means that there is no meat in the house, and that your diet will be damper and tea, with an egg or two—damper being a heavy unleavened cake baked in the ashes, and so called, no doubt, from the damp it puts on your digestion. Hospitality, however, a hearty welcome, and the best that can be had, never fail in the Australian bush.

But, at times, one gets into queer places, and meets with odd incidents. Archbishop Polding was sleeping one night in a log hut, with open rafters above. Awaking, he saw two small lights in the upper roof, and was puzzled to make out what they were. They looked like two greenish stars peering through the shingles. But the mystery was solved by a cat pouncing down from the beams and seizing him by the nose. Having a sick call from Sydney to Illawara, a ride of eighty miles, a very heavy rain came on, and I stopped at a wooden hut for shelter. As the downpour continued the good people offered to lend me a beautiful blue cloth cloak, which hung up in the room and which someone had left there for a time. When it was taken off at the house where I stopped the whole inside of it was covered with bugs, as if it had been sown with pearls, and it had to be hung upon a tree and swept with a broom. The sick woman whom I went to visit, and whom the messenger, who had ridden all the way to Sydney, reported to be near death, came and opened the door. She was quite well, and had only had a fit of ague. I stopped the night at a log hut in the neighbourhood, and was awakened the next morning by a very loud and extraordinary noise. Shrieks and wailings were predominant, whilst a certain harmonious discord in two parts ran through the shrill notes. I got up and inquired, and was told that it was *the settler's clock ;* a species of kingfisher that lives on snakes, against which it is protected by a ruff of feathers round its neck. Owing to its destroying so many poisonous snakes the bird is held sacred. From the extraordinary dialogue of sounds with which the male and female salute the rising sun, Governor King gave it the name of *the laughing jackass*, by which it is commonly called. Returning from that most beautiful district at the ascent of Mount Keera, the forest was on fire on both sides : a not unusual occurrence after a high wind on a very hot day. I stopped to examine if it was safe to proceed, and, looking to the horse's feet, found a kangaroo rat, which is the exact copy of the larger kangaroo in miniature, cowering under the horse's hind legs for protection from the fire. On the same ascent is the celebrated hollow tree, to which I once conducted Bishop Polding for shelter from heavy rain : it kept us and our horses perfectly dry, and there was still room enough for two more horses.

Breakfasting at Bathurst in a hotel after saying Mass, a young lady came to me in great distress of mind. She had but recently arrived alone in the Colony, and had brought me a letter of introduction. " Whatever are you doing," I asked, in some surprise, " in this remote place ? " Through her tears she told me that she had come with the view of buying land; but that she was lodging with a Catholic farmer in the neighbourhood, who would not let her have her horse, and was trying to force her to marry his son. " Do you really mean to say that you have ridden all the way from Sydney, and have crossed those lonely Blue Mountains without any guide or protector?" So it was, however. "Go back at once to your lodgings," I said, "and tell the people that I shall be there in two hours' time." On my reaching the door the whole family came out. They were so sorry, but the lady's horse was loose in the bush, and could not be caught. I said to my man: "Put the lady's saddle on your horse; then go back to the hotel, get another horse, and follow us as soon as you can over the Connoll Plains. As to you (turning to the settler), see you send that lady's horse and things to the Bathurst Hotel by to-morrow morning, or you will hear through the magistrate." No sooner was she mounted than I gave her a canter of some eight or ten miles, when I deposited her with a worthy surgeon and his wife, who kindly undertook to see her off to Sydney by the next public conveyance, and to send a trusty man with her horse. I thus lost a day in rescuing a distressed damsel from toils woven by her own folly.

Wherever we got the loan of a court house up the country as a chapel I invariably found a Bible on the bench for administering oaths, on one back of which a paper was pasted the full length in the form of a cross; most commonly consisting of two crossed pieces of coarse brown paper. When anyone had to be sworn, the clerk asked : " Are you Protestant or Catholic?" If Protestant, the book was opened and its pages kissed ; if Catholic, the brown paper cross was presented to be kissed. I wrote a letter to the Governor, pointing out both the indecency and the illegality of this practice, as well as the prejudice which it caused. By a circular to the magistrates the abuse was put an end to.

At Sydney we did our outdoor work in gigs, as well to save time as on account of the heat. Besides the usual flock, forming a fourth of the population, we had to look after the prisoners' barracks, a huge jail to which the convict men were sent on their first landing, and to which they were returned from every part of the Colony for punishment. We had also to attend the felons' jail, where some forty executions took place yearly. We had to look after a large chain-gang upon an island in Sydney Cove. We had to visit a large convict hospital at Sydney; another at Parramatta, fifteen miles off; and another at Liverpool, at a distance of twenty miles. Again there was the Benevolent Asylum, a refuge for decayed people; for there was no Poor Law, nor was it needed in those days. The funerals, also, which were outside the city, required to be attended to at least every other day. Parramatta had to be served regularly from Sydney, and Liverpool from time to time. Father McEncroe and I had to bear the brunt of this work.

Another field of occupation was examining and signing the papers of the large convict population. No one could obtain his ticket of leave, or his free pardon, or leave to marry, or the privilege of having wife and children sent out at Government expense, unless the document he presented was signed by a clergyman of his communion. Then there were duties for the Vicar-General as head of the department; duties and correspondence with the Colonial Office, with the Surveyor's Office, with the Architect's Office, with the Audit Office, with the Treasury, and with the military, as well as with the Convict Department.

There were grants of land to be obtained for churches, schools, or presbyteries; payments to be arranged or certified for priests or school teachers; aid to be sought for new buildings; arrangements made for duties to the military, as well as for the convicts; favours to be solicited in exceptional cases that seemed to call for mercy; special journeys in Government services by land and sea, such as attending executions. I always found the heads of departments friendly and obliging. The official dinners at Government House tended to strengthen this good understanding ; and on those occasions his Excellency was always considerate in inviting the Protestant Archdeacon and Catholic Vicar-General on different days, so that each in his turn had the place of honour, and said grace.

CHAPTER IX.

RELIGIOUS EXPANSION.

AFTER his arrival in the Colony, Sir Roger Therry opened a correspondence with Mr. Blount, then member for Steyning, on the religious wants of that distant penal settlement. Mr. Blount, in consequence, made an energetic appeal to Parliament upon the injustice and cruelty of sending away the criminals of the country to the other extremity of the world without providing them with adequate provision for their religious instruction or requirements. He dwelt with strong emphasis on the religious destitution of the Catholics. Meanwhile, Sir Richard Bourke was devising a systematic plan for meeting those wants, which ultimately took shape in his celebrated despatch to Lord Stanley, at that time Secretary of State for the Colonies, of date September 3cth, 1833. About the same date I addressed a letter through the Governor to his Lordship, asking for four additional Catholic chaplains. His Excellency begins his despatch by stating that he has received the order of the King in Council for dissolving the Protestant Church and School Corporation; but without any information of the views of His Majesty's Government as to the future maintenance and regulation of churches and schools within the Colony. His Excellency then points out that there are large bodies of Roman Catholics and Scotch Presbyterians, and that probably one-fifth of the whole population of the Colony were Catholics. "The charge on the public treasury next year would be : for the Church of England, £11,542 ; for the Scotch Presbyterians, £600 ; and for the Catholic chaplains and chapels, £1,500. The Catholics possess one large and handsome church at Sydney, not yet completed, and to aid its completion the Government had given donations at different times amounting in all to £1,200. The sum of £400, included in the £1,500, had been appropriated in aid of private subscriptions for erecting Catholic chapels at Campbell Town and Maitland. A chapel was begun in Campbell Town and in Parramatta some years ago ; but neither have been completed for want of funds. Such an unequal support cannot be acceptable to the colonists, who provide the funds from which the distribution is made."

Sir Richard then proposed the following arrangements, to be applied equally to the Church of England, the Catholics, and the Scotch Presbyterians. That whenever a congregation applies for the erection of a church and clergyman's residence, on their subscribing not less than £300 and up to £1,000, the Government shall give an equal subscription, the building to be invested in trustees. That where a hundred adults, including convict servants living within a reasonable distance, shall subscribe a declaration of their wish to attend that church or chapel, £100 a year shall be paid out of the Treasury to the clergyman of that church. That when two hundred adults so subscribe, £150 a year shall be paid ; and that when five hundred adults so subscribe, £200 a year shall be paid ; beyond which no higher stipend shall be paid by the Government. Thus the three great national denominations of England, Ireland, and Scotland were to be treated alike and on the same footing. Before the warrant was issued for payment by the Treasury, a certificate was required from the religious authority at the head of each denomination that the clergymen were in performance of their duty. In the same despatch his Excellency was pleased to say a kind word of the Catholic Vicar-General, preliminary to stating that "he thought £200 a year too low for the office, and that it might advantageously be raised to £400, to enable him to visit frequently the chapels in the interior." Before this despatch was sent the Governor kindly gave me an opportunity, through Sir Roger Therry, of seeing it. I could only express my gratitude for a scheme so well calculated to meet all requirements, whilst it left ecclesiastical authority in such perfect freedom. Sir Richard had privately expressed his opinion that the result of this scheme would be to provide the Colony with all the clergy required, after which the Government, supported by popular opinion, would cease to give its support to any religious denomination, and thus the several communions would support their own churches. To use his own phrase, "they would roll off State support like saturated leeches." And so it has come about.

The scheme received the complete approval of the English Government, and was passed as an Act of Legislative Council on July 29th, 1836. About the same time a scheme of denominational education was arranged, in which the schools were supported by the Government, partly by a fixed annual sum, partly regulated by the numbers in attendance.

On making my application the year previous for four additional priests I had more than one object in view. I strongly felt that a bishop was required for Australia. I had written some time before to Bishop Morris in the Mauritius, by one of the very few ships that ever went to that island, and had explained to him the very unsatisfactory state of things in Van Dieman's Land. I had also sent to him certain cases requiring dispensations, to which

my special faculties did not extend. In reply I received a
letter, stating that he was sending another priest to Van
Dieman's Land, and that the faculties would come by
another letter. The letter never came or the priest either.
New Zealand was but one thousand miles distant, and
though Protestant missions had been established there for
a considerable time, no priest had ever reached it. Norfolk
Island was a penal settlement, quite as far off, but no priest
had ever visited it. Moreton Bay (now Queensland) was
another penal settlement far to the north of Sydney, which
had only been once visited by Father Therry. A new
colony was also beginning to be formed in the extensive
region which finally took the name of Victoria.

Under the clear conviction that so large a responsibility
required the immediate superintendence of a bishop, I
wrote to the Superiors at Downside, explained the case,
mentioned the application I had made to the Home
Government for additional priests, and urged them to move
for the appointment of a Bishop of Sydney. Lord Stanley
had sent a copy of Sir Richard Bourke's despatch to Mr.
Blount, and stated that he should consult Bishop Bramston
as to the priests to be sent out; and thus the way was
opened.

In May, 1834, my old Novice-master, Father Polding,
was appointed first Bishop of Sydney by Gregory XVI.
He undertook to provide the other three priests applied for,
and the four received the usual passage and outfit provided
by Government. Meanwhile Lord Stanley had replied
to my letter, not only approving my application, but
adding that, should our wants increase, he would be happy
to attend to any further recommendation supported by the
Governor of the Colony. Not long after, Sir Richard
Bourke received a letter from Lord Stanley, announcing
the appointment of the four priests, one of whom, Dr.
Polding, was invested with the dignity of a bishop. He

then expressed his regret at my being superseded, and proposed that I should go to Hobart Town with the same stipend. When Sir Richard read the letter to me, I laughed, and said : " Your Excellency will understand our ways better than Lord Stanley. I should be of material use to the Bishop in the beginning. Let him take the stipend of £400 a year which you recommended for the Vicar-General, and let me take the ordinary stipend of a priest." " Well,' he said, " there is no other man in the Colony who would have made such an offer." So I remained in my old position, and the Bishop received the £400 a year. My next point was to secure a proper residence for the Bishop before his arrival, a residence that would suitably represent his dignity as the head of the Catholics of Australia. I succeeded in renting a large and stately house, built for the first Protestant Archdeacon, and which at that time alone occupied the Vale of Woolomooloo, with an extensive domain attached to it. It joined the Sydney Park, in which stood his Cathedral.*

* In the preface to a volume of sermons published in 1842, Dr. Ullathorne alludes to the various places in which these sermons were delivered, contrasting their condition then with that in which they were at the above date : " They were preached," he says, " in the 'old court house' in Sydney, where there is now a large Cathedral, a magnificent parish church, two chapels, and ten thousand Catholics ; the jail at Parramatta, where the only light except the candles on the altar came from the opening of a wooden shutter, which gave the priest a prospect of a busy tavern over the way, where now is a handsome church, flanked by a school and convent ; an old barn at Windsor, where is now a goodly church, with a congregation of eight hundred persons, besides free schools, a boarding school, and an orphanage ; an assembly room at Bathurst, beyond the Blue Mountains, placed over some livery stables, now is a church ample for one thousand persons, and served by two priests ; in the police court of Maitland, which now contains two churches ; in a public-house on Patrick's Plains, or a room in the hospital at Liverpool, or the public inn at Appin, or the court house at Wollongong, all which places now have their churches and clergy." It is needless to say that the contrast here drawn out is indefinitely greater at the present day, when the Church in Australia has taken developments not dieamed of when the above remarks were written.

Meanwhile, having had to remove the priest from Windsor for six months, I had unexpectedly heavy Sunday duties to perform. I went to Windsor, a distance from Sydney of forty-five miles, and put up at a Protestant tavern. The next morning at six o'clock I had to say Mass, preach and administer the Sacraments, to attend the convict and military hospitals; then to ride to Parramatta, a distance of twenty miles, there to put up at the Woolpack Inn, and perform the same duties in the military guard house, a long dark room without a single window, erected over the prison of a chain-gang. The only light I had was from the opening of a wooden shutter at the back of the temporary altar. Before me I had the prospect of a busy public-house. When I turned to the people I got a Rembrandt view of the first row, whilst the rest of the congregation were buried in darkness. On one occasion two Catholic ladies were on a visit at the Governor's country residence. On Sunday they prepared to come to Mass. The Governor and his suite insisted that they could not appear in such a place. They insisted that they must go. So an aide-de-camp was sent to the barracks to secure two steady Catholic sergeants to kneel behind them for their protection. After this duty I attended the military and convict hospitals, about a mile from each other, and then to breakfast at the inn. After which I rode to Sydney, fifteen miles further, to preach in the evening. The next morning by eleven o'clock came on the sense of fatigue, from which I recovered by lying for a couple of hours on a sofa with a light book. On one of these occasions at Windsor, I had a sick call after night came on, which was a couple of miles beyond the river Hawkesbury. When I and my man reached the river, there was no getting the ferry-boat across for a very long time. The convict ferry-men were sleeping in their hut on the other side of the river, and were unwilling to hear with all our shouting. It was a cold, sharp night in the open air, and we got back to the inn at a quarter to twelve. I was hungry, with fasting till one o'clock the next day before me. Everyone else was in bed, so I searched all about the house till I found a piece of bread and a jar of pickled walnuts, of which I made a hasty supper before midnight, which I had to regret the next day.

Father McEncroe generally attended the executions at Sydney, and prepared the condemned for death. It is a fact that two-thirds of the Protestant criminals sought the aid of the Catholic priests after their condemnation to the gallows. This at last produced such an impression that the Protestant Archdeacon printed and circulated a thousand copies of a pamphlet on the subject, in which, among other things, he said that this fact ought not to awaken any surprise. That these poor creatures had very little religion, and that the soothing ways of the priests, and their less guarded system of confession, acted as a fascination on criminals in their last moments. *A propos* of these and similar remarks, I remember having been summoned to a bushranger immediately after his sentence. My first words to him were : " You are not a Catholic— why have you sent for me ? " He was a finely-formed young man, with an intelligent face, and in full vigour of life. With tears he replied : " Sir, I want to tell you what is on my mind ; and if I tell it to a parson he will tell it again." I felt the Archdeacon's pamphlet would do more good than harm, so I took no notice of it.

Two men, after their condemnation, were sent by sea to Newcastle, to be executed on the scene of their crimes. It was for beating an overseer to death in the midst of a chain-gang employed in making a breakwater. One of them, though not a Catholic, applied for a priest, and I went with them a distance of about seventy miles from Sydney. On arrival at the jail at Newcastle I was told by the Governor of the jail that the Protestant chaplain

particularly desired to see me.   I thought it singular, because, though a stranger to me, he had recently written an
attack upon me in a Wesleyan magazine.   On his entrance
he was embarrassed, and told me that as he had to attend
one of the men, and this kind of duty was new to him, I
should greatly oblige him if I would give him some
guidance what to do.   I gave him such hints as I thought
would be useful to the poor man, and he left me with
thanks.   The execution was to take place early next
morning on a promontory, upon which a lofty scaffold
was erected, that it might be visible to a thousand men,
forming a chain-gang.   These men were dressed, as usual,
in alternate brown and yellow clothing of frieze, were all
in irons, and were guarded by a company of soldiers.   The
execution took place soon after sunrise, because the Deputy
Sheriff and executioner had afterwards to proceed up the
river to hang some blacks.   I was therefore very early at
the jail.   We had to walk with the condemned about a
mile to the scaffold, and it was blowing a furious gale of
wind from the sea.   The Anglican clergyman again wished
to see me.   He asked what I should do on the way and
on the scaffold?   I told him that my poor man was well
instructed, that on the way I should repeat a litany which
he would answer, and I should occasionally address words
to him suited to his state.   "Very good, Sir ; and what
will you do on the scaffold?"   "The man," I replied, "is
well taught to offer his life to God for his sins, which he
will do with me in the words I have taught him.   And
when the executioner is quite ready for the drop, he will
give me a sign, and I shall descend the ladder and pray
for his soul."   "Very good, Sir, will you please to walk
first with your man?"   "Certainly."   He followed in a
nervous condition, and when we reached the scaffold each
knelt at the foot of a very tall ladder.   The wind blew
tremendously, and sent my ladder down, falling across the

back of my Anglican friend; but I seized him by the coat laps, and just saved him from the descending blow. The ladders were then tied, and I mounted first. What a spectacle were those upturned faces on that desolate rocky promontory! The scaffold shook in the wind, and I had to put one foot against the framework and to hold the man from being blown off, speaking to him, or rather praying with him, whilst the executioners made their preparations. The young man was bent on speaking to his comrades below, but I would not let him: for such speeches at the dying moment are commonly exhibitions of vanity. He obeyed me, I pressed his hand, and he was cast off. After all was over I walked back with my Anglican friend, who said to me: "Sir, this is a painful and humiliating duty. Had I known that I should be subject to it I should never have taken Orders."

About this time I received a letter from Father Connolly, asking for a priest to visit Hobart Town; and after weighing the matter I thought it best to go myself. I took, as was my wont, the first vessel that offered, and it proved to be a small coasting schooner. The voyage was of some eight hundred miles, and the vessel was heavily laden. I found three women and seven children cooped in the small cabin, and no one to talk to except a young artist. We encountered a heavy gale with adverse winds off Bass' Straits. The small craft laboured heavily under the storm, the bulwarks were stove in, an anchor was unshipped, and several casks of brandy were washed overboard. We drove to leeward some hundred miles in twenty-four hours. The women and children were in a sad state, with scarcely room in which to move. At last, after some days in this critical state, the wind moderated and veered round, and we ran into port. I found things much as I had left them, and after a fortnight returned to Sydney. My return voyage was in a large Scotch ship from India manned by Lascars. We reached Sydney Heads in the night, and could get no pilot off, though we fired gun after gun. The captain had never been there before. However, I was able to point out where the danger lay, and we ran through the Heads and came to anchor.

CHAPTER X.

NORFOLK ISLAND.

IN the year 1834 a conspiracy was formed among the convicts in the penal settlement of Norfolk Island, to overmaster the troops and take possession of the island. A larger number than usual pretended sickness, and were placed in hospital for examination. Those employed at the farm armed themselves with instruments of husbandry, and the gang proceeding to their work were to turn upon the guard. The guard was assailed by the working gang, those who had feigned sickness broke their chains and rushed to join their comrades, but the men from the farm arrived too late. In the skirmish which ensued one or two men were shot and a dozen were dangerously wounded, of whom six or seven died. A great number of men were implicated in the conspiracy. A Commission was sent from Sydney to try them, and thirty-one men were condemned to death. After the return of the Commission the Governor sent for me, told me that a new Commission was about to proceed to Norfolk Island, that there were several men to be executed from the last Commission, that he had engaged an Anglican clergyman to go for the occasion, that I should oblige him if I also would consent to go, and that we should receive hospitality at the mansion of the Commandant.

As the Government brig which conveyed us was limited in its accommodation, the captain, a Catholic, kindly gave me

his cabin. Our voyage lasted a fortnight, during which time
I had several private conversations with my Anglican companion. He was of Cambridge University, was an amiable
man, but held some peculiar doctrines. For example, he
maintained that the efficacy of baptism depended on the
prayers of the parents and sponsors. In a special case, he
told me he had sent away the applicants without giving
baptism, because he did not think them in a becoming
state to pray for the child. I asked him if he had taken
care to have that child baptised afterwards ; he replied
that he did not think it necessary. I cannot but think that
one of our conversations had a material influence on his
conduct on the island. My remarks in substance were to
this effect : " I cannot understand how you gentlemen profess
to be healers of souls, when you know nothing about your
patients. You seem to me like a medical man who goes
into the wards of a hospital, takes a look round, directs
that all shall be clean and well aired, and then prescribes
one and the same medicine to all the patients. Now we
examine the condition of our patients one by one, and give
the remedy required by each." I think the result of this
conversation will be seen later on.

I have given a description of Norfolk Island in my
pamphlet entitled " The Catholic Mission in Australia,"
which may perhaps be inserted here.

" Norfolk Island is about a thousand miles from Sydney. It is
small, only about twenty-one miles in circumference ; of volcanic
origin, and one of the most beautiful spots in the universe.
Rising abruptly on all sides but one from the sea, clustering
columns of basalt spring out of the water, securing at intervals its
endurance with the strong architecture of God. That one side
presents a low sandy level on which is placed that penal settlement
which is the horror of men. It is approachable only by boats
through a narrow bar in the reef of coral, which, visible here,
invisibly encircles the island. Except the military guard, and the
various officers and servants of Government, none but the prisoners

are permitted to reside on the island ; nor, unless in case of great
emergency, can any ships, but those of Government showing the
secret signals, be permitted to approach. The land consists of
a series of hills and valleys, curiously interfolded, the green ridges
rising above one another, until they reach the shaggy sides and
crowning summit of Mount Pitt, at the height of 3,000 feet above
the level of the sea.

The establishment consists of a spacious quadrangle of buildings
for the prisoners, the military barracks, and a series of offices in
two ranges. A little further beyond, on a green mound of Nature's
beautiful making, rises the mansion of the Commandant, with its
barred windows, defensive cannon, and pacing sentry. Straying
some distance along a footpath, we come upon the cemetery closed
in on three sides by close thick melancholy groves of the tear-
dropping manchineel, whilst the fourth is open to the restless sea.
The graves are numerous and recent—most of the tenants having
reached by an untimely end the abode to which they now con-
tribute their hapless remains and hapless story. I have myself
witnessed fifteen descents into those houses of mortality, and in
every one lies a hand of blood. Their lives were brief, and as
agitated and restless as the waves which now break at their feet,
and whose dying sound is their only requiem.

Passing on by a ledge cut in the cliff that hangs over the
resounding shore, we suddenly turn into an amphitheatre of hills,
which rise all round until they close in a circle of the blue
heavens above—their sides being thickly clothed with curious
wild shrubs, wild flowers, and wild grapery. Passing the hasty
brook and long and slowly ascending, we again reach the open
varied ground. Here a tree crested mound, there a plantation of
pines ; and yonder below a ravine descending into the very bowels
of the earth, and covered with an intricacy of dark foliage inter-
luminated with chequers of sunlight until it opens a receding vista
to the blue sea. And now the path closes, so that the sun is
almost shut out ; whilst giant creepers shoot, twist, and contort
themselves upon your path, beautiful pigeons, lories, parrots,
parroquets, and other birds, rich and varied in plumage, spring
up at your approach. We now reach a valley of exquisite beauty in
the middle of which, where the winding, gurgling stream is jagged
in its course, spring up—the type of loveliness—a cluster of some
eight fern trees, the finest of their kind, which with different incli-
nations rise up to the height of fifteen or twenty feet, a clear black
mossy stem from the crown of which is shot out on every side one
long arching fern leaf, the whole suggesting the idea of a clump of

8

Chinese umbrellas.   Ascending again through the dark forest, we find rising on every side, amongst other strange forest trees, the gigantic pine of Norfolk Island, which ascending a clean stem of vast circumference to some twelve feet shoots out a coronal of dark boughs each in shape like the feathers of the ostrich, indefinably prolonged until rising, with clear intervals, horizontal stage above stage, the great pyramid cuts with its point the clear ether at the height of two hundred feet.   Through these we at length reach the crown of Mount Pitt, whence the *tout ensemble* in so small a space is indescribable, of rock, forest, valley, cornfield, islets, sea birds, land birds, sunshine, and sea.   Descending, we take a new path to find new varieties.   Emerging after a while from the deep gloom of the forest, glades and openings lie on each side, where among many plants and trees the guava and lemon prevail.   The fern tree springs gracefully out, and is outstripped by the beautiful palmetto raising "its light shaft of orient mould" from above the verdant level, and at the height of twenty-five feet spreading abroad in the clear air a cluster of bright green fans.   In other places the parasite creepers and climbers rise up in columns, shoot over arch after arch, and again descend in every variety of Gothic fantasy. Now they form a long high wall, which is dense and impenetrable, and next comes tumbling down a cascade of green leaves, frothed over with the white convolvulus.   Our way at last becomes an interminable closed in vista of lemon trees, forming overhead a varied arcade of green, gold, and sunlight.   The orange trees once crowded the island as thickly, but were cut down by the wanton tyranny of a former Commandant, as being too ready and too great a luxury for the convict.   Stray over the farms, the yellow hulm bends with the fat of corn.   Enter the gardens, especially that delicious retreat, "Orange Vale"; there by the broad breasted English oak grows the delicate cinnamon tree—the tea, the coffee, the sugar plant, the nutritious arrowroot, the banana with its long weeping streamers and creamy fruit, the fig, all tropical fruits in perfection, and English vegetables in gigantic growth.   The air is most pure, the sky most brilliant.   In the morning the whole is drenched with dew.   As the sun comes out of his bed of amber, and shoots over a bar of crimson rays, it is one embroidery of the pearl, the ruby, and the emerald; as the same sun at eventide slants his yellow rays between the pines and the mountain, they show like the bronzed spires of some vast cathedral flooded in golden light."

All who have seen Norfolk Island agree in saying that it

is the most beautiful place in the creation, but it is very difficult of access. There is no harbour, and the only approach to the settlement is by boats over a bar in the coral reef that girdles the island, and which can only be crossed in calm weather. If the weather is unfavourable for landing at the settlement the vessel must proceed to the opposite side of the island, and there put off a boat, which lands the passengers on a ridge of rock that is slippery with wet seaweed. We had to adopt this last course on the present occasion.

Reflecting in my own mind that this was the first time a clergyman had ever visited the island, I resolved to be the first to land, for which I had grave reasons, which will appear directly. We were told to be ready to jump one by one, as the boat approached the rocks, as the oars would be at once reversed to prevent the boat being staved by the rock. I got into the stern sheets and sprang the first, when back went the boat. Major Anderson was there with his tall figure, at the head of a company of soldiers, drawn up in honour of the Commission. Before anyone else had landed, I walked straight up to the Commandant, and after paying my respects asked leave to go at once to the prison where the condemned men were confined. I requested to be furnished with a list of those who were to be reprieved and of those who were to be executed. These were kindly furnished me, as they had just reached his hand from the vessel. I then asked how many days would be allowed for preparation of the poor men who were to die; and after kindly asking me my thoughts on the subject, five days were allowed. A soldier was then appointed to guide me to the prison. We had to cross the island, which was about seven miles long by four in breadth. The rest of the passengers, when landed, proceeded to Government House.

And now I have to record the most heartrending scene

that I ever witnessed. The prison was in the form of a square, on one side of which stood a row of low cells, covered with a roof of shingles. The turnkey unlocked the first door and said : " Stand aside, Sir." Then came forth a yellow exhalation, the produce of the bodies of the men confined therein. The exhalation cleared off, and I entered and found five men chained to a traversing-bar. I spoke to them from my heart, and after preparing them and obtaining their names I announced to them who were reprieved from death, and which of them were to die after five days had passed. I thus went from cell to cell until I had seen them all. It is a literal fact that each man who heard his reprieve wept bitterly, and that each man who heard of his condemnation to death went down on his knees, with dry eyes, and thanked God. Among the thirteen who were condemned to execution three only were Catholics, but four of the others put themselves under my care. I arranged to begin my duties with them at six o'clock the next morning, and got an intelligent Catholic overseer appointed to read at certain times under my direction for those who could not read; whilst I was engaged with the others. Night had now fallen, and I proceeded to Government House, where I found a brilliant assembly, in strange contrast with the human miseries in which my soul had just been steeped. It may seem strange to the inexperienced that so many men should prefer death to life in that dreadful penal settlement. Let me, then, say that all the criminals who were executed in New South Wales were imbued with a like feeling. I have heard it from several in their last moments, and Father McEncroe, in a letter to me, which I quoted to Sir William Molesworth's Committee on Transportation, affirmed that he had attended seventy-four executions in the course of four years, and that the greater number of criminals had, on their way to the scaffold, thanked God that they were not going to Norfolk Island.

There were two thousand convicts on the island, all of them men, all retransported for new crimes, after having been first transported to New South Wales. Many of them had, at one time or other, received sentence of death. They were a desperate body of men, made more desperate by their isolation from the outer world; by being deprived of access to all stimulants; by the absence of hope; by the habitual prospect of the encircling sea that isolated them from other lands by the distance of a thousand miles; and by the absence of all religious or other instruction or consolation. Besides the criminals, only the military force and officials with their wives were permitted on the island. No ships, except those despatched by Government, and exhibiting the secret signals, were allowed to come near the land. Everything was on the alert, as in a state of siege. I had an opportunity of witnessing this. I was walking with the Commandant in a wood; he was conversing with secret spies he had among the convicts, when suddenly a shot was heard from a distance. Off went the shots of the sentries in all directions. The Commandant ran off to his post, and I after him. The troops were moving in quick time to their stations; and then came the inquiry. To our relief, it turned out that a young officer, just arrived by our vessel and ignorant of the rules, had been amusing himself by firing at a bird. But what an ear-wigging the young officer got! The rule was that no shot be fired on the island except to give alarm. A ludicrous scene occurred in the Court when the shot was fired. The Commissioner was sitting with a military jury, but the moment the gun was heard, the officers and soldiers rushed out to their posts, leaving the judge and the two lawyers alone with the prisoners on trial.

So sharply were all on the alert, for there had been three attempts by the convicts at different times to take the island, that I never ventured to move after nightfall without having a soldier with me to answer the challenges. A little incident that I witnessed made the sentries all the sharper. I was walking in the evening with the Commandant, when a sentry at some distance from us presented arms instead of giving the challenge. The old soldier, who had been a warrior from his seventeenth year, and had been in fifty battles, from Alexandria to Waterloo, was a martinet, and was up to the sentry in a moment. "Why did you not challenge?" "I knew the Commandant, and presented arms." "You deserve a court-martial. Anyone might have put on my clothes. You ought to have challenged, and if I did not come up at the second call and give the password, it was your duty to fire at me."

I spent the first week in preparing the men for death, and inquiring into the condition of the convicts generally. This took me daily from six in the morning to six at night. Then came the executions. The Commandant had received orders that all the convicts, to the number of two thousand, should witness them. As he had only three companies of infantry, some contrivance was required to prevent a rush of the convicts on the troops, as well as to conceal their number. Several small, but strong, stockades were erected and lined with soldiers, between the scaffold and the standing ground of the convicts, whilst the rest of the force was kept in reserve close by, but out of sight. The executions took place half one day and half the next. One thousand convicts divided into two bodies were brought on the ground the first day, and the other thousand on the second day. Thus all passed off in tranquillity. I had six of my men put together in one cell and five in another,* one of which parties was executed each

* This implies that the writer had charge of *eleven* convicts. He has stated above that *seven* of those condemned to die had placed themselves in his hands. It is to be supposed that the additional *four* must have been of the number of those condemned by the earlier Commission.

day, and executed in one group, whilst the Protestants were executed in another. My men asked as a special favour, the night before, to be allowed some tobacco, as with that they could watch and pray all night. This indulgence was granted.

When the irons were struck off and the death warrant read, they knelt down to receive it as the will of God ; and next, by a spontaneous act, they humbly kissed the feet of him who brought them peace. After the executioner had pinioned their arms they thanked the jailers for all their kindness, and ascended the ladders with light steps, being almost excitedly cheerful. I had a method of preparing men for their last moments, by associating all that I wished them to think and feel with the prayer, " Into Thy hands I commend my spirit ; Lord Jesus, receive my soul." I advised them when on the scaffold to think of nothing else and to say nothing else. The Catholics had a practice of sewing large black crosses on their white caps and shirts. These men had done so. As soon as they were on the scaffold, to my surprise, they all repeated the prayer I had taught them, aloud in a kind of chorus together, until the ropes stopped their voices for ever. This made a great impression on all present, and was much talked of afterwards.

As I returned from this awful scene, wending my way between the masses of convicts and the military, all in dead silence, I barely caught a glance of their suspended bodies. I could not bring myself to look at them. Poor fellows ! They had given me their whole hearts, and were fervently penitent. They had known little of good or of their souls before that time. Yet all of them had either fathers or mothers, sisters or brothers, to whom they had last words and affections to send, which had been dictated to me the day before. The second day was but a repetition of the first. The Protestant convicts were executed after

the Catholics. The Anglican clergyman had three to
attend to each day. Then came the funerals, the Catholics
at a separate time from the Protestants. A selected number
of the convicts followed each coffin to the most beautiful
cemetery that the eye of man could possibly contemplate.
Churchyard Gully is at some distance from the settlement,
in a ravine that opens upon the sea, being encircled on the
land side with dark thickets of manchineel, backed by the
bright-leaved forest trees, among which lemon and guava
trees were intermingled. Beyond there the ravine ascended
and was clasped in by the swelling hills covered with wild
vines and grapes. Above all this was a crown of beautiful
trees, beyond which arose Mount Pitt to a height of 3,000
feet, covered with majestic pines of the kind peculiar to
Norfolk Island. Arrived at the graves, I mounted a little
eminence, with the coffins before me and the convicts
around me ; and being extraordinarily moved, I poured
out the most awful, mixed with the most tender, conjura-
tions to these unfortunate men, to think of their immortal
souls, and the God above them, Who waited their repent-
ance. Then followed the funeral rites. So healthful was
the climate, that all who lay in the cemetery had been
executed, except one child, the son of a Highland officer,
over whose tomb was the touching inscription : " Far from
the land of his fathers."

After the return of the procession, it was found that the
men who composed it were sore and annoyed. The
executioner had followed the coffins as though chief
mourner, at which they were indignant. Yet the man did
it in simplicity, and had a friend among the dead. He was
a man whom Sir Walter Scott would have liked to have
had a sketch of. A broad-chested, sturdy-limbed figure,
broad-faced and bull-necked ; who had won his freedom
by taking two bushrangers single handed at Port Maquar-
rie. But in the struggle he had received a cut from a

hanger, across the mouth, that opened it to the ears, and left a scar over his face that was alternately red and blue. Yet he had good-natured eyes. Whilst pinioning the arms · of one of the men, he suddenly recognised him, and exclaimed : " Why, Jack, is that you ? " " Why, Bill," was the answer, " is that you ? " He then shook his old friend by the hand, and said : " Well, my dear fellow, it can't be helped."

After the executions I devoted the rest of the time to the convicts, instructed all who came together for the purpose, and got a man to read to them, whilst I heard about one hundred confessions. Many of them had not seen a priest for some twenty years, others since they had left their native country. I had also duties at the military barracks, where I said a second Mass on the Sundays. As Major Anderson was much engaged with his despatches for the returning ship, Mrs. Anderson, a most kind and accomplished lady, on my return from my long labours, seeing me worn and exhausted, used to have horses and a groom in readiness, and rode with me herself through the beautiful island before dinner. She saw that my burden was heavy, and wished to give me a diversion. I shall never forget the extreme kindness of these excellent people. They saw their other guests in the course of the day, but I could only see them in the evening. The hospitable dinners and social converse at the large evening parties, however agreeable, completed my exhaustion ; so that one night, towards the end of my visit, I arose in a state of extreme sickness, with my spine as cold as an icicle. However, I rallied the next day and completed the work before me. But when I got on board the vessel I was in that state of exhaustion that the powers of my mind were completely suspended, and I felt little beyond the sense of existence. If I took a book up I could see the letters, but not the sense, and moved as in a dream.

By the time, however, that we reached Sydney, in the course of some fourteen days, my powers had gradually returned. It was not merely the mind, but the feelings, that had been greatly drawn upon.

Before the executions the Commandant asked me privately, if I had any reason to believe that there was a conspiracy to escape from the prison. To which I replied: " My dear Major, of what I know of those men, I know less than of that of which I know nothing." He replied : " I beg your pardon, I did not think of it." I was not surprised at the question, for my Anglican friend had repeated at table the histories that he had got from his men : to the surprise of his auditors, who did not conceal the displeasure it gave them. But after the executions were over I drew the Major aside and told him that the men had authorised me to let him know that there had been a plan for escape. That they had got a piece of a watch-spring concealed in the heel of one of them, had passed it by an agency from cell to cell, and had sawn all the fetters ready for snapping ; and that their plan was to mount one on the back of another, to tear off the shingles from the roof, and so escape in the night to the thick bush, hoping in time to get a boat into their power. But on the arrival of the clergy they gave it up. " And now," I said, " if you will go and examine the fetters you will find them sawn and filled up with rust and bread crumbs." On going to examine, the turnkey was confident that the fetters were sound, and tinkled them with their keys. But the Commandant said, " I am sure of my information ;" and on closer examination it was found that they were all cut.

My last act before leaving the island is worth recording, as an example that the most desperate men ought not to be despaired of. The Major at breakfast told me of a case that gave him a great deal of solicitude. Among the convicts was one who was always in a round of crime

or punishment. He was one of those who had been reprieved, and yet was already again under punishment. I
asked if he were a Catholic. He thought so. "But
how can I see him : we are just about to sail?" "If you
will see that man," he said, "I will send a message on
board that they are not to sail until I have been on board;
and I will send you notice at the last moment." I found
the man chained in a cell with three others, and I asked
him to come out awhile, as I wanted to speak with him.
He was a tall, strong-built man, and I saw he was one of
those proud spirits that would not seem to cave in before
his comrades. I told him the turnkey would take off his
fetters if he would only come out. He replied : " Sir, you
are a kind gentleman, and have been good to them that
suffered, but I'd rather not." I turned to the others and
said, "Now, men, isn't he a big fool? You would give anything to get out of this hot place ; but because I am a
priest, he thinks you will take him for a softy, and chaff
him, if he talks to me. I have got something to tell him,
and then he can do as he likes. He knows I can't eat
him. What do you say?" "Why, Sir, you are such a
kind gentleman, he ought to go out when you ask him."
"And you won't jeer him as a softy because he talks with
me?" "Oh, no, Sir." "Well, take off his irons." I wanted
to get him into a private room, but he would not go out of
eyeshot of the other men, and nothing could induce him.
I did not like to shut the door on them, lest it might be
taken for a trick. I said : "Let's go into the turnkey's
room." No, he would not. So we walked up and down
the yard, with a sentry on each side a short distance off.
I found he was a Catholic, made an earnest appeal to
his soul ; but he held himself still, and I seemed to make
no way. A sailor came up : "Anchor short hove, Sir.
Governor waiting in the boat." I felt bitter : it was the
first time I had found a soul inaccessible. I threw up my

arms, looked him full in the face, and poured out the most terrible denunciations upon him for neglecting the one opportunity of saving his soul : for I never expected that he would have a chance of seeing a priest there again. But though I did not know it until fifteen months afterwards, his heart was changed. As soon as I left he asked to be put in a cell by himself, got a turnkey, who was a Catholic, to lend him books, and became a new man. In going on board I said to the Commandant : " You must not mistake that man. There is nothing mean about him. He would not tell a lie. Under other circumstances he would be a hero But if he says he will thrash an overseer, he will do it. And if the man resists he will kill him." The hint was taken. After a time one chain was taken off him, then the other. And on my return, after fifteen months, I met him smiling as he worked among the flowers in the Government garden ; and he proved most useful among his fellow-convicts. He ultimately got his liberty, and became a respectable man.*

Soon after my return to Sydney I placed the state of the convicts at Norfolk Island before Sir Richard Bourke, and strongly represented the great evil of their being locked up at night in the dark, without any division between the men or any watchman to control their conduct. I earnestly pointed out the necessity of partitions, lights, and watchmen under proper superintendence. But that was not effected until long afterwards, when the representa- tions of Bishop Wilson prevailed. But I put my attempt

* A singular circumstance in connection with this story deserves recording. As Bishop Ullathorne was in the act of penning the above lines a letter reached him written by the very person referred to therein, and relating his subsequent history. After alluding to the last occasion on which they had met, the writer went on to say that after recovering his liberty he had settled in another colony, where he had gradually risen to a position of some eminence, and was bringing up his family in various professions. He had remained faithful in the practice of religion, and acknowledged all the happiness of his changed life as due to the impressions he had received from Dr Ullathorne.

on record in my evidence before Sir William Molesworth's Committee in 1838.

At this time an effort was made to upset the denominational system of education, and to establish in its place a general system with the Bible as a prominent class-book. A public meeting was called in the great room of Pultney Hotel, presided over by a certain philanthropist named Backhouse, who was visiting the Colonies partly on a benevolent expedition, partly as a botanical explorer. The Governor did not approve of the scheme, and hinted that he should like Sir Roger Therry and myself to oppose it, which we were already prepared to do. The Chief Justice, Sir Francis Forbes, was also in opposition. The platform was occupied with Anglican clergymen, Dissenting ministers, and their friends. The moment we appeared in their front a commotion took place among them; they put their heads together, and it was announced that no one should speak for longer than a quarter of an hour. I arose immediately after this announcement, and stated that a public meeting demanded full and free discussion; that I represented a large interest in question; and that a quarter of an hour would barely enable me to state the case, without leaving time to argue it. One after the other we gave them their quarter of an hour, until they were perplexed what to do, when Sir Roger Therry proposed as a resolution, that the scheme was not adapted to the wants and wishes of the people. This their own Secretary, a Dissenting minister, got up and seconded. So it passed, and we retired to another room, when we heard a great clamour, for they attacked the Dissenting minister as an enemy of the Bible. But what could the poor man do? They wanted to get rid of us, and it was the only way open. I published a pamphlet entitled, "On the Use and Abuse of the Scriptures," and the new education scheme died away.

CHAPTER XI.

ARRIVAL OF THE BISHOP.

ON September 13th, 1835, the Right Rev. Father Bede Polding, Bishop of Hierocœsarea, Vicar-Apostolic of New Holland and Van Dieman's Land, arrived in Sydney, accompanied by three priests and four ecclesiastical students. He had stayed for a time in Hobart Town, where he was received by Governor Sir George Arthur with marked courtesy and hospitality. He found things in the same state in which I had found them ; but left there a Benedictine priest, the Rev. Father Cottram, and an ecclesiastical student, afterwards Dean Kenny, to open and teach a school for the people.

The Bishop's house was ready for his reception. The Catholic population received him with great joy, and presented him with a handsome carriage and pair as expressive of their wish to maintain him in his dignity. He was well received by the Governor and the chief officials, to most of whom he was the bearer of letters. He received a stipend of £400 a year, and I retained mine and remained to assist him in my former office.

Everything in the Church now began to assume larger proportions. The Bishop took a position which gradually raised the tone and spirit of the whole Catholic body. We had pontifical functions with as much solemnity as our resources could command, which much impressed the people, to whom they were new. Then the vast body of the

Catholics, who had never been confirmed, received this Sacrament. As the Bishop's house was large, he turned half of it into a boarding school, over which I presided for a time. Thus was begun a solicitude for raising the sons of the settlers who were acquiring property, that they might take their suitable position. As the Bishop was inexperienced in official correspondence, and as the work began to increase, I continued that duty under his direction to the end. When resident, later, at Parramatta, I rode once or twice a week over to Sydney, to perform this duty under the eye of the Bishop, and to call at the Government offices when business required it. I had also to look after the completion of the church begun at Maitland, and to start another at Parramatta. I had the assistance of the Government architect in devising the plans. But what was my surprise, on arriving one day at Maitland, to find that without my knowledge Father Therry had been there, and had doubled the number of windows in the walls. This was one of his singularities, to put as many windows in a building as the walls would allow of, without any consideration for the intense glare of heated light. Thus in the old Cathedral of Sydney he put seventy large windows, two rows in one wall. At Campbell Town his church was like a cage. At Maitland he spoiled what would have been a well-proportioned nave in the old lancet style. His taste in architecture was for what he called *opes ;* if a plan was brought to him, his first question was : " How many more *opes* would it admit of?" He could not understand the principle of adapting the light of a building to the climate.

Riding at Maitland along the fertile banks of the river Hunter, it was impossible not to admire the beauty of those primitive forests and the fertile abundance produced by the deep and rich alluvial soil. Then there were the varied notes of the birds. I was riding through the wood with

Mr. Walker, the chief supporter of our religion in that locality, when I heard at some distance first a whistle, then the crack of a whip, then the reverberation of the lash. I asked : " What road is that over there ? " " There is no road," he replied. " But I heard a man driving, and there again." " Oh ! that's the coachman." " But a coachman must have a road." " The coachman's a bird," said he ; and a bird it was, exactly imitating the whistle of a coachman and the crack and lashing of his whip. Then the bell bird rang its silver bell, and another species cried like a child in trouble, whilst the flocks of parrots made a croaking din, and flights of black cockatoos spread over the fields of maize with a noise like the rusty hinges of an old castle all flapping together in the wind.

The Bishop himself began that wonderful course of missionary labour among the convicts which attracted so much attention, produced so great an influence, and, more than any other part of his ministry, drew so great a veneration towards him. He had not merely the heart of a father, but the heart of a mother towards them. When they came into his presence he wept over them, and they could never resist the influence of his words. The first step he took was to obtain leave from the Government for all the Catholic prisoners, as they arrived by ship, to be retained in the convict barracks of Sydney for ten days before they were sent up the country. When a ship arrived from Ireland there would be as many as three hundred to look after. They were brought to the church at six in the morning and remained until eleven ; again marched to the church at three and remained until six. It was a kind of retreat adapted to their circumstances. The Bishop was there the whole time, assisted by the Sydney clergy. After an address by the Bishop, they were classified by the clergy into those who had not performed their religious duties for one, for three, for five, or for ten years. After the clergy had examined into the amount of instruction which each possessed, they were re-classified for instruction, the ecclesiastical students acted as catechists, and some of the men were picked out as monitors. Then began the confessions, in which the Bishop took his large share. He gave most of the instructions, and after the religious duties were completed by Holy Communion, a special course of instruction and advice was given to them regarding their position as convicts, what power their masters had over them, how the law affected them, to what dangers they were exposed, and how they would most effectually succeed in obtaining mitigation, good treatment, and their ticket of leave ; after this they proceeded to their assignment.

I need scarcely say that this system produced a most beneficial result which was widely recognised. In my evidence before the Parliamentary Committee on Transportation in the year 1838, I was able to quote a letter from the Bishop, stating that, of 1,400 prisoners who had already gone through this system, only two had found their way into the Sydney Jail; and that, whereas hitherto our clergy had attended not less than twenty executions yearly, during the six months since this system was adopted only one Catholic had been executed, and he for a crime of three years' standing. In short, it was a common remark among the clergy, that those whom they had in hand on their arrival very rarely found their way into jail.

This was but a part of the Bishop's labour among the convicts. At regular intervals he visited the felons' jail, instructed the Catholics, heard their confessions, and said Mass for them in the press room. Shortly after he had said his first Mass there, the head jailer, a good Catholic, and a man of mild manners though of resolute will, said to me : " I will tell you something, Sir, and you will tell it to no one else. You know how this place is infested with small vermin, so that even our rough men can hardly

9

stand it. Well, when we are crowded we are obliged to put a lot of men in the press room of a night to sleep. But ever since the Bishop has said Mass there, there is a rush of men to get to that end of the room, because there have been no vermin there since that time." If there were men to be executed he always prepared them, although a priest attended them on the scaffold.

Every Sunday morning, the convicts, from their barracks, were marched to the last Mass in the Cathedral, where they crowded to the Bishop's confessional ; and when he had to officiate, the congregation had consequently to be detained a long time before the service began. Occasionally it became my duty to represent the great inconvenience to the congregation. He would then weep, and say : " Any one else I could put off, but I cannot resist these poor creatures." After the Sunday Vespers, he would mount his horse and proceed to a large chain-gang on Goat Island, or perhaps to some other chain-gang working on the roads, but boxed up in wooden huts on Sundays. There he would have the Catholics drawn out, and after an earnest address to them would use some retired place for a confessional. After the hard labours of the Sunday were over, he delighted to have all the Sydney clergy at his house to a late dinner, and took that opportunity to invite any lay gentleman to whom he wished to show respect.

When he went up the country the convicts were always his first care, and he got as many to Mass as he could and spent much of his time with them. When they knew he was coming, the Catholic settlers met him on the confines of the district, on horseback, and conducted him to the church, if there was one, or to the temporary place where he was to officiate. He made it a point, before leaving, to ride through the district in company with the priest, calling at the house of every free Catholic or Emancipist who respected himself, and was of good conduct.   But if a man was not living properly, or neglected his duty to his family, he rode past his house without taking any notice of him. He thus inspired the Emancipists to respect themselves, and with the same view he established respectable schools for their sons and founded a Catholic newspaper, which taught them their public rights and duties.

Having such an influence over the convicts they ran to him, as to a father, in their hours of distress.   Let me give an example.   He was walking in his large garden on a certain day, saying his office, when a man in a wretched plight came from his hiding-place among the trees and knelt before him.   He then told his story.   He had absconded from service 150 miles up the country, because the overseer had been down upon him, and had unjustly reported him so often to his master that he had been flogged several times.   He then showed his back covered with wounds and scars, and declared he was so miserable that he could bear it no longer.   He had come all that way, avoiding the roads, and had had nothing to eat for three days but a green cob of maize, for he was obliged to keep in hiding.   After questioning him closely, the Bishop sent him to the kitchen for food, and went straight to the Principal Superintendent of Convicts, an officer of great authority.   To him he told the whole tale, expressed his conviction of the truth, and pleaded for mercy.   The Superintendent replied : "The man must be sent to the barracks, and must be punished ; but I promise you he shall be sent to another master, and to one who will do justice."

The Bishop's servants were mostly convicts, and, of course, he was kind to them.   There was an old man among them, who worked in the garden, who was very simple, and, in the main, honest ; but seeing the Bishop's jewelled mitre, wrapped it in a cloth, carried it to the principal hatter in the city, said it was a curious Indian cap, and asked the master of the shop what he would give for it. The master suspected at once that it was something belonging to the Catholic Bishop. He detained the old man, and sent a messenger to the Bishop's house. A priest went to the shop, took possession of the mitre and the old man, and on his arrival at home he was saluted with general laughter. No more notice was taken of it. The old man worked on, but never heard the last of the mitre from his fellow-servants.

Our wants of all kinds increased so much that the Bishop thought it desirable that I should go to England, and thence to Ireland, and do the best I could to provide for them. As, however, things were in a very unsatisfactory state in Hobart Town, his Lordship wished me first to accompany him thither, and so start on the long voyage from that port. We accordingly proceeded thither on May 10th, 1836.

CHAPTER XII.

VOYAGE TO ENGLAND.

AFTER completing affairs in Hobart Town, I took the first ship that offered for England. It proved to be a heavy tub, with not only an uncultured, but an incompetent captain, and we were full six months on the voyage. I found the cabin passengers to be a surgeon of the navy, who had taken out a shipload of convict women to Hobart Town, a pleasant companion; a young Englishman, educated in Germany and equally agreeable; an uncultured Scotch Presbyterian minister, who had originally been a carpenter—a kind man, but going home in trouble; a young Scotch settler, who, though a Presbyterian, looked to me for guidance; and a Jewess, who was a widow with her two young daughters.

So unskilful a navigator was the captain, that he ran us into sixty-six degrees south latitude, far beyond Cape Horn, where we were entangled among icebergs for nearly a fortnight. The men lost all confidence, got low spirited, and proposed to the chief mate that he should take command of the ship. He very properly told the captain, and so the conspiracy was stopped. I counted more than seventy icebergs in sight at once; and we must have passed through some two thousand of them. Some of the largest, as measured by the quadrant, were 150 feet in height above the sea, and a quarter of a mile long, but most of them were much smaller. The weather was squally as

well as foggy, and a look-out had to be kept day and
night from the foreyard. It was intensely cold, but we
passengers agreed to have no fires, but to wrap warm and
take plenty of exercise. All our live stock, sheep, pigs,
goats and poultry died of the cold ; and the shrewd old
surgeon watched the dying moments of the creatures, to
see that they were thrown overboard and not brought to
table. After clearing the icebergs we ran to Cape Horn,
and, strange to say, were becalmed off Staten Island for
a whole day.

Four little Cape pigeons accompanied us during the
whole way from the coast of New Zealand to the Horn ;
they never rested on the ship, but sometimes on the water,
and flew about in the whole run, picking up anything the
cook threw overboard. At the Horn they left us, and
another came about us with a string tied to its leg. In a
fortnight we ran from Cape Horn to the Brazils, where, in
rapid change from cold to heat, most of us caught cold.
After a long spell at sea the sense of smell becomes acute
on approaching land. We were in a fog and could see
nothing, but the odour of land was rich with perfumes.
Suddenly the mist cleared, and the land revealed itself
covered with orange trees in flower and fruit. Our next
object was to make for Rio Janeiro, to obtain fresh provisions. But the captain again blundered. He had clear
observations the day before, sighting the bold land about
Rio Janeiro, but mistook it, and sailed back some sixty
miles, when he fairly confessed he knew not where he was.
We got a man off in a boat from the shore, and I was able
to understand him. We were near, he said, to the Bay of
Angra deis Reis. He undertook to pilot us into the bay,
and there we came to anchor off the town. I landed with
the captain, to assist him to find a ship agent. We found
a respectable young Englishman acting as American
Consul, and he undertook to provision the ship.

Two hills rose above the town, on one of which stood a large Benedictine monastery, and on the other a Carmelite convent of men. The next day I took my young Scotch friend as a companion, and went up to the Benedictine monastery. The Prior received us with true Religious courtesy and hospitality, and we stayed the night that I might say Mass next morning. There were but few Religious to take care of the property ; for the Religious Orders had been suppressed through the influence of the Freemasons. My Scotch companion was awestruck with all he saw ; and was quite nervous as we passed through the long cloisters, lighted by a single lamp, to our rooms. The negro slaves of the property, about forty in number, were chanting the *Salve Regina* after returning from their work. There was an Irish medical man married to a native Portuguese, who possessed considerable wealth, and had built for himself a beautiful mansion outside the town. In this mansion he invited me and my companion to take up our quarters, and assembled a party to meet us. I found religion at a low ebb generally, and most of the clergy in a low condition. This was in part a consequence of the revolution, and I have reason to believe that there has been considerable improvement of late. But at that time scarcely anyone went to the Sacraments, unless in danger of death. I found one parish priest, however, who was truly pious and earnest, and paid him all the attention I could.

The public school was in beautiful order ; but this priest assured me they were not allowed to teach religion in it ; not even the doctrine of the Holy Trinity. Angra deis Reis is the great coffee-growing district. I was impressed with the modest demeanour of the slaves ; both men and women, on the roads, even with loads on their heads, stood still as we passed and asked a blessing in the name of Christ. We entered a large barn-like place in a coffee plantation, where an old negro woman had care of the infant negroes ; and a strange sight it was to see such a number of little blackies crawling all over the long floor with very slight clothing in the great heat.

Our host invited us to a good long ride into the country to visit a collegiate establishment. The soil was wonderfully rich, abounding in plantations of coffee, sugar, and tapioca. Palm, orange, and cocoa trees were profuse on the roadsides, and the pineapple grew everywhere, like a common weed. The head of the College was an excellent Portuguese Oratorian, a man of considerable attainments as well as piety. He read a little English, and showed me his English books. There was specimens of our science, and of our literature, as he told me. The first was an odd volume of an old " Repertory of Arts and Sciences," the second was Harvey's " Meditation on the Tombs," the third was Miss Bordenham's " Mrs. Herbert and the Villagers." He was surprised when I told him they were not fair samples of English thought and letters. Just as we were sailing I received by a messenger a letter from this good Father, written in beautiful Latinity. He sent me some money, asking me to purchase with it and send him some good books in English. I was obliged to return it, as I could not reach him without some address at Rio Janeiro. He also sent me a present of a large bird, which, he said, was a stranger in that country. It proved to be a very fine specimen of the great horned screamer, so called from having two large horns in front of each of its wings. I had hoped to take it home as a present to the Zoological Society, but knowing nothing of its habits we could find nothing it would eat, and so it died. I gave it to the surgeon to stuff for the Army and Navy Surgeons' Museum.

Nothing particular occurred during the rest of the voyage, except that the young man who was teaching me

German had a quarrel with the big carpenter, a Shetlander, whom he throttled and nearly strangled ; when I had to interfere and restore peace. I contrived to make a sort of retreat, as I always did on long voyages. I also wrote some chapters on the convict system, which afterwards proved of use. But when I afterwards found that so little was then known in England about the Australian Colonies, I regretted that I had not prepared a book on the subject. Indeed, I was urged by a friend at Hobart Town to return first to Sydney to gather materials. But duty urged expedition, and I left Sydney at a day's notice. I landed in my native country towards the close of 1836.

CHAPTER XIII.

VISIT TO ROME.

ALTHOUGH it was some time after my arrival in England before I proceeded to Rome, it will be better to dispose of that visit first. The occasion was a letter received from Cardinal Weld, requesting me to go to Rome and make a report to the Holy See on the Mission of Australia. At Paris I met some of the devout Catholics of that city, and amongst others the future President of the Society of St. Vincent de Paul, then a young man, who kindly drove me to the principal churches and charitable institutions. I also made the acquaintance of the Venerable Abbé Ducot, who had been long in India, but had published a discouraging book about its missions, as they were at that time. Father O'Meara, then tutor to the present Mr. Hornyhold, also introduced me to several of the leaders of Catholic affairs whom it was interesting to know. At Chalons-sur-Saône I met the celebrated Abbot Guéranger on the steamer, in company with Father Brandis, afterwards Novice-master at the great Monastery of Einsiedeln, and author of several Benedictine books. They were on their way to Rome to obtain approval for the new foundation of French Benedictines which Guéranger was establishing. I was the first professed Benedictine they had ever seen, and they asked me if I belonged to the monastery near Bath. They were going to the Monastery of St. Calisto in Rome, expecting that the Procurator of the

English Benedictines, who lived there, would be of use to them. I also was going to the same house, and we joined company. I found the Abbot well versed in the Fathers and Church history, and we had much interesting conversation. He maintained the authenticity of the works ascribed to St. Dionysius, and spoke of writing on the subject. He had completed the first volume of his " Origines Ecclesiæ Romanæ," of which he had copies for Rome ; but his great contest for restoring the Roman Breviary to its integrity in France, and his magnificent work, the " Institutions Liturgiques," prevented its being ever completed. He was an enthusiastic lover of art and a valuable companion in visiting Genoa, Pisa, and Florence.

At Lyons I was introduced to the managers of the Society of the Propagation of the Faith, then in its early years. I do not forget the kind attention which I received from them. At their request I drew up a full account of the Australian Mission and of the convict system, to which I added a description of the country and of its most curious productions. It filled nearly a number of their " Annals," and being so completely new, was said to have advanced the interests of the Society. The Society voted a handsome allocation of money to Australia, and it was continued for many years.

We arrived at San Calisto in Rome on the morning of Holy Saturday, 1837. As there was no Benedictine Cardinal at that time the suite of rooms for the use of that dignitary were vacant, and the Fathers put them at my disposal. So soon as I was refreshed I went out with Father (afterwards Bishop) Collier to see St. Peter's and attend the Pontifical functions in the Sixtine Chapel. When he brought me in front of the Colonnade, I said : " This is not St. Peter's, you have deceived me ; it is some miniature of it." It was so dwarfed by distance that I really believed it to be nothing else. But as we approached it

grew upon the eye into the enormous temple it is. We
entered the Sixtine, but I had no sooner got a glimpse of
the Pope than I was turned out by the Swiss Guard. " Is
this the Roman welcome ? " I said to Father Collier.
" Coming from the far end of the world to report a new
continent for the work of the Church, I am at once turned
out of the Pontifical Chapel." He then, however, recollected that the frock-coat was the sin I bore upon me. I
ought to have been in the habit of my Order. But that I
had never worn, and it had yet to be made. The Pontifical
Chapel is part of the Pontifical Court, and requires some
kind of Court costume.

When I was presented to the Cardinal Prefect of Propaganda, the mild and gentle Cardinal Franzoni, as Vicar-
General of Australia, His Eminence, after a quiet inspection,
exclaimed : " Qual giovane ! " And after answering a few
questions, I retired. On my presentation to Pope Gregory
XVI. by the same title, His Holiness uttered the same exclamation : " Qual giovane !—What a youth." But he was
truly paternal, and expressed a hope to see my report.
On fire as I was, and that habitually, with the interests of
the Australian Mission, and anxious to awaken a like
interest in Rome, these receptions considerably cooled me.
I felt I was looked on as a mere boy, and I therefore kept
out of sight, and set to work with my report. I drew it
up at considerable length, in four parts. It was put into
Italian by Dr. Collier, and was revised by Abbot Peschiatelli. I presented it one part at a time, until I knew
that the whole had been printed at the Propaganda Press.
I then called upon the Cardinal Prefect, who expressed
warm interest in the report, and became very cordial. He
also informed me, to my great satisfaction, that a Canon of
the Cathedral of Vienna, moved by what he had heard
of that country, had given a foundation for the maintenance
of a priest at Norfolk Island. I think that his informant

must have been the late Baron von Hügel, who in his early days had made the tour of the Australian Colonies, and whom I had the pleasure of meeting with his family, in England, in later days.

I took the opportunity to observe to the Cardinal Prefect, that as both His Holiness and himself had remarked, with apparent surprise, upon my youthfulness, I begged to observe that I had not sought the office, that it was imposed upon me, and that I was most ready to resign it. His Eminence replied that the report I had given was fully approved, that I had worked the Australian soil a good deal, and that I was not to suppose there was any dissatisfaction. His Holiness also directed that I should receive the diploma of Doctor in Divinity. I then began to understand Rome in a way that long experience has confirmed. When persons go there with great ecclesiastical or religious interests to be settled, they are commonly treated with a certain reserve, if they are strangers, until their spirit and character are seen through, when, if satisfactory, they are treated with every kindness and consideration.

As Cardinal Weld had invited me to Rome, he gave me a cordial welcome. At his table I met his son-in-law, Lord Clifford; the Miss Clifford who was afterwards first Prioress of St. Scholastica's, Atherstone; and the present Cardinal di Luca, then secretary to Cardinal Weld. The next day the Cardinal was taken ill; he was repeatedly bled, according to the medical system of Rome at that time, against which all the English exclaimed; and in the course of a week he died. His departure caused universal regret. His great piety, his charity, and his edifying and recollected demeanour, so marked on all occasions, had drawn towards him a very high degree of respect. Besides the solemn *Requiem* at his funeral, at which the Pope himself assisted, Lord Clifford had a

Requiem celebrated at San Carlo in Corso, to which the English in Rome were invited, and at which Dr. Wiseman read a long oration recounting the history of the Cardinal's life. This gave rise to a singular scene for so solemn an occasion, and that in a Roman church. The music was the celebrated *Requiem* of Mozart, performed by the best singers, with instrumentation. Mozart is rarely heard in Roman churches, and it attracted the artists and musicians. But when the thrilling tones of Mozart had become interrupted for a long time by the monotonous reading of Dr. (afterwards Cardinal) Wiseman, in the harsh sounding English language, however interesting to the English, the Italians could stand it no longer, but set up a hissing all over the church. After a few moments Dr. Wiseman got a hearing, and by a few words of grave and dignified rebuke restored silence until the lecture was completed.

This was the only time at which I ever knew Italians misbehave in a church. As to the misconduct of the English, it was at that time proverbial. On the very next day after my arrival, which was Easter Sunday, I saw an Englishman striving against the Swiss Guards, to force his way into the dress circle at the Pontifical Mass. The Captain of the Guard came up to remonstrate, when the Englishman squared his fist at him. The captain clapped his hand on his sword, but three halberdiers quietly put their shoulders against the Englishman and as quietly moved him back out of the way. Just before my arrival a most disgraceful thing occurred. The ground was very wet, and the Pope, in his white robes, was taking a walk at some distance from his attendants, when three brothers, Englishmen, and gentlemen so-called, met him where there was but a narrow path with a puddle on each side. The three brothers linked their arms together and met His Holiness full face. The Pope stopped and pointed to the puddle, they only laughed and went right on, and His Holiness stepped into the puddle, as he said, almost to his knees, and got away before the attendants joined him. The carriage then came up and the Pope entered it. The Pope sent for Cardinal Weld and narrated the whole affair. The Cardinal's brother-in-law, Mr. Bodenham, from whom I had the story, went straight to their lodgings. The sister appeared, but they got out of the way. On hearing his statement she expressed her indignation at such a charge. He replied : " Madam, it is true, and I have come in kindness, after conferring with the Marquis of Anglesea, to say that their passports will arrive directly; but unless they leave Rome at once you will have your house filled with the police."

Dr. Wiseman was then head of the English, Dr. Cullen of the Irish, and Dr. Grant of the Scotch College, from all of whom I received great kindness. Bishops Walsh and Griffiths were also on their visit to Rome, and were lodged at the English College. The Pope treated them with particular attention. I was invited to accompany them, under the guidance of Dr. Wiseman, over the roof of St. Peter's, and on ascending the dome we four just filled one quarter of the metal ball beneath the cross. There was one Cardinal whose kindness to me, a young stranger, ought not to be forgotten. Cardinal Castrocani not only took a great interest in all my proceedings, but called on and presented me with a valuable painting, which he said had been bequeathed him by another Cardinal: an "Assumption of the Blessed Virgin," supposed to be by Guido Reni. This picture I gave to the Sisters of Charity whom I took out to New South Wales.

I had a brief interview with Monsignor (afterwards Cardinal) Mezzofanti, the great linguist, in company with Abbot Guéranger. He was waiting to accompany the Pope in a walk through the Vatican Library. I was as much struck with the wedge-like form of his brow, as with his singular meekness and modesty, and with the remarkable pliability of his mouth, which so readily gave itself to every form of language and dialect. It was one of those faces that could never be forgotten, expressive of a character unique and thoroughly simple.

Another most interesting visit was made to the cele-brated Christian artist, Overbeck. Being introduced by · his intimate friend, the Abbot Peschiatelli, I was allowed to see his works still in progress, which, as a rule, he never allowed to be seen, but only his finished cartoons and paintings. He was then at work on his chief picture, representing the influence of religion on the arts, now in the Frankfort Gallery. His face was like that of one of his own refined ideals. He spoke with warmth of the missionary life, and considered his own calling as a kind of mission to souls, and quite warmed me with his gentle enthusiasm.

The tranquillity of the Benedictine monastery, the great kindness, courtesy, and refinement of the Fathers, and the religious influence of Rome, were very grateful after the rough work of Australia, and the toils and solicitudes that followed my return to England. Then, though I had been a professed Benedictine for a dozen years, owing to the Penal laws it was the first time that I had ever worn or even seen the Benedictine habit ; and I found it a valuable control on rapidity of movement, and even of thinking. The gentle-hearted Father Glover, of the Gesù, was my confessor ; and after kneeling by his side in his cell he invited me to sit down, and I obtained useful information from his well-informed mind. It was he that put into my hands the books, published in America, that first opened my eyes to the secret mysteries of Freemasonry, up to its highest grades, as practised on the Continent, and which were published after the murder of Morgan for betraying its secrets, had produced so great a sensation. This enabled me to comprehend in a practical way the mischievous machinations of that secret society, which is so little understood in England.

Searching everywhere for devoted priests for Australia I was told of a priest who, in or near Turin, had founded a new Institute of Missioners of self-denying and laborious men. Now one thing that fretted me in Italy was to see such a vast number of priests, many of them, apparently, with little to do, whilst in Australia souls were perishing without pastors or Sacraments. I could not help talking of this. But I soon ascertained that the really competent men in Rome were engaged in one important occupation or another, and that a certain class of priests, then numerous, were men on their little patrimonies, or chap- laincies, mere Mass-saying priests, who would have been more in our way than a help to work like ours.

I asked Father Glover's opinion about the new Institute of Missioners near Turin. He said the name of the founder was Rosmini, but that his writings were suspected of having a taint of novelty and unsoundness. I then asked if there had been any reply to them, and he mentioned the works of Gioberti, which could be got at Genoa. But when I inquired of the booksellers at Genoa, they told me that his books were prohibited by the State, and he himself sent into exile. In the year 1848 I sailed in the same vessel with Gioberti from Genoa to Civita Vecchia, and was surprised to observe his extremely nervous state of body ; his head and limbs shook con- tinually, and I was told by those who knew him that he was always in more or less of fever, which appeared to be confirmed by the red and inflamed condition of his eyes. I never could understand his fundamental position in ontology (of which the American, Brownson, made so much), that in every affirmative proposition were affirmed *ens creat existentias ;* for creation is a free act of the Divine will, and is not, therefore, an object of our mental

10

intuition ; and St. Paul teaches that " by faith we know
that the world was created by the word of God." Then
existences are contingent, and of contingencies we have no
mental intuition.

On the invitation of the Cardinal Prefect of Propaganda,
I stayed at Rome for the festival of Corpus Christi and
witnessed the great procession at St. Peter's, which
impressed me, more than anything I had seen, with the
religious grandeur and resources of Rome.   At my farewell
audience, the Sovereign Pontiff gave me words of encouragement, and recommended me to learn to speak
Italian before my next visit to Rome.   I bid farewell to the
Benedictine Fathers, who gave me letters of introduction
to all the monasteries of the Order that were on my way
back to England ; and on my subsequent visits to Rome
though I did not reside with them, I always experienced
their fraternal charity and hospitality.

Father Brandis had told me that there was an excellent
young priest, the son of a magistrate of the district of
Bellinsona, who desired to go on the foreign missions, and
he gave me a letter to the father.   I therefore returned by
way of the Alps, and made my way to the house of Signor
Leoni, the father of the young priest in question, situated
in a beautiful country by the lake Lugano.   Here I presented the letter of Father Brandis, and was most cordially
and hospitably received.   But before I proceed let me
record my last meeting with this good Father.   In 1857,
being an invalid, I was sent by medical advice to the snows
of Switzerland, and among many interesting places, I paid a
visit with my reverend companion to the great Monastery of
Einsiedeln, venerable with the history of a thousand years.
On arrival I sent in a card and asked for a Father who
could speak either French or Italian.   A Father came, and
said : " You are no stranger here.   We know your history
as a missioner, and the book I hold in my hands is your

book on 'La Salette,' translated. We will send for your luggage to the hotel. Our best apartments are at your disposal." But as he was conducting us to the apartments reserved for dignitaries, the Father stopped suddenly at a door, and said : " Here is a Father who speaks French fluently." The door opened, and there stood the Novice-master in a circle of his novices. I looked at him, he looked at me ; then he threw his arms around me. It was my old friend Father Brandis. I found him to be a truly spiritual man, full of zeal for Benedictine piety. We spent delightful days in the Abbot's quarters and witnessed the pilgrimages constantly flowing to the sanctuary. On parting, Father Brandis gave me his translations of the "Rule and Life of St. Benedict," and his "Manual of Bene-dictine Piety."

The family Leoni received me with warm welcome. The old magistrate was a man of patriarchal simplicity, living among his children and grandchildren, all under one roof, after the old mediæval manner of Italy. I was much edified during my three days' stay with the simplicity and unity of this large family. There was a purity of thought and a piety of heart, a gentle yet free courtesy, in this happy society which was very endearing. The head of it was a mild, firm, and benevolent character, evidently much respected all the country round. On Sunday was the monthly procession of the parish round the church, when the old magistrate was distinguished from the rest by carrying a larger and more ornamented candle, and walking last. The young priest, however, was not at home, but with his brother, the principal architect of Turin. I therefore drove to the Lago Maggiore, crossed to Savona, and took the diligence to Turin. During this journey I was much taken with the gentle simplicity of a young Franciscan friar ; wherever we had to pay fare he quietly asked a passage for the love of God, and obtained it. At Turin I stayed some days with the Leonis, who took me everywhere. I called to see Rosmini, not losing sight of his missionary institute ; but he had gone to visit his mother, who was ill. I found the young priest more heavy and less spirited than the rest of his family ; but as he was eager to go I took him, his brother paying the expenses. But at London he lost courage and returned home.

CHAPTER XIV.

Work in England and Ireland.

ONE of the first things I did in England was to publish, in pamphlet form, the "Catholic Mission in Australasia." This at once awakened a warm interest in the missionary work of that remote country.* Several English priests offered themselves for the work, but their Bishops could not spare them. Besides publishing five editions of that pamphlet, I took to lecturing on the same subject, and generous contributions flowed into my hands. I then went to Ireland, and met its Bishops assembled at Maynooth, who took such an interest in the wants of Australia that several of them promised that if any of their young priests were willing to offer themselves, they would account every year served in Australia as two towards obtaining a parish, in the event of their ultimate return. Several bishops invited me to visit them at their homes ; but from none of them did I obtain more earnest co-operation than from Archbishop Murray, of Dublin, and Bishop Kinshela, of

---

* In this pamphlet, Dr. Ullathorne writes : " Over the whole range of New South Wales there are at present but seven missionaries. Sydney alone would require three, yet the Bishop is sometimes left alone with its duties added to his own. Vast districts, such as that of Bathurst, covered with Catholics, are without a single priest. Van Diemen's Land requires seven priests at least, and has only two. The south and western colonies, stretching along a line of 2,500 miles, have never seen a priest." This was written in 1838. The provinces here spoken of are now governed by five Archbishops and sixteen Bishops, with a corresponding number of clergy.

Ossory. I also received very great assistance from Dr.
Montague, the President of Maynooth, a remarkably
shrewd man, who possessed a surprising knowledge of
the character of every priest in Ireland, and who could
point out where the most devoted men were to be found.
Nor must I forget the extreme kindness that I met with
from all the professors of the College. Dr. Gaffney, the
Dean of Discipline, was of special service in recommending
students to me, and at his request I gave a spiritual re
treat to the students in preparation for ordination.

At that time the Irish prelates were seriously thinking
of founding a college for educating priests for the British
Colonies and foreign settlements, and the Primate, Archbishop Crolly, asked me to draw up an estimate of the
probable number that would be required. This I did and
gave it into his hands. I also made the intimate
acquaintance of the Franciscan Fathers of Dublin, who had
recently completed their large church, still called " Adam
and Eve," owing to a tavern which formerly occupied the
site and bore that sign. Two of the Fathers volunteered
for the Australian Mission, Fathers Geoghehan and
Coffey, the first of whom went out with me, and the latter
later on. It was in this Religious house that I contracted
a close friendship with Father McGuire, the celebrated
controversialist. Few people in these days will recollect
the famous platform controversies of Pope and McGuire,
and of Gleig and McGuire. But at that time he was
giving a great course of controversial lectures at the new
Franciscan church, which was most densely crowded four
nights in the week by an audience most eager to hear him.
What struck me most in these lectures was the wonderful
amount of freshness and vigour which he gave to old
familiar texts. As his lectures were long, though intently
listened to, and very energetic, Father McGuire descended
from the pulpit his garments saturated with perspiration.

He had immediately to change them ; after which he descended into the common room of the Fathers, where he was met by a number of his friends. A red-hot poker was in the fire, a tumbler of whisky and water on the table. He seized the poker, plunged it into the beverage, and drank it off hissing ; after which he was safe from the consequences of his exertions. Then followed colloquial interchange of wit and learning for some two hours, such as I never witnessed before or since ; after which I drove Father McGuire to his lodgings before I went to my own.

The famous controversy between Pope and McGuire has a history attached to it, which, as it is very little known, I may as well repeat. Richard Coyne, the well-known publisher in Dublin, had an extensive knowledge of controversial books down from the time of the self-styled Reformation. At the beginning of that public controversy he was unacquainted with Father McGuire, but went, through curiosity, to see what was going on. He soon detected that Pope was using " Leslie's Case Stated," and that McGuire was not acquainted with the book. He then got introduced to McGuire and asked him to come and dine with him on Sunday. McGuire alleged in excuse that on Sunday he must go to Maynooth to extract from the Fathers. " I will give you the Fathers in a nutshell," replied Coyne. Accordingly he accepted the invitation. I give what follows in the words of Coyne, addressed to me in the presence of McGuire. As soon as McGuire arrived at his house Coyne put an old book into his hands, open at the subject at which the controversy then stood. This book was Manning's " Leslie's Case Stated," into which the Catholic controversialist had inserted the whole of Leslie's book, word for word, and had answered it point by point, not only with great ability, but with a pleasant humour, especially in his powerful appeals to the principles of his adversary. " He no sooner had read a few pages," continued Coyne, "than, in his humility, that man (pointing to McGuire) dropped on his knees, lifted his eyes to Heaven, and thanked God for the gift." Pope was equally ignorant of Manning's reply, and the subsequent history of the controversy is this: Pope daily rested on a bed after his exertions, whilst a friend read to him "Leslie's Case Stated"; McGuire took a long walk in the Phœnix Park with Coyne, and worked into his mind Manning's reply. After the controversy was over, and published, Mr. Pope retired from all future controversy, took up his residence at Bangor, and an affectionate correspondence was maintained between the two combatants become friends so long as both lived. Coyne then published a new edition of Manning's "Leslie's Case Stated," which he dedicated to Father McGuire as the "Bossuet of the British Churches."

In all future platform controversies and lectures McGuire never felt satisfied without having Coyne close by him; whilst in their familiar hours McGuire always called Coyne his father and Coyne called McGuire his son. It was most amusing to hear the tall ecclesiastic calling out to the little layman: "Dicky, my father," and then the reply: "What, Tom, my son?" I had one especial opportunity of being entertained with this style of colloquy. At leisure times I was fond of searching into old book shops, picking up what I thought might be useful in Australia, where books in those days were very scarce. In Dame Street, Dublin, I thus picked up a great rarity, no less than the collection of the original tracts, pamphlets, and sermons of Martin Luther, without any of those expurgations of his abusive language and obscenities which were effected in the collected editions of his works. They were bound up in a dozen quarto volumes. The woodcuts in the several title pages showed how his publisher had progressed with the author. The earlier tracts were ornamented with the tiara, the Papal keys, and other Catholic emblems, which belonged to the printer's old stores, but as time went on, the printer could afford to change them for satirical pictures, until they became obscene and even blasphemous. I showed this rare collection to Coyne, and told him how little they had cost me. He at once set his heart upon them, but in vain: they were unobtainable. He then tried another move. He invited Father McGuire and a number of lay friends to meet me at dinner. After the cloth was removed, and the claret had circulated (I never touched wine in those days, it refused to agree with me) Mr. Coyne tapped the table and called out to McGuire at the opposite end of it : " Tom, my son." " What, Dicky, my father ? " " Here is Dr. Ullathorne, who has got possession of a rare collection of the original unexpunged tracts of Martin Luther ; and I am sure he agrees with me that they can be in no way better placed than in the hands of the great controversialist of Ireland." McGuire was profuse in thanks, and the whole table applauded. After silence had returned, all looked at me, so I rose and said : " My dear Father McGuire, I know how much value you would set on such a collection and how useful it would be in your controversies. The mere exhibition of the wood-cuts would be sufficient to reveal the base character of the foul heresiarch who has cast so much confusion into the world. I also know how much my friend, Mr. Coyne, with his great knowledge of controversial books, appreciates the possession of such a book as this. I only know of one copy more of it ; and as we are all three agreed upon its value, I think we shall further agree that it is desirable that there should be a copy at each end of the world. My copy will be packed shortly for Australia."

The friendship which I enjoyed with the clergy of Dublin, and the opportunities which this gave me of observing their life of duty, led me to a high estimation of their learning and zeal, as well as of the religious influence which they exercised over their people. The charities of the city of Dublin were to me wonderful. I preached in the Jesuit Church for the Institute of the Good Shepherd, which then bore another name; made acquaintance with the Foundress of the Sisters of Mercy; and arranged with Mrs. Aikenhead, the Foundress of the Sisters of Charity, for a filiation of five Sisters to accompany me to Sydney, for which the approval of Archbishop Murray was readily obtained. At his house I had the pleasure of meeting that very laborious prelate, Bishop Scott, the first Vicar-Apostolic of Glasgow. To converse with a man of his energy and experience was no common gain.

But it was Bishop Kinshela, of Ossory, who took me strongly by the hand. His house at Kilkenny was like a home to me. He took me with him to visitations, ecclesiastical conferences, and on other occasions, and initiated me into the whole working of the Irish Church. He gave me the run of his Seminary, with leave to take as many young men as offered themselves for Australia. I selected one priest and five students, who afterwards turned out valuable priests. Thus, whilst working in the interests of Australia, I was gathering useful experience for myself.

In the midst of this work, in the early part of the year 1838, I was summoned to give evidence before Sir William Molesworth's Committee on Transportation. The pamphlet I had written on the Australian Mission had awakened attention; and without my knowing it, Dr. Lingard, the historian of England, had written a letter to a member of Parliament, recommending that I should be examined before that Committee. On my arrival in London, Sir W. Molesworth invited me by note to a private interview. I went to his house, and was amused to find him in a dandy silk dressing-gown covered with flowers like a garden, and tied tight with a silk cord with flowing tassels. He had my pamphlet before him, and tried to coach me up as to the best way of giving evidence. When we came to one embarrassing point, I told him it was doubtful whether I ought to speak on it. He pulled up his head, gave me a menacing look, and said : " Do you know how grave would be the consequences of your refusing ? " I looked into his eyes whilst replying : " You have read that book, and ought to know that I am not a man to be talked to in that way." He tried to laugh it off, and I said to him gravely : " At present I have conscientious doubts whether I ought to speak on that subject. I will consult some of the best theologians and act on their advice." The printed evidence itself will show in what manner both the chairman and myself approached that subject, and how I contrived to throw the weight of the testimony on other shoulders. Before the Committee, being in a new position, full of matter, and like a young soldier for the first time under fire, somewhat excited, I spoke with such rapidity that I had to be repeatedly stopped by the members, that the reporter might be able to record the words. The Report of that Committee forms a large volume, and in the Appendix will be found a good deal of my correspondence with the Secretary for the Colonies, concerning the clergy whom I sent out from time to time.

Knowing the importance of interesting members of Parliament in my transactions with the Government, I made it a point to sit in the Strangers' Gallery on most nights of that winter during the debates. Sometimes Mr. Philip Howard would come up and sit with me, sometimes Mr. O'Connell, sometimes others ; but the man I found most difficult to converse with was Mr. Shiel, who then held office, but who was too quick and restless to listen to details and wanted to jump at once at conclusions. Avoiding obtrusiveness, I took every opportunity of studying men and things. But I learnt more of the ways of Parliament in its routine business,

than during debates ; although Parliament was very different then to what it is now.   Then during great debates
everyone was absorbed and there was no speaking to anyone.   I witnessed remarkable scenes and exhibitions of
character in the old house of St. Stephen's, but this is not
the place in which to record them.   I must not forget to
notice the invaluable services which I received from Mr.
Howard, of Carlisle, during the whole of my mission to
England ; he was always at my service with his kindness
and industry.   And I took the first opportunity on my
return to inform the Catholics of Australia of what he had
done for them.

At this time Sir Richard Bourke was attacked in certain
letters to the *Times*, to which I wrote a reply that was well
received in New South Wales.   I had one curious bit of
correspondence with Lord Glenelg, the Secretary for the
Colonies.   I had applied for a stipend, passage money, and
outfit for a priest for Norfolk Island.   This was granted.
There had been a great difficulty in obtaining an Anglican
chaplain for that destination, and the Governor of New
South Wales had written to Lord Glenelg that no Anglican
could be induced to go there, and that in consequence he
had been obliged to send a Dissenting minister.   What,
then, was my surprise when I received no more than
£100 for passage and outfit of the priest for Norfolk Island,
whilst for each of those sent out to New South Wales I
received £150.   I at once paid the priest appointed to that
penal settlement £150, and sent him on his way.   I then
wrote to Lord Glenelg, told him what I had done ; represented the much greater sacrifices that awaited him, besides
his having to undertake a second voyage ; and added that
unless the additional £50 were paid I should have to beg it
of friends, and that I was sure it was not the intention of
Government that I should fit out the servant of Government with the beggings of charity.   The result was that

the other £50 were paid. Having occasion to call on Sir George Grey, who was then new in the office of Under Secretary, I was received with an amusing check. Instead of waiting to hear my business, by the time I had reached his official table he had pulled himself up into what some people would call great dignity, and said : "We never inter-fere between a priest and his bishop." " Pardon me," I said; " I am well aware of that. But I call as the repre-sentative of the Catholic Bishop of Sydney, and am known to Lord Glenelg, with whom I have had several trans-actions." He then entered into business.

I must here mention that I had obtained the services of the Rev. Francis Murphy, then senior priest of St. Patrick's, Liverpool, who, having been educated at May-nooth, went over to that College, and there induced several young priests to join him. I obtained their passage and outfit, and they proceeded at once to Sydney. On again returning to Dublin, Mr. Drummond, secretary to the Lord-Lieutenant, and a most popular man in Ire-land, sent me a request to call on him. He repre-sented to me how completely the Irish people were in the dark respecting the sufferings and trials that attended transportation to the Penal colonies. They had heard of the final success of a few men who had been banished to Australia, and were completely deceived as to the painful lot of the great multitude. He then asked me to write something that might open their eyes. I told him that, as I had heard similar sentiments expressed by many priests, I would write a popular tract on the subject. I then wrote the tract entitled " The Horrors of Transpor-tation," got Mr. Coyne to put it in type, and sent a copy to Mr. Drummond, with the information that it stood in type at Mr. Coyne's, and was entirely at his disposal. He sent it to London for the Lord-Lieutenant's approval, which having obtained, he ordered a very large number of copies, which were sent in packets to the parish priests and to the prisoners.

I then gave a course of lectures on the Australian Mission and the condition of the convicts, in the churches of Lancashire, which, as they had been preceded by my pamphlet on the subject published in Liverpool, awakened a great deal of interest. The churches were densely crowded, and collections reached a sum considerably beyond the average. Ladies occasionally put their jewels on the plates. In the course of six weeks I collected some £1,500. The Fathers of the Society of Jesus were particularly cordial in co-operation. I then met the English Bishops assembled on their affairs at York. They took a kind interest in the Australian Mission, although they could not spare us any priests. I also assisted at the opening of the chapel of New Oscott, at which all the Bishops were present, as well as a hundred priests. On that occasion the more ample form of vestments was first introduced in place of the old form derived from France. Pugin, with his dark eyes flashing and tears on his cheeks, superintended the procession of the clergy, and declared that it was the greatest day for the Church in England since the Reformation. Dr. Weedall preached an elaborate discourse on Catholic education.

CHAPTER XV.

HAVING already sent two companies of priests on their way to Sydney, as well as several school teachers, three remaining priests, the five Sisters of Charity, and five ecclesiastical students assembled in London, and we embarked on board the *Sir Francis Spaight* towards the end of July, bound direct for Sydney without any intermediate stoppage. Among the reverend clergy whom I had engaged for the Mission were the Rev. Francis Murphy, who afterwards became the first Bishop of Adelaide; the Rev. F. Geoghehan, who became the second Bishop of Adelaide; and the Rev. T. A. Gould, O.S.A., who became first Bishop and afterwards the first Archbishop of Melbourne. I had secured the stern cabin for the Sisters, with one room in which they could meet, and a large cabin for myself, in which an altar could be fixed, and where I could assemble our whole company for Mass in moderate weather. Having good sea legs and a quick sense in the feet of the coming movements of a ship, I felt secure at all times; but had a priest strapped at one end of the altar, to hold the foot of the chalice whilst it was on the altar. The chief difficulty was to manage the confessional for the nuns. I did not think it expedient that they should come to my cabin, so every Saturday morning I went openly, with a book under my arm, to the cabin where they could assemble, and they came one by one. The passengers concluded that I had some special instruction to give at that time. I used my own cabin, also, for giving a course of logic to the ecclesiastical students, giving them a free day whenever the topsails were reefed, the meaning of which they soon found out.

Dr. Heptonstall, the Procurator of the English Benedictines in London, who had assisted the other priests at their departure, remained with us to the last moment. He was a most valuable friend, acting gratuitously as agent for the Australian Mission in London at all times. After seeing all those under my charge settled in their quarters, I took a survey of the passengers and a measure of the captain. The passengers were a very mixed society, and the captain a big, soft sort of man, without much strength of character, and I therefore anticipated trouble, which failed not to come. The first mate proved incompetent to manage the crew, and was therefore put aside; and the second mate, a brother of the captain, whom all respected, was put in his place.

Twice a day I arranged for the Sisters to come on deck for an hour or two, when it soon became understood that a part of the deck should be left exclusively for them, whilst I always contrived to be near them or with them. For there was an American on board with his family, a reckless bully, who came on board with one name and at sea appeared under another, and who enjoyed making mischief in which he sometimes made young and thoughtless men his tools. Nor was the captain the man to control him. As he took the carving, for example, at one end of the table, he contrived to insult one person after another of humbler condition, by sending them lumps of fat, or something they could not well eat. I watched and corrected this as much as I could. There was one poor woman whose husband was shy, and whom I interfered to protect on several occasions until at last the husband lost all patience and struck the American the moment they came on deck. I was in my cabin, but the daughter of the man rushed down to me screaming: "Oh, Dr. Ullathorne, do come up, Mr. —— has struck my father, and he has drawn a big knife." I went up, the poor man was cowering by the man at the wheel, and the American, sitting behind the companion with a malignant face, was whetting a large knife on his boot. I walked up and down between them, and kept my eyes upon the American until he shut up the knife and put it in his pocket. I then got the other man down to his cabin; after which I called upon the captain to preserve peace.

After a time the captain got into trouble. Losing his temper one day with the man at the wheel, he struck him. The man said very quietly: "Captain, if you strike again, I must strike in self-defence." He did strike again, and the man returned the blow: he was then put in irons. But this was not all: two more men got drunk on grog, imprudently given them by steerage passengers—a common fault in a long voyage. As they were riotous and backed the man already in irons, we had three men ironed on the quarter-deck for some days. The captain was very anxious, for the men held out, and the crew sympathised with them. At last the two senior Sisters asked leave of the captain if they might speak to the men, and try to make peace. The captain was too glad of the offer, and had the imprudence, in his anxiety, to peep through the cabin window to see how they succeeded; and the men perceived him there, which spoiled the whole thing. But when the Sisters came before the men, they rose and pulled off their caps, with the greatest respect, and listened to them with great attention, after which one spoke for the rest. "Ladies, we know you are true ladies and servants of God, and give your lives to the poor people; and I can't tell you how we and all the men respect you. We are not worthy to stand in your presence; but we believe we have been wronged, and all our mates desire us to stand firm and to bring our case into court at Sydney." Their pleading was thus a failure. The next day I went of my own motion, and sat among them, and said something like this to them. " Now, mates, I have been a sailor like you, and have furled many a topsail. My heart always warms to a sailor. The captain was wrong to strike the man at the wheel, but I don't think you know how to go about these things. I know Sydney better than you. If you land as prisoners you will have the ship agents, the consignees, against you ; they will get learned lawyers, and you'll have nothing but land sharks. And you'll get all the worse for holding out against your duty. If your irons are taken off, and you return to your duty, you will still have your case, if you choose to follow ; and won't be in a worse, but in a better position." I then went to the captain and said : " Now, captain, if you will send your mates to take off those men's chains, and you say quietly to them : ' Now, men, will you go to your duty ? ' I think they will obey you." This was done, and being good-hearted fellows they soon forgot all about their grievance.

Yet, despite these disagreeables, we had many pleasant days. The majority of the passengers were simple, inoffensive people, only they had not spirit enough to combine and protect themselves from being annoyed. We had also our diversions. In calm weather we were surrounded by the albatrosses, some of those majestic birds flying in the air, others resting on the waves, some hauled on deck with fishing lines, other poor wretches shot with rifle balls. Whilst surrounded with them, I read to the Sisters Coleridge's " Ancient Mariner;" and they were touched with the wondrous tale, and murmured long after the closing lines :

> He prayeth best who loveth best
> All things both good and small ;
> For the dear God Who loveth us
> He made and loves them all.

Another day, under half a breeze with the sea moderate, a sperm whale rose from the depths and struck the ship right under her keel. The vessel lurched and hove as if upon a rock. The man at the helm thoughtlessly ran to look over the counter. A thundering volley of oaths soon brought him back with another to help him. The captain was terribly excited and the crew in consternation. The monster at last disentangled himself and lifted his huge head close up to the side of the ship. I got the Sisters up to view him, and they could almost touch his head bestrewed with weeds and barnacles. He then got himself clear of the ship, and how he did snort and blow and spout after his accident! A smart young fellow called out, " I should not like to sleep in the same cabin with him !" " Why not ? " " If that is his breathing, what must be his snoring ! " The laugh at this joke set all minds free again. The captain, though alarmed, was prompt in handling his ship ; for though a soft man, he was a good seaman. The only thing like this that I remember was when a lad in the Mediterranean. It was fine weather, and we were most of us below at tea, when the brig was suddenly struck as against a rock. We rushed up, and there was a big grampus that had struck the vessel amidships ; he raised his giant body into the air, fell splash upon the water, and went on blowing with redoubled energy. He had left his mark, however, on the copper.

Many years ago a whaler was actually sunk by a sperm whale. She was a cranky old craft, commanded by Captain Rankin. When a calf-whale is caught the cow-whale will follow the ship. It was so in this case ; the mother-whale, furious at having lost her young one, attacked the ship, came again and again at her hull, until with her ivory horn she stove in her timbers, and as the vessel was sinking the crew took to their boats and had to pull some three hundred miles before reaching the Australian coast : after which

Captain Rankin gave up the sea and established a cheese dairy near Bathurst, the only one of any importance in the Colony ; and in my days Rankin's cheese was to Australians what Stilton is to Englishmen. On December 31st, 1838, we reached Sydney, having been five months and a-half on the voyage.

CHAPTER XVI.

AT WORK AGAIN IN AUSTRALIA.

WHEN the Sisters were lowered into the boat by a suspended chair, to reach the land, all the men spontaneously arranged themselves along the bulwarks, to show their respect and address them in a low voice in the words: " God bless you, ladies! God bless you, ladies!"

I had scarcely landed a day when I found myself the object of universal indignation, not only in the Colony, but in other penal settlements.* Several other officials from the Colonies had given evidence on the convict system as well as myself, including the Chief-Justice, Sir Francis

° All manifestations of public feeling were not, however, so hostile. The Bishop has forgotten to allude to a great meeting of Catholics, held on January 6th, 1839, in the course of which many fervent expressions of gratitude were offered in acknowledgment of his great services to the Church in Australia. Alluding to his recent visit to England, Mr. Justice Therry reminded them that it had been undertaken solely for the spiritual benefit of the Catholic community, and not for the advancement of any commercial interest. " I will venture to say," he continued, "that my reverend friend never once inquired how wool sold at Garraway's." In his reply Dr. Ullathorne took up this remark. " Mr. Therry has observed," he said, "that whilst in Europe I never mentioned the price of wool, though doubtless I was often questioned about it. This is quite true. 'How is land selling in New South Wales?' some persons would ask me ; and I would reply that I had been so much occupied with the cultivation of sheep that I had not paid much attention to land. 'Well, then, how is wool selling?' 'Why, you will think it strange,' I would reply, ' but though my flocks are very numerous, they don't bear wool, and if they did we should not fleece them.'"—Kenny, "History of Catholicity in Australia," p. 155.

Forbes; and they had spoken in language as plain as mine. But I was selected by the newspapers as the scapegoat for all. Then, besides my plain evidence, there was the little book on the Australian Missions which had been given, according to the wont of hostile newspapers, in garbled extracts with sinister comments. They concluded, however, falsely, that I had abused the system of assigning convicts to private service for my own purposes, and with a view to obtaining assistance, in which they proclaimed that I had succeeded, at the cost of the Colony. It must be remembered that the Australian press was to that of England, in those days, what Australian was to English society. There was no mincing of terms. I had deeply wounded both freemen and Emancipists in two most sensitive points—in their pride and in their pockets. I had made the degrading state of things widely known, not only at home, but throughout Europe. I had exposed the vicious results of the assignment system, yet others had gone further than I. The land derived its value from the number of convicts placed upon it ; the settlers got work without paying wages ; and the more criminals the more wealth. Moreover, trade, manufactures, and even domestic service, depended on the same resource.

After the evidence given against it, the system had been vigorously attacked by Parliament and by the British press, and its reformation was already looming in the distance. In the Colonial Legislature the subject of the evidence was discussed before my return ; and my dear old friend, Attorney-General Plunkett, expressed his regret at my vivid style ; and as he was a man of the highest character, and the only Catholic in the Assembly, this did not mend matters. As my pamphlet had been much misrepresented, the Bishop had had a thousand copies of it printed in Sydney with the view to correcting these false statements by its issue ; but as the assault grew more furious, he did not venture to put it out, and I found all the copies carefully stowed away in a storeroom.

My landing was the signal for the storm to burst out anew, and for some six months I had about half a dozen columns of abuse allotted daily to my share. No one defended me. The Bishop and the clergy were dismayed : all held their tongues—and so did I—except that one of the senior clergy, whom I had sent out, told me that they would never have peace so long as I stayed in the Colony. Only Mr. Judge Therry, who was more versed in the criminal history of the Colony than any other man, solemnly declared to me that every word that I had uttered was true ; and that if I retracted a syllable of it he would never forgive me. I had another curious testimony in my favour. Going one day upon a steamer, a settler, a stranger to me, came up and said : " Sir, we shall never forgive you." I asked: " Why not ? " " Because all that you said is true, and it will ruin us. We could have dealt with a pack of lies like the Major's." This referred to a man who had published an infamous book in England, libelling the most respectable persons in the Colony.

One step, however, we took, which resulted in great advantages to the Catholics of the country. Hitherto the Catholics had supported the *Australian*, a paper written by a clever barrister, the son of Judge Stephens. But this paper attacked us more malignantly than the rest, even than that edited by the notorious Dr. Lang, the chief Presbyterian minister, a violent politician. Stephens went so far as to attack our Bishop, and to hold him up to ridicule as well as myself. In consequence of this I went to the office, in company with another priest, to let them know that if they continued this policy we should establish a newspaper of our own. " I," I said, " am fair game, but you have no right to attack the Bishop ; what has he done to offend you ? " They evidently did not believe that we could establish a newspaper. An apology appeared for the attack on the Bishop ; but they adopted my words, that " I was fair game." But the Catholics would stand this no longer. The leading laymen met, put down a sufficient sum of money, and a Catholic paper was started, and was edited by Mr. Duncan, a keen-witted, clever convert from Presbyterianism, whom I sent out as a schoolmaster, and who ultimately rose to be Commissioner of Customs. He gave them blow for blow ; and the chief value of this was that the Catholics had now an organ and a voice which exercised a considerable political influence.

By desire of the Bishop I took up my abode at Parramatta, as well with the view of building a church there, establishing a school, and forming a mission, as to take charge of the Sisters of Charity, who were placed in a house and garden purchased by Mr. William Davis expressly for them. I went over to Sydney at least once a week to attend to the correspondence and other business with the Government. At that time Sir Richard Bourke had resigned, and Sir George Gipps was Governor of the Colony. We had business with the Colonial Office; with the Surveyor-General's Office, for grants of land ; with the Auditor-General's Office, for payment of stipends ; with the Treasury ; with the Superintendent of Convicts' Office ; and with the military authorities, for attending the troops. I left all this correspondence docketed in pigeon-holes, but I doubt if it has been preserved. Liverpool was attended from Parramatta, and I had a young priest to assist me. At Liverpool, Mass was still said in the convict hospital, as we had no chapel there yet. A curious incident, the effect of imagination, occurred to this young priest on one of his first journeys. He was new to the Colony; and riding one night to Liverpool, to officiate next morning, darkness came on, and with the darkness an unaccountable fear that the blacks were around him. He backed his horse under a tree, and there he sat all the night in the rain, expecting every moment that the blacks were coming to spear him. I saw on his return that he was very pale and worn ; and then the story came out. Yet there were no natives about : it was entirely the effect of imagination.

Besides the school, the principal work of the Sisters was in the great female prison, called the Female Factory. This was the head-quarters of all the female convicts. They were assigned to service from there. They were returned there for punishment. There were commonly as many as 15,000 women in this prison, distributed into three wards or classes. The first class consisted of those who were ready for assignment ; the second of women sent in with illegitimate children when they had no nurse ; the third class was of those who had to undergo severe punishment, and who, on their entrance, had their hair cut off, an operation not unfrequently attended with the most violent scenes. As there were generally some five hundred Catholics among these unfortunate women, the Sisters went to instruct and influence them five evenings in the week. They sat in chairs in the midst of one of the yards, and the women sat on the flags in groups around them, except private interviews were required, when they resorted to rooms assigned to their use. It was sometimes difficult to prevent these poor creatures from making complete confession to the nuns. They wanted to unburden their minds, and said they would as soon speak to a nun as to a priest. The reverence with which the Sisters were regarded by all these women was quite remarkable, and the influence which they exercised told, not only in the prison, by the greater order and the easier management of these numerous and excitable women, but after a time it was felt throughout the Colony, and was repeatedly expressed by the magistrates from the bench. The whole establishment was bettered by their influence. There were no more of those violent outbreaks which marked its earlier history. For example, the convict women once broke out to see the races, and it took several days to get them all back again. Old Mr. Marsden, the senior chaplain of the Colony, magistrate, and Chairman of the Committee of Management, told me that the women were once in such a state of rebellion that, in his perplexity, he sent for a company of soldiers, who had no sooner entered the yard and were drawn up than the third class, whose occupation was breaking stones, began to pelt the men with stones. The captain in command said to the magistrate: "What are we to do? We can't fire upon the women or charge them with the bayonet." The clerical magistrate replied: " Drive them in with their own weapons." And the men drove them into their quarters with stones, where they were locked up.

It was my duty to say Mass for the Catholic women once a week, and to hear all whom the nuns had prepared and sent to me. Although this work was very beneficial, and changed the habits of many a poor soul, the labour, which was long, and took more than one day in the week, often left me completely sick and exhausted. Another duty in that factory was of a singular character. When convict men obtained their ticket-of-leave and a permit to marry, or got their freedom, some of them would come to the female prison, exhibit their papers, and ask for a wife. This was made known to the women of the first class, who were ready for assignment. Some of them would present themselves in the room where the man was waiting. After taking a survey of them, he would beckon one to him. The two had a private conversation, and, if they agreed to marry, which was commonly the case, they were married by their own clergyman on the spot. It is a fact that many of these marriages, especially if they went to live in the country, turned out well.

On one occasion, however, there was a great disturbance in the factory, of which I was the unconscious cause. The long room in which I was giving the Catholic women an instruction was only separated by a wall from another long room in which the second class were nursing their children. Quarrels often arose among them about little things concerning the wants of their offspring. Suddenly there arose such a clamour and a swearing and cursing among these women, that it pierced the wall and put the women I was instructing into a state of excitement. They murmured, groaned, drew long sighs, and expressed their feelings aloud. I seized the occasion to improve it. I told them they need not affect to be horrified, but had better look at themselves in this conduct, for that when my eye was not on them they did much the same at certain times of excitement ; and there I left them. Somehow they got the notion into their heads that the disturbance had been got up to insult their priest. That night they broke into the other ward, and there was such a fight between the two classes of women that several of them had to be carried on shutters to the hospital, seriously injured. The matron told the whole story to me, and the women told it to the nuns.

Sir George and Lady Gipps showed their appreciation of the Sisters by repeatedly calling upon them, when at their country house at Parramatta ; sent them presents from their garden, and would have invited them in a quiet way to their mansion, only they received hints that it would be against their rule. And here I may mention that, on their arrival the Governor expressed to me his readiness to allow them pensions ; but as they refused to accept their passage and outfit from the Colonial Office, to the great surprise of Lord Glenelg, so they declined the offer of the Governor, thinking it best to keep themselves independent.

I forgot to mention in its proper place a rather curious

encounter with Bishop Broughton, after he had been raised from the rank of Archdeacon to that of Bishop of Australia. There is always a great levee at Government House on the Queen's birthday.   The Catholic Bishop presented himself in rochet and mozzetta.   The next day the Protestant Bishop sent in a protest to the Governor against his having received Dr. Polding in robes appropriate to a Roman Catholic bishop.   Sir Richard Bourke sent for me.   He had evidently no personal objections, for he said the only thing that struck him was that it was a very pretty dress.   But he was aware that the Bishop was backed in his protest by a party of zealous Anglican officials, and as his protest had received but little attention he requested that it should be referred to the Home Government.   Consequently, we sent a document to the Governor, in which it was stated that, properly, the robes in question were the domestic wear of a Catholic bishop, and so far from being *appropriate* to a bishop, they were worn by certain other ecclesiastics of lower rank, and even by canons.   The two documents were sent home together, and in course of time the reply came from the Colonial Office, that as the Catholic Bishop had stated that the robes worn at the levee were not appropriate to a bishop, there was no question to go before the legal adviser of the Crown.   But, to prevent all further nonsense on the subject, the Bishop went henceforth to the levee in coat and feriola.

I have also omitted stating in its due place, that at the close of 1836 I again visited Norfolk Island in company with a Special Commission, consisting of judge, lawyers, and a military jury.   I was received with joy by my former penitents, most of whom had persevered in their resolutions, and had stood to their religious practices despite of the ridicule of their companions.   Nearly sixty of them had learnt to read their prayers.   The Commandant whose hospitality I again enjoyed, assured me that crime had considerably diminished, and to my delight I found that for the fifteen months that had passed since my first visit, there was not a single Catholic brought before the judge.

I admitted the former penitents to Holy Communion ; and during the fifteen days that we remained on the island three hundred confessions and twelve conversions were the reward of my labours. The penitents, now become the majority of the Catholics, petitioned to be placed in separate wards, that they might say their prayers together. The one with whom I had formerly had the greatest difficulty was now free from chains and working in the garden of the Commandant, and every official commended him.

The assaults of the Press still went on, and every new piece of intelligence that reached us from England, whether of reform recommended in the transportation system, or of discussions on the subject in Parliament, awakened anew the animosity of which I was the object. A certain Miss Byrne arrived in the Colony from Ireland, professing to be the niece of a priest, and was taken under protection by an anti-Catholic party, and employed in lecturing on the horrors of Popery. To her lectures I gave a public reply. It so happened that two ruffians, looking out for plunder in the neighbourhood of Parramatta, met with this woman and attacked her on the road where she was walking. Fortunately they were caught. My adversaries in the Press seized the occasion to associate me with it, and one flaming article was headed : " Dr. Ullathorne and Blood." So great was the excitement caused, that when these men were brought before the Supreme Court, the judge thought it expedient to warn the jury that I was in no wise connected with the case before the trial proceeded.*

* At this period it would seem as if the public were disposed to take part in any attack on Dr. Ullathorne, however unjust or extravagant. At the desire of the Bishop he had published a sermon " On Laying the Foundation-stone of a New Church," which opens with the following sentence : " Ceremonies may be said to be the religion

Two of these newspapers wrote some gross libels upon the Rev. Father Brady, a grave and holy man of mature age, who, educated in France, after having served for twelve years in the Isle of Bourbon, was placed at Windsor, on the Hawksbury, where he built a church. He afterwards became the first Bishop of Perth. To these libels I replied. But as the editors persevered in their attacks, an action was brought against them. One of the papers was ruined in consequence. The editor subsequently established a paper in Melbourne, and became a defender of the Catholic cause in that Colony.

Father Geoghehan had been sent to Melbourne to found the Church in the Colony of Victoria ; and though the gold mines had not yet been opened, he succeeded in building a large church. The Bishop wished me to pay a visit to Adelaide, the capital of the new province of South Australia, with the view of ascertaining what Catholics there were in that Colony and what could be done for them. Father Lynch, one of the young priests that I had brought from Ireland, took my place at Parramatta ; and according to my custom, I took the first vessel that offered. She was a small coasting schooner, and the only passengers I found on board were an uneducated woman with a number of children who occupied the main cabin. Leaning over the bulwarks, I was thinking what a dreary passage of some eight hundred miles I should have, when a respectable young man came and leant near me. Turning to me, he said : " The last time we met was

of the body, as faith is the religion of the mind, and prayer and the love of God the religion of the heart." No sooner did it appear than Dr. Lang, the minister of the chief Scottish church in the Colony, assailed it, and sought to expose the (supposed) monstrous admission of the assertion that " Ceremonies are the religion *of the body*," by which words, apart from the context, he represented the meaning of the writer to be that they were the religion of the body Catholic ; and on this supposition raised a fabric of solemn invective against a system so unspiritual.

at the hotel by the leaning tower of Bologna, and your conversation at that table that day decided me on settling in Australia. I am on my way to my property at Adelaide." I then remembered him, and was glad of someone to converse with. When we landed at Adelaide, the city, a few miles from the Port, was in the fourth year from its foundation. Like the old Etruscan cities, it had been regularly laid out from the first in a square. The straight streets were, many of them, only marked out by rough roads and chippings on the trees ; and the houses were, here and there, not yet brought into line. I was hospitably received by Mr. and Mrs. Philips and their family, whose house, beautifully situated, looked over the great level plain, rich with grass and most beautiful flowers, upon the precipitous range of Mount Lofty. My first point was to see the Governor ; my second to obtain a room in which to assemble the Catholic population. I wrote to the Governor's Secretary, but obstacles were put into the way of an audience on pleas that seemed to me trifling. I next called with Mr. Philips on the Chief Commissioner : for the Colony was founded by an association on speculation, and was under the management of their Commissioners, as well as under the rule of Colonel Gawler, the Governor appointed by the Colonial Office. The Chief Commissioner at that time was a Scotch Presbyterian. I asked leave for the use of a building which had been lent to every denomination until they had a place of worship of their own. I was received respectfully, but dryly, and was told that I should receive an answer by letter. The answer was a refusal, without reason assigned. It was evident that the authorities were against the presence of a Catholic priest, if they could manage it. The refusal soon got wind among the population ; and a Protestant, who kept a china shop, was so indignant at this treatment, that he offered to put his china into his cellars and to give

up his shop to our use twice a week, on Sundays and
Thursdays. There I erected an altar and said Mass,
preaching and catechising morning and evening on those
two days in the week. I found that the Catholics were not
more than fifty in number.

I now wrote direct to the Governor, informed his Excellency of my official position in the Australian Colonies,
and that I had brought out a letter from the Colonial
Office recommending me to the Governors of those
Colonies. I requested the honour of an audience. This
was at once granted, but the interview was very formal. I
got no more notice from Government House than this
quarter of an hour's conversation. As there were no convicts in this Colony there was no ground for applying to
the Government for the maintenance of a priest. Besides
which, the Bishop had wisely made it a rule never to put
one priest alone where he could not be in a position to visit
another priest the same day. So that in Norfolk Island,
when it came to have a chaplain, two priests were placed
together. And in the vast and thinly populated districts
of the interior of New South Wales, two priests were
placed together, one of whom remained at home whilst the
other travelled through half the territory; and, on his return,
the other started through his course over the other half of
the district, visiting all the settlements and holding stations
wherever the people could be gathered together. I remember one priest reporting from the Mimeroo Plains, that
in the course of a year he and his companion had travelled
10,000 square miles.

I made one very interesting acquaintance in Adelaide.
Next door to my host resided Captain Sturt, the celebrated Australian explorer, who had then nearly lost his
sight from what he had gone through. From him I
learnt many interesting details of his expeditions. I was
particularly struck with his account of the time when,

after a long course of thirst, they had to drink the blood of their horses. Their men lay prostrate and groaning; not excited, they were past that, but half dead, and despairing. He wondered how ever he was able to keep himself up.

After baptising the last-born child of my hospitable hosts, I bade them farewell and returned to Sydney. After that youngest daughter had been baptised I said: "Now, remember, this child must be a nun." Twenty years after Mrs. Philips wrote to me from Sydney, and reminding me of what I had said, informed me that this child had actually become a Benedictine nun in the Convent near Parramatta.

I might as well tell here how the Mission to South Australia finally came about. On the first establishment of the Australian Hierarchy, of which more hereafter, the Holy See appointed me to Adelaide, but I succeeded in obtaining exemption from the appointment. The Rev. Francis Murphy was then appointed; but as there were no means in the Colony for his maintenance, a collection was being made in New South Wales to aid the first beginning. Just at that time Mr. Leigh, of Woodchester, who, after his conversion, was residing at Leamington, called on me at Coventry and expressed his desire to found a Catholic bishopric at Adelaide. He then explained that he had some property there, and had once intended to give one acre of town allotment in Adelaide and a hundred acres in the country, together with the sum of £4,000 towards founding a Protestant bishopric; but that since his conversion he wished to give this donation towards the Catholic bishopric. I said to him: "This is most providential, for a bishop has been appointed to Adelaide, whilst at present there is not even support for a priest." Not only did Mr. Leigh carry out his intention, but he also obtained plans for a small cathedral, which was erected on his town grant.

I puzzled my friends in Sydney by telling them that the

streets in Adelaide were fitter for the study of astronomy than for commerce. The fact was that miles of newly marked-out streets were unmade, and after heavy Australian rain were full of pools of water, through which my good hostess waded to the china shop for evening service, and in which the brilliant stars of the southern hemisphere were reflected.

At this time I wrote my " Reply to Judge Burton," the most important of my Colonial publications ; for it has become the text-book for the early Catholic history of New South Wales. Judge Burton had been a sailor in his youth, as well as myself, and he was full of Protestant zeal. On a visit to England he had published a large book, in which he advocated Protestant ascendancy in the Colony ; maintained the old scheme of devoting one-seventh of the lands of the Colony to the maintenance of the Protestant Church and Protestant education ; and in which he had not spared us. He had also delivered certain judgments from the bench, reversed, indeed, afterwards, by his brother judges sitting in *banco ;* but which, had they stood, would have invalidated all Catholic marriages up to a recent period, would have illegitimised the children of those marriages, and have upset the tenure of their property. This he had done on the mere plea of the applicability of English laws, which were in no wise applicable to the Colony.

On these two themes I wrote, and not only handled his delinquencies plainly, but with considerable severity ; for the Judge had shown a strong animus, and it was necessary to produce an impression. The pamphlet did produce a sensation. Judge Burton was still in England, and one of his brother judges sent him the sheets as they were printed. We took care to send several copies to the Colonial Office in England, and to the library of the House of Commons. He returned just before I left the Colony. His friends gave him a public dinner, and did their best to smooth things over. But soon after he was removed to India, where he remained eighteen years : after which he returned as Chief Justice to Sydney for a time. But this stern policy did not improve the feelings of the High Church people towards me; nor did the lawyers, as a body, like to have one of their ornaments attacked. A leading barrister, who ventured to say at a public meeting that this pamphlet was only unanswerable because no one thought it worth answering, was hissed into silence by the general sense of the assembly.

Another conflict in which I was concerned was with the Tract Society. This was something new in our Colonial history. Hitherto we had been accustomed to go on our own way without interference. But through Sir Richard Bourke's Act providing for religion, we had an influx of clergy of all kinds, and this brought in a good deal of old English anti-Catholic prejudice, to which we had hitherto been strangers ; and we had to assert that position of perfect equality which the policy of the Government had assigned to us. From the Tract Society anti-Catholic tracts began to be distributed even at the doors of Catholic houses. We noticed that even Government officials made themselves active in this Society ; and not only subscribed to it, but made speeches in its assemblies. To meet this and other machinations, we established a Catholic Association, with monthly meetings. The Bishop generally presided, and opened the subject, leaving the exposition and enforcement to me, who had a previous understanding with the chief speakers as to how the discussion was to be guided to its conclusion. Thus when these tracts began to fly about I advised the Catholics to accept the next that was offered and bring it to me. A quantity came. I then made extracts from them of passages that were insulting to Catholics, and drew up a list of the Government officials who supported the Society. We then called a great meet-

ing of the Catholic population and proposed to them that,
as this Tract Society was promoting enmity and division
between two classes of Her Majesty's subjects, and as
several of the Government officials, instead of promoting
peace, were co-operating in this method of disturbing the
peace of society, a list of those gentlemen, together with
extracts from those tracts, should be forwarded to Her
Majesty's Secretary of State for the Colonies.   This was
done, and it cleared the rooms of the Society of these
gentlemen.

The Bishop wished me to take the lead in this conflict,
to receive all blows aimed at his authority, and thus to
keep the Episcopal office free from attack.   This I readily
assented to as proper to the office of Vicar-General.   But
the Press coupled all this with my evidence on the Transportation system, and dubbed me with the title of the Very
Rev. Agitator-General of New South Wales.

In the year 1838, Bishop Pompallier arrived in Sydney
from France, on his way to begin the Mission in the
Islands of Oceanica, and was accompanied by several
Fathers of the Marist Institution.   From Sydney they proceeded to New Zealand, where they first began their
labours.   And this recalls to mind the conversion of a New
Zealand chief, which took place some years before in
Sydney.   A worthy Irishman wished to marry the daughter
of this chief, but being a truly religious man desired first to
make her a Christian.   He brought her and her father over
to Sydney, and then came and told the Bishop that he
wished to present them to him, in the hope of their conversion.   The Bishop fixed the time, and received them in
rochet and mozzetta, attended by two priests.   The Irishman acted as interpreter.   The man was told that the Chief
of the Christians received with respect the Chief of the
Maori, which was duly acknowledged.   After some more
conversation in the way of politeness, the Bishop took a

large crucifix and held it before his eyes. The chief gazed at it for some time, after which the Bishop said : "You are accustomed to revenge the wrongs of your tribe." The chief nodded his head. "And your people are accustomed to bear torture bravely?" Again he nodded his head. "Well, this is a case of revenge, and a case of torture. Did you ever see torture like this?" Still gazing, the chief shook his head. Then the Bishop slowly said, and the Irishman interpreted : "The Great God of Heaven, Who made all men, was angry with man, and would not destroy him. But the Great God had a Son like Himself, and He made a man of Him, and He revenged the wickedness of men on His Son. And this was what His Son suffered. And for the sake of what His Son suffered, He is ready to pardon every man who begs pardon of Him and obeys His laws." The chief was deeply moved and tears flowed from his eyes. The essential point of the mystery of Redemption had entered his mind. He and his daughter received a course of instruction, were baptised, and the daughter married to the Irishman.

I was thinking over this incident, before writing it, in the year 1888, when I received a visit from my friend, Dr. Redwood, Archbishop of Wellington. To him I repeated what I have just written. The Archbishop asked : "Do you remember the name of that Irishman?" I confessed that I could not recall it. "Was it Paynton?" "Now you mention it, I am confident that was his name." "Then," said the Archbishop, "he and his family have always been good practical Catholics, and the chief as well. It was in his house that Bishop Pompallier was first received on his landing. It was in that house that he said the first Mass ever said in New Zealand. And that house was always looked on with respect by all the Catholics, until it was burnt down not so very long ago."

Later on came another group of Marist Fathers, on their way to the South Sea Missions. And among them I particularly remember Father Batallion, who converted the Wallis Islands, became the first Bishop of Central Oceanica, and whose life has been recently published in France. I also remember making the acquaintance of the Blessed Father Chanel, who was martyred for the faith in the Island of Futuna, and who has been recently beatified : but wherever met, I do not remember, unless it were in New Zealand. I also remember calling upon the Bishop and his companions, destined for New Guinea, and whispering to Dr. Heptonstall : "Look well at the heads of those men." When we had left them, Dr. Heptonstall asked : "Why did you tell me to look at those men's heads ? " " Because," I replied, " I know something of the savage race of New Guinea, and am confident that some of their heads will be knocked off before twelve months are out." And it did occur, that landing in a boat, from the vessel that took them from Sydney, the savages met them in the water with their clubs, battered the Bishop's head to pieces and his body was taken back to Sydney.

In the year 1841 the foundation was laid of a second church in Sydney, the history of which is truly interesting. Mr. William Davis, the same worthy man who had given the first convent at Parramatta, offered his own house and garden as a site in Sydney on which to build a church. That house had a remarkable history. It was the house in which Father Flynn had officiated until he was unlawfully seized, committed to jail, and sent out of the country. He was arrested so suddenly that he was unable to consume the Blessed Sacrament. That was left in the house of Mr. Davis, and the Catholics went there on Sundays to say their prayers. This continued for two years, there being no priest in the Colony, until a French expedition of discovery arrived ; when the chaplain of the expedition said Mass in the house, and consumed the Host that had been left. This house may therefore be considered to have been the first Catholic chapel in Australia. It was situated on elevated ground close by St. Philip's, at that time, too, the only Protestant church in Sydney.

Mr. Davis was a truly religious man. Transported on the charge of having made pikes for the insurrectionists of Ireland in 1798, for he was a blacksmith by trade, he had suffered much for his faith. Twice he had been flogged for refusing to go to the Protestant service, and for the same refusal was so long imprisoned in a black hole that he almost lost his sight. But no sooner had he obtained his freedom, than by his industry and integrity, where good mechanics were few, he began to succeed in his trade. Then his house became like that of Obededom, and God blessed him, so that when I first became acquainted with him he had become a man of landed property, and had accumulated a considerable amount of wealth, and having no immediate dependents was much disposed to assist the advance of religion. How often have I heard him exclaim, in his earnest simplicity : " I love the Church."

It happened that at this time a scheme was being agitated for establishing a general system of elementary education on conditions which no Catholic could have accepted ; in consequence of which, the Bishop and myself had an interview with the Governor, Sir George Gipps, on the subject. After considerable discussion, the Governor brought the interview abruptly to a conclusion by saying : " In short, I must adhere to the strongest party, and I don't think that you are the strongest." After that we determined to make a public demonstration ; for we knew that, if not the strongest by numbers, we were by our union. We took the opportunity of laying the foundation of St. Patrick's Church. The Catholic population was in a state of exalted enthusiasm, in looking forward to it. The procession started from the Cathedral, and had to pass through the principal parts of the town. Bands of music were provided. The cross preceded, magnificent banners following along the line. Three hundred girls clothed in white followed the cross, the rest of the children forming a long line. Then came the Catholic people, who were 14,000 out of a population of 40,000. After them the acolytes and the clergy in their sacerdotal vestments, whilst the procession was closed by the Bishop in mitre and cope with his attendants. Such a procession had never been seen in Australia. The whole population filled the streets, and as we reached the place of the new church, on one of the highest points in Sydney, by every descent you might have walked on the heads of the people, among whom voices were heard saying : " We can't do this ; we must consent to come second." The foundation-stone was suspended in the air, visible to the multitude. At the Bishop's request I was mounted upon it, and thence I gave the touching history of the house which had now disappeared, which had been the centre of Catholic devotion in our days of trial and persecution, and which had now made way for the church which was there to rise on the most elevated point in Sydney. It was on the very catacombs of the Catholics that this church was to repose.

This was a revelation to the Colony of our strength, and our reply to the Governor's remark. It must be remembered that, in those days, we had to meet the long cherished traditions of Protestant supremacy, and to *assert* that equality before the law, which the law itself had given us.

CHAPTER XVII

ON my final return from the Australian Mission a good deal of curiosity was awakened as to the reason for this step. It was widely known that I had much to do with the organisation of the Church in that remote country, and this brought me sundry letters of inquiry from friends, to which I gave but general answers : for I did not think it expedient at the time, when I had returned to monastic obedience, to indulge what I looked upon as mere curiosity. But I have the document before me at this moment, in the year 1889, in which I clearly laid my reasons before Bishop Polding in the year 1840.

The mission next in importance to that of New South Wales, in those days, was that of Van Dieman's Land, now Tasmania. It was in a very unsatisfactory state, was a convict settlement, and was a thousand miles away from Sydney. Hence it could neither be properly superintended nor, properly, be provided for by the Bishop of Sydney. This had long dwelt on my mind, and I urged upon the attention of the Bishop, repeatedly, how necessary it had become that he should apply to the Holy See for the appointment of a Bishop to Van Dieman's Land. But absorbed as the Bishop was in missionary work, especially among the convicts, it was long before he entered into the plan. But when at last he saw the necessity of another Bishop clearly, he showed me a list of names recommended

for that office, and I found my own at the head of it. I at
once declared that I could not accept of it.   I had seen sufficient of bishops, I said, to compassionate them, but not
to envy them ; and that unless his Lordship consented to
remove my name, with the understanding that it was not
to be replaced, I should have no resource left me but to
return to my monastery in England.   An additional,
though accidental reason, was, that owing to a long course
of anxieties I was at that time much wasted and worn down
in health ; so much so that, in looking back to that time, I
find that in the speeches I had to make in public assemblies,
I had repeatedly to apologise for brevity on that account.
Persons from England who had met me, reported to my
friends there how weary and worn I looked : for I had
many solicitudes and many things to combat which it is
unnecessary here to record.   It was a maxim of the
Bishop, as I have already stated, that it was the business
of the Vicar-General to meet all the blows, and to keep his
principal in the good odour of peaceful reputation.   I will
give one or two examples.

On St. George's Day the English gentlemen of the
Colony gave a great dinner to the Irish and Scotch.   The
chairman invited the Bishop and myself as his guests.
The Bishop declined appearing, but wished me to go as his
representative.   I went accordingly.   I had to return thanks
for the Bishop and the clergy.   What I said was warmly
applauded, until I happened to allude to our great ancestry
as a Church.   It was but a transient remark, nor was it
noticed except by an Indian judge, who happened to be
there as a guest.   But he, in his anti-Catholic feeling, gave
vent to some sour exclamations, to everyone's annoyance.
Immediately opposite him sat the Chevalier Dillon, a
well-known Irishman, who had been titled by the King of
France for having discovered the remains of the celebrated
navigator, La Perouse, on the Fiji Islands.   Dillon seized

hold of an apple, and said to the judge : "If you don't stop, I'll drive this down your throat!" This quieted the judge, and there the matter ended. As soon as I was seated, I turned to my next neighbour, Captain (afterwards General) England, a man of good judgment, and said : "Tell me frankly; did I say anything inappropriate?" "Upon my honour," he replied, "if I thought so I would tell you ; but I thought nothing of the kind." But the hostile papers, ever on the look out for the old offender, represented me as having caused what approached near to a fracas among gentlemen. It might have been well to have avoided the allusion in a mixed company, but in the warmth of speaking one sometimes lets slip what is not acceptable to all hearers.

The laying the foundation-stone of St. Patrick's Church had long been looked forward to. Collections for the building had been made for years, committees were formed, and weekly meetings held. As the time approached a warm national feeling had been raised among the Irish-Catholic population, and they resolved to make an exhibition of national emblems. Hitherto national distinctions had been instinctively avoided in the Colony ; all prided themselves on being Australians. The rumours afloat about this exhibition of nationality alarmed the governing authorities ; they were afraid of its ending in reprisals, and of its becoming the beginning of national parties. The Governor sent for the chief police magistrate and expressed to him his apprehensions. The magistrate came to me, and conjured me to prevent the religious procession from being turned into a national demonstration. "Suppose," he said, "that orange flags are lifted up, what will be the state of Sydney? Hitherto we have all gone on so peacefully together." I asked the opinion of the Attorney and Solicitor-General, both Irish Catholics, and our leading men among the laity. They thought that, however innocently intended, things were going too far. I felt compelled to take the matter in hand, and made full representations to the Bishop. His Lordship felt reluctant to oppose the ardent feelings of the people. I retired to another room and wrote him a letter, stating that I had now done all I could in the way of representation, both to himself and to the clergy, and felt myself free from further responsibility ; but that, as the whole object of the procession was to conduct his Lordship to the foundation-stone, and not to make a national demonstration, I felt that the representations of the authorities ought to be attended to. He then sent for me, and asked what I recommended, as he did not see his way. To this I replied that, without compromising him, if he would leave it to me I thought I could find a way through the difficulty. And it was left to my judgment.

This was the eve of the day appointed for the ceremony A meeting of the general committee was then being held, and I got Mr. Therry, the Solicitor-General, and some other gentlemen, to accompany me to the assembly. It was densely crowded, and excited speeches were going on. In a speech of an hour's length I gradually worked the assembly round until I came to the point: and then the chief leader of the popular voice arose, and called upon the assembly to comply with my advice, and for the sake of peace to withhold from the procession those marked national emblems, however much they had cost ; for peace was better. Thus the point was gained. Mr. Therry, who had been one of O'Connell's leaders in the great meetings for Emancipation, was much struck with the whole affair, and with the way in which that vehement excitement in one direction was turned, by degrees, into another. When I informed the Bishop of the result, he expressed great satisfaction, and declared that it set his mind in peace. How successful that procession was, as a Catholic demonstration, I have already stated.

After various plans had been considered, Bishop Polding decided to go himself to Rome, and obtain what further assistance he could of men from England and Ireland. As there was still reason to apprehend that my name might be put before the Holy See for Van Dieman's Land, I decided to accompany him to England; and Dr. Gregory completed the party as attendant on the Bishop.

We engaged our passage in a Chilian brig, bound, in the first instance, for Korarika, in the Bay of Islands, New Zealand, our object being to visit Bishop Pompallier and his missioners in that settlement; the French Bishop having long wished for such a visit, for the sake of the influence on the natives. Thence we were to sail for Talcuhana, in Chili, with the intention of riding over the Pampas across South America, and taking shipping for England on the other side. For this purpose we had taken English saddles as part of our equipment.

The Catholics prepared a magnificent demonstration in honour of the Bishop on his departure, and a large sum of money was collected to cover the expenses of his journeys. I was asked what I should like, but I told the delegates that I would on no account interfere with the testimonial to the Bishop; they might give me some trifle as a remembrance, such as a snuff-box. And I was consequently presented with an address accompanied with a snuff-box filled with sovereigns.

On the morning of departure I said Mass for the nuns whom I had brought to the Colony, now increased in number, who had come from Parramatta to Sydney for a blessing, and to bid us farewell. I had hitherto had the entire guidance of them, and I loved them in God as a father loves his children. Dear souls, it was a touching scene, and they wept the whole Mass over their separation from their friend and guide. It is only a fortnight from writing this that I celebrated with them, the breadth of the world between us, a singular jubilee of thanksgiving. They wrote to remind me that on December 31st, 1888, it would be fifty years since I firsr landed them in Sydney, and asked me to join them in their thanksgiving for all the benefits they had received, and, I may add, for all the good God had enabled them to do during those past fifty years. But the most interesting part of their letters recorded the present state of their Congregation in Australia.

There are now 110 members. They have a large hospital in Sydney, with 150 beds, which is well supported; another hospital in Parramatta in the house in which I placed them; an orphanage at Hobart; a young ladies' college in a well-constructed building; and they teach 3,000 children besides. They are also about to erect a hospital at Melbourne, towards which they have received a sumptuous offering. Of the five members who landed with me, one alone survives, who is still Superior of the orphanage, at the advanced age of eighty-nine years. Here is a theme for gratitude.

The departure was marked by an extraordinary scene. The Catholics accompanied the Bishop from the Cathedral to the harbour, the population crowded the shore, the ships hoisted their colours, salutes were fired, and steamers, with the chief Catholics on board, with bands of music, accompanied the vessel to the Head. The affectionate respect shown the Bishop was loud and hearty on all sides. At last we were alone on the wide sea, and the coast of Australia vanished from our eyes.

After we had become familiar with the captain, who was an Englishman, and part owner, naturalised in Chili, and who had sailed wlth Lord Dundonald in his famous conflicts with the Spaniards, he said to me one day: " I was never more surprised than when I first met such a great man as you are. From all I had heard and read in the newspapers I expected to meet a great, big-boned man,

with a passionate temper, and a big shillalah in his hand."
So, on meeting some military officers from India, after
acquaintance, they said laughingly : "We know all about
you in India ; your Bishop is an angel, but you are the
Agitator-General."

One thing I did before I left Sydney, which ought to be
recorded. It was something very obvious, to me at least,
but no one else seemed to see it. A great deal of speculation was going on, and land in Sydney and other townships
rose enormously in favourable positions. It was said that
land had been sold in one principal street at a higher price
per foot than it had ever been sold at that time, in
Cheapside, London. Many millions of paper money had
floated from the banks : but at that time the Government
Gazette" published the amount of specie in the Colony,
which did not amount to more than £600,000. Anyone
with a little knowledge of finance ought to have seen the
consequence : but no notice was taken of it. I then wrote
three letters in the *Australian Chronicle*, the Catholic paper,
addressed respectively to his Excellency the Governor, to
the city of Sydney, and to the Colony at large, in which
I predicted that great troubles were in the wind, and that
a great deal of property must soon change hands. I regret
I have not a copy of those letters, I lent them to the British
Consul at Talcuhana and never recovered them. They
were received with incredulity ; but after a time came the
crash, and many failures. Land ran down rapidly in price,
and sheep, the staple of the Colony, came from twenty-five
to five shillings a head, and even to half-a-crown. Nor did
the Colony fully recover itself until the discovery of gold.
Meeting my old friend, Sir Roger Therry, long years after,
on his return to England, he said : "We did not believe your
letters, we were rather amused at them : but we were
awfully punished."

If I were asked how I was affected by those long and

persistent attacks of the Press, by the opinion thus gene-
rated, though it never touched the Catholic circle, I should
say that, being then a young man I was not without an
annoying consciousness of it, especially as I was left to
bear the brunt alone ; yet it was less the object of thought
than of a certain dull pressure as from the enduring of
hostile elements. But it was a valuable training, as it made
me indifferent to public opinion, where duty was concerned,
for the rest of my life.   In my book " On the Management
of Criminals " I have spoken of the way in which the Colony
ultimately did me justice.   The time at last came when all
the inhabitants of New South Wales, as well as of the other
Australian Colonies, came round to my way of thinking.
I was probably sitting in my room at Birmingham pursuing
some tranquil occupation, unconscious of what was passing
at Sydney, when 100,000 people met under their leaders
from all parts of the Colony in that park I had so often
traversed—in front of that Cathedral where I had minis-
tered—to proclaim with one voice the convict system an
abomination and a pollution of the land, which must be got
rid of at all cost, and to utter the solemn resolve that never
again would they allow a convict ship to touch their shores.*
Among the speakers who addressed that great assembly
was my old friend, Archdeacon McEncroe.   Then arose
three cheers for the old advocate of their new views ! Such
is opinion, that queen of the world who has so often to
revise her judgments.

* This meeting was held at Sydney in the year 1850.

CHAPTER XVIII.

NEW ZEALAND.

WE left Sydney on the brig *Orion*, on November 16th, 1840. Captain Sanders, a warm-hearted man, not only paid us every attention, but entertained us greatly with his anecdotes of Lord Dundonald and the War of Independence. I took advantage of his collection of Spanish books; and after about a fortnight's sail we cast anchor before Korarika, in the Bay of Islands. The town at that time consisted of a native pah, a small British settlement, and the French Mission. We were met on board by Mr. Waterton, brother of the celebrated naturalist, who was residing with the missioners and spent his time in botanical excursions. On reaching the mission house we found that Bishop Pompallier was absent on a tour among the islands of the Pacific in his little schooner. The Fathers of the Marist Congregation, who had received our Bishop's hospitality on their way out, received us with joy. Their residence was of wood, and their little wooden church, bright with green paint, stood adjoining: small as it was, it had its font, confessional, and all appointments complete. Soon after our arrival the evening service began for the native tribes, and, of course, we attended the service in the church. A chief object of our visit was to remove an impression made by the Anglican and Wesleyan missioners upon the natives, that the Catholic religion was not the religion of Englishmen, but the religion of a people with whom they had nothing to do.

13

This statement they had embellished with fantastic stories of the old anti-Catholic type, seasoned for the New Zealand palate with horrible stories of the cast of Foxe's "Book of Martyrs." To give an example: An Irish gentleman went to New Zealand with the view of purchasing land, and on his return to Sydney he told me that as he was travelling about, with a native Catholic as a guide, he came upon a crowd of natives listening to a man who was preaching to them from a stump. He had a flaming torch in his hand, which he waved about with great energy. My friend asked the native guide to explain what he was saying, and this was the substance of it. He told them that the Catholics—*Picopos* he called them—were a cruel people, who worshipped wooden gods. That they came from a place called Roma; and that at Roma they tore people to pieces with wild horses if they would not be Catholics; and they took fire and burnt them under their arms and on their bodies, which acts he imitated with his torch. In short, he applied the history of the pagan persecutions to the Roman Catholics. How the Fathers were looked upon by people thus instructed I had an opportunity of observing. I was walking on the hills with some of them when we came near to a large wooden school used by some English missioners. I expressed a curiosity to see it, and we went towards it. But the moment the native women inside caught sight of the soutanes and three-cornered hats of the Fathers they rushed up in a fury and slammed the door against them.

One Father read the prayers before the altar in the native language, which the people answered, and then another Father intoned the hymn, which the people took up. It was the *O Filii et Filiæ*, adapted to the New Zealand language, but in the old simple notes. How they did · sing ! with voices harsh, stentorian, and vehement, beyond European comprehension. They had but few notes and no music in their voices. They sang in jerks. The Alleluias that end the stanzas became *Arr-a-oo-yah.* With a strong grinding on the *rr*, and a great jerk at the final *yah.* But however vehement, as I have always observed among the South Sea Islanders, they drop their voices to their lowest pitch at the end of their song, as if exhausted by the effort, which makes all their singing plaintive. After this earnest act of devotion, the senior missioner addressed them. We could not understand what he said, but he every now and then pointed to us, and we heard the word *picopo;* he then pointed to himself, and again we heard the word *picopo*, and all eyes were bent upon him. After the service we asked the Father the meaning of the word *picopo.* He then explained that *picopo* meant bishop and also meant Catholic. When Bishop Pompallier began his mission he had to invent new words for the expression of ideas new to his neophytes. Their language, chiefly formed of vowels and liquids, contained but thirteen letters, and there was in it the peculiarity that two con-sonants could not be brought together and that every word must end with a vowel. The word bishop, or *évêque*, was unpronounceable, so that he took the Latin word *episcopus*, and changed it into *picopo* to designate himself, and it became the name of his religion as well. The Father was explaining to the natives how they saw before their eyes English Catholics as well as French Catholics. When he spoke of English Catholics he called them *Picopo poroyaxono* (*poroyaxono* meaning an Englishman, and taken from Port Jackson, the harbour of Sydney, which many of them had visited in the whaling ships) ; but French Catholics he called *Picopo Wee wee*, a name given them by the natives from their so constantly repeating the words *Oui, oui.*

We visited the tribe the same evening, in their low huts, creeping inside, where we could sit, but not stand. The *Maori*, who form the principal race, are a magnificent race

in height, strength, and intelligence. They could all read
and write, even at that time. When a few obtained these
acquirements they rapidly communicated them to the rest.
Their chiefs were singularly fine looking men, and the tattoo
on their faces gave depth to their expression. The women
were coarse in features for their sex, but were animated
with an incessant cheerfulness that often broke into laughter.
The costume of both sexes was still the old woven mats,
often coloured in good taste. We found the chief under
taboo; having had his hair cut that day he was prohibited
from using his hands until the day following. He politely
explained that he could not rise, for the same reason, but
must keep seated with his hands across his breast.* His
wife sat on one side of him and his daughter on the other,
feeding him with his supper. A skillet, containing about
half a peck of boiled potatoes, stood before him ; his wife
peeled one with her fingers and put it into his mouth, then
his daughter peeled another, and put that into his mouth.
So the meal went on, irresistibly reminding me of his mouth
being a potato trap. The potatoes of New Zealand are
among the largest and best in the world, but dark in colour.†
He was a grand specimen of his race, and was as polite as
circumstances would allow, and explained to us that if he

---

* The Bishop does not say whether it was with this or another chief
that he enjoyed the honour of rubbing noses. He found the illustrious
nose very blue and very cold. In his last illness, when someone spoke
of his feeling cold, he replied with his usual humour, " Not so cold as
the nose of a New Zealand chief; that is the coldest object in nature
that I know of."

† Not only the potatoes, but the pork also of New Zealand was often
praised by the Bishop as superior to anything of the kind known in
Europe. He used to relate how both these comestibles figured on
the occasions when peace was established between two tribes after a
period of war. The ceremony in use at such times was peculiar. A
wall was built, composed of roast pork and potatoes, mixed together ;
the rival tribes established themselves at either end of the wall and
steadily ate their way through it till they met in the middle ; and when
this happened, the peace was considered as concluded.

was not fed in that way he would be obliged to go without food when he was under taboo.

The missioners explained to us that, in consequence of their recent cannibalism, the Bishop had found it expedient not to explain to their neophytes the doctrine of the Real Presence until they were completely prepared for Baptism ; but that in this respect they followed the discipline of the early Church : so that when the neophytes assisted at Mass they were only told that it was the highest degree of worship, the meaning of which they would understand later. And before they were baptised it was committed to them as a profound secret of the faith. Meanwhile, whilst assisting at Mass, one of the priests said suitable prayers with them.

The next day we went up the Bay some miles, in a boat, to pay our respects to the Governor, Captain Hobson, R.N. The British settlement had only recently begun, and the Bay of Islands was still the head-quarters. The Governor talked freely about the influence of Bishop Pompallier with the natives. The Bishop had taught Mrs. Hobson the native language, and she spoke with great respect of him. But Bishop Polding was not a little perplexed when the Governor launched out with his grievance, sailor-like, against Bishop Pompallier, for the illegal way in which he sailed his missionary schooner. He described her as an American craft sailed by a French commander and crew from an English colony, without regular papers, and exhibiting a fancy flag. "If I met her at sea," concluded the Governor, "I should certainly seize her as a pirate and take her into port." To me, as an old sailor, the surprise of our Bishop at this language was amusing. He attempted a defence, but knew no more of marine law than the Bishop of New Zealand. At a later period the Bishop got his vessel registered as belonging to New Zealand, and hoisted the British flag.

The Governor's residence was near to a native *pah*, which was placed on a lofty rock, scarped and strongly fortified, and even the water approach defended by well-constructed palisades made of the trunks of trees. Within the *pah* was the armed tribe. In front of it were several companies of British troops under tents. It was believed that the natives were disposed for a conflict with them. The Governor mentioned this, and added that he had a native in prison for a murder, that he had contrived that the man should escape, but that the natives had brought him back again, wanting a reason for a conflict, and that he only wished he could get rid of him. The officers at the camp invited us to lunch with them. They were anxious about the state of things, and said that as they had no artillery they could only get at the *pah* with rockets.

Next day, on the recommendation of Mr. Waterton, Dr. Gregory and I made an excursion to examine a remarkable geological formation. Accompanied by two of the missioners and Mr. Waterton, we went up some way along the long winding ridges and across the valleys which characterise that part of New Zealand. At last we came to a broad valley, with a stream rushing through it, on the bank of which was a native village. Not a soul was at home, they had all gone to a distance to cultivate their potato plots. There was nothing in it alive but a dog. The provisions of corn belonging to the villagers were stored in huts raised on long poles to preserve them from the rats. To protect them from human aggressors these stores were tabooed, in sign of which bunches of feathers were suspended from them. To violate a taboo is death.

On the flank of the village arose a mountain of marble, which extended for some half a mile along the valley. This mountain exhibited itself in most fantastic shapes, like the ruins of huge Gothic castles and abbeys, close upon each other.   Trailing plants and mosses covered the whole ; whilst here and there caverns opened from the ground, as if they were the vaults and dungeons of this gigantic mass of ruins.   The marble itself, when broken, was white, with salmon-coloured veins.   One of these caverns was tabooed at the entrance.   The Fathers explained that this was the village cemetery, and that we might enter notwithstanding the taboo, as Europeans were excused from the law, on supposition of their ignorance of it.   We entered, but found nothing but an old musket and a stench of human remains.

Passing through a wood on our return, we met an old woman, who, as soon as she caught sight of the Fathers, began a wailing cry of joy.   They had made her a Christian, but she had not seen them for some time.   After they had talked kindly to her, we left her still wailing and crying in her joy as long as we could hear her voice in the lonely wood.   The natives invariably express any deep-felt joy by wailing and crying.   Whilst at the mission house, a father and mother arrived in a boat to visit their son, who was studying with the Fathers ; and during the interview, which lasted an hour, they never ceased their wailings for joy.

The Rev. Mr. Williams, the head of the Protestant Mission, had a good house with ornamental grounds on the opposite side of the Bay.   He courteously crossed the Bay in a beautiful boat, manned by natives, to pay us a visit, and that visit we returned.   He had been twenty years on the island, and had accumulated considerable property.   The extent of land and stock which the Anglican missioners had acquired had been the theme of attack, both in the Sydney press and in the Legislative Council.   Before there were any settlers, and twenty years before there was any Catholic Mission, they held possession and obtained a quantity of the best land for mere trifling considerations. It was also said that the Anglican and Wesleyan missioners had carried on an extensive commerce with the natives in blankets, spirits, and even in New Zealanders' heads. These heads were the trophies of war. They were baked, then hardened in a current of cold air, and kept on shelves as proofs of bravery. They were sought after for museums and surgical collections. But the trade in them became a cause of war for their possession, and after a time the Australian Government made them contraband. In defending the missioners against this charge, the Protestant Bishop of Sydney once committed himself, in the Council, to the following statement: "That these gentlemen were bound to provide for their families ; and that, by the blessing of God there were no people who had larger families than the missioners of the South Sea Islands "—a statement which not a little entertained the daily press.

The natives soon discovered that the French missioners never entered into traffic, or cared for land beyond the small quantity required for their dwellings. Their one care was for the souls of the people : and about 40,000 of them had already come under the care of the Catholic missions. Bishop Pompallier told me, at a later period, that they soon found the most horrible stories propagated among the people about Catholic acts and doctrines. For example : the priests were taken for a sort of magicians, who profess to conjure bread into Christ, and were a sort of cannibals professing to eat human flesh. On his visit to a distant tribe for the first time, they stared at him as he seated himself, with his tall and handsome figure, before them. Then he said to them : " I am going to eat you, but let me first make you a present of a blanket apiece." Then he explained to them that he had not come to eat their bodies, but to bring their spirits to the Great Spirit. And as he became familiar with them they told him that the missioners always sold their blankets very dear. My friend, Mr. Lett, of Sydney, in travelling about New Zealand, found his best introduction at the Catholic villages in telling the people he was a *picopo* and making the sign of the Cross. But on one occasion he committed the mistake of addressing a Protestant chief in this way. Immediately the man looked very grave, shook his head, and said : " God very good—Maria very bad." My friend asked him : " What do you mean by Maria ? " He pointed upwards, and said : " The woman—very bad."

I was curious to see one of these wealthy missionary establishments, that I might speak of them from knowledge. Father Bataillon, afterwards Bishop of Wallis Island, which he converted, undertook to accompany Dr. Gregory and myself. We started in a boat for a long pull over the length of the vast Bay, and so up the principal river for a distance of some six or seven miles. Our crew consisted of the tailor of the mission, a French youth, and a young native, who was to leave us at the other end of the Bay. We calculated on sailing back with the evening breeze. We pulled the whole way, and took our first rest on a rock, which we found covered with small oysters, and refreshed ourselves with what Italians call the " fruit of the sea," cutting our hands pretty freely in the operation of detaching them. We next pulled to a Catholic village upon the shore. The moment the three-cornered hat was seen the chief, with all his tribe of both sexes, came crying with joy to meet us. The salutes were made without interrupting the crying ; and the tall and burly chief rubbed his large nose against both sides of mine—a nose that was blue and cold as that of a dog. Then we all knelt on the grass, and Father Bataillon said prayers in their tongue, to which they answered with their usual energy ; after which followed a merry gossip with the good Father, that was Sanscrit to us.

Meanwhile the wind had freshened to a gale, the water was getting rough, and it was judged on all hands unsafe to proceed further: it would be as much as we could do to get home, though we had a leading wind, or nearly so. After holding council we decided on making for an island which was some distance to windward, hoping to carry sail from there into the harbour of Korarika. We found the island beautiful, with a single cottage on it and a vegetable garden. The inhabitants were a young Scotchman and his wife, who showed us every attention. After reaching England, I found it recorded in a newspaper that soon after this the young couple had been murdered and their place plundered. We launched again and set sail. the gale increased, our lee gunwale touched the water, and one of us had to bail the water thrown over the bows Feeling the position critical I got the Father to let me steer the boat, held the sheet of the sail in my hand ready to let go in case of a squall, and put her before the wind. We then began to sing the Litany of the Blessed Virgin, and never was it sung more earnestly. The vessels in the harbour were watching us through their glasses, anxious for our safety; alert, expecting a capsise. But after dark we finally reached a point half a mile below the harbour, hauled up the boat, and got safely home.

One excursion must be related for its amusing incident. Bishop Polding, Dr. Gregory, a son of Mr. Justice Therry, whom we were taking to college, myself, and two of the missionary Fathers started in the boat to visit a first class *pah* and to see the country. The *pah* was a formidable structure, square in form, as usual, enclosing a considerable population; its defence consisting of upright stems of trees driven into the soil, bound together, and at the angles of the fortress grotesque figures, carved and coloured, surmounting still larger stumps of trees. Stockades protected the entrance, and when these were passed the difficulty was far from being surmounted, for you only found yourself in a narrow passage which wound its way to the interior centre before you could obtain an entrance ; and this passage left you at the mercy of the rifles or spears that could be used by the warriors from the chinks and loopholes on both sides. A hostile tribe or confederation of tribes might lie in ambush for months, watching an opportunity to gain entrance by scaling, breaking, slipping through, or undermining.

On our return we came to the bend of a river, which we must cross to reach a native village. A woman brought a bark canoe across, too frail to take more than one passenger at a time, and leaky as the ferry-boat of Charon, for the water already covered the precarious footing that it offered. One of the Fathers crossed, standing upright. The Bishop followed the example ; but as the frail craft cockled from side to side, he was obliged to clap himself down at the bottom of the canoe amidst the water, where, in his purple stockings and shovel hat, he presented a singular spectacle. The woman who rowed him burst out laughing, and we could not help joining in the chorus. We all got over at last, and were much interested in watching the native women cooking a dog. Their style of cooking, if simple, is perfect. The following is the recipe : First make a hole in the ground of convenient size, then pave it with good round stones. On the stones make a wood fire until the stones are thoroughly heated. Prepare other heated stones at the same time. When all is ready, cover the heated stones with leaves. Lay the dog, duly prepared, upon them, cover it up with leaves, and then place the other hot stones upon it. Let experience regulate the time for the cooking, and then when you take up the baked animal you will not only find it the tenderest of food, but every drop of the gravy will be contained in it.

We had now to make our way to our boat, and I set my mind on gaining it by a range of hills covered with wood. The natives shook their heads, and declared we could not go that way. The Fathers declared we could not safely neglect their admonition. But in a headstrong mood, I resolved to try, and persuaded Dr. Polding to join me, taking young Therry with us. The missioners and Dr. Gregory took another way. From the hills we had to descend, and soon found ourselves up to the knees in black mud, treacherously concealed under long grass. The further we went in a worse condition we found ourselves. Young Therry lost his boots, and we had to carry him on our backs by turns. In the midst of our difficulties at last their appeared a tall and half naked New Zealander. He had a brace of wild ducks in his hand, and waving them about as he stood on the verge of the bog, he shouted out : " One talera, two talera, three talera." " Yes, yes," we were ready to give him a dollar a head to help us out of our trouble. He then came near. I mounted on his shoulders, and he landed me on a green mound, when I could see the boat on the river and the Fathers in it. But when I turned again to look for the Bishop, I saw him mounted on the tall copper-coloured native, his purple-stockinged legs, covered with mud, sticking out before. Upon his shoulders, over the shovel hat, rode young Therry, and from his hands hung the brace of wild ducks. This human pyramid, advancing with solemn pace on the two long copper-coloured legs, caused a hearty laugh, after which we joined the boat.

One missionary anecdote from the lips of Bishop Pompallier, and then we will leave this interesting people. A daughter of one of the principal chiefs had been a follower of certain Dissenting missioners,· and her name was Hoke. But, coming under the influence of the Bishop, she became a zealous Catholic. She was intelligent and well instructed.

The missioners, concerned at losing such an influential proselyte, came and remonstrated with her. They said : "Well, Hoke, we are surprised at your going to those *picopos* who will not give you the Holy Book "—and on that theme they enlarged. Meanwhile Hoke sat and listened with her arms across : for they are very polite. When they had finished, Hoke arose to speak, and they had to sit and listen. She began : " You mickoners, you say you come from God ; but if you come from God you don't tell lies." She then said to a girl attending her, " Fetch my books." She took up one little book and said : " Look, that teaches all I have to believe. It explains the Apostles' Creed. Look ! " She laid it down and took up another. " Look, that explains all I have to do. It explains the Ten Commandments. Look ! " She then took up a third, and said : " Look, that explains all I have to ask of God. It explains the Lord's Prayer. Look ! If I was blind, of what use would be the Holy Book ? But the *picopo* came, and he spoke to my ear living words, and the words went to my heart, and the light of God came with them, and I saw and believed. And now you have told lies—go, go, go ! "

CHAPTER XIX.

SOUTH AMERICA.

AFTER a very interesting fortnight at Korarika we set sail for Chili. Our captain had failed in disposing of much of his remaining cargo of jarke (*chaire cuite*), or sun-dried Chilian beef. For the pork of New Zealand, fed in the woods, was so abundant and so much superior to anything of the kind fed in England, combining the qualities of veal and wild boar with that of pork, that the settlers never grew tired of it. This great supply of hogs had sprung from three left by Captain Cook. Before his arrival they had no quadrupeds, besides rats, except the dogs left by the Spaniards, which still retain the Spanish name of *perro*. The cannibalism formerly in practice was associated with the notion that in eating a warrior they partook of his warlike qualities.

On leaving New Zealand we found ourselves on the broad Pacific, where a strong wind is almost always blowing in the direction of Cape Horn. In the Bay of Aranca I read over again the celebrated epic of Ercillas, and dwelt on his fine vision in those waters. Passing Juan Fernandez on a bright day, with a fine breeze, it was impossible not to recall Selkirk and Robinson Crusoe. The lofty island still abounded with goats ; but Chili had made it a penal settlement, a sort of second Norfolk Island, which destroyed its poetry. The Andes towered up at a great distance on our right, and volcanic ashes fell in fine dust upon our deck, though we saw nothing of volcanoes. At last we turned into the Bay of Talcuhana, where the friends of our captain, whose brother-in-law was Governor of the town, came crowding on our deck.

We soon learnt that there was a furious civil war raging in Columbia, and that it would not be safe to take our proposed route across the Pampas, owing to the confusion on the other side of the continent. The city of Conception was seven miles inland from the port; a new bishop had just been appointed, and he was on his way to receive consecration at St. Jago, the capital, attended by fifty horsemen, on a ride of some six hundred miles. As there was no suitable inn at Talcuhana, we remained on board, going ashore to say Mass and to look about the country; for both the city of Conception and the town of Talcuhana had been utterly destroyed by an earthquake seven years previously to our arrival, and this was the third destruction by similar causes. On the last occasion a great wave came upon Talcuhana and washed it into the sea: and the first town of that name lay at the bottom of the Bay.

Being English, the people could not get rid of the notion that we must be Protestants, and that young Therry was the Bishop's son. Even though they saw us say Mass in their churches, they only concluded that the Protestant service was very like their own. We had also to encounter a prejudice on the part of the Governor of the Province, which came of a very innocent cause. Colonel Frere, a member of a wealthy family near Talcuhana, had been exiled, with some of his companions, for their share in one of the numerous insurrections which from time to time agitated the country. They were sent off to one of the South Sea Islands in a gun brig. Calling at Sydney on their way, our Bishop heard of them, with his usual kindness called upon them, offered them hospitality, and sent them presents of provisions which might conduce to their comfort. The governing authorities of Chili heard of this,

mistook the courtesy of a Catholic bishop to Catholic gentlemen under a cloud for sympathy with their cause. The
Bishop, therefore, on arriving received no attention, except
from the family of Freres, who did all they could to show
their gratitude, and put their finest houses at our disposal.
But Captain Saunders and his friends bustled about, explained the spirit and intent of the Bishop, and went to
the Governor at Conception to lodge an explanation with
him, and told him what a disgrace it would be if the Bishop
were neglected because of a pure act of humanity. We
were consequently invited by General Bulnoz to his
mansion in the city of Conception. Bulnoz was the brother
of the hero who had conquered the Peruvians on their own
soil, and who was at that time President of the Republic.

We started on the beautiful horses lent by the Freres,
accompanied by our captain and the British Consul, and
after a ride of seven miles reached the splendid mansion of
the Governor, which had been rebuilt since the earthquake,
and covered a large space of ground, as the whole was on
the ground storey, a precaution against new earthquakes.
On surveying the city we found that it had been utterly
destroyed : all that remained of the once most magnificent
cathedral in South America were the broken steps of the
high altar. All the churches as well as the convents had
been completely destroyed. The population for several
years had lived in tents. The town was being gradually
reconstructed, but all on ground floors. The bells of the
provisional church were suspended in low wooden cages.
It was curious to notice the sparkles of gold in the broken
bricks of the ruins, but they were not worth extracting.

The heads of the clergy, of the Religious Orders of men,
and the chief notables were invited to meet us ; and such a
dinner was laid on the table as only Chilians or Peruvians
could understand. The courses were endless, and eating
went on for seven hours and a-half, from four o'clock to

half-past eleven. None of the party spoke any language but their native Spanish, except the clergy, who spoke to us and interpreted for us in Latin : for though we under-stood their speech pretty well we did not venture to smatter in it. So Don José, one of the canons, was our chief interpreter. Towards the end of the dinner, at which the sweets were introduced in the middle and the meats followed anew, a negro servant undertook to produce an English dish in our honour. The dish was produced amidst general expectation, and consisted of five boiled ducks floating in hot water, with skins as tight as the skins of ripe goose-berries. Altough it was the etiquette to taste of each dish, everybody rebelled against the English dish, and it was taken away. After the prodigious labour of this dinner, we rose from table at near midnight. We left the Bishop in a suite of handsome rooms, and Dr. Gregory and I took our way to the British Resident, where we found accommodation On our way thither we met first one then another of the city police, mounted on horseback, trotting along and blowing a whistle all the way, except when it was interrupted by chanting *Ave Maria purissima* or calling the hour, with the cry *Viva Chili.* It struck us as an effective way of warning the thieves and evil doers to get away.

The next morning the Bishop said Mass in the principal provisional church ; but the people still believed that he was a Protestant, and that they were assisting at a Protestant service. We then, under clerical guidance, made a round of visits to all the Religious houses, both of men and women, accompanied by a curious crowd, the bells all ringing in honour of the Bishop throughout the city. The decora-tion of the churches was unpleasantly tawdry. Religion was confessedly at a low ebb in the country, and the Sacraments but little frequented. We did not visit the convents without getting a penance, though most kindly intended. At every house of nuns or friars we were pre-

14

sented with a cup of thick chocolate and a sugar biscuit, from which we could not escape by any apology, so that we were nearly choked. The Trinitarian Nuns, a large and flourishing Community with a respectable boarding school, threw open the folding doors of their enclosure and received us in a body, standing on one side of the enclosure whilst we stood on the other. Benedictines though we were, they insisted on our receiving the Trinitarian scapular, and sent for their chaplain to confer it in their presence. As the Bishop tamely submitted to the function, we, of course, followed, however uncanonical the proceeding.

After luncheon with the Governor, his Excellency proposed to drive the Bishop back to Talcuhana. A great company, consisting of the chief clergy, Superiors of Religious houses, military officers, and gentlemen assembled on horseback with a guard of honour. A singular vehicle, consisting of a sort of tub with the sides and seat mounted on four wheels, was produced ; and the Governor, an enormously stout man, mounted together with the Bishop, and we were ranged in order and proceeded. It was a strange and variegated scene, and the English Consul and I soon dropped behind that we might talk freely and enjoy the spectacle. It reminded us of Flaxman's procession of the Canterbury pilgrims. Military men were mixed with civilians in their broad sombreros, and the cloaks and scapulars of the Religious men flew out in the wind, whilst their heads were covered with large-brimmed straw hats. After going about a mile the seat of the carriage broke down between the big wheels, evidently owing to the immense weight of the Governor. The two riders disentangled themselves. After examination the vehicle was pronounced incurable, and to the great relief of the Bishop, who was a famous horseman, led horses were brought forward for them to mount. On approaching Talcuhana we were met by another escort, headed by the chief men of the town when bidding farewell to our entertainers we returned to our ship.

In the harbour was a French whaler which, after two years in the Pacific, was returning to Havre de Grace. We arranged for a passage in her, the mates and harpooners giving up their cabins for a small share of the fare, and we were soon once more at sea. They kept the crow's nest at the masthead, as they were not full, and still hoped to fall in with a whale or two, but were disappointed. The captain was an able man, well-mannered and agreeable. The numerous crew were light-hearted, easily amused, and always gay. They had no allowance of rum, as on board an English ship, but drank spruce beer, made on board from twigs of the spruce tree. They had neither the economy nor the industry of English sailors, with whom not an inch of rope is wasted. As we neared France coil after coil of rope was thrown overboard, which English sailors would have been employed in turning into spinyard, knittles, etc. The reason alleged was that they would have everything new for the next voyage. Yet with all their leisure they never quarrelled.

One night we were awakened in our cabins by an awful scream from aloft. It had begun to blow, and a light youth was furling a maintop-gallant sail when he slipped from the yards and hung suspended by his hands to the foot rope. The captain, a little wiry man, was on deck, and shouted out: " Hold on a minute." He then threw off his pea-jacket, ran up aloft like a cat, got astride the yard like lightning, seized the man by the collar, flung him over his shoulder like a child, and brought him down on deck. This was the third life he had saved in the course of his maritime career.

During the early part of the voyage I thought much on the religious requirements of Australia. There were then five colonies, at great distances from each other, as well as the distant penal settlements of Port Macquarrie and Norfolk Island. And yet the one bishop was entirely occupied with New South Wales, and could know little of what passed in the other colonies. Until they had each a bishop they were not likely to have a due provision of priests. It appeared to me that what was wanted was an Australian Hierarchy with an Archbishop at its head. I thought, also, that the Bishop would enter into the scheme of multiplying bishops more readily if a Hierarchy could be gained instead of Vicars-Apostolic. I therefore drew up a scheme for a Hierarchy, alleging the reasons for it that I thought expedient, specifying the sees to be gradually filled up. I presented my scheme to the Bishop, and urged the subject on his attention until he became disposed to see its importance and to enter into it. This document Bishop Polding afterwards took to Rome, and he informed me that it was made the basis of the plan afterwards approved by the Holy See. Archbishop Nicholson, then a Carmelite Father, also told me that it was through his influence, knowing the ways of Rome, that the plan became successful at Propaganda. But of this later on. Let us proceed on our voyage.

The Bishop never lost an opportunity of drawing souls to God. I remember his telling me that he thought the sublimest act of his ministry was on a dark night travelling through Illawarra. He was being guided through the bush by the son of an Irish settler, and conversing with him as he rode along beside the horse, the Bishop found that for a long time he had not been to his religious duties. It was very dark and pouring with rain, but the Bishop got off his horse, tied him to a tree, sat on the fallen trunk of another tree, got the boy to kneel on the wet ground, and heard his confession. The next time he went that way he inquired for the boy, and found that he had been killed whilst felling a tree.

On board the French whaler the Bishop got a word first with one man, then with another, and gradually formed a little class that came down into the cabin for instruction. The class grew until it embraced the whole crew, officers included, who came down in their watches below. To one or other of us, as their choice suggested, they came to confession. At twelve o'clock on Easter Eve, lying in my cabin, I heard the men creeping into the cabin in their stockings, and when assembled those simple-hearted men went on their knees and sang the cantique, *Réjouissez-vous, O Chrétiens*, as a greeting to the Bishop at the dawn of Easter Day. Next morning, the weather being fine and the sea smooth, an awning was stretched over the main deck, an altar erected, and the Bishop, with Dr. Gregory and myself as assistants, sang High Mass for the crew, all of whom went to Holy Communion. Having most of them been choir boys, when young, in their village churches, they sang the Mass in plain chant, and acquitted themselves well. At the offertory the cook unexpectedly presented himself on his knees with a loaf on a cloth, especially prepared for the *pain bénit*, to be eaten after Communion according to French custom. Often after that day did we hear the men singing pious cantiques, especially during the night watches.

On crossing the line we gave a festival to the crew, handing them some of our Chilian sheep and sundry dozens of light wine. But the sheep of Chili have not too much meat on their frames ; when dressed and hung up, if you put a light inside them they make excellent red lanthorns, and reveal their whole anatomy. Still the men enjoyed their dinner of fresh provisions, were exceedingly gay, and danced and sang without cessation the whole day. Their instrumental music consisted of an old speaking trumpet and some bars of metal, on which, with the help of their mouths, they contrived to accentuate their favourite tunes.

These rough men were so simple and childlike! How they enjoyed our entering into their amusements, and talked to us of the pleasure it would be to their mothers, wives, and sisters, to hear from them that the Bishop had promoted and witnessed their fête. I could not resist inserting this little event, it struck us as showing what Christianity could do to make the hearts of men of a rude occupation, simple. It was such a contrast to what English rustics would have been under like circumstances. But sailors, even English sailors, are incomparably more simple and genuine, as a class, than their brethren ashore; if only religion could be brought to them when afloat, they could be guided as children are guided when off their element.

The captain was a steady and religious man, who always made his Easter duties. The only one who hung back was the young surgeon. One saw that it was nothing but a little of the pride of the *esprit fort*, and that more in show than in reality; for he was really a good-hearted young man. One smooth day, Dr. Gregory asked him to go up with him into the maintop, there to lie down and have a talk in the cool air. After a time Dr. Gregory, who was a strong, muscular man, seized him by the collar, as if going to pitch him into the sea. The little doctor, startled, called out, "Ah, Monsieur Gregory! *Tenez, tenez.*" "What is the matter," said Dr. Gregory. "There must be something not right in your conscience that makes you afraid. The fact is, the Bishop has sent me for you, he wants to speak to you in his cabin. "Oh, Monsieur Gregory, will you make my apology?" "Certainly not. Is that your French politeness? Go and make it yourself." They came down; the little doctor reluctantly descended to the Bishop's cabin. Dr. Gregory pushed him in and closed the door. After an interval he came out with a happy face and went to Communion soon after, to the delight of the crew. He then told Dr. Gregory that he had been piously brought up, and that his first Communion day had been the happiest of his life ; but that he had been diverted from the exercise of his religion through the influence of certain college companions, though never in his heart had he abandoned the faith.   On our reaching Havre de Grace the ship's company presented the Bishop and his companions with a grateful and touching address drawn up, and read by the doctor, which appeared in the Havre newspapers.

About three hundred miles off the river La Plata we encountered a gale such as I never elsewhere experienced. It had been blowing already and the sea was rough, when there came a tremendous gale that laid the sea flat, the foam running over the surface like cream.   We put before the wind under bare poles, and as it became more moderate the sea rose furiously.   On sounding the pumps there were twelve feet of water.   We took our spell with the men at the pump handles, but after twelve hours' pumping it was found that there was no leak : it was the result of the strain upon the hull for the time.

As our vessel entered the Channel we got an English newspaper from a pilot-boat, and the first thing on which my eyes fell was the failure of the Wrights' Bank.   This was sad news for the Catholics of England and for Catholic institutions, and we were apprehensive for our own small resources.   But our agent, Dr. Heptonstall, had divined the state of things, and had drawn everything out just in time.

CHAPTER XX.

In England and Ireland.

TOWARD the close of May, 1841, we reached Havre, and got to London in time for the aggregate meeting of the Catholic Association, at which O'Connell made one of his great speeches. The Bishop was particularly solicitous to appear at that great assembly, as an opportunity for bringing the Catholic affairs of Australia before the Catholics of England. He said to me: "I will skirmish, if you will explain our great wants systematically." The Bishop spoke, but Lord Camoys, who was in the chair, overruled my speaking in the committee room, on the plea of want of time ; and though repeatedly called upon I thought it prudent to sit still. However, the meeting brought us into contact with the leaders of the English Catholics.

At the request of the Bishop I then proceeded to Maynooth without delay, to endeavour to obtain more ecclesiastics; or, rather, to prepare the way for the Bishop's obtaining them, whilst the Bishop himself went to assist at the opening of St. Chad's Cathedral in Birmingham. Very kindly received by my old friends, the President and professors of Maynooth, I was asked by Dean Gaffiney to give the annual retreat to the students, prior to ordination and the break-up of the College. This, with the help of the works of St. Alphonsus, I did ; and took an opportunity, with the President's approval, of giving a lecture on the

Australian Mission. This led sundry of the students to offer themselves to the work of the Australian Church. I wrote to Bishop Polding, telling him how important it was that he should be on the spot without delay, as the vacation was so near; that otherwise my work would be frustrated. He replied that he would leave Birmingham immediately after the opening, and that, as I suggested, he would not even wait for the assemblage of the leading Catholics from every part of England in the Town Hall afterwards. Yet though his Lordship faithfully complied with my request thus far, from being inexperienced in railway travelling he reached Liverpool too late for the boat. He was advised to go to Holyhead, reached there too late again for the boat, returned to Liverpool, and at last reached Dublin after the vacation had commenced. This misfortune was serious, as the freshness of the call to Australia wore off before another opportunity came round.

We made a journey together to the South of Ireland, where the Bishop had many friends and I not a few. We received a genuine welcome at Carlow, where the College was having its exhibition, and there met the celebrated Bishop England, of South Carolina, as also Bishop Clancey, of Demerara. Thence we paid a visit to the Cistercian Monastery of Mount Mellerai, where for the first time I found myself in a centre of that ascetic life to which I had once aspired. The monastery was large, the Community numerous, the church capacious; but everything bore the signs of Cistercian simplicity and poverty. A large school was under the care of the Fathers, who taught agriculture as well as literature. We resolved to assist at the midnight office, and nothing to my heart was more impressive. The office was long, for everything was solemnly chanted. The two long choirs of the white-robed monks alternately sang the psalmody in three simple, but sweet, notes that never varied, with long pauses for reflection in the middle of each verse. The lessons and even the Gospel were sung in the same tones, and the Abbot gave the Benediction, still in the same notes, from the rood-loft· The sweet accents, with solemn pauses of silence, of that never tiring monotony of rise and fall, under which the ever-varying sense of the psalmody advanced, seemed to express the acquirements of an unchangeable peace and patience of soul ; whilst the whole of the changeable movement was interior and contemplative. It seemed to realise that sentence of St. Augustine : " Join thyself to eternity and thou shalt find rest."

Next day we parted with the courteous and hospitable Abbot, and proceeded through the beautiful scenery by the Blackwater until we reached the hospitable roof of Father Fogarty, the parish priest of Lismore, and a friend of the Bishop and of the Australian Mission. But, habituated as we were to tropical climates, the chill of the night watch in the monastic choir had struck into our very bones, and although we were near the end of a bright July, we begged of Father Fogarty, as the greatest charity he could do us, to make a good roaring fire. And highly amused was he as he piled wood upon burning wood, and watched our pale faces and shivering frames, until a good dinner combined with the glowing flames to put us to rights. And yet that Cistercian choir clings to memory, recalling men dead to the world, but alive to God.

At Clonmel we met the excellent Dean Burke, and had an opportunity of thanking him for the good care he had taken of the convicts sent from the prison of that town to New South Wales. Making our way across the bogs in an open car, we met groups of men, every now and then, all alive with excitement at the General Election for Parliament then going on. The country was enjoying the first-fruits of Catholic Emancipation and the Reform Act. We stopped and talked with those we met, and the Bishop impressed on them the advantages for steady men of emigration to the Australian Colonies. At Kilkenny, walking from the Black Monastery, as the old Dominican Monastery—still in the hands of the Dominican Fathers—is called, we met John O'Connell in company with the Mayor; and they gave us a beautiful specimen of the freedom of election. They told us they had just come from the bulk of their voters securely locked up in a large barn, to keep them safe from the rival candidate, and with plenty of whisky to amuse them until safely conducted by sure friends to the poll. They invited us to go and address them and cheer them up, which, of course, we declined as politely as we could.

At Cork, Father Mathew received us with the heartiest welcome, and became our guide through the city, which gave us an opportunity of witnessing his wonderful influence and popularity as the Apostle of Temperance. On first meeting he started back and said: " I expected to meet a venerable man with a white head, and not a man of your age. I have printed 20,000 copies of your sermon on drunkenness. You are entitled to the silver medal." And he gave me one. The Temperance Movement was at its height. The house of Father Mathew was turned into an office for temperance purposes. He had three secretaries constantly engaged. He told us that he had spent £1,600 in aiding temperance bands alone ; and that the medals he had given away and his extensive correspondence were sources of great expense to him. His work involved a complete system of administration. He conducted us to the celebrated Convent of Blackrock, of which he was the temporal Father, and we spent a pleasant day there. We also met him at the Bishop's, Dr. Murphy, whose large collection of books covered every wall of his house, from the entrance to the attics. Our chief object in visiting Cork was to see the Rev. Father England, brother of the

Bishop of South Carolina, the man who had done more than any other on this side of the world for the convicts embarked for Australia.   He was chaplain to the convict establishment at the Cove of Cork, and a man of more indefatigable zeal and untiring charity there could not be. We knew when a convict ship arrived from Cork that half our work was done.   He heard every man's confession, gave books to all who could read, and letters to all who deserved particular attention.   We were disappointed in not finding him—he had recently died.   We saw his sister, the Superioress of the first Convent of the Presentation, founded by Miss Nagle.   We went to visit an emigrant ship preparing to start for Sydney, and the emigrants were delighted to have a few words and a blessing from their future Bishop.

We went by coach from Cork to Killarney, and stopping to change horses at an intermediate town a large group of electioneering men, armed with shillalahs, came up to the coach and asked if there were any Tories there.   A foolish young Englishman answered from the top of the coach : " I'm a Tory."   In an instant two men climbed to the top of the coach and pulled him down into the middle of the group, and every stick was quivering over him for a blow. I quickly cried out to the Bishop, who was at the other side from what was going on : " Get out your cross, jump down, or they will kill the man."   I pushed the coach door open and shouted to the men: " Stop !   Here is the Catholic Archbishop of Sydney, a great friend of Irishmen, who wants to speak to you."   They stopped, listened to the Bishop, gave three cheers for him, and let the man go. Pale and trembling he came up to the Bishop, and asked if he might know to whom he was indebted for his life.   The Bishop gave him a stern rebuke for his folly, and said to him : " You little know the meaning which those words convey to the minds of those poor people."   At last a man of more respectable appearance came up, who was evidently the leader : he gave his pledge that the young man should not be disturbed. We sailed over the Lakes of Killarney with the usual enthusiasm, and witnessed some exciting election scenes, which the temperance movement saved from degradation. All was good natured and good humoured.

On our return to England we separated, each on our own way. Some letters passed between us on my proposed appointment to the Bishopric of Hobart Town, against which I was as averse as ever; and even more so, because I felt that, good priest as he was, as Father Therry had been placed as Vicar-General in Van Dieman's Land, I should have the same difficulties to meet there as I had on my first arrival in Sydney, owing to his want of management in temporal affairs. The result was that I received a letter informing me that our relations were at an end. This was partly a surprise, but still more a relief. I wrote to the Secretary for the Colonies, announcing my retirement from office, settled with the Colonial Agent, and immediately returned to my Monastery at Downside. I then wrote to the President-General, the truly venerable Dr. Marsh, informed him of what I had done, and awaited his directions. The President wrote me a very kind letter in reply, saying I should be glad of a rest after my labours.

Father Wilson was then Prior. He gave me some teaching to do; and among other things I had the spiritual instruction of a young class. I found this class inclined to be restless and troublesome over their spiritual reading. I asked them to tell me plainly the reason of it. They told me that for some time they had been set to read the first book of St. Francis of Sales on the "Love of God," and that they could not understand it. It was evident that to lads of twelve and fourteen years those disquisitions on the mental and moral faculties were pure metaphysics, so I got the book changed to their great relief. But I had myself a lesson to learn. Accustomed almost since my ordination to exercise my free judgment on matters of importance, and to direct and lead the way in new undertakings, when ordered to do little things by my Superior I felt a jump in my lower nature, which led me to look down and say to myself: "Hallo! what is the meaning of that?" No doubt others, under similar circumstances, have experienced the same. I then learnt the difficulty there is at first in passing from an active life of authority to the observance in subjection of regular discipline. But in a short time that passed away. Soon after, the President-General directed me to place myself under the authority of the Provincial of the South. Father Bernard Paillet, a devout religious man, had been appointed to the mission of Coventry, but was seized with an attack of the nerves on his way, which deprived him of sight, and I was instructed by the Provincial to take his place.

CHAPTER XXII

The Mission at Coventry.

I FOUND the mission of Coventry in a desolate condition, and the small mission house under the care of a young girl. The chapel, of no great age, was small and plain, with large cracks in the walls, which were afterwards explained when it was taken down ; for it had been built on deal planks laid almost on the surface of a bed of sand.* The house was so small that there was barely space enough in the rooms for a little table and half a dozen chairs. But there was a good school which had been built by Father Cockshoot during his administration. And though an old man had the sole charge of the school, he was a good schoolmaster of that time. Father Pope, a celebrated musician, had served the mission in his last and infirmer years, had exerted himself much, and had infused a spirit of piety into his little congregation ; but he was succeeded by one, a good man, but of infirm mind, who had been twice in an asylum, and who, though devout, was utterly incapable of taking care of a congregation. Hence there had been a considerable falling away. But I found them

---

* "The chapel of Coventry," he writes in the preface to a volume of sermons published in 1842, "is raised on a sloping bed of sand. The walls are broken and giving way, the ceiling in a very bad condition. The foundations on one side were recently taken out to be repaired, and were found to rest on rotten piles. The interior walls, specially of the sanctuary, are covered with wet, and the whole interior is a scene of cold and naked desolation, contrasting strangely enough with the fervour of its poor, but zealous, congregation, whose rapidly increasing numbers it will scarce contain."

to be a good, simple people, only anxious to have the mission restored; and I did my best to put them right with my Superior. Four sergeants on the recruiting staff were particularly complained of; but I found them to be excellent men, truly religious, and regular at their religious duties; two of them were afterwards raised to lieutenancies. Excepting one very respectable farmer, and the Town Surveyor, they were almost all of the decent class of weavers or watchmakers, and were truly devoted to the Church. The furnishing of the chapel was very poor, nor had I ever saved money that I might put it right; but Mrs. Amherst, of Kenilworth, aided me to set things in order. I soon obtained an assistant in Father Clarkson, and the work went on.*

Meanwhile I received a letter from Bishop Polding at Rome, informing me that the plan I had drawn up for an Australian Hierarchy had been accepted; that as I had raised so much objection to the See of Hobart Town, Prior Wilson, of Downside, had been appointed to that see, and that I had been appointed to the See of Adelaide in South Australia. Prior Wilson declined the appointment. I kept mine to myself for some time, meditating upon it, until I received another letter from Bishop Polding—now Archbishop of Sydney—requesting a reply, by signifying my acceptance. Resolved, as I was, to decline the episcopate in any shape, I wrote in reply that, with leave of my Superior, I would come to Rome and plead my own cause, as I was still in the mind not to accept any such appoint-

---

* Writing to Bishop Brown, of Wales, shortly after his arrival at Coventry, he says : "I am now in full occupation and very happy in the midst of it. I am surprised to find with what facility I have begun to plod. I trust I shall never have any other than my present duties, or those of a similar character." And again, after referring to some vexatious public affairs : "When will all this weary work cease? Who would exchange the quiet I experience, plodding among my poor Coventry people, for all these cares and heart-burnings ?"

ment. I went to Rome, and after an interview with Cardinal Franzoni, the Prefect of Propaganda, I was freed from the appointment to Adelaide, and the Rev. Francis Murphy was appointed. At Rome I made the acquaintance of Father Nicholson, an Irish Carmelite, afterwards Archbishop of Corfu. Having a considerable knowledge of the business ways of Propaganda, and influence as well, he had been of great use to Archbishop Polding in obtaining the establishment of the Hierarchy. It had raised the reputation of the Archbishop, and Pope Gregory XVI. showed him a mark of confidence by sending him on a special commission to Malta. The Archbishop had asked Father Nicholson to go with him to Sydney as his Vicar-General. He consulted me on the subject, and put the question: "Suppose Dr. Gregory were to take different views from mine, what would be the consequence?" I replied that though Dr. Gregory was a most attached friend and follower of the Archbishop he would never interfere in matters of that kind. But the Father declined the invitation, and on later reflection I did not think it would have answered. The Archbishop and he were both sensitive men by nature, and would have come together in matured life with different habits of viewing things.

At my farewell audience with Gregory XVI. His Holiness told me how much the Archbishop of Sydney regretted that I could not be one of his suffragans, and gave a special blessing to my mission in England. At a later date I learnt that Father Nicholson had advised Cardinal Franzoni to keep me in view for any vacancy in England; and this explains a letter that I received from His Eminence in the following year, in which he announced that a see had been constituted at Perth, in Western Australia, and offering me the appointment, adding, however, that if I was not inclined to accept it, he wished me to recommend some suitable person for that appointment.

15

As that diocese was the most suitable for a mission to the blacks, I recommended Father Brady, who had had a long experience in the Island of Bourbon among the negroes, was an excellent missionary, and had a great attraction for the aboriginal population. He was appointed. But later on the Archbishop called on the Spanish Benedictines to establish a mission to the blacks in that quarter. The Queen of Spain took an interest in the work, and sent them out in a frigate. One of them was appointed Bishop. The two Bishops did not pull well together, probably from want of sufficient defining of their respective jurisdictions, and Dr. Brady retired. But the mission to the blacks has been a great success.

On my departure from Rome I was asked by Dr. Grant, of the Scotch College, if I would travel home with an elderly lady, Mrs. Hutchinson, of Edinburgh, for her protection. Mrs. Hutchinson, the widow of Colonel Hutchinson, had been, before her conversion, a leader and sort of centre of the Irvingites of Edinburgh; but, after her conversion to the Church, had become the chief founder of St. Margaret's Convent, in whose interest she was now in Rome. I consented to travel with her, and the more readily as she wished to go by the Tyrol, and to visit the Adolorata and the Ecstatica, then exciting a great deal of attention. At Assisi we stayed two days, deeply interested in all that was associated with St. Francis and St. Clare. The mountains and plains of that austere region breathed of the heroic poverty and ecstatic detachment of these wonderful Saints. After visiting the proto-convents of the two Saints, we stayed at the Hospicium of the Portiuncula. The old King of Bavaria was there at the same time.

At Perugia I had a letter to the Abbot of the celebrated Benedictine Monastery, and as I could not remain there a guest, having a lady under charge, the Abbot kindly put his carriage at our disposal, and sent a Father to be our guide. At the hotel we met the celebrated Mrs. Gray, who opened the English mind to the ancient Etruscan remains, and found her full of enthusiasm with her discoveries. In the still loftier placed city of Cortona, after visiting the shrine of St. Margaret, I made special inquiries respecting the Ecstatica of Sansovina, of whom the Earl of Shrewsbury had written in the second edition of his book. The Bishop was absent, but I was given to understand that he had given it no especial countenance, except to allow her daily Mass and Communion in the house. A grave Canon with whom I conversed was inclined to use discouraging language : he thought it a case of catalepsy. But the Franciscan Fathers at St. Margaret's assured me that it was a remarkable case, and well worth a visit. We resolved to go to Sansovina, and one of the canons kindly gave me an introduction to the Archpriest who was the director of the person in question. Like Cortona, Sansovina was situated on very high ground, and we had to get oxen to help our horses up the steep ascent. At the rude inn I asked a servant girl if many strangers visited the place. She said : " Until lately, very few ; but now a great many." I asked why they came. She answered : " *A cosa di questa ragazza.*" (Because of this lass.) And she added : " *Un gran Principe di Londra e venuto.*" This was Lord Shrewsbury. The peasantry of Italy generally imagined in those days that England was somewhere in London. After I was Bishop of Birmingham, a bishop asked me in the Papal sacristy of the Vatican : " *Monsignor, sta questo Birmingham in Londra o in Scozzia ?*" And when I assured him that it was in the very centre of England, he still wished to know whether this Birmingham was in England or in America. Geography in those days was not a strong point, even with learned Italians.

In the evening we called on the Archpriest, who struck me as having a great resemblance to the famous O'Connell, both in size and figure, as it had also struck Bishop—afterwards Cardinal—Wiseman as he told me at a later time. He received us very kindly, and said he would gladly give us an opportunity of observing what was most remarkable in the young person under his care, if we attended the Mass next morning, which he should say in her room. I then asked for a private interview with him, and asked him to tell me candidly what were his own observations of the case, as far as he could properly communicate them. He told me that he had made it a rule never to volunteer any remark, but that he would frankly answer any questions. In reply to mine, the Archpriest sketched her history and that of her poor parents, and how her infirmities had come upon her after great solicitude in attending her mother in an illness. Did she take much food? She lived on the air, water, and a little lettuce. Was she supposed to have the stigmata? She had the sense, but not the manifestation of them. She had prayed much that they might not appear. She also had peculiar relations with the Ecstatica of the Tyrol, Maria Möerl, knowing much of what passed with her. What were the chief singularities that distinguished her? These I might observe for myself at the Mass next morning. I wished him good evening, thanking him for his kind attentions, and one of his curates showed us through the town. He was not very communicative on the subject which chiefly interested us, but prudently referred me to the Archpriest. Yet he warmly defended the innocence and purity of her character, despite the stories about her being deluded or a deceiver.

Next morning we went early to the house, and were shown into her small bedroom. Besides ourselves, there were two female pilgrims from Loretto, in their pilgrim's costume. The Archpriest was preparing to say Mass, with a curate to assist him, at an altar placed against the wall opposite the end of the bed. On the bed lay the poor girl,

robed in a long, white, cotton dress covered with a sheet
On one side sat her mother, on the other a female relative.
I at once observed that her head and brow were large and
well proportioned, and that her nervous predominated over
her muscular system. I had no particular recollection of
Lord Shrewsbury's statement, but in a critical spirit I
knelt in the position most favourable for observations. She
was very pale, and with closed eyes recollected. At the
offertory she suddenly sprang up erect, without any aid
from her arms, and expanded her arms in prayer for the
length of a minute, and then slowly descended backwards,
until again reclined on her bed, when the sheet was drawn
over again by her attendants. At the consecration she
did the same, praying longer than before. I then observed
that she rested on her toes. The curate, who was by me,
whispered : " Blow towards her." I did so, and her figure
wavered like a reed in the wind. I further observed that
in descending it was with the same slowness even when
naturally the muscles ceased to support the back. After
receiving Holy Communion she rose three times in prayer
but it was no longer towards the altar, but in the direction
where I was kneeling. I thought : " What is the meaning
of this ? Is she showing herself ? " But it was afterwards
explained to my question, that as the Blessed Sacrament
was no longer on the altar she made her thanksgiving
towards the parish church, and that she rose as many times
after Communion as she had special prayers to offer.

So soon as the Archpriest was unvested, I went to him
and asked : " May I speak to her now, and that in private ? "
The room was at once cleared, and I went to her and said :
" This exhibition of yourself is very dangerous for your
soul. I cannot imagine the depth of humility you need
for your security." She calmly replied : " Indeed I need
humility. Pray for me in your charity." " But," I rejoined, " to be talked about by thousands and gazed at by

hundreds, as if you were something singular, and to be attacked by others as a hypocrite, really this is perilous for your soul." She replied in the same gentle tones: "Gladly would I be walled round from all mankind, but this is permitted for my greater confusion." "But," I said (in substance), " do not many people, as I hear, come to see you, and to ask your prayers, and to consult you, as if you were inspired? And is not this dangerous for a sensitive young woman like you?" She kept very tranquil under the attack, and whispered, with a tear trickling from her eyes: "The more need I have that all the world should pray for me. I speak only when my director commands me to do so." I then asked her two or three questions kindly, respecting myself, to which she replied briefly and appositely. Then I asked her prayers and left her to her recollection.

At Florence, among other acquaintance we met the Misses O'Farrell, sisters to the Governor of Malta, and Father Nicholson, the Carmelite, who was on a visit to them. They invited us to join them in a visit to the church which contained the incorrupt body of St. Mary Magdalen of Pazzi, of which they had been promised a private inspection. It was only publicly exposed on her festival. But the fact that it was going to be exposed got wind, and we found the large church so crammed with people that it was with considerable difficulty that we reached the high altar under which it lay. On our way from the church the Misses O'Farrell heard of a remarkable case of sanctity and suffering. After some inquiry we found the house, and ascended to the second storey. We found an aged mother bound by her infirmities to an armchair, and her daughter, aged about thirty-five, upon a bed, whilst a young woman attended upon them both. We were cautioned not to go suddenly near the bed, lest we should cause a shock to the sufferer. Whilst the ladies talked to the mother, I slowly approached the daughter, whose sufferings were such as I had never in my life witnessed. We were told that her legs were literally turned up upon her back, and that upon them she lay. The expression upon her features of patient suffering was indescribable. Her head and every limb shook and thrilled, whilst her lips moved in prayer. Catching sight of me at the bed-foot, contemplating her, she gave a little start; I slowly raised my eyes and finger towards Heaven; she raised her eyes in the same direction and went on with her prayer. Her whole frame seemed to be tortured as with a fire running through her nerves. The mother told us that her daughter had prayed long for the gift of suffering, and that she had been in this state of suffering for seven years. That, seeing her sufferings had made her so holy, at last she herself prayed for the gift of suffering, and that some time after she had begun that prayer she had lost the use of her limbs and was now bound to her chair. The neighbours, she said, and many good people were very good to them, and had provided them with the girl we saw, who served them very affectionately. A good priest, she added, had been exceedingly kind to them, had obtained the privilege of an altar in their room, where he said Mass for them every day; "and this (she said) has rewarded us for all our sufferings." The good priest had also taken an interest in obtaining relics for them, and if we opened the folding doors that closed in the altar we should see them. On opening the doors we were surprised at the extraordinary number of relics that covered the back of the walls, the sides of the altar, and the back of the folding doors, like swarms of bees. I never saw so many authenticated relics together before. This spectacle of devout and patient suffering impressed me far more deeply than what I had seen at Sansovina, although suffering was not absent in that case.

We went on to Bologna, and from there by the mail towards Mantua; but when we arrived on the Austrian frontier at Mollia Gonsaraga, the Commissary of police, after examining our passports, declared that the lady could proceed no further. " Why ? " I asked.   He declined giving a reason.   The place was but a village.   We were travelling by the postal courier.   There was neither hotel in the place, nor vehicle to be had.   I stepped down, took the commissary aside, and asked him : " If you were in my place, in charge of this lady, what would you do? "   He replied : " I think the best thing you can do is to leave the lady here and go to Mantua yourself and see the First Commissary of Police."   " Are you a married man ? " I asked.   " Yes," he said, " and live with my family in that house."   " Then will you take charge of this lady until I return ? "   He promised to do so, and was very civil.   He gave me a letter.   I left Mrs. Hutchinson in company with his wife and went on to Mantua with the courier.   Arriving there, after some search at midnight I found the First Commissary supping at the hotel.   After reading the letter I presented, he said : " If the expense is no consideration, send a carriage for the lady, but stay here yourself and I will see whether she can go on or not."   I did so, and Mrs. Hutchinson arrived under care of the Commissary with whom I had left her.   It soon appeared that she was under his surveillance.   He was a respectable man, and showed himself really inclined to be of service to us, so I made a friend of him, and invited him to dine with us.   On visiting the First Commissary at his office, he looked at her passport, cast his eyes over Mrs. Hutchinson, and said: " This lady cannot go on."   " Why? " I asked.   He was not at liberty to say.   " What, then," I asked, " is to be done ? "   He offered so to arrange my passport that I might return in her company.   But how was I to obtain her luggage, which had been taken possession of by the

Custom House. Guided by the officer from Mollia Gon-saraga, I made my way to the Custom House, leaving Mrs. Hutchinson at the hotel, no doubt still under surveillance. But she was calm though troubled, not knowing a word of Italian, and unable to understand the cause, which was a great mystery to me. I found three officials installed at the Custom House, all of whom were ready to speak together, and all positive that it was a grave case, that there was some great difficulty, and that the matter required time. I was referred to the police office. On our way we met a tall, genteel-looking young man, and my friend whispered to me that if I could secure his influence all would come right. He introduced me, but I found him stiff and formal, and he put difficulties in the way that I could not comprehend; but he let it escape that it was *una cosa politica.* I immediately took out my notebook and recorded the words, with their date. Seeing, however, that neither I nor my friend from Mollia Gonsaraga could produce any impression, I hinted to him to drop behind and leave us together. I then began to tell him that I was a Catholic missioner returning from Rome, and to speak of the wonders of Australia. This interested and softened him, and he ended by saying that if I and the lady with the Commissary were ready at six o'clock in the morning, when the returned courier arrived, he would take care that all should be right for our departure.

On our arrival next morning at the office, Mrs. Hutchinson's luggage was produced, thoroughly searched, and a long protocol produced, which we, the commissary, and the courier, had to sign, and then we received our passports, with a note upon mine which had further consequences. We engaged a carriage to take us back, and on leaving the commissary at Mollia Gonsaraga, I thanked him for all his kindness, and presented him with a couple of sovereigns,

saying to him : " Tell the First Commissary that this is
only the opening of the game ; he will hear more of it later
on." On arrival at the gate of Parma the police, after
inspecting the passports, declared that the lady could not
enter the city. " Why ?" I asked. " Because it is recorded
on your passport that you are returning because she is not
allowed to enter the Austrian territory." " But this," I said,
" is not Austrian territory." " True," he replied, " but the
lady's passport is not *visé* for return." " Where is the chief
officer of police ? " I asked. " He is absent, and will not be
home till late to-night." " Where is the lady to stay meanwhile ? " I asked. " Here," he replied. It was in one of
the towers of the gate, without even a roof that I could
see. " You have our passports," I said, " and we can't
move without them." I then called to the coachman :
" Drive as fast as you can to the Eagle Hotel." Off we
went, and two police after us. We reached the hotel in
time to put Mrs. Hutchinson in a private room before the
police came up. I met them at the door, and told them
they could watch the exits as much as they liked, but, on
the word of an Englishman, if they attempted to annoy
the lady it would be at their peril. Late at night we saw
the chief of police. He was a thorough gentleman. He
said there was undoubtedly some great mistake ; but that
when the Austrians began to *finesse* there was no end of it.
He thought it would be best to give us both new passports
to Florence, where we could see our own Ambassador.

On arriving at Florence, our Ambassador, Lord Holland,
explained the whole affair at once. He said that as Mrs.
Hutchinson had given the name of Mrs. Colonel Hutchinson, after the Scotch fashion, they had mistaken her for
the Mrs. Colonel Hutchinson of the Irish family, who had
assisted in the escape of Lavallete from prison in 1817,
although she had been dead seven years. He himself, he
added, was on the long list of prohibited persons, in conse-

quence of his father's sympathy with Napoleon, until he was made Ambassador at Florence. He advised us to take boat at Leghorn to Genoa.

We found Genoa in a high state of festivity, celebrating the coming of age of the son and heir of King Charles Albert. On that evening the magnificent Bay of Genoa was to be illuminated, and never did I see such a spectacle of the kind! Meeting my old friend, Mr. Bodenham, of Herefordshire, there, he joined us in a boat; but finding the boat too low for the view we got on board an English ship. All the vessels were drawn out in two rows, displaying their colours, with a long lane between, through which the Royal Family was to pass on to a floating island covered with a garden of plants and flowers. The Bay was covered with boats filled with spectators, each having a lantern in shape of a large coloured tulip at the head of its mast, so that as the night darkened the Bay looked like a large bed of tulips. At a signal gun from a frigate in the offing, the King and his family advanced down the channel between the shipping on a barge in the form of an immense swan, which came majestically along, moved by silvered oars beneath its wings; and the Court followed in other barges. The whole party landed on the island in the middle of the bay. At the next signal the long quays sent up a succession of fireworks, with clusters of fire balloons. The next signal brought out a superb panorama; all the mansions on the heights around the Bay were brought out in brilliant light, as well as groups of trees. This magic scene drew forth immense applause that mingled with bands of music upon the water. The lighthouse, on its lofty rock, at the entrance of the Bay, was next covered—both rock and lighthouse—with flames of fire; and my friend, in his enthusiasm, cried out: "Well done lighthouse!" The next addition to the vast scene was a volcano thrown between the lighthouse and city! (Finally, amidst sounds of music, Milan Cathedral rose up from the water, covered with light, in all its stateliness and grandeur.

We joined a steamer in the early morning that had come from Civita Vecchia on its way to Marseilles ; and there found Archbishop Polding fast asleep on the deck, with Dr. Gregory standing beside him, and got the last news from him of Australian affairs in Rome

On our arrival in London I drew up a statement of our treatment at Mantua, which Mrs. Hutchinson sent to her brother, one of the Scotch Lords of Session.   He submitted it to Lord Aberdeen, the Minister for Foreign Affairs, who opened a correspondence with Prince Metternich on the subject.   The Prince sent an ample apology, assuring Lord Aberdeen that the officials at Mantua had been severely rebuked ; yet, he added, they could not be altogether blamed, as the lady *was so very much like* the Mrs. Colonel Hutchinson in question : forgetting, if he ever knew, that she had been dead seven years.   However, one good resulted, that all the proscribed names of English persons were expunged from the list.

Some time before I left Coventry for Rome Mrs. Amherst, of Kenilworth, had strongly recommended to my attention a person then residing at Bruges, whom she described as very religious, and possessing remarkable powers, and as distinguished for her wisdom as her charity; and who, she thought, would be of great value to the mission of Coventry.   This was the celebrated Mother Margaret Hallahan.   I begged Mrs. Amherst to do her best to secure her services, for she was the very person that I stood in need of.   She accepted the invitation, and when she was introduced to me by Mrs. Amherst I was much struck, not only by her remarkable figure, but still more by her great modesty, intelligence, and vigour.   At her own suggestion she made a spiritual retreat in preparation for the work before her, and then I appointed her to teach

the girls' school.* But very soon afterwards I had to make
the journey to Rome, and left her to make her own way.
On my return I was gratified to find that " Sister Margaret," as she was already called by the people, had
gathered a hundred girls into the school, had found out all
the sick and distressed people of the congregation, and was
taking great care of them, and had already associated
several respectable young women with her, who were
devoted to her and her works of charity. But for an
ample account of her zealous and most fruitful labours, I
must refer to the well-known " Life of Mother Margaret
Hallahan."†

* Dr. Ullathorne's first impressions of Mother Margaret are thus
expressed in a letter written to Bishop Brown, of Wales, dated
May 8th, 1842, just before starting for Rome : " I leave this
mission," he says, "just when it had begun to develop. I have
recently received a very valuable aid in a person—a sort of Sister
of Charity—from Belgium ; she is English, able to teach my
girls' school, visit the sick, and give instructions ; and I had calculated on having two more very soon, whom I should have found no
great difficulty in supporting. It would probably have been the germ
of an institute. This person will remain till I return." Two years
later (January, 1844) he writes to the same friend : " Being now free
from Adelaide I shall feel at liberty to work on, providing for the
wants of this great population. I hope to have a third poor school
in operation before long. The work that I have most before me at
this moment is the commencement of a convent. I propose establishing and applying the Third Order of St. Dominic as Sisters of
Charity, through the instrumentality of Sister Margaret. I am waiting to see the Provincial, and so soon as I have his concurrence
I am ready to begin with four excellent persons, all thorough
workers, with good sound sense and solid devotion. Sister Margaret
is invaluable. The quantity of good works and charities that pass
through her hands is almost inexplicable. The manner she is
spiritualising this congregation is admirable ; and all this amidst a
good deal of personal suffering."

† It was during the earlier part of his residence at Coventry that
Dr. Ullathorne published a volume of sermons with a remarkable
preface on the subject of preaching. This volume contains, amongst
others, the famous sermon on drunkenness which has often since
been reprinted. Referring to it in one of his letters he says : " The
sermon on drunkenness was taken in part from St. Chrysostom.
There was a man at Sydney to whom it was given by one of the

Soon after, I was honoured with the visit of two distinguished prelates. Archbishop Polding had appointed
to meet Monseigneur de Forbin-Janson, a Prince in his
own right as well as a bishop, at my poor cottage, where
I gave them the best hospitality I could. Their object in
meeting was to visit the Earl of Derby at his country
mansion, to plead for the release of the Canadian prisoners
transported to New South Wales for their part in the
Canadian insurrection. They were all respectable men,
farmers or farmers' sons, of French descent; their main
object was to protect the property of the Church. They
were kept aloof from the criminal convicts, placed at a
Government farm, and had conducted themselves with
great propriety.

As I found the Archbishop in difficulties as to whom to
recommend for the Bishopric of Hobart Town, I took the
opportunity strongly to recommend Father Willson, of
Nottingham, to his attention, pointing out his remarkable
qualities and his singular fitness for that Penal settlement.
He was consequently recommended to the Holy See, was
appointed, and ultimately placed under obedience to accept
the office. With Father Willson I was intimately acquainted.
He had taken a great interest in the Australian Mission on
my first visit to England in 1837 and 1838. I had often
visited him, had seen his great influence, and the way in
which he worked his mission. I paid him a visit whilst he
was building the Cathedral of St. Barnabas, and observed
his skill in matters of business.

On that occasion he expressed a great desire to know
the nature of the Institute of the Fathers of Charity,
founded by the celebrated Rosmini, who had recently
established their head-quarters at Loughborough. On that

priests, and who after reading it attentively remarked, 'the gentleman
who wrote this must have been *a hard drinker in his day*,' little
thinking that it had been written by one who by necessity, no less
than inclination, had always been a water drinker."

hint I went over to visit them, and told Dr. Pagani, then their Superior, that I had visited their Founder in Turin with the view of proposing a filiation in Australia, but had missed finding him, and that I had heard adverse remarks, and wished therefore to know the real nature of their Institute. Dr. Pagani said that I was the first person to make inquiries of them, and that he would be glad to give me the fullest information. He put the Rule into my hands, and also the Meditations in manuscript which their Founder had drawn up for the retreats of his disciples. I was struck with a certain originality in the Rule, and with a singular freshness in the Meditations ; and I spent the greatest part of two days and nights making extracts from them ; and was then able to give an account of their system to Father Willson. Later on I made a spiritual retreat at Loughborough, under Dr. Gentili, and we had much conversation, not only about the English Mission, but specially on the great importance of beginning a series of missions or retreats to the people under the approval of the Bishops. I found him quite prepared for such a work, and, as I was then publishing a volume of sermons with prefaces, in the general preface I introduced the subject. This led Dean Gaffney, of Maynooth, to write to me, re-commending me to begin the work, and offering to pick out from the College young and duly qualified men to assist me. But I already had my engagements under obedience. Being invited by Mr. de Lisle to preach at the blessing of the Calvary erected by him on the Grace Dieu Rocks, I again met Dr. Gentili, and we renewed the subject of preaching missions. Soon after he was invited by Father Willson to make a beginning at Nottingham, and not long after, in 1845, he and Father Furlong gave the great mission at Coventry which I have described in the Appendix to his Life.*

Before Bishop Willson consented to be consecrated, it

* This mission was begun on May 21st, 1845.

was arranged that the Archbishop of Sydney should meet him at my house, for the purpose of settling certain affairs, in which I was requested to arbitrate between them should it become needful. The principal point insisted upon was that Father Therry should be recalled from Hobart Town before the Bishop's arrival. This was agreed to, but unfortunately was not done, which occasioned the Bishop many and long troubles : for although Father Therry was a good man, he was not a man of business. For an account of Bishop Willson's successful episcopate in that penal settlement, I must refer to the memoir of him which I wrote in the *Dublin Review* of July, 1887.

There is a passage in the life of Mother Margaret Hallahan, in which she takes credit for having prevented my return to Australia with Bishop Willson, through the prayers of the people. This seems the proper place in which to tell the whole of that story.

The consecration of Bishop Willson took place at the Birmingham Cathedral, and, at the Bishop's request, I acted as his secretary, and read his Brief. After the rite was completed, and I was assisting at his unvesting in the sacristy, I said to him : " Now that the mitre is on your head, and not on mine, I have no objection to go out and help you." He looked up at me, and said : " Are you in earnest ?" I replied : " As long as I am safe from the mitre, with leave of superiors, I am indifferent where I am sent." He said: "I shall certainly write to your President-General." About a week after, I received a letter from Dr. Barber, then President-General, saying that he had received an application from Bishop Willson for my services, and asking my own mind on the subject. I replied that my sole object in leaving Australia was to avoid the office of Bishop, but that, exempt from that peril, I was completely indifferent as to where I was placed, subject to my Superior's approval. Dr. Barber wrote, in reply, that he felt I might, with my experience of the Colonies, be very useful to the new

Bishop ; that Coventry was now on a fair footing to go on, and that, if the Bishop renewed his application, he would feel it his duty to let me go with him. I then told Mother Margaret that I expected to be summoned to return with Bishop Willson to Australia. Her reply was : " No, you will not. The Blessed Virgin will take care of that." Having her assembly of pious people for the Rosary that night, she sent messages through them to the houses of the Catholics, requesting them to watch during the whole of that night, and to pray especially for her intention. After that, I heard not a word more either from Dr. Barber or from Bishop Willson. I did my best to assist him in his preparations, and bade him farewell ; but not a word of explanation escaped from his lips.

After he had visited the Archbishop of Sydney he wrote me a letter, in which, among other things, he said : " The next time I see you I shall have to go down on my knees." The Bishop came to England to lay the condition of Norfolk Island before the Government, soon after my consecration to the Western District. We met at Prior Park, where we dined together. Talking by ourselves after dinner, I asked him : " Why did you write to me that, when you saw me, you would have to go on your knees ?" He started up, burst into tears, and said : " I will go on my knees directly." " No," I said, " I will not allow it. But what did it mean ?" He then told me that he was just going to write for me to Dr. Barber, when he suddenly reflected : " Why is this man here ? He began the work in Australia and ought to be there. There may be something wrong. And knowing that I was intimate with Dr. Gentili, he went over to Loughborough to consult him on the subject. They could neither of them explain the mystery, and the Doctor said : " You had better not risk it." " But," concluded the Bishop, " I had not been in Sydney two days before I saw through the whole of what you must have gone through ; and I only wonder that it did not kill you."

16

CHAPTER XXIII.

COVENTRY CHURCH.

THE congregation of Coventry began rapidly to increase; the little chapel was excessively crowded, and it became necessary to think seriously of building a church in its place. As its position was by no means central, I examined various situations in more central positions, but could find none that were purchaseable that would not have involved the removal of buildings that would have made the ground very costly. There was ample space in the garden attached to the old missionary premises, and I therefore resolved, with the approval of the Provincial, to build the church in the old position. Mr. Charles Hansom was a young Catholic architect and Town Surveyor of Coventry; but he was more acquainted with the Greek and Palladian than with the Gothic styles. However, we put our heads together, made a study of the Gothic, visited and measured the old Catholic churches in several counties, made a tour through Belgium and on to Cologne, and, finally, fixed on the lancet style of the thirteenth century for the nave, which I proposed should be developed into the Early Decorated for the chancel and later chapels. But the funds had to be raised for the work, and after establishing a weekly collection in the congregation I went forth and solicited alms over the most populous parts of England.* This was a new experience, and one that taught

* The foundation-stone of Coventry Church was laid on May 29th, 1843. In that and the following year Dr. Ullathorne travelled over many parts of England collecting alms. He writes from London :

me many useful things.   Happily, I received a large contribution from Mr. Charles Eyre, of Bruges, an old friend
of Mother Margaret Hallahan's, which helped us much.   I
had left a considerable library in Sydney ; this, I thought,
ought not to be removed from a country where books of
that valuable kind were scarce.   I therefore proposed to
the Archbishop of Sydney to leave them there on condition of receiving £150 to buy a set of the Fathers.   But
the sum went to the building account.

The nave was built first with the tower, and was con-
structed with unusual solidity for the time.   Our great
difficulty was to find a sculptor, for architectural sculpture
was, at that time, a lost art, that was only beginning to be
revived under the celebrated Welby Pugin.   However, we
found a farmer's boy, who, though untutored, had a genius
for that kind of art, and with the help of casts with which
we provided him he succeeded tolerably well.   It was in the

"Hitherto begging has been pleasant enough ; I suppose I shall find
its pleasures diminish as time goes on.   I walk some twenty miles a
day on the London pavements without any excessive fatigue, because
I have nobody to talk balderdash about it at the end."   From York
(July, 1844) he writes : "Father Mathew has been here, and has made
a great sensation.   He is making a tour through England.   I should
have no difficulty in bringing him to Coventry, but I have not decided,
nor do I at present feel disposed to do so, though we might easily have
St. Mary's Hall, and a great sensation would be the result.   But I
scarcely know how far it would be prudent to engage myself in what
is called the temperance movement.   I shall consider the two sides
of the question before I decide.   It is rarely I have to deliberate on
any subject ; but there really are two sides to this question as regards
this country ; yet I feel a bias towards the temperance movement,
though it be in excess and attended by accidental dangers of
delusion."
He also made a tour in Belgium, where he received considerable
subscriptions.   It appears to have been his first visit to that country,
and at Bruges he was equally delighted with the church architecture,
and indignant with the modern ornaments added in French and
Roman style to the mediæval Gothic.   "How I should like," he says,
"to grind the noses off the faces of the men who are changing so
many of the fine old Gothic fronts of the houses into modern flat
ones !"

early time of transition from the old chapels to churches ;
St. Chad's and the church at Derby were alone completed,
and no one of the later generations can realise the shifts
to which we were put for funds as well as for builders to
realise our designs.   But when Pugin examined the plans,
and afterwards the completed structure, he not only commended its solidity, but considered it to be a pure revival
of the style of the thirteenth century.   The nave was first
completed with the chancel arch bricked up, and then, with
a temporary altar, we took possession of it.   We had now
a great deal more space which soon filled, and, at the evening
services, became closely packed, every standing place being
filled as well as the seats.   At those evening services I
adopted the method of the Fathers, and gave expositions
of large portions of books of Holy Scripture.   I gave
lectures on the beginning of Genesis, and explained the
Creation : this drew a number of Freethinkers as well as
others.   I explained the Epistles of St. Paul to the
Romans and to the Galatians : this drew a considerable
number of Dissenters.   I took the history of the Patriarchs,
and this awakened general interest.   But though I gave
out the text of Scripture part by part as I advanced, I was
not so tied to the text as not to expatiate freely on any
point of doctrine or moral teaching that the text suggested,
after the manner of the Fathers.

I found not only that this method was effective in
drawing full congregations, but that it led to many conversions.   And I have no hesitation in saying that, for
evening lectures, whoever is versed in the Holy Scriptures
and in the manners and customs of the Holy Land, will
find this method one of the most effective that can be
adopted.   It was the method of the Church for 1,200
years.   But here let me tell an anecdote.   After I was
removed to the See of Birmingham, I adopted much the
same method of Scriptural instruction in the Lenten

evening lectures at the Cathedral. Some, however, of the reverend clergy did not relish this revived method of instruction, though the people delighted in it. As there was not a little twittering among them about it, I resolved to put an end to it. So on ascending the pulpit on Sunday evening, I said to the congregation : " You, my brethren, who are of opinion that your Bishop should instruct you according to his own judgment, and not according to the judgment of other persons, please to hold up your hands." A thousand hands were lifted up, and I heard of no more objections.

Sometimes curious cases would occur. For instance, a girl who had lost her mother became a pious convert in the school, but her father was a complete infidel. He came with her to church sometimes, but there was no getting him to say a prayer. He was a working man, who had dabbled in the ologies. He talked to me about his love and worship of nature, and the four elements. " Elements," I asked, " what elements ? " " The four elements," he replied. " You, a chemist," I answered, " and talk of the four elements ! Come to the church on Sunday and hear what I shall say to you." He came, and I took for my text, " From invisible things all things visible were created." I went into the subject of invisible causes ; from that I passed to the one supreme cause, and so to Creation and Providence ; and illustrated my theme by showing how all visible and material things are convertible into invisible elements by the application of science, when they are more the objects of science than in their concrete forms. After the instruction the man came to me in the sacristy and said : " Sir, I shall be ever grateful to you. You have proved me to be a fool." " Just what I wanted you to know," I said. " It is the first step to your becoming wise. Now you must begin to say your prayers." He did so ; but a fortnight afterwards there was a violent knocking at the door at midnight. I went down, and found the same man there in a state of vehement excitement. He said : " Feel my heart." It was beating like a hammer. I got him inside, soothed and tranquillised him, and then he said : " I can't pray ; I have no belief." I told him to go home and rest, and come to me next day. He was quieter then, and I asked him : " Have you more confidence in my knowledge than in yours ? " " I have," he said. " Well, on my knowledge begin again to say your prayers with your daughter, and come to me for instructions." He did so, and became a steady Christian.

Another opportunity for instruction arose in the school-room. After Mother Margaret arrived, she had a devotional little altar placed in the girls' school, and put a triptich upon it, in which she enshrined her favourite.little statue of the Blessed Virgin. Three nights in the week she got a number of girls and women together, and they sang the Litany of Loreto and said the Rosary. The number of persons drawn to this devotion increased until the girls' school had to be opened into the boys' school, and the two rooms became crowded with men as well as women. Strangers came in numbers, and as the weekly collections for building the church were paid there every Monday night, I went to the school, and after the devotions were ended and the collections received I sat down and gave a familiar sort of fireside talk. At one time I took the people in imagination to Rome, and described to them the churches and devotions. At another, I got them to the Holy Land, and described the holy places. Now we went into the Catholic antiquities of Coventry and its old religious customs ; then some sketches of voyages and travels were given ; at another time it was the picturesque life of some Saint, or a series of anecdotes, or the invention of a parable or two. On these familiar talks the ears of the people hung with attention, and the place was generally crowded. Then the young women devoted to Mother Margaret would ask this or that woman, when they saw her to be a stranger and interested, if she would like to speak to Mother Margaret. This led to interviews after the rest were gone away, when a few pithy words would often lead to conversions. Sometimes men also asked friends they had brought to come and have a word with me. What then passed in the schoolrooms got talked about in the town, and in the ribbon factories, which drew other persons to come and listen.

After the church was completed it drew numbers of people of all classes to see it when unoccupied. It was a new thing to see a Catholic church, with all its Catholic appointments, just like the old churches as they were furnished in the Middle Ages ; and I had a person there to let me know when there were several visitors. I then went in and explained to them both the church and all its symbolism, with which the congregation was made thoroughly acquainted. This sometimes led to interesting conversations on the Catholic religion, and catechisms were accepted.

In instructing converts, I never brought them into classes ; I observed that this made them shy, and that they preferred coming alone. I found also that by instructing them one by one it was easier to adapt even a shorter instruction to their individual states of mind and several characters. But I had a remedy for those briefer times of instruction, which I found very valuable. If the neophyte was a man, I introduced him to some Catholic man of the same class on whom I could rely ; if a woman, she was introduced to some devout Catholic woman. These I appointed as sponsors ; they had them by them in church, taught them Catholic customs and manners, answered their questions, and made them acquainted with

other Catholics—so that they did not come into the church
as isolated persons. Those were happy days. The
growing congregation was united like a family. I had all
sorts of help, including, after the church was built, two
Reverend Fathers, instead of one. We said Mass at
Kenilworth also on Sundays and festivals, which was the
beginning of that mission. We had a lending library in
the school, and books were given out and received each
Sunday afternoon, when many of the people spent their
time about the enclosure round the church, to which they
were devoted. At the time when I was called from
Coventry to other work we were receiving converts at the
rate of a hundred a year.

Before the chancel could be begun it was necessary to
pull the house down, and I rented a house of considerable
size in an adjoining street. My reason for this was that
Mother Margaret and I had already planned the beginning
of a Religious Community of Dominican Tertiaries, and
this required a series of rooms and a chapel for their use ;
and it became expedient to place the other clergy in other
lodgings. This was not done without the formal approval
both of the Provincial and of the Bishop. The novitiate
was begun, and was conducted under my general
directions ; Mother Margaret, who was already a professed
Tertiary, managing the details of observance, and infusing
her vigorous religious spirit into the novices, who already
began their active works of charity as part of their formation.

When the chancel was completed, and the partition
wall removed, the people on their entering the church on
the following Sunday, were struck with wonder and
admiration at the scene presented to them. The deep
sanctuary, the large east window, rich in colour with its
Saints and tracery ; the light rood screen, with its rood
loft, holy rood, and impressive figures ; the beautiful lateral
arches opening into parclosed chapels, to the expenses of

which they had specially contributed ; the high altar, richly decorated ; and the stalls for the clergy and the choir, filled them with delight and rewarded them for all their sacrifices. For the first time in their lives they saw a real Catholic church, and never tired of being taught what, in all its details, it symbolically expressed to their senses. It was consecrated by Bishop (afterwards Cardinal) Wiseman in the year 1845, and on the following day all the Bishops of England assisted at the solemn opening, which was attended by many of the Catholic gentry of that and neighbouring counties. In the afternoon a great entertainment was given to the Bishops and the visitors in the old Catholic Guild Hall, which was filled with guests.

On that occasion I first put on the full Benedictine habit, and in that costume received those who came to the opening, and put them in their places. But the habit had been unknown in England since the time of Queen Mary, and some of those who came to the opening did not relish its appearance. About that time I was invited to preach at the opening of the Church of St. Edmund, Liverpool ; but when I replied that as a Benedictine I always preached in the habit of the Order, I received a reply from the venerable Father at the head of that church that " another preacher would be provided." On being asked to preach at the old Sardinian Chapel in London, I went up to the pulpit in the habit of my Order, as a matter of course ; but on returning to the sacristy I encountered a sharp rebuke from the senior priest, who was warmly indignant. Much of the old timidity of the persecuting days was still to be found in England, but in the Colonies we had learned greater freedom. Cardinal Wiseman was also teaching the English Catholics to bring forth all our religious practices openly and without disguise.*

* About this time Dr. Ullathorne paid a visit to Downside, and his feelings on revisiting his old Monastery are expressed in an interesting

As there once at least existed an impression on the mind of some of our leading ecclesiastics that I was a devoted follower of the philosophy of Rosmini, I think it well to leave on record what had always been my real views on that subject. From the time that I formed acquaintance with his disciples at Loughborough, I admired the Rule of the Order, as I have said, and also the Founder's system of spiritual exercises, and made more than one reteat under the Fathers. But Dr. Gentili spoke much to me about a book by their Founder, still in manuscript, called the "Cinque Piaghe." When that book was published in Italy and I had read it, I wrote to Dr. Pagani, telling him that I thought there were very grave points in it: I believe my observations were sent to the author. This was some time before it was placed on the Index. The Fathers in their kindness sent me all the works of Rosmini as they were published. In the order of their publication I read them, and as they made a large display of books on my shelves this probably led to the impression of my being a follower of his philosophy. But though I found much to admire in those writings, in his philosophy I detected what I considered to be grave and fundamental errors which would not stand by the common teaching of the Church. The first thing to which my attention was awakened was a doctrine in the first volume of his psychology where he describes the generation of man. He there describes the formation of the soul as being a touch of Divine light upon the *materia*

etter written from thence, and dated "Saturday after Ascension, 1884":—" I have been here since Thursday night, and must leave on Monday. Everything here edifies: good discipline, perfect obedience and observance, silence at all due times, and an admirable spirit of fraternal charity. Downside was never in better order. I attend choir, meditate, and think over all that has passed since I left this peaceful and happy abode, and would be glad to remain here always. Everything tells me how much I have lost, gaining in nothing but this poor world's wisdom and conceit, since I left the cloister some fourteen years ago."

deposita, upon the embryo. This description evidently left out any created spiritual substance of the soul, and the context left the meaning clear. I then wrote to Dr. Pagani and had repeated conversations with Dr. Berletti, in which I asked how the spiritual substance of the soul was to be accounted for. My difficulty was sent to Rosmini himself. In reply, I was always told that I must wait for other books still in manuscript, the titles of which were mentioned.

I waited for one book after another, but the explanation did not come. At last the volume " De Reali " appeared, and on receiving it I was told that I should find in it what I sought. But instead of finding the desired explanation, to my astonishment I found this doctrine, that " Creation is division in God ; that this was not Pantheism because Pantheism taught that all things were God." Soon after discovering this error, so fundamentally opposed to the teaching of the Church respecting Creation, I received a letter from a secular priest, in the West of England, telling me that he had long been devoted to Rosmini's philosophy but that he had had doubts and misgivings about it for some time past, and asking me to give him my mind on the subject. In reply I wrote a long letter, telling him of the fundamental errors which I had observed in that philosophy Many years later on I received a letter from Cardinal Newman, informing me that a letter had come to him from the then representative of the Order in Rome, asking him as a particular favour for a letter that might be a support to him in a special audience with the Sovereign Pontiff. Apprehensive that this audience might concern the writings of Rosmini, I recommended His Eminence to be cautious what he wrote, and gave him an account of the grave errors to be found in his philosophy. This must have been about the time when the second examination of these works began, including the posthumous publications. For about two or three years later came forth the Decree of the

Holy Office condemning forty propositions contained in these works. I must not dismiss the subject without bearing testimony to the religious spirit and energetic labours of the Fathers of Charity in this country.

Bishop Baines, of the Western District of England, died suddenly in July, 1843, on the night after he had officiated at the opening of St. Mary's Church, Bristol. And I was informed at a later time, by Dr. Grant, then secretary to Cardinal Acton, that Propaganda proposed to Gregory XVI. that Bishop Brown of the Welsh District should be transferred to the Western District, and that I should be appointed to succeed Bishop Brown in Wales. This was confirmed by a letter received from Bishop Brown at the time, in which he asked me whether, in the event of my being appointed to succeed him, I would take to the house which he was about to engage for his residence at Chepstow. In my reply I said that I thought it very unlikely that I should be appointed, and even more unlikely that I should accept ; but that, as he had put a definite question, I ought not to leave him without a definite answer. That my opinion had always been that a Vicar-Apostolic should live in the principal town or city of his district, where he could exercise most influence, be surrounded by a body of clergy, and perform the episcopal functions in the most becoming way. Chepstow would not, therefore, be a place that I should choose for a residence.

But when this proposal was carried to the Sovereign Pontiff, His Holiness immediately replied : " No, no, questo Monsignore Baggs."

Dr. Baggs was Rector of the English College in Rome, was well known to the Pope, and a favourite. He was appointed to the Western District, and I escaped for the time. But only for a time. For when Bishop Baggs took the district in hand he found things in great confusion, and was so severely tried that it hastened his end. He died on

October 16th, 1845. But before he died he gave to the Rev. Mr. Parfitt a letter, which was to be delivered to his successor. That letter came, of course, into my hands. In it he wrote of the great trials he had gone through, and stated that it had been his intention to go abroad (to Rome, I suppose), and there to resign his office.

The office remained vacant for an unusual time. But in the month of May, 1846, I received a letter from Cardinal Acton, informing me that I was appointed to the Western District, urging me not to refuse the appointment, and pointing out that in these days the episcopate, in England, was more a burden than an honour. This was a great blow to my feelings. All was going on so well at Coventry, making those the happiest days of my life. The house had just been completed and I had designed it for a small Community of Fathers, hoping to show in the course of time that with the endowment already existing, and with the adjoining population in the colliery district, work and maintenance might be found to support a little Community. The Dominican Sisters had been recently professed, and I was looking out for a position at the other end of the city in which to place them in a convent of their own. Were all these plans to come to an end? I went to Mother Margaret in the school, and gave her a look which she at once understood. She put a child down from her knee, followed me to the house, and said : " I see you are made a Bishop." " Not," I replied, " if I can get out of it." On the same day I went to Stanbrook, to lay the case before Dr. Barber, my old Prior, and now my Provincial. He was a grave, elderly, and spiritual minded man, and had long been my confessor before I went to Australia. Before him I laid all my objections, after which he represented to me the confusion and trouble that had so long prevailed in that district, the difficulties to be surmounted, and gave it as his decided opinion that the experience I had obtained would enable me to surmount what a less experienced person would not be able to manage so well. But on my saying that I never would accept a mitre except under obedience, my Superior answered : " As far as I can I give you that obedience." This settled me : and I wrote to Cardinal Acton that I submitted to the burden. Bishop Walsh came over from Birmingham in great kindness to encourage me and give me some useful hints about the consecration. Bishop Griffiths, of London, was also kind and brotherly. Bishop Wiseman sent me the Bishop of Bellay's book, "The Practice of a New Bishop," which with Barbosa's chapters on the spiritual qualities required in a bishop, in his work " De Episcopate," assisted me in making the preparatory retreat.

During this retreat I reflected much on the importance of obtaining a change from the provisional state of Vicars-Apostolic to that of Hierarchical Ordinaries, as had been already accomplished for Australia. I also thought much of the importance of establishing Ecclesiastical Seminaries on the principles laid down by the Council of Trent, in which the ecclesiastical sciences might be learnt, and the discipline of a diocese acquired under men exclusively devoted to that work, instead of those mixed colleges in which secular studies were, as a matter of course, the predominant feature. These views took strong possession of my mind.

My consecration as Bishop of Hetalona, appointed Vicar-Apostolic to the Western District, took place at Coventry on Sunday, June 21st, 1846. Bishop Briggs, the senior Vicar-Apostolic, was the consecrating Bishop ; Bishops Griffiths and Wareing were the assistants, and Bishop Wiseman the preacher. It was on the same day on which Pope Pius IX. was crowned. All the Bishops of England were kind enough to be present, also Dr. Brady, the Bishop of Perth, in Western Australia. Dr. Newman and his companions, recently received into the Church, and but just arrived at Oscott, were also present. I can never forget the light and sense that streamed upon my mind when, after the consecration was completed, the mitre was placed by the three Bishops on my head, or the resolutions I then formed, never to rest until the Hierarchy of Ordinary Bishops was obtained. I would gladly have had the sacred rite followed by three days of deep silence for the sake of reflection, as prescribed by St. Benedict to be observed after religious profession, instead of having to entertain the Bishops and other visitors at an hotel. But hospitality was an especial duty; and the Bishops had received me into their number with the open-hearted confidence of their brotherhood.

Although freed at my appointment from the Coventry Mission, I had to provide for the future of Mother Margaret and her Dominican Community; and upon an understanding with Bishop Walsh, I arranged to bring them into the Western District so soon as I could find a suitable place for them. I had next to part with the good and pious congregation, which had been so great a consolation to me. I knew them all so well, with all their little histories, and had received many of them into the Church. But few of them had ever caused me any trouble, and being mostly of one class—industrious ribbon weavers or watch-makers—they were like one family. They presented me with a beautiful chalice, for which they subscribed £40, and invited Father Aylward, the Dominican, from Hinckley, to be their spokesman. We parted at a great meeting outside the church, where the chalice was presented, not without many tears; and I promised that I would use their gift at the altar to remind me of them, a promise I kept for forty years.

CHAPTER XXIII.

THE BEGINNING OF MY EPISCOPATE.

AT the time when I succeeded to the Western District, Dr. Brindle was Vicar-General of that district as well as President of the College of Prior Park, which had been the residence of the two former Bishops. I had written to him to say that I should proceed to Prior Park, and should remain there a month to show my interest in the establishment; but that I should afterwards take up my residence in Bristol. My reason for this was that Bristol is the most populous city in the district; that it appeared to me to be the most suitable centre for the diocese, and that there was room amid the population for several missions and for expanding the influence of religion. As to Bath, it was already in possession of my Benedictine brethren. But, as Bishop, it was my duty to place myself at the head of the secular clergy who had no other Superior, and gradually to gather a staff of picked men around me.

The extensive and imposing range of buildings which form the College of Prior Park were built by an Italian architect in the reign of Queen Anne, as a mansion for the celebrated Mr. Allen, a man of great wealth derived from the West Indies. The grounds amid which it is placed are very beautiful, and the whole presents a striking, and even classical, picture from the city of Bath. Its name of Prior Park is much older, it having been the site of the country residence of the Prior of Bath, which in the olden time had its chapter of Benedictines. As the mansion of

Mr. Allen it was much visited by Pope, Fielding, and other literary men ; and Mr. Allen was the prototype of Squire Allworthy in Fielding's "Tom Jones." It finally passed into the hands of a speculator, who was said to have nearly paid the purchase-money with the magnificent timber he cut down. From him Bishop Baines bought the whole property, intending the central mansion for the episcopal residence, and the two wings, with their double corridors of communication, for two distinct colleges (the one devoted to the study of the humanities, and the other for the sciences). · This required a great deal of alteration and new construction ; in fact, something approaching to a University was contemplated.

After Prior Park had been occupied for a certain time as a college, the interior and central roof of the mansion were burnt down by a great fire. But the Bishop bought an unfinished and highly ornamental mansion that was for sale in Bristol, and with the help of its materials restored the mansion in greater splendour than before, raising the central hall up to the very roof of the building. This very much increased the debts and difficulties.

Prior Park exhibited a striking example at that time of what I have seen in a less degree in other places. It was originally intended as a palatial residence, and was still exhibited as a show place twice a week to the visitors at Bath. Externally it was a magnificent pile ; internally it was adorned with many pictures and other costly furniture. But when an institution intended for laborious work is surrounded with much material magnificence the men engaged on it are too apt to depend rather on material display than on the character of the work which should give life and power to the establishment. It was the weakness of the Jews rebuked by the Prophet Jeremias.* They too often measured the greatness of their religion by the magnificence

* Jeremias vii. 4.

17

of the Temple in which it was enshrined. When buildings are plain and simple men feel that they must rely on themselves for success.*

Dr. English, afterwards Archbishop of Trinidad, came to Coventry to accompany me to Bath, where I stayed with Mr. Robert Tichborne, and the next day went up to Prior Park in his carriage, attended by Father Cooper of Bath, and Father Vaughan, afterwards Bishop of Plymouth, who was at that time President of St. Paul's College, the Rev. Mr. Parfitt being President of St. Peter's. On my arrival I was publicly received according to the ritual, and a large party of clergy and laity were invited to meet me at dinner. There were at that time at Prior Park, teaching the classics, Messrs. Neve, Estcourt, Collins, and Capes ; all recent converts. Mr. Northcote and Mr. Healy Thompson were residing at Bath, but had not as yet taken any share in the work of the College. I invited Mr. Northcote to the College as Prefect of Studies, and Mr. Healy Thompson as professor, taking Mr. Estcourt as my secretary. At this time I received a letter from Archbishop Polding, just

---

* There is one authentic anecdote, often related by Dr. Ullathorne connected with some of the architectural adornments of Prior Park, which is too amusing to be passed over. The original architect had placed a series of stone statues of the pagan gods over the corridors that formed the communication between the central mansion and the wings. Bishop Baines called in an artist, who, with the help of canvas and plaster, transformed these figures into representations of Saints, which were ranged on the two sides of the broad flight of steps leading up to the chief entrance. Thus Jupiter was changed to St. Peter in cope and tiara, whilst Hercules did duty for St, Gregory the Great. There is a tradition that storms of rain made sad havoc of these transformations, revealing the stone gods underneath. Horrified at these exhibitions, Dr. Gentili, who resided at one time as professor at Prior Park, resolved to pull them down. He procured a long rope, tied it round the neck of Jupiter, and got a number of the College boys to lay hold of the other end. When all was ready he called to the boys, " Now when I say the third time, ' Come down, you great *monstere*' (speaking in his broken English), all pull together." He had said it once, when hearing the shout the Bishop threw up a window and put a stop to the contemplated demolition.

arrived in London from Sydney, expressing great regret at having arrived too late, as his principal object in coming to Europe was to solicit the Holy See to appoint me to be his Coadjutor. I invited him to Prior Park, and he was present at the College Exhibition. I had promised to reside at Prior Park for the first month, but I did not slumber there. I visited Bristol and Clifton, and sundry missions and convents. In short, I took a survey of the district which then included the two present dioceses of Clifton and Plymouth. At the invitation of the Earl of Shrewsbury, I assisted at the opening of the magnificent church at Cheadle. I also consecrated an altar at the opening of the church at Blackmore Park. Mr. Charles Hansom was the architect and I had something to say to that design.

Before long I began operations in Bristol and Clifton. I called Mother Margaret Hallahan and her little Community of Dominicanesses from Coventry, and after a time placed them in a house in Queen Square, Bristol, where they opened a school, and began to visit the sick. As the only two churches in Bristol were close together, I made a survey of the whole extent of Bristol, and had a plan drawn up in four divisions in which I proposed to establish four missions, two of which would still require churches and schools. In one of these I secured ground and began a school in it, to be used provisionally as a chapel. I also organised two annual collections throughout the district to assist undertakings of this kind. The plan of the four missions was completed by my successors.

The Clifton Mission involves a history. It was begun by Father Edgworth, a Franciscan, long before my time. He purchased a large plot of ground in a commanding situation, and built, in the first place, on one side of it, a small convent, intended for a Community of active nuns, the chapel of which was used temporarily for the mission, and the residence for the priest. He then began a magnificent church in freestone on the central ground, and that at a time when we had nothing in England but the old chapels, with the exception of the church at Moorfields, in London. It was planned to stand on a basis more extensive than itself, something not unlike in character to the Madeleine. The basis consisted of crypts rising, because of the inclined ground, considerably above the ground on one side. Upon those crypts the large church was raised, the walls were nearly completed, and the greater part of the columns for a lofty porch in front, when the whole property was taken possession of by the Glamorganshire Bank for money advanced. Such was the state of the Clifton Mission when I came to the district ; the church, a great ruin, stood conspicuous to all eyes and a disgrace to the Catholics.

My earnest desire was to build a large church and attach the Bishop's residence to it, so as to serve for a cathedral. Father Vaughan, the Vicar-General, and Mr. Estcourt searched for a site for the purpose in vain. At last the Vicar-General suggested the repurchase of the ruin from the Bank. It was reported that there was some intention of purchasing it to make a market-place of it ; and after some negotiations the whole property was purchased of the Bank for £3,000, including a mortgage, which a Catholic lady had upon it. Of this sum £1,000 was paid by the Dominican Sisters for the little convent that stood apart on one side of it. Mother Margaret and her Sisters took possession of the convent, and in course of time greatly enlarged and beautified it. Schools were opened in the crypts, both for boys and girls. I took a house adjoining the premises, in which the Vicar-General, my secretary, and another priest resided with me.

The walls of the church had been long exposed to the weather, without any roof, and it was of so great a breadth without interior supports that the architects of Bristol declared it could never bear a roof. But I sent for Mr. Charles Hansom, my former architect, then residing at Clifton, and said to him : "I know that these walls will not bear the expanse and weight of timber required for the roof, nor will the vaulting of the crypts bear pillars of stone. You must put your ideals of architecture in your pocket and do just as I advise you. You must put long sleepers of timber upon the crown of the two series of vaults, and upon them raise pillars of timber to the height of the wall, which can be cased and capped in wood, and from those pillars carry circular arches of wood lengthwise and across, upon which to receive the roof." Mr. Hansom saw its feasibility and carried it out with success. Windows were cut in the walls, and a chancel was formed with stalls for a chapter, as I never gave up the hope of seeing the Hierarchy re-established. The church held a great many people, and in consequence of dignified functions and careful preaching it soon began to fill, so that more priests were required. But among the greatest religious attractions were the popular devotions in the convent chapel, where the priest said the Rosary three nights in the week. The Litany was sung, and sermons given in the evening, both in English and French ; and this formed an attraction which drew a number of Catholics to reside at Clifton quite as much as the church.

The next step taken was to build a house adjoining the church for the residence of the Bishop and clergy, and the rest of the ground in front of it was cleared for a garden. But this house was not completed until after I was translated to Birmingham. Meanwhile funds had to be raised for these works, and the Catholics residing in Clifton were very generous.*

* The subsequent history of Prior Park need not be here recapitulated. In consequence of the complicated difficulties which had grown up in the diocese in connection with this establishment, Bishop

Meanwhile good work was going on at Bristol and Clifton. A mission was carried on for a fortnight in the old chapel at Trenchard Street by Dr. Gentili and Father Furlong, which, being the first ever given in the Western District, drew many souls to their religious duties. But this did not satisfy Dr. Gentili. In his ardour he longed to give another mission, which should last a month, observing that those who most required to be instructed came crowding in at the end of the fortnight, when there was no time to do much for them. It was therefore arranged that at a later period a mission should be given by the two Fathers for a whole month at the Church of St. Mary's. This was done in the early part of

Ullathorne proceeded to Rome in the spring of 1847 to lay a full report before the Holy See. A Commission of Bishops was appointed by Propaganda to investigate the case, but it was not until after Bishop Ullathorne's removal to the Central District that the affairs of the College were finally brought to a conclusion. The College was broken up, and the property passed for a time into secular hands, whence it was at a later period recovered by Dr. Clifford, Bishop of Clifton ; and now again flourishes as one of our Catholic colleges. This visit of Bishop Ullathorne to Rome in 1847 was the occasion of his first presentation to Pope Pius IX., of whom he speaks in one of his letters as " truly a man raised up by God." "Mr. Estcourt and I scramble about in the afternoons to churches, shrines, and convents. I see Rome in altogether a new light from my former visits. Not a single association of its pagan and classic times can I think of : it seems to me completely saturated with the blood of the Martyrs and the prayers of the Saints at every step. But its fine things, even its finest churches, except the very old ones, do not penetrate the soul like our own Gothic churches." He returned to England early in June, 1848. The first anniversary of his consecration found him once more at Bristol, whence he addressed a touching letter to the Dominican Community he had planted there, giving a glimpse of his own interior, so seldom laid bare to the eyes of others. " A year of Episcopacy," he says, "is a fearful account. I solemnly and sadly feel that I have failed in many things for which I had light ; and have slackened from many things for which I was not without some strength, and which the prayers of God's better servants had obtained for me. I should like to do better, but if you had not prayed for me I should most certainly have done worse. Every glance at the crucifix before me strikes my heart with a keen reproach. Every recollection of the sentiments and light of this day twelve months does me the same

1848.* But, however successful, these labours were very exhausting to the missioners, and especially to Dr. Gentili, who would insist on living and sleeping in the sacristy, that he might lose no time, but be ready at everyone's call, early and late. His mind was also very much tried at that time by the revolutionary agitations which were shaking all the thrones of Europe ; whilst Charles Albert had begun his conflict with Austria, and the Sovereign Pontiff was surrounded with those perils which ultimately drove him from Rome. His occasional conversations with me showed how much these things were agitating him in the midst of his work.

He also poured out to me his regrets at having completely mistaken the spirit of the English clergy as a body during his earlier knowledge of the English Mission. His first experiences were at Prior Park; his next was in working an English country mission at Sheepshead, where everything had to be begun, and where he was much isolated. But when he began to give retreats in missions already established, his eyes were opened. He saw that the

good office. If it is a difficult thing to be a good Sister of Penance, how much more difficult is it to be a good Bishop ! Pray that you may have a better Father, for at present he is but the watch-dog at the feet of St. Dominic, who holds the flaming torch in his mouth, and looks up at the bunch of lily flowers which the Saint holds in his hands ready to consume whatever may threaten its purity !"

* "This mission," says Dr. Ullathorne, in one of his letters, "began a new order of things in Bristol." It had its amusing features, to which the Bishop often referred. In one of his instructions Dr. Gentili had spoken strongly against the vice of drunkenness, specially denouncing the intemperance of women. "If a man has a wife who gets *dronk*," he said, "he should take the stick to her." His words bore immediate fruit, and the next day several women presented themselves with broken heads, complaining that their husbands had not been slow to put the missioner's exhortation into practice. He felt the necessity, therefore, of somewhat qualifying his words. "Last night," he said, "I told you that if a man had a wife who got *dronk*, he should take the stick to her. But I did not mean that he should beat her with a great thick stick. It may be a leettle, thin one, what you call cane."

priests, as a rule, thoroughly understood their work, and, whilst laborious, knew how to adapt themselves to the English mind by avoiding haste and awakening public excitement, which only roused up adversaries to counter-act their efforts. I had had ocular proofs that he had made representations to Rome under his earlier impressions. He admitted this; but hoped, he said, to do justice to the English clergy, to their steady, quiet, and prudent labours, and their self-denial, in letters to be written as soon as he could have leisure for the purpose.

But that leisure never came. Their Superior, Dr. Pagani, came to see the two Fathers before they left Bristol, and I represented to him in what an exhausted condition they were, especially Dr. Gentili, and how hazardous it would be for them to take up other work until they had some rest. Mother Margaret, who with her Dominican Sisters had worked hard, under Dr. Gentili's directions, among the women and children during the whole mission, made similar representations. The answer was, that arrange-ments had been made for their immediately beginning other missions in Dublin ; but that when these were concluded the Fathers should have proper time for rest. They went and what they did in Dublin, and how Dr. Gentili died, in the midst of that work, is matter of history. Yet however great the grief, however immense the loss to the English Mission, I was not surprised, for he was half dead from mental and moral exhaustion before he began his work in Dublin ; and the toil and excitement that came upon him with the rush of that fervid people to hear his discourses, and to reach his confessional, was too much for his mortal strength.

CHAPTER XXIV.

The Hierarchy.

Not to dwell longer on the details of administration in the Western District, my administration of which lasted scarcely for the term of two years, during which I had twice to go to Rome, I now come to the most important and eventful of those labours which mark the track of my episcopal life. But this will require a short preface.

From the time of Queen Elizabeth the desire was constantly growing for the restoration of the normal state of Episcopal government in the Church that still remained in England, though so diminished in the number of its members, and under so fearful a persecution. I have given the history of that movement in the work that I published in the year 1871, entitled " The History of the Restoration of the Catholic Hierarchy in England." I will only add here that I wrote that book after the movement began in Parliament for the repeal of the Ecclesiastical Titles Act ; my object being to prove to the members of Parliament, that before that Hierarchy was re-established, every possible precaution had been taken by the Holy See to avoid giving offence to the Government and people of England ; for which purpose I give a minute account of every step in the negotiation and preparation for that great act, as between the representative of the English Vicars-Apostolic and the Holy See, drawn as well from the documents upon which it was based as from notes taken at the time of the conversations and discussions as they occurred, day by day, with all their circumstances. To that book I refer for the fullest and most authentic details. All I shall do here will be to give the briefest sketch of those transactions.

The Constitution by which the Church in England had hitherto been regulated was drawn up by Pope Benedict XIV., one of the greatest of canonists ; it was published in 1756, and was known by the name of its first words, *Apostolicum Ministerium.* But we had long outgrown the provisions of that Constitution. It was drawn up when we were still under heavy Penal laws, and liberty of conscience was denied to us ; when our Colleges were abroad, and all our clergy trained abroad ; when the Religious Orders had not a house in England ; when there was nothing resembling a parochial division ; but the few places of worship were private chapels, and the clergy who served them were the chaplains of noblemen or gentlemen. But the Penal laws had been now removed, we had obtained freedom of action, the Catholics of England had grown important by increase of numbers and of churches; all the institutions belonging to the Church had been reinstated among us, except the ordinary Government belonging to a Province of the Church, and the power which that implies of making Synodal laws for our regulation. The Church in America had obtained its Hierarchy, Australia had obtained its Hierarchy ; the West Indies had obtained a Hierarchy ; the Catholics of England were still left to be guided by the old rules of the Penal times, which were no longer applicable as of old.

In the Apostolic Letter constituting the Hierarchy it is stated that many petitions had come from England in favour of its establishment. From the days of Mr. Pitt, English statesmen had repeatedly expressed their wish to see the Catholic Bishops in England made Bishops in Ordinary, as being more conformable to the principles of the British Constitution than Vicars of the Pope. In the report of the Episcopal meeting in London in 1845 I find Bishop Griffiths proposing to petition the Holy See for the restoration of the Hierarchy. The Bishops assembled agreed to this proposal, and Bishops Wiseman and Baggs were requested to draw up a statement of the reasons for, and the difficulties that would attend the change, for transmission to Rome.

At the annual meeting of 1847, the first at which I assisted, it was found that confusion had reached its height. Certain laymen had made grave representations to Propaganda, as unjust as they were unfounded, against the venerable Bishop Griffiths, and had become active in thwarting the councils of the Vicars-Apostolic with respect to obtaining legal provision for the security of our ecclesiastical property ; I refer especially to Romilly's Bill for Settling Catholic Trusts, on which advice had been sought from Rome, and which, through the intervention of these persons, was set aside altogether.

With these facts before them the Bishops resolved to request Bishops Wiseman and Sharples to proceed to Rome, as well to explain matters on the part of the Vicars-Apostolic as to feel their way towards obtaining a Hierarchy. In conversing with Cardinal (then Monsignor) Barnabo, Secretary of Propaganda, and representing the serious existing embarrassments, he said : " You will always have these troubles till you ask for the Hierarchy: ask for it, and I will support you." The Revolution was then making rapid progress in Italy, and both Bishops were obliged to return to England, where, shortly afterwards, Bishop Griffiths died. But the question had been mooted, and the Vicars-Apostolic received a letter from the Holy See, requesting them to draw up a scheme for dividing the eight Vicariates into at least twelve Bishoprics. Dr. Wiseman had succeeded Bishop Griffiths as Pro-Vicar-Apostolic of the London District, and at an episcopal meeting held in November, 1847, a scheme to this effect was actually drawn up. At another, which opened in London on May 2nd, 1848, we were requested by the Holy See to present three names to Rome for a Coadjutor to Bishop Walsh in the Central District, and also names for a successor to Bishop Riddell. The difficulties before alluded to still existing, it was thought desirable to send some priest of standing and capacity to Rome to represent these difficulties, and act as an agent for pressing on the Hierarchy. After various proposals, Bishop Brown, of the Welsh District, suggested that a bishop would be the best envoy, and that I should be requested to undertake the work. As all the other bishops promptly united in this request, I put myself at the service of my brethren. I was to present a memorial to the Holy See, signed by all the bishops, exposing their sentiments with regard to the representations made at Rome by discontented persons ; I was to endeavour to obtain the early appointment of a new Vicar-Apostolic in the North, and I was to press on the affair of the Hierarchy. After making a few arrangements at Clifton, where I left Father Hendren as my Vicar-General, I started for Rome in the May of 1848. Whilst at Paris an attempt was made to establish the Red Republic, and I was an eye-witness of the chief scenes of that event. ·

The Republic established after the overthrow of King Louis Philippe was still on foot, under its three heads, and its Constituent Assembly : but committees of the Red Republican school were sitting here and there, with truculent fellows keeping sentry at the doors, red-capped, red-sashed—the very scum of the populace. The day · before the attempt they conducted a funeral procession of men who had died of their wounds received on the barricades in the first conflict. The whole affair was evidently a scene got up to move the populace. After the two hearses followed a number of wounded men, bandaged and crawling along; and then came the wives and children of the dead or wounded. The procession was flanked by Red Republicans in their ordinary clothes, but with red sashes, and some of them with red caps, carrying their muskets with fixed bayonets as a guard of honour. They were all of a piece, a dirty, ghastly procession; and in sepulchral tones they called upon all persons to take off their hats as they slowly passed through the streets.

The next morning I was taking an early walk when, crossing the Place de Carousel, I saw a group of some twenty men in blue blouses, with a tall, well-made man in their centre, evidently the commander of the group, a man of respectable as well as commanding appearance, head and shoulders above the rest, wearing also a blue blouse over his suit of black broadcloth. They at once recalled to my mind St. Real's description of the appearance and bearing of the conspirators of Venice before their outbreak. They walked on with rapid step, a firm purpose in each movement, their heads bent forward, their hands tightly grasping the bludgeons with which each of them was armed. I stood gazing at them, astonished that no one of the many passengers across the great Palace Square seemed to take any especial notice of them that the sentries of the National Guard and the police eyed this strange group with indifference. As to the regular army, it had been removed by the Republican Committee from the city to the suburbs. I was myself quite certain that these men were proceeding to some rendezvous, in contemplation of some desperate act; and this in connection with the Red Republican exhibition of the previous day.

Some hours later, I think about eleven o'clock, I was passing, in company with Dr. Nicholson, in a hired carriage by the doors of the Legislative Assembly, when we saw those very men, accompanied by others of a like description forcing their way into the House. The alarm was at once given, an officer seized our horse's head, turned us round and directed us to proceed back over the bridge. We did so, and on reaching the Place de la Concorde I got out, leaving my companion, who was of a nervous disposition, to go on his way, I myself being curious to see what would come next.

The drums were beating the reveille all over Paris, and regiments of National Guards and Gardes Mobiles (the latter consisting of the *gamins* of Paris, with no other military costume than their native rags, though completely armed and regimented) came marching into the Place de la Concorde and around the Legislative Chambers, till in little more than an hour there were 100,000 men under arms concentrated there. Placed on the high ground above the Place I saw all that passed. Beneath me the General commanding the National Guard dismounted, came in front of a regiment, waved his sword, and said a few words, when cries arose from the regiment full of bitter resentment and indignation. The men rushed from the front rank upon him, and tore off his epaulettes. In the next morning's papers I learnt that he had ordered them to ground arms and unfix bayonets : and that they had proclaimed him a traitor and renounced his command. He was in the conspiracy.

That evening I dined with a party at the Miss O'Farrell's, in the Rue Rivoli. As Paris was in a great state of excitement, when the rest of the party had retired I stayed for the protection of the ladies, in case of any emergency, till late at night. A few doors from them was the house occupied by Sobrière and his gang of conspirators. A considerable force was concentrated here, and the police entered Sobrière's house to arrest him and his companions. But for some time he was not to be found, till at last they pulled him down by the legs from inside the chimney.

The ladies and myself watched all that went on in the streets from the window. The National Guards exhibited their bourgeois qualities to perfection. They sang the first lines of " Mourir pour la Patrie," and other such rhapsodies —never getting beyond the second line from defect, it seemed, of memory—and they talked in short, hurried sentences with one another, as they marched along in very wavering lines.

One regiment had a soft-looking stout man at its head, with whom a man of the street tried to enter into controversy, asking what all this meant, etc.; to which the weary marching man replied, obviously annoyed, yet incapable of resisting the spirit of colloquy : " C'est assez qu'il y a quelque chose." Then, turning to his men, he said : " Ne repondez pas." But this questioner was tenacious, and a group was gathering around him. Suddenly a pistol was fired in the colonnade close to the house from which we were looking on, when the regiment, apparently without orders, halted, faced round to the colonnade, and levelled their muskets. I then requested the ladies to retire to the back room, which they did very reluctantly, wishing to see the continuation of the fun. The soldiers, however, soon recovered arms, faced to their first position, and marched on. At last we heard cries of " Vive la ligne !" and saw a regiment of the regular cavalry advancing amid the cheers of the people. It was evident the bulk of the population did not want the Red Republic. That night orders were given that the windows should be illuminated to furnish light to the streets for military operations. There was apprehension also lest the city should be set on fire. But, the night passed quietly, the chief conspirators being already under arrest at the Hôtel de Ville.

Next morning I went out early. The troops of the line were bivouacked in the streets ; and a strong force of cavalry guarded the approaches to the Place de la

Concorde and the Legislative Assembly. A few hours later there was a great concentration of the National Guard round the Hôtel de Ville, and I saw the prisoners carried off, accompanied by a strong force, to Vincennes. It was amusing to see the bourgeois soldiery carrying their loaves of bread, and sometimes their sausages, on their bayonets, where they roasted and fried in the sun, and were likely when eaten to require a good deal of help to get them down—from the wine-casks of the vivandières, who were in great force on the occasion. One poor girl I observed in her regimentals halting along with a lame leg, and with difficulty keeping her place. The citizen forces were in high glee at their bloodless victory.

I went on the same evening towards Marseilles, and at every town we came to the officials, with tri-coloured badges across their breasts, were vigilant in inspecting passports and examining the features of travellers.

[The history of the negotiations for the restoration of the English Hierarchy, and of the part taken therein by Bishop Ullathorne, has been published by him in his little volume, entitled "The Catholic Hierarchy in England," which is in great measure drawn from this portion of his autobiography, and which, therefore, it is unnecessary to reprint here. Although these negotiations were concluded in the year 1848, the Revolution in Rome and the absence of the Pope, from the November of that year until the April of 1850, necessarily suspended all business. It was not, therefore, until the September of 1850 that the Brief for erecting the Hierarchy was published. Before this took place, however, important changes had taken place in England. On the death of Bishop Walsh, Bishop Ullathorne was appointed to be his successor in the Midland District, in spite of his own remonstrances and his attachment to his first episcopal home.]

In leaving Clifton for Birmingham (he says), it was with painful regret that I parted with those of the clergy, and with those convents that had so zealously and loyally stood by me and supported me in my difficulties. My plans for Bristol and Clifton were coming into practical shape, and I greatly regretted leaving them unfinished. The Community of my own Dominican children, who had followed me from Coventry, and whom I had cherished with so peculiar a care, were now expanding in numbers and discipline, as well as in their works ; and these also I had to leave behind, promising, however, to establish a filiation of them under my own jurisdiction as soon as I could see my way to it. My last act was to commend them to the care and kindness of my successor, Bishop Hendren. My faithful friend and coadjutor, Mr. Estcourt, accompanied me to Birmingham, where he continued to act as my secretary.

On arriving at Birmingham I was received by the main body of the clergy of the district in St. Chad's Cathedral ; * Dr. Newman and the Oratorian Fathers, who had recently taken possession of Old Oscott, were also present. The clergy dined with me, and Dr. Weedall addressed me, in their name, in a beautiful discourse, in which his loyalty and that of his brethren, the clergy, to the one appointed over them by the Holy See, was cordially expressed and cordially received ; and what is much more, that loyalty was realised to the letter. At this crisis in my agitated life I found myself placed in a peaceful jurisdiction over a united clergy, conspicuous for their devotion to the episcopal authority. And my difficulties in my new responsibility were not so much of a moral as of a material character.† It is not my intention, however, to carry this

* August 30th, 1848.

† " From causes that need not be specified," says a writer in the *Oscotian* (July, 1866), " the temporal administration both of the

narrative into the administration of the Central District, or
of the Birmingham Diocese, nor will I dwell on the delirious
excitement into which the crafty writings of a certain
newspaper, and the intemperate letter of a certain states-
man, threw the minds of many of our countrymen during
the six months that followed the promulgation of our
Hierarchy in 1850. The first Provincial Synod of Westminster was held, for greater convenience, at St. Mary's
College, Oscott, during the month of July, 1852. The
conducting of this Synod was the masterpiece of Cardinal
Wiseman. He it was who drew up the Decrees, excepting

missions (in the Central District) and of Oscott College were sadly
embarrassed. Bishop Ullathorne saw but one way for restoring the
balance of accounts to a healthy condition. He resolved to take the
clergy into his confidence, and to gain their consent to a general
reduction of income." He moreover set before his people the
necessity for economy in a series of financial Pastorals, explaining that
so long as the existing embarrassments continued it was necessary
that instead of expending money on new undertakings every resource
should be husbanded till the claims of justice could be satisfied. It
is due to his memory to say that before his death the great burden
of debt which he had inherited from his predecessors was entirely
liquidated. At what personal sacrifices, and with what a persevering
exercise of prudence and self-control this was done, is probably known
to few. To confidential friends he has more than once said that so
great was his sense of the obligation that thus lay on him that if so
much as £5 came into his hands of which he was free to dispose, it
was always laid aside and applied to the one great object. "Never
despise small sums," he would say; "all great debts are discharged,
as they are for the most part incurred, by the accumulation of small
sums." How severely this duty, however, told on him, in his long
and patient labours to fulfil it, may be guessed from one passage in a
letter written to Bishop Brown (1856), in which, after giving certain
explanations, he thus concludes : " It has been my misery ever since I
wore a mitre to have to deal with debts and difficulties ; and if it had
not been for the good state of the clergy of this diocese I know not how
I could have gone through with it. Nothing but the inward fear that
it would be a cowardly running away from the will of God has kept
me from secretly departing from the diocese, and either burying
myself in some lonely place in a remote country, like the old hermits,
or labouring there for my daily bread. I am quite aware that this
was a temptation, and it has gone ; but it will show you how the
administration of this diocese has pressed on me."

the Constitutions for the Cathedral Chapters, which were committed to Bishop Grant and myself, though their main substance is the work of Bishop Grant. The unity and harmony which pervaded that Synod is one of the most delightful reminiscences of my episcopal life. Certainly no one but Cardinal Wiseman, who concentrated his whole capacious mind upon it in one of his happiest moods, could have brought it to so successful an issue, or have given it so great an amount of ecclesiastical splendour. And thus the rule and precedent was established for the conducting of our future Synods.

With the completion of our Hierarchal Order I close these reminiscences, uncertain whether at a future period I may resume them or not.

WORKS BY
ARCHBISHOP ULLATHORNE.

A Popular Edition of Archbishop Ullathorne's three great works:

"GROUNDWORK OF THE CHRISTIAN VIRTUES,"
"THE ENDOWMENTS OF MAN,"
AND
"CHRISTIAN PATIENCE."

Price 7s. each ; or 21s. the set of three volumes.

" A good and great work by a good and great man. This eloquent series of almost oracular utterances is a gift to men of all nations, all creeds, and all moral systems."—*The British Mail.*

" Books which breathe the spirit of the Apostles, but are ' down to date ' in all the accumulated facts and experiences of modern life."—*Weekly Register.*

ECCLESIASTICAL DISCOURSES.
Crown 8vo, 6s.

" We do not hesitate to say that by the publication of the discourses Dr. Ullathorne has conferred a boon, not only on the members of his own communion, but on all serious and thinking Englishmen. The treatment of the whole subject is masterly and exhaustive."—*Liverpool Daily Post.*

MEMOIR OF THE LATE BISHOP WILLSON,
First Bishop of Hobart, Tasmania.
With Portrait, 2s. 6d.

" The compassion of the Bishop for the convicts and the noble firmness with which he besieged the authorities, until he obtained an amelioration of their condition, will draw forth the admiration of every Philanthropist, Catholic, Protestant, or Agnostic."—*Weekly Register.*

CHARACTERISTICS FROM THE WRITINGS OF ARCHBISHOP ULLATHORNE,

Together with a Bibliographical Account of the Archbishop's Works. By the Rev. M. F. GLANCEY. Crown 8vo, cloth, 6s.

"The Archbishop's thoughts are expressed in choice, rich language, which, pleasant as it is to read, must have been additionally so to hear. We have perused this book with interest, and have no hesitation in recommending our readers to possess themselves of it."—*Birmingham Weekly Mercury.*

SELECTION

FROM

BURNS & OATES'

Catalogue

OF

PUBLICATIONS.

LONDON: BURNS AND OATES, L<small>D</small>.

28 ORCHARD ST., W., & 63 PATERNOSTER ROW, E.C.

NEW YORK: 12 EAST 17TH STREET.

1892.

NEW BOOKS.

Saint Ignatius Loyola and The Early Jesuits. By STEWART ROSE. With more than 100 Illustrations by H.W. and H.C. Brewer and L. Wain. The whole produced under the immediate superintendence of the Rev. W. H. Eyre, S.J. Super Royal 8vo. Handsomely bound in Cloth, extra gilt. Price 15s. net.

"This magnificent volume is one of which Catholics have justly reason to be proud. Its historical as well as its literary value is very great, and the illustrations from the pencils of Mr. Louis Wain and Messrs. H. W. and H. C. Brewer are models of what the illustrations of such a book should be. We hope that this book will be found in every Catholic drawing-room, as a proof that 'we Catholics' are in no way behind those around us in the beauty of the illustrated books that issue from our hands, or in the interest which is added to the subject by a skilful pen and finished style."—*Month.*

The Letters of the late Father George Porter, S.J., Archbishop of Bombay. Demy 8vo. Cloth, 7s. 6d.

"Brimful of good things. . . . Will instruct and amuse widely-differing classes of readers. In them the priest will find a storehouse of hints on matters spiritual ; from them the layman will reap crisp and clear information on many ecclesiastical points ; the critic can listen to frank opinions of literature of every shade ; and the general reader can enjoy the choice bits of description and morsels of humour scattered lavishly through the book. It would be hard to find a correspondence which, in style, more closely observes the golden rule of letter-writing—'write as you speak.'"
—*Tablet.*

Ireland and St. Patrick. A study of the Saint's character, and of the results of his Apostolate. By the Rev. W. B. MORRIS, of the Oratory. Crown 8vo. Cloth, 5s.

May be called a sequel to the author's "Life of St. Patrick," being a study chiefly in the 5th, 12th, 17th, and 19th centuries of those influences which have preserved the Faith in Ireland, and obtained for that country the exalted, if unintentional praise of Lord Macaulay, when he says, "Alone amongst the Northern Nations Ireland adhered to the Ancient Faith."

Immediately.

The Wisdom and Wit of Blessed Thomas More. Edited, with Introduction, by the Rev. T. E. BRIDGETT, C.SS.R., author of "Life of Blessed Thomas More," "Life of Blessed John Fisher," &c.

Aquinas Ethicus; or, the Moral Teaching of St. Thomas. A translation of the principal portions of the second part of the *Summa Theologica*, with Notes. By the Rev. JOSEPH RICKABY, S.J. Quarterly Series.

The Spirit of St. Ignatius, Founder of the Society of Jesus. Translated from the French of the Rev. Fr. XAVIER DE FRANCIOSI, of the same Society.

Succat ; or, Sixty Years of the Life of St. Patrick. By the Very Rev. Mgr. ROBERT GRADWELL.

SELECTION

FROM

BURNS AND OATES' CATALOGUE
OF PUBLICATIONS.

—❯❯❯✦❮❮❮—

ALLIES, T. W. (K.C. S.G.)

Formation of Christendom. Vols. I., II., and III.,
(all out of print.) . . . . . .
Church and State as seen in the Formation of Christen-
dom, 8vo, pp. 472, cloth   .   (out of print.)
The Throne of the Fisherman, built by the Carpenter's
Son, the Root, the Bond, and the Crown of Christ-
endom. Demy 8vo   .   .   .   .   . ; £0 10 6
The Holy See and the Wandering of the Nations.
Demy 8vo. 0 10 6
Peter's Rock in Mohammed's Flood. Demy 8vo. . 0 10 6

"It would be quite superfluous at this hour of the day to recommend
Mr. Allies' writings to English Catholics. Those of our readers who
remember the article on his writings in the *Katholik*, know that
he is esteemed in Germany as one of our foremost writers."—
Dublin Review.

ALLIES, MARY.

Leaves from St. John Chrysostom, With introduction
by T. W. Allies, K.C.S.G. Crown 8vo, cloth   . 0 6 0
"Miss Allies' 'Leaves' are delightful reading; the English is remarkably pure and graceful; page after page reads as if it were
original. No commentator, Catholic or Protestant, has ever sur-
passed St. John Chrysostom in the knowledge of Holy Scripture,
and his learning was of a kind which is of service now as it was at
the time when the inhabitants of a great city hung on his words."—
Tablet.

ALLNATT, C. F. B.

Cathedra Petri. Third and Enlarged Edition. Cloth 0 6 0
"Invaluable to the controversialist and the theologian, and most
useful for educated men inquiring after truth or anxious to know
the positive testimony of Christian antiquity in favour of Papal
claims."—*Month.*

Which is the True Church ? Fifth Edition   .   . 0 1 4
The Church and the Sects 0 1 0
          Ditto,   Ditto.   Second Series. .   .   . 0 1 6

ANNUS SANCTUS:

Hymns of the Church for the Ecclesiastical Year.
Translated from the Sacred Offices by various
Authors, with Modern, Original, and other Hymns,
and an Appendix of Earlier Versions. Selected and
Arranged by ORBY SHIPLEY, M.A.
Plain Cloth, lettered 0 5 6
Edition de luxe 0 10 6

ANSWERS TO ATHEISTS : OR NOTES ON

Ingersoll. By the Rev. A. Lambert, (over 100,000 copies
sold in America). Tenth edition. Paper. . . . £0 0 6
Cloth 0 1 0

B. N.

The Jesuits : their Foundation and History. 2 vols.
crown 8vo, cloth, red edges 0 15 0

"The book is just what it professes to be—*a popular history*,
drawn from well-known sources," &c.—*Month.*

BAKER, VEN. FATHER AUGUSTIN.

Holy Wisdom ; or, Directions for the Prayer of Contemplation, &c. Extracted from Treatises written
by the Ven. Father F. Augustin Baker, O.S.B., and
edited by Abbot Sweeney, D.D. Beautifully bound
in half leather 0 6 0

" We earnestly recommend this most beautiful work to all our
readers. We are sure that every community will use it as a constant
manual. If any persons have friends in convents, we cannot conceive
a better present they can make them, or a better claim they can have
on their prayers, than by providing them with a copy."—*Weekly
Register.*

BORROMEO, LIFE OF ST. CHARLES.

From the Italian of Peter Guissano. 2 vols. . . 0 15 0

" A standard work, which has stood the test of succeeding ages; it
is certainly the finest work on St. Charles in an English dress."—
Tablet.

BOWDEN, REV. H. S. (of the Oratory) Edited by.

Dante's Divina Commedia : Its scope and value.
From the German of FRANCIS HETTINGER, D.D.
With an engraving of Dante. Crown 8vo . . 0 10 6

"All that Venturi attempted to do has been now approached with
far greater power and learning by Dr. Hettinger, who, as the author
of the 'Apologie des Christenthums,' and as a great Catholic theologian, is eminently well qualified for the task he has undertaken."—
The Saturday Review.

BRIDGETT, REV. T. E. (C.SS.R.).

Discipline of Drink 0 3 6

"The historical information with which the book abounds gives
evidence of deep research and patient study, and imparts a per-
manent interest to the volume, which will elevate it to a position
of authority and importance enjoyed by few of its compeers."—*The
Arrow.*

Our Lady's Dowry ; how England Won that Title.
New and Enlarged Edition. 0 5 0

"This book is the ablest vindication of Catholic devotion to Our
Lady, drawn from tradition, that we know of in the English language."—*Tablet.*

BRIDGETT, REV. T. E. (C.SS.R.)—*continued*.

Ritual of the New Testament. An essay on the principles and origin of Catholic Ritual in reference to the New Testament. Third edition . . . £0 5 0

The Life of the Blessed John Fisher. With a reproduction of the famous portrait of Blessed JOHN FISHER by HOLBEIN, and other Illustrations. 2nd Ed.   0 7 6
"The Life of Blessed John Fisher could hardly fail to be interesting and instructive. Sketched by Father Bridgett's practised pen, the portrait of this holy martyr is no less vividly displayed in the printed pages of the book than in the wonderful picture of Holbein, which forms the frontispiece."—*Tablet.*

The True Story of the Catholic Hierarchy deposed by Queen Elizabeth, with fuller Memoirs of its Last Two Survivors. By the Rev. T. E. BRIDGETT, C.SS.R., and the late Rev. T. F. KNOX, D.D., of the London Oratory. Crown 8vo, cloth,   0 7 6
"We gladly acknowledge the value of this work on a subject which has been obscured by prejudice and carelessness."—*Saturday Review.*

The Life and Writings of Sir Thomas More, Lord Chancellor of England and Martyr under Henry VIII. With Portrait of the Martyr taken from the Crayon Sketch made by Holbein in 1527 .   0 7 6
"Father Bridgett has followed up his valuable Life of Bishop Fisher with a still more valuable Life of Thomas More. It is, as the title declares, a study not only of the life, but also of the writings of Sir Thomas. Father Bridgett has considered him from every point of view, and the result is, it seems to us, a more complete and finished portrait of the man, mentally and physically, than has been hitherto presented."—*Athenæum.*

BRIDGETT, REV. T. E. (C.SS.R.), Edited by.

Souls Departed. By CARDINAL ALLEN. First published in 1565, now edited in modern spelling by the Rev. T. E. Bridgett 0 6 0

BROWNE, REV. R. D.:

Plain Sermons. Sixty-eight Plain Sermons on the Fundamental Truths of the Catholic Church. Crown 8vo 0 6 0
"These are good sermons. . . . The great merit of which is that they might be read *verbatim* to any congregation, and they would be understood and appreciated by the uneducated almost as fully as by the cultured. They have been carefully put together; their language is simple and their matter is solid."—*Catholic News.*

BUCKLER, REV. H. REGINALD (O.P.)

The Perfection of Man by Charity: a Spiritual Treatise. Crown 8vo, cloth. 0 5 0
"We have read this unpretending, but solid and edifying work, with much pleasure, and heartily commend it to our readers. . . . Its scope is sufficiently explained by the title."—*The Month.*

CASWALL, FATHER.

Catholic Latin Instructor in the Principal Church Offices and Devotions, for the Use of Choirs, Convents, and Mission Schools, and for Self-Teaching.
1 vol., complete £0 3 6
Or Part I., containing Benediction, Mass, Serving at Mass, and various Latin Prayers in ordinary use . 0 1 6
May Pageant : A Tale of Tintern. (A Poem) Second edition 0 2 0
Poems 0 5 0
Lyra Catholica, containing all the Breviary and Missal Hymns, with others from various sources. 32mo, cloth, red edges 0 2 6

CATHOLIC BELIEF: OR, A SHORT AND

Simple Exposition of Catholic Doctrine. By the Very Rev. Joseph Faà di Bruno, D.D. Tenth edition . . . . . Price 6d.; post free, 0 0 8½
Cloth, lettered, ... 0 0 10
Also an edition on better paper and bound in cloth, with gilt lettering and steel frontispiece 0 2 0

CHALLONER, BISHOP.

Meditations for every day in the year. New edition. Revised and edited by the Right Rev. John Virtue, D.D., Bishop of Portsmouth, 8vo. 6th edition . 0 3 0
And in other bindings.

COLERIDGE, REV. H. J. (S.J.) *(See Quarterly Series.)*

DEVAS, C. S.

Studies of Family Life : a contribution to Social Science. Crown 8vo 0 5 0
"We recommend these pages and the remarkable evidence brought together in them to the careful attention of all who are interested in the well-being of our common humanity."—*Guardian.*
"Both thoughtful and stimulating."—*Saturday Review.*

DRANE, AUGUSTA THEODOSIA, Edited by.

The Autobiography of Archbishop Ullathorne. Demy 8vo., cloth 0 7 6
"Admirably edited and excellently produced."—*Weekly Register.*
"Told in manly, vigorous English, and filled with bits of descriptions of sea-life that are quite as good as anything Dana ever wrote, and characterized by a certain quaint humour that has frequently reminded us of the writings of Charles Waterton, the naturalist ; this autobiography is certainly the most entertaining book that has been added to Catholic literature for many a long year."—*Caxton Review.*

EYRE, MOST REV. CHARLES, (Abp. of Glasgow).

The History of St. Cuthbert : or, An Account of his Life, Decease, and Miracles. Third edition. Illustrated with maps, charts, &c., and handsomely bound in cloth. Royal 8vo 0 14 0
"A handsome, well appointed volume, in every way worthy of its illustrious subject. . . . The chief impression of the whole is the picture of a great and good man drawn by a sympathetic hand."—*Spectator.*

FABER, REV. FREDERICK WILLIAM, (D.D.)

All for Jesus	£0	5	o
Bethlehem	o	7	o
Blessed Sacrament	o	7	6
Creator and Creature	o	6	o
Ethel's Book of the Angels	o	5	o
Foot of the Cross	o	6	o
Growth in Holiness	o	6	o
Hymns	o	6	o
Notes on Doctrinal and Spiritual Subjects, 2 vols. each	o	5	o
Poems (a new edition in preparation)			
Precious Blood	o	5	o
Sir Lancelot	o	5	o
Spiritual Conferences	o	6	o
Life and Letters of Frederick William Faber, D.D., Priest of the Oratory of St. Philip Neri. By John Edward Bowden of the same Congregation	o	6	o

FOLEY, REV. HENRY, (S.J.)

Records of the English Province of the Society of Jesus. Vol. I., Series I.	net	1	6	o
Vol. II., Series II., III., IV.	net	1	6	o
Vol. III., Series V., VI., VII., VIII.	net	1	10	o
Vol. IV. Series IX., X., XI.	net	1	6	o
Vol. V., Series XII. with nine Photographs of Martyrs	net	1	10	o
Vol. VI., Diary and Pilgrim-Book of the English College, Rome. The Diary from 1579 to 1773, with Biographical and Historical Notes. The Pilgrim-Book of the Ancient English Hospice attached to the College from 1580 to 1656, with Historical Notes	net	1	6	o
Vol. VII. Part the First: General Statistics of the Province; and Collectanea, giving Biographical Notices of its Members and of many Irish and Scotch Jesuits. With 20 Photographs	net	1	6	o
Vol. VII. Part the Second: Collectanea, Completed; With Appendices. Catalogues of Assumed and Real Names: Annual Letters; Biographies and Miscellanea	net	1	6	o

"As a biographical dictionary of English Jesuits, it deserves a place in every well-selected library, and, as a collection of marvellous occurrences, persecutions, martyrdoms, and evidences of the results of faith, amongst the books of all who belong to the Catholic Church."—*Genealogist.*

FORMBY, REV. HENRY.

Monotheism: in the main derived from the Hebrew nation and the Law of Moses. The Primitive Religion of the City of Rome. An historical Investigation. Demy 8vo.	o	5	o

FRANCIS DE SALES, ST.: THE WORKS OF.
Translated into the English Language by the Very Rev.
Canon Mackey, O.S.B., under the direction of the
Right Rev. Bishop Hedley, O.S.B. .   .   .
    Vol. I.   Letters to Persons in the World.   Cloth   . £0   6   0
"The letters must be read in order to comprehend the charm and
sweetness of their style."—*Tablet.*
    Vol. II.—The Treatise on the Love of God.   Father
    Carr's translation of 1630 has been taken as a basis,
    but it has been modernized and thoroughly revised
    and corrected.   0   9   0
"To those who are seeking perfection by the path of contemplation
this volume will be an armoury of help."—*Saturday Review.*
    Vol. III.   The Catholic Controversy.   .   .   0   6   0
"No one who has not read it can conceive how clear, how convinc-
ing, and how well adapted to our present needs are these controversial
'leaves.'"—*Tablet.*
    Vol. IV.   Letters to Persons in Religion, with intro-
    duction by Bishop Hedley on "St. Francis de Sales
    and the Religious State."   0   6   0
"The sincere piety and goodness, the grave wisdom, the knowledge
of human nature, the tenderness for its weakness, and the desire for
its perfection that pervade the letters, make them pregnant of instruction for all serious persons. The translation and editing have
been admirably done."—*Scotsman.*
    ⁎ Other vols. in preparation.

GALLWEY, REV. PETER, (S.J.)
Precious Pearl of Hope in the Mercy of God, The.
Translated from the Italian.   With Preface by the
Rev. Father Gallwey.   Cloth   0   4   6
Lectures on Ritualism and on the Anglican Orders.
2 vols.   (Or may be had separately.)   .   .   0   8   0
Salvage from the Wreck.   A few Memories of the
Dead, preserved in Funeral Discourses.   With
Portraits.   Crown 8vo.   0   7   6

GIBSON, REV. H.
Catechism Made Easy.   Being an Explanation of the
Christian Doctrine.   Eighth edition.   2 vols., cloth   0   7   6
"This work must be of priceless worth to any who are engaged in
any form of catechetical instruction. It is the best book of the kind
that we have seen in English."—*Irish Monthly.*

GILLOW, JOSEPH.
Literary and Biographical History, or, Bibliographical
Dictionary of the English Catholics.   From the
Breach with Rome, in 1534, to the Present Time.
Vols. I., II. and III. cloth, demy 8vo .   . *each.*   0 15   0
    ⁎ Other vols. in preparation.
"The patient research of Mr. Gillow, his conscientious record of
minute particulars, and especially his exhaustive bibliographical information in connection with each name, are beyond praise."—*British
Quarterly Review.*
    The Haydock Papers.   Illustrated.   Demy 8vo.   .   0   7   6.
" We commend this collection to the attention of every one that
is interested in the records of the sufferings and struggles of our
ancestors to hand down the faith to their children. It is in the
perusal of such details that we bring home to ourselves the truly
heroic sacrifices that our forefathers endured in those dark and
dismal times."—*Tablet.*

GROWTH IN THE KNOWLEDGE OF OUR LORD.

Meditations for every Day in the Year, exclusive of those for Festivals, Days of Retreat, &c. Adapted from the original of Abbé de Brandt, by Sister Mary Fidelis. A new and Improved Edition, in 3 Vols. Sold only in sets. Price per set, ... £1 2 6

"The praise, though high, bestowed on these excellent meditations by the Bishop of Salford is well deserved. The language, like good spectacles, spreads treasures before our vision without attracting attention to itself."—*Dublin Review.*

HEDLEY, BISHOP.

Our Divine Saviour, and other Discourses. Crown 8vo. . . . . o 6 o

"A distinct and noteworthy feature of these sermons is, we certainly think, their freshness—freshness of thought, treatment, and style; nowhere do we meet pulpit commonplace or hackneyed phrase —everywhere, on the contrary, it is the heart of the preacher pouring out to his flock his own deep convictions, enforcing them from the 'Treasures, old and new,' of a cultivated mind."—*Dublin Review.*

HUMPHREY, REV. W. (S.J.)

Suarez on the Religious State: A Digest of the Doctrine contained in his Treatise, "De Statû Religionis." 3 vols., pp. 1200. Cloth, roy. 8vo. . . . 1 10 o

"This laborious and skilfully executed work is a distinct addition to English theological literature. Father Humphrey's style is quiet, methodical, precise, and as clear as the subject admits. Every one will be struck with the air of legal exposition which pervades the book. He takes a grip of his author, under which the text yields up every atom of its meaning and force."—*Dublin Review.*

The One Mediator; or, Sacrifice and Sacraments. Crown 8vo, cloth . . . . o 5 o

"An exceedingly accurate theological exposition of doctrines which are the life of Christianity and which make up the soul of the Christian religion. . . . A profound work, but so far from being dark, obscure, and of metaphysical difficulty, the meaning of each paragraph shines with a crystalline clearness."—*Tablet.*

KING, FRANCIS.

The Church of my Baptism, and why I returned to it. Crown 8vo, cloth . . . . . o 2 6

" A book of the higher controversial criticism. Its literary style is good, its controversial manner excellent, and its writer's emphasis does not escape in italics and notes of exclamation, but is all reserved for lucid and cogent reasoning. Altogether a book of an excellent spirit, written with freshness and distinction."—*Weekly Register.*

LEDOUX, REV. S. M.

History of the Seven Holy Founders of the Order of the Servants of Mary. Crown 8vo, cloth . . o 4 6

"Throws a full light upon the Seven Saints recently canonized, whom we see as they really were. All that was marvellous in their call, their works, and their death is given with the charm of a picturesque and speaking style."—*Messenger of the Sacred Heart.*

LEE, REV. F. G., D.D. (of All Saints, Lambeth.)

Edward the Sixth : Supreme Head. Second edition.
Crown 8vo   .   .   .   .   .   ,   .   .   £0   6   0

"In vivid interest and in literary power, no less than in solid historical value, Dr. Lee's present work comes fully up to the standard of its predecessors ; and to say that is to bestow high praise. The book evinces Dr. Lee's customary diligence of research in amassing facts, and his rare artistic power in welding them into a harmonious and effective whole."—*John Bull.*

LIGUORI, ST. ALPHONSUS.

New and Improved Translation of the Complete Works of St. Alphonsus, edited by the late Bishop Coffin :—
Vol. I. The Christian Virtues, and the Means for Obtaining them. Cloth   0   3   0
Or separately :—
  1. The Love of our Lord Jesus Christ   .   .   .   0   1   0
  2. Treatise on Prayer. *(In the ordinary editions a great part of this work is omitted)*   .   .   .   0   1   0
  3. A Christian's rule of Life   0   1   0
Vol. II. The Mysteries of the Faith—The Incarnation ; containing Meditations and Devotions on the Birth and Infancy of Jesus Christ, &c., suited for Advent and Christmas.   0   2   6
Vol. III. The Mysteries of the Faith—The Blessed Sacrament   0   2   6
Vol. IV. Eternal Truths—Preparation for Death   .   0   2   6
Vol. V. The Redemption—Meditations on the Passion.   0   2   6
Vol. VI. Glories of Mary. New edition   .   .   .   0   3   6

LIVIUS, REV. T. (M.A., C.SS.R.)

St. Peter, Bishop of Rome ; or, the Roman Episcopate of the Prince of the Apostles, proved from the Fathers, History and Chronology, and illustrated by arguments from other sources. Dedicated to his Eminence Cardinal Newman. Demy 8vo, cloth   .   0   12   0

"A book which deserves careful attention. In respect of literary qualities, such as effective arrangement, and correct and lucid diction, this essay, by an English Catholic scholar, is not unworthy of Cardinal Newman, to whom it is dedicated."—*The Sun.*

Explanation of the Psalms and Canticles in the Divine Office. By ST. ALPHONSUS LIGUORI. Translated from the Italian by THOMAS LIVIUS, C.SS.R. With a Preface by his Eminence Cardinal MANNING. Crown 8vo, cloth   0   7   6

"To nuns and others who know little or no Latin, the book will be of immense importance."—*Dublin Review.*
"Father Livius has in our opinion even improved on the original, so far as the arrangement of the book goes. New priests will find it especially useful."—*Month.*

Mary in the Epistles ; or, The Implicit Teaching of the Apostles concerning the Blessed Virgin, set forth in devout comments on their writings. Illustrated from Fathers and other Authors, and prefaced by introductory Chapters. Crown 8vo. Cloth   0   5   0

MANNING, CARDINAL.

England and Christendom	£0 10	6
Four Great Evils of the Day. 5th edition. Wrapper	0 2	6
Cloth	0 3	6
Fourfold Sovereignty of God. 3rd edition. Wrapper	0 2	6
Cloth	0 3	6
Glories of the Sacred Heart. 5th edition	0 6	0
Grounds of Faith. Cloth. 9th edition. Wrapper	0 1	0
Cloth	0 1	6
Independence of the Holy See. 2nd edition . .	0 5	0
Internal Mission of the Holy Ghost. 5th edition .	0 8	6
Miscellanies. 3 vols. . . . . the set	0 18	0
National Education. Wrapper	0 2	0
Cloth	0 2	6
Petri Privilegium	0 10	6
Religio Viatoris. 4th edition, cloth . . .	0 2	0
Wrapper	0 1	0
Sermons on Ecclesiastical Subjects. Vols. I., II.. and III. . . . . . . each	0 6	0
Sin and its Consequences. 7th edition . . .	0 6	0
Temporal Mission of the Holy Ghost. 3rd edition	0 8	6
Temporal Power of the Pope. 3rd edition . .	0 5	0
True Story of the Vatican Council. 2nd edition .	0 5	0
The Eternal Priesthood. 9th edition . . .	0 2	6
The Office of the Church in the Higher Catholic Education. A Pastoral Letter . . .	0 0	6
Workings of the Holy Spirit in the Church of England. Reprint of a letter addressed to Dr. Pusey in 1864 Wrapper	0 1	0
Cloth	0 1	6
Lost Sheep Found. A Sermon	0 0	6
On Education	0 0	3
Rights and Dignity of Labour	0 0	1

The Westminster Series

In handy pocket size.

The Blessed Sacrament, the Centre of Immutable Truth, Wrapper	0 0	6
Confidence in God. Wrapper . . .	0 1	0
Or the two bound together. Cloth . .	0 2	0
Holy Gospel of Our Lord Jesus Christ according to St. John. Cloth	0 1	0
Holy Ghost the Sanctifier. Cloth . . .	0 2	0
Love of Jesus to Penitents. Wrapper . .	0 1	0
Cloth	0 1	6
Office of the Holy Ghost under the Gospel. Cloth	0 1	0

MANNING, CARDINAL, Edited by.

Life of the Curé of Ars. Popular edition . . .	0 2	6

MEDAILLE, REV. P.

Meditations on the Gospels for Every Day in the Year. Translated into English from the new Edition, enlarged by the Besançon Missionaries, under the direction of the Rev. W. H. Eyre, S.J. Cloth £0 6 0
(This work has already been translated into Latin, Italian, Spanish, German, and Dutch.)
"We have carefully examined these Meditations, and are fain to confess that we admire them very much. They are short, succinct, pithy, always to the point, and wonderfully suggestive."—*Tablet.*

MIVART, PROF. ST. GEORGE (M.D., F.R.S.)

Nature and Thought. Second edition .   .   .   0 4 0
"The complete command of the subject, the wide grasp, the subtlety, the readiness of illustration, the grace of style, contrive to render this one of the most admirable books of its class."—*British Quarterly Review.*
A Philosophical Catechism. Fifth edition .   0 1 0
"It should become the *vade mecum* of Catholic students."—*Tablet.*

MONTGOMERY, HON. MRS.

Approved by the Most Rev. G. Porter, Achbp. of Bombay.
The Divine Sequence : A Treatise on Creation and Redemption. Cloth 0 3 6
The Eternal Years. With an Introduction by the Most Rev. G. Porter, Achbp. of Bombay. Cloth. 0 3 6
The Divine Ideal. Cloth 0 3 6
"A work of original thought carefully developed and expressed in lucid and richly imaged style."—*Tablet.*
"The writing of a pious, thoughtful, earnest woman."—*Church Review.*
"Full of truth, and sound reason, and confidence."—*American Catholic Book News.*

MORRIS, REV. JOHN (S.J.)

Letter Books of Sir Amias Poulet, keeper of Mary Queen of Scots. Demy 8vo 0 10 6
Two Missionaries under Elizabeth 0 14 0
The Catholics under Elizabeth 0 14 0
The Life of Father John Gerard, S.J. Third edition, rewritten and enlarged 0 14 0
The Life and Martyrdom of St. Thomas Becket. Second and enlarged edition. In one volume, large post 8vo, cloth, pp. xxxvi., 632, ...   0 12 6
or bound in two parts, cloth 0 13 0

MORRIS, REV. W. B. (of the Oratory.)

The Life of St. Patrick, Apostle of Ireland. Fourth edition. Crown 8vo, cloth 0 5 0
"The secret of Father Morris's success is, that he has got the proper key to life the extraordinary, the mysterious life and character of St. Patrick. He has taken the Saint's own authentic writings as the foundation whereon to build."—*Irish Ecclesiastical Record.*
"Promises to become the standard biography of Ireland's Apostle. For clear statement of facts, and calm judicious discussion of controverted points, it surpasses any work we know of in the literature of the subject."—*American Catholic Quarterly.*

NEWMAN, CARDINAL.

Church of the Fathers £0 4 0
Prices of other works by Cardinal Newman on
application.

PAGANI, VERY REV. JOHN BAPTIST,

The Science of the Saints in Practice. By John Bap-
tist Pagani, Second General of the Institute of
Charity. Complete in three volumes. Vol. 1,
January to April. Vol. 2, May to August. Vol. 3,
September to December . . . . each   0 5 0

"'The Science of the Saints' is a practical treatise on the principal
Christian virtues, abundantly illustrated with interesting examples
from Holy Scripture as well as from the Lives of the Saints. Written
chiefly for devout souls, such as are trying to live an interior and super-
natural life by following in the footsteps of our Lord and His saints,
this work is eminently adapted for the use of ecclesiastics and of religious communities."—*Irish Ecclesiastical Record,*

PAYNE, JOHN ORLEBAR, (M.A.)

Records of the English Catholics of 1715. Demy 8vo.
Half-bound, gilt top 0 15 0

"A book of the kind Mr. Payne has given us would have astonished Bishop Milner or Dr. Lingard. They would have treasured it,
for both of them knew the value of minute fragments of historical
information. The Editor has derived nearly the whole of the information which he has given, from unprinted sources, and we must
congratulate him on having found a few incidents here and there
which may bring the old times back before us in a most touching
manner."—*Tablet.*

English Catholic Non-Jurors of 1715. Being a Summary of the Register of their Estates, with Genea-
logical and other Notes, and an Appendix of
Unpublished Documents in the Public Record
Office. In one Volume. Demy 8vo. . .   1 1 0

"Most carefully and creditably brought out . . . From first to last,
full of social interest and biographical details, for which we may
search in vain elsewhere."—*Antiquarian Magazine.*

Old English Catholic Missions. Demy 8vo, half-bound.   0 7 6

"A book to hunt about in for curious odds and ends."—*Saturday
Review.*

"These registers tell us in their too brief records, teeming with interest for all their scantiness, many a tale of patient heroism."—*Tablet.*

POOR SISTERS OF NAZARETH, THE.

A descriptive Sketch of Convent Life. By Alice Meynell.
Profusely Illustrated with Drawings especially made
by George Lambert. Large 4to. Boards . .   0 2 6
A limited number of copies are also issued as an *Edition
de Luxe,* containing proofs of the illustrations printed
on one side only of the paper, and handsomely bound.   0 10 6

"Bound in a most artistic cover, illustrated with a naturalness
that could only have been born of powerful sympathy; printed clearly,
neatly, and on excellent paper, and written with the point, aptness,
and ripeness of style which we have learnt to associate with Mrs.
Meynell's literature."—*Tablet.*

QUARTERLY SERIES Edited by the Rev. H. J.
Coleridge, S.J. 77 volumes published to date.

Selection.

The Life and Letters of St. Francis Xavier. By the
Rev. H. J. Coleridge, S.J. 2 vols.   .   .   .   £0 10 6
The History of the Sacred Passion. By Father Luis
de la Palma, of the Society of Jesus. Translated
from the Spanish. 0 5 0
The Life of Dona Louisa de Carvajal. By Lady
Georgiana Fullerton. Small edition   .   .   .   0 3 6
The Life and Letters of St. Teresa. 3 vols. By Rev.
H. J. Coleridge, S.J.   .   .   .   .   . each   0 7 6
The Life of Mary Ward. By Mary Catherine Elizabeth
Chalmers, of the Institute of the Blessed Virgin.
Edited by the Rev. H. J. Coleridge, S.J. 2 vols.   0 15 0
The Return of the King. Discourses on the Latter
Days. By the Rev. H. J. Coleridge, S.J. .   .   0 7 6
Pious Affections towards God and the Saints. Medi-
tations for every Day in the Year, and for the
Principal Festivals. From the Latin of the Ven.
Nicolas Lancicius, S.J. 0 7 6
The Life and Teaching of Jesus Christ in Meditations
for Every Day in the Year. By Fr. Nicolas
Avancino, S.J. Two vols. 0 10 6
The Baptism of the King : Considerations on the Sacred
Passion. By the Rev. H. J. Coleridge, S.J. .   0 7 6
The Mother of the King.   Mary during the Life of
Our Lord. 0 7 6
The Hours of the Passion. Taken from the *Life of
Christ* by Ludolph the Saxon 0 7 6
The Mother of the Church. Mary during the first
Apostolic Age 0 6 0
The Life of St. Bridget of Sweden. By the late F. J.
M. A. Partridge 0 6 0
The Teachings and Counsels of St. Francis Xavier.
From his Letters 0 5 0
Garcia Moreno, President of Ecuador. 1821—1875.
From the French of the Rev. P. A. Berthe, C.SS.R.
By Lady Herbert 0 7 6
The Life of St. Alonso Rodriguez. By Francis
Goldie, of the Society of Jesus 0 7 6
Letters of St. Augustine. Selected and arranged by
Mary H. Allies 0 6 6
A Martyr from the Quarter-Deck—Alexis Clerc, S.J.
By Lady Herbert 0 5 0
Acts of the English Martyrs, hitherto unpublished.
By the Rev. John H. Pollen, S.J., with a Preface
by the Rev. John Morris, S.J. 0 7 6
Life of St. Francis di Geronimo, S.J. By A. M. Clarke.   0 7 6

QUARTERLY SERIES—*(selection) continued.*
VOLUMES ON THE LIFE OF OUR LORD.
The Holy Infancy.

	£	s.	d.
The Preparation of the Incarnation	£0	7	6
The Nine Months. The Life of our Lord in the Womb.	0	7	6
The Thirty Years. Our Lord's Infancy and Early Life.	0	7	6

The Public Life of Our Lord.

The Ministry of St. John Baptist . . .	0	6	6
The Preaching of the Beatitudes	0	6	6
The Sermon on the Mount. Continued. 2 Parts, each	0	6	6
The Training of the Apostles. Parts I., II., III., IV. each	0	6	6
The Preaching of the Cross. Part I. . . .	0	6	6
The Preaching of the Cross. Parts II., III. each	0	6	0
Passiontide. Parts I. II. and III., each . . .	0	6	6
Chapters on the Parables of Our Lord . . .	0	7	6

Introductory Volumes.

The Life of our Life. Harmony of the Life of Our Lord, with Introductory Chapters and Indices. Second edition. Two vols.	0	15	0
The Works and Words of our Saviour, gathered from the Four Gospels	0	7	6
The Story of the Gospels. Harmonised for Meditation	0	7	6

Full lists on application.

RAM, MRS. ABEL.
"Emmanuel." Being the Life of Our Lord Jesus Christ reproduced in the Mysteries of the Tabernacle. By Mrs. Abel Ram, author of "The most Beautiful among the Children of Men," &c. Crown 8vo, cloth   0   5   0
"The foundation of the structure is laid with the greatest skill and the deepest knowledge of what constitutes true religion, and every chapter ends with an eloquent and soul-inspiring appeal for one or other of the virtues which the different scenes in the life of Our Saviour set prominently into view."—*Catholic Times.*

RICHARDS, REV. WALTER J. B. (D.D.)
Manual of Scripture History. Being an Analysis of the Historical Books of the Old Testament. By Rev. W. J. B. Richards, D.D., Oblate of St. Charles; Inspector of Schools in the Diocese of Westminster. Cloth.   0   4   0
"Happy indeed will those children and young persons be who acquire in their early days the inestimably precious knowledge which these books impart."—*Tablet.*

RYDER, REV. H. I. D. (of the Oratory.)
Catholic Controversy: A Reply to Dr. Littledale's "Plain Reasons." Sixth edition   0   2   6
"Father Ryder of the Birmingham Oratory, has now furnished in a small volume a masterly reply to this assailant from without. The lighter charms of a brilliant and graceful style are added to the solid merits of this handbook of contemporary controversy."—*Irish Monthly.*

SOULIER, REV. P.
Life of St. Philip Benizi, of the Order of the Servants of Mary. Crown 8vo   0   8   0
"A clear and interesting account of the life and labours of this eminent Servant of Mary."—*American Catholic Quarterly.*
"Very scholar-like, devout and complete."—*Dublin Review.*

STANTON, REV. R. (of the Oratory.)
A Menology of England and Wales ; or, Brief Mem-
orials of the British and English Saints, arranged
according to the Calendar. Together with the Martyrs of the 16th and 17th centuries. Compiled by
order of the Cardinal Archbishop and the Bishops
of the Province of Westminster. Demy 8vo, cloth   £0 14 0

THOMPSON, EDWARD HEALY, (M.A.)
The Life of Jean-Jacques Olier, Founder of the
Seminary of St. Sulpice. New and Enlarged Edition.
Post 8vo, cloth, pp. xxxvi. 628   .   .   .   .   0 15 0
" It provides us with just what we most need, a model to look up to
and imitate ; one whose circumstances and surroundings were suffi-
ciently like our own to admit of an easy and direct application to our
own personal duties and daily occupations."—*Dublin Review.*
The Life and Glories of St. Joseph, Husband of
Mary, Foster-Father of Jesus, and Patron of the
Universal Church. Grounded on the Dissertations of
Canon Antonio Vitalis, Father José Moreno, and other
writers. Second Edition. Crown 8vo, cloth .   .   0 6 0

ULLATHORNE, ARCHBISHOP.
Endowments of Man, &c. Popular edition.   .   .   0 7 0
Groundwork of the Christian Virtues : do.   .   .   0 7 0
Christian Patience,   .   .   do. do.   .   .   0 7 0
Ecclesiastical Discourses 0 6 0
Memoir of Bishop Willson. 0 2 6

VAUGHAN, ARCHBISHOP, (O.S.B.)
The Life and Labours of St. Thomas of Aquin.
Abridged and edited by Dom Jerome Vaughan,
O.S.B. Second Edition. (Vol. I., Benedictine
Library.) Crown 8vo. Attractively bound .   .   0 6 6
"Popularly written, in the best sense of the word, skilfully avoids
all wearisome detail, whilst omitting nothing that is of importance
in the incidents of the Saint's existence, or for a clear understanding
of the nature and the purpose of those sublime theological works
on which so many Pontiffs, and notably Leo XIII., have pronounced
such remarkable and repeated commendations."—*Freeman's Journal.*

WARD, WILFRID.
The Clothes of Religion. A reply to popular Positivism.   0 3 6
"Very witty and interesting."—*Spectator.*
"Really models of what such essays should be."—*Church Quarterly
Review.*

WATERWORTH, REV. J.
The Canons and Decrees of the Sacred and Œcumenical
Council of Trent, celebrated under the Sovereign
Pontiffs, Paul III., Julius III., and Pius IV., tran-
slated by the Rev. J. WATERWORTH. To which
are prefixed Essays on the External and Internal
History of the Council. A new edition. Demy
8vo, cloth 0 10 6

WISEMAN, CARDINAL.
Fabiola. A Tale of the Catacombs. . . 3s. 6d. and   0 4 0
Also a new and splendid edition printed on large
quarto paper, embellished with thirty-one full-page
illustrations, and a coloured portrait of St. Agnes.
Handsomely bound. 1 1 0

www.ingramcontent.com/pod-product-compliance
Lightning Source LLC
Chambersburg PA
CBHW060607030726
47498CB00005B/1579